EX LIBRIS

VINTAGE **CLASSICS**

THE SECRET AGENT

Józef Teodor Konrad Korzeniowski was born in the Ukraine on 3 December 1857. His parents were Polish and had both died in exile by the time Conrad was eleven years old. His uncle became his guardian and looked after him in Krakow until he was sixteen when he went to sea. He worked on both French and British ships before he became a British citizen in 1886 and changed his name to Joseph Conrad. In 1896 he married Jessie George and they later had two sons. His first novel, *Almayer's Folly*, was published in 1895 and he went on to write many more, as well as short stories, essays and a memoir. His most famous work, *Heart of Darkness* (1899), was inspired by his experiences working on a steamboat in the Congo. *The Secret Agent* was first published in 1907. Joseph Conrad died on 3 August 1924.

OTHER WORKS BY JOSEPH CONRAD

Almayer's Folly

An Outcast of the Islands

The Nigger of the 'Narcissus'

Lord Jim

Heart of Darkness

Youth

Typhoon

Nostromo

The Mirror of the Sea

Under Western Eyes

Chance

Victory

The Shadow-Line

The Rescue

The Rover

JOSEPH CONRAD

The Secret Agent

A Simple Tale

WITH AN INTRODUCTION BY
Giles Foden

VINTAGE BOOKS
London

Published by Vintage 2007

8 10 9 7

Introduction © Giles Foden 2007

The Secret Agent was first published in 1907
The author's preface was first published in 1920

Vintage
Random House, 20 Vauxhall Bridge Road,
London SW1V 2SA

www.vintage-classics.info

Addresses for companies within The Random House Group
Limited can be found at: www.randomhouse.co.uk/offices.htm

The Random House Group Limited Reg. No. 954009

A CIP catalogue record for this book
is available from the British Library

ISBN 9780099511533

Penguin Random House is committed to a sustainable future for
our business, our readers and our planet. This book is made from
Forest Stewardship Council® certified paper.

Printed and bound in Great Britain by Clays Ltd, St Ives plc

CONTENTS

———

INTRODUCTION

The beginning of *The Secret Agent: A Simple Tale* (1907) is laden with what, on the surface, seem like mysterious references to hair. There is the 'black wig with a white cap' worn by the widowed mother of Winnie Verloc, the full-busted, broad-hipped heroine of the book who has married Verloc, the secret agent of the title, simply to find a material way to look after her mentally retarded brother, Stevie. There is Winnie's own hair, 'very tidy', and apparently significant of otherness: 'Traces of the French descent the widow boasted were apparent in Winnie too . . . in the extremely neat and artistic arrangement of her glossy dark hair.' The preoccupation is not a solely female one. There is also Verloc's own 'dark, smooth moustache', first spotted over bedclothes pulled up to his chin and covering 'thick lips capable of much honeyed banter'. And finally there is Stevie, the 'growth of thin fluffy hair . . . [that has] . . . come to blur, like a golden mist, the sharp line of his small lower jaw.' All this in a first chapter!

It is a chapter in which the principal players in Conrad's intense family drama are expertly introduced through a tour of Verloc's premises – 32 Brett Street, Soho: a shop whose door is always half ajar. The business is selling contraceptives – those 'closed yellow paper envelopes, very flimsy, and marked two-and-six in heavy black figures' – together with pornography and anarchist literature. For, of course, *The Secret Agent* is not just a family drama but also a political one. Revolutionary terrorists meet in Verloc's shop, unaware that its proprietor is reporting on their activities to the embassy of a great foreign power. (The Russian embassy seems most likely, though Prussia would do just as well. In calling Verloc's two controllers Baron Stott-Wartenheim and Mr Vladimir, Conrad seems to be hedging his bets.)

The shop is where Verloc sets out from for his appointment with Mr Vladimir at the embassy, leaving his 'ostensible business' in the hands of Stevie. The clue to the mystery of the hair lies in that 'ostensible', for hair is what covers up, what disguises. But the agency that is secret is not just Verloc's work as an informer and agent provocateur for Mr Vladimir, nor yet the more or less violent anarchist plans of Michaelis, Ossipon, Yundt and the Professor. It is Winnie's working marriage in the interests of her brother; it is the Assistant Commissioner keeping his own wife happy; it is Chief Inspector Heat's private mission to lock up all the anarchists regardless of habeas corpus. It is, most of all, the mass of mankind, 'mighty in its numbers', swarming 'numerous like locusts, industrious like ants, thoughtless like a natural force, pushing on blind and orderly and absorbed, impervious to sentiment, to logic, to terror too perhaps.' Their secrecy relates to their indifference, and to the fact that the mass of humanity is an unpredictable entity, the sum effect of whose actions is incalculable.

The previous quotation shows Conrad at his rhetorical best, dispelling those doubters who say he relies too much on abstract language. For here are they not, those much-maligned abstract nouns, moving across the periodic rhythm of the sentence just like a surging crowd? The mighty mass thus signified, the unheeded proleteriat of all nations, is certainly the subject of this book, which to my mind is among the greatest in the English language yet written. Its object is sociological, what it's concerned to show – nothing less than the ineffability of the human multitude, the unutterable burden of their desires and fears, their nightmares, hopes and dreams.

The 'wisdom of crowds' it might not be, but whatever it is, this ineffability is oblivious to policemen and terrorists alike. The dean of British Conrad critics, Robert Hampson, has called it 'the novel's own anarchic subversion of systems', and this seems very right to me. In the presentation of opposing political views, for that matter in the presentation of each perceiving consciousness, something like a process of mixing or turbulence is going on. It is as if Conrad is saying it's impossible to limit things off. Everything is interrelated (the book's plot expertly shows this in the round), and private and professional motives cannot be divided.

These interrelations apply to classes, to the very idea of classes in dialectical opposition as conceived in Marx's programmatic fashion. In offering up the implacable totality of the modern urban crowd – perhaps in counterpoint to the implacability of the sea in his earlier work – Conrad is keen to show how near that crowd is to his middle- and upper-class readers. The 'era of reconstruction' – the building of Trafalgar Square and Shaftesbury Avenue in the late 1880s, mentioned on the book's first page – has by no means cleared London of its slums. No, the hard city is 'just there' in *The Secret Agent*, and the threat of it is conceived as an inanimate one, as inimical to slum-dwellers as to anyone else. This is made clear in the text. Returning from his visit to the embassy, a depressed Verloc (the book is also one of the great masterpieces of the depiction of male depression) slips off his braces and, pulling up the venetian blind, leans his forehead 'against the cold window-pane – a fragile film of glass stretched between him and the enormity of cold, black, wet, muddy, inhospitable accumulation of bricks, slates, and stones, things in themselves unlovely and unfriendly to man.'

The same sentiment is expressed in John Buchan's novel *The Power-House* (1916): 'You think that a wall as solid as the earth separates civilization from barbarism. I tell you the division is a thread, a sheet of glass. A touch here, a push there, and you bring back the reign of Satan.' Another London novel (of inferior quality to *The Secret Agent*), *The Power-House* is about a secret society whose ultimate goal is world domination. Though coming from very different directions – Buchan from Presbyterian Scotland and London's clubland, via South Africa; Conrad from a family whose father was imprisoned and exiled for his part in a radical uprising against Czarist rule – they were both acutely aware of the sinister potentialities of revolution.

So far as the London aspects of Conrad's novel are concerned, they share more with the down at heel, anomie-ridden London of T.S. Eliot's 'Prelude' (1915) and *The Waste Land* (1923) than Buchan's Pall Mall, though the salon of Michaelis's patroness is in Piccadilly and the Assistant Commissioner operates in Whitehall and Westminster. This mixing of dingy, fashionable and political society is one of the most striking characteristics of *The Secret Agent*. Geometrically speaking it is a circle, like one of those Stevie endlessly draws, not a line: everything comes round in the end. The mathematical construction of the book might be a good subject for a Ph.D since its refusal of classes applies to types of mental conception as well as social divisions. As Mr Vladimir puts to Verloc: 'Since bombs are your means of expression, it would be really telling if one could throw a bomb into pure mathematics.'

There is something in that remark of the lesson Conrad learned from Henry James about narrating different quantities through their opposites. As the latter said, in the preface to his short story

'The Altar of the Dead' (1895), 'the spirit engaged with the forces of violence interests me most when I can think of it as engaged most deeply, most finely and most "subtly" (precious terms!)'

That impact of violence against subtlety, represented in *The Secret Agent* by science, got a dry run with violence impacting art in 'The Informer', a story of Conrad's about anarchists published in *Harper's Magazine* in 1906, while he was writing *The Secret Agent*. 'The Informer' is narrated by a collector of Chinese bronzes and porcelain who is introduced to 'Mr X', a famous revolutionary writer. Another collector, X lives in luxury while proclaiming: 'There's no amendment to be got out of mankind except by terror or violence.' X tries to prove there is no contradiction between the luxury of his life and his destructive propaganda by telling the tale of a young woman, a bourgeoise 'Lady Amateur', one of the 'idle and selfish class' who dabbles in revolutionary activities. It is a figure whose type we know from Henry James's terrorism novel *The Princess Casamassima* (1886) though there, as with Michaelis's patroness in *The Secret Agent*, the Lady is a full-blooded aristocrat. In James's novel, the protégé Hyacinth Robinson (who blows himself up) is a bookbinder; before he became a revolutionary celebrity, Michaelis was a locksmith. Both are professions which give access across barriers.

James's novel and 'The Informer', together with another Conrad short story, 'An Anarchist' (1906), are part of the essential literary background of *The Secret Agent*, but its real roots lie in the author's own physical wanderings. Practically speaking, the anonymity of the city in the novel derives from periods Conrad spent in London between ships, a lonely Polish sailor lodging in various districts in 1880 (Finsbury Park and Stoke Newington), 1889 (Pimlico) and 1891 (Victoria); that is to say exactly the time during which *The Secret Agent* is set. As he puts it in his Author's Preface: 'I had to fight hard to keep at arm's-length the memories of my solitary and nocturnal walks all over London in my early days, lest they should rush in and overwhelm each page of the story.'

The influence of these walks on the construction of the novel cannot be overestimated. In his memoir, *A Personal Record*, Conrad recalls exploring 'the maze of streets east and west in solitary leisurely walks without chart or compass'. Could it be that it was Brett Passage or Brett Road, London E8 – just to the east of his

Stoke Newington digs at 6 Dynevor Road – that provided the name for Verloc's shop on a fictional 32 Brett Street in Soho?

Who knows, but one retains on reading *The Secret Agent* a strong sense of Conrad, like Dickens before him, as an urban *flâneur*, a strolling spectator absorbed by crime, grime and grandeur. The Polish peregrinator dissects the city on foot but – being an outsider everywhere – refusing the divisions it normally employed to explain itself, keeping his equanimity in front of this place 'of marvels and mud', as London seems to Winnie.

To modern eyes some of those divisions and regions need explaining, as although the character of Soho has intensified (despite the efforts of Westminster Council), others have changed utterly. One is Islington, where the Professor lives in the novel, that 'unwholesome-looking little moral agent of destruction'. In the 1880s and 90s, Islington was a powerful source of 'unhygienic labour' as Conrad calls the working class in the book. It wasn't anything like today's 'New Labour' zone until 100 years later. Until at least 1992 the atmosphere was bohemian, sometimes downright disreputable. I saw the transformation myself while living in Islington at that time as a young writer and enthusiastic drinker, watching as the white working-class gangster's club on my street (Riley's, on Westbourne Road: it was full of 'the unbalanced nervous fury of the age of bar-rooms' that characterises Winnie's plunging blow) was slowly overwhelmed by the agglomeration of lawyers and media people moving into houses nearby. *The Secret Agent* was prophetic in seeing London as a place of changing properties, but even Conrad could not have foreseen the extent to which the city's inhabitants would be in thrall not to secret agents but estate agents, and its landscape changed not by the commune's raising of barricades but by those raised in the process of gentrification.

Conrad's anarchists, who do not believe in private property at all, have a different idea of reconstruction. They want everything to change very quickly indeed. The Professor is the only of them who is dangerous, terrifyingly so, with his padlocked wardrobe full of explosive chemicals and a rubber-ball detonator in his pocket. But ironically he, 'lost in the crowd, miserable and undersized', is the most affected of all by the ineffability of mass human movement. At home in Islington and in finer parts of the city, the 'limits of the horizon' might be 'hidden by enormous piles of bricks', but the immense multitude can be perceived. What if nothing could move them? That is the terrorist's fear. As Conrad implies, the problem of the novelist is not so very different.

The Professor is one of a number of characters in the book whose interiority is suddenly displayed to us – as internal lumber, in his case. After meeting blond, 'robust', curly-haired Tom Ossipon, womaniser and fellow conspirator, he glances into a shop window on his way home to N1: 'Facing the only gas-lamp yawned the cavern of a second-hand furniture dealer, where, deep in the gloom of a sort of narrow avenue winding through a bizarre forest of wardrobes, with an undergrowth tangle of table legs, a tall pier-glass glimmered like a pool of water in a wood.' It is as if Conrad were trying to explain the Professor's motivation in terms of a fairy tale, but like so much else in *The Secret Agent*, the clarity of the old tale has been made 'winding', 'bizarre', 'tangled' by modernity; and from that involution something perverse, psychologically speaking, has come.

The moment of self-recognition (the Professor is spooked by the mirror) is thematically fitting. In the ever-changing city even the terrorist, with his padlocked cupboard, will be disturbed. The Professor cannot remain in 'the hermitage of the perfect anarchist'. Very shortly after looking into the furniture shop he will be found by Chief Inspector Heat, if only to be told he is not sought. The suicide bomber warns the policeman that 'you may be exposed to the unpleasantness of being buried together with me', perhaps the most sickly evocation of mixing in the whole book.

The sense of permeable architectural limit that the novel so elegantly displays has its psychological counterpart. Just as different regions and inhabitants of the city will always interpenetrate, even if not bodily, so there will be a mixing of mental states. Once again it's a case of furniture, mental and actual. Mr Verloc does not really notice Winnie's mother taking away furniture for her new lodging in the almshouse ('his intense meditation, like a sort of Chinese wall, isolated him completely from the phenomena of this world of vain effort and illusory appearance') but the leaving of the remainder at Brett Street and more importantly Stevie ('somewhat in the same way as the furniture') will open his reserve like a key. Widow Verloc's departure does just as much to trigger the tragedy as Mr Vladimir's order as it is involved in the changed set of domestic circumstances that causes Winnie to ask Verloc to take Stevie out with him a little, which in turn puts the idea of using Stevie at Greenwich in Verloc's head as he frantically searches for an accomplice.

On coming in after the bombing and being asked serenely by Winnie if he has been to see Stevie, Verloc might slam the 'glazed parlour door' between the shop and the house – the door that divides the two parts of his life – but he will now no longer be able keep them apart. From this moment on come a series of brilliantly handled scenes that are half French farce, half Greek tragedy. First the Assistant Commissioner then Heat turn up at Brett Street, slowly Winnie realises the awful truth, and the climax that is the result of the mixing of personal and political is inescapable. In Aristotelian, structural terms, the rising towards the moment of tragic crisis and the falling away from it (the Ossipon-Winnie scenes), have never been better done in all fiction.

The coming tragedy is made all the more poignant by Verloc's ironically resonant babbling ('I have no mind to get . . . a stab in the back directly') and the presence of the joint of beef, acting like 'funereal baked meats for Stevie's obsequies' but also standing in for Stevie himself, in reality lately gathered up with a shovel by a constable ('blown to small bits: limbs, gravel, clothing, bones, splinters – all mixed up together'). Far from being evidence of sordidness and moral squalor, as some contemporary reviewers averred (Conrad rebuts them in his Author's Preface), the generic and the physical mixing is of a piece with the Heraclitean 'every-thing flows' ethos of the novel – even if it is mostly a dirty kind of flow, as noted by the description of the Assistant Commissioner's visit to Soho as being 'a descent into a slimy aquarium from which the water had been run off'.

The Assistant Commissioner is the unacknowledged hero of the book. Surely it is in his and the minds of other characters in this 1907 book (in particular Verloc's), not Leopold Bloom's in *Ulysses* (1922) or Clarissa Dalloway's in *Mrs Dalloway* (1925), that we find the first signs of indirect free style turning into stream of consciousness as an emerging trend in literature in English. See here, as skulking in the shadows the Assistant Commissioner takes then loses account of a more junior copper:

> The policeman on the beat projected his sombre and moving form against the luminous glory of oranges and lemons, and entered Brett Street without haste. The Assistant Commissioner, as though he were a member of the criminal classes, lingered out of sight, awaiting his return. But this constable seemed to be lost to the force forever. He never returned: must have gone out the other end of Brett Street.

A lot hangs on the omission of the pronoun 'he' before 'must have'. The Assistant Commissioner's musing thought about the beat constable's disappearance is recorded as part of the third person narration but with a much stronger sense than usual in Conrad of the stream of a single character's momentarily charged psychology breaking through. It might be thought fitting in a novel which is all about mental and physical breakthroughs, from the penetration of Verloc's indolent self-isolation (not least of which is his belief that he was married for himself and not for Stevie) to Winnie's conviction that 'life doesn't stand much looking into'.

That is not to say that the examined life might be any more nurturing. With as warming lights only the Assistant Commissioner's professionalism (and in even that there is a self-serving element relating to his own domestic circumstances) and Winnie's love for Stevie (and that receives from its background too much of what the author in his Preface calls 'sombre colouring' to be truly warming), Conrad's vision is powerfully nihilistic.

Given that nihilism, it is no wonder commentators such as John Gray (in his book *Al Qaeda and What it Means to be Modern* (2003)) and Pankaj Mishra (in an article on the literature of terrorism published in the *Guardian* on 19 May 2007) have drawn parallels between Conrad's anarchists and the followers of Osama bin Laden. For what is the Professor but a prototype for a suicide bomber of the type with which we are now all too familiar? And it is no wonder that *The Secret Agent* was not just the favourite book of that homegrown American terrorist Theodore J. Kaczynski, aka the Unabomber, but a kind of working manual for his activities.

Al Qaeda actually drew some of its philosophy from nineteenth-century European revolutionaries like the Professor and his crew. As for the Unabomber (a former mathematics professor who had read Conrad's works a dozen times, according to his lawyer), Kaczynski used 'Conrad' or 'Konrad' as an alias on at least three occasions while staying at a hotel in Sacramento from where he mailed bombs. He lived a hermit's life in his Montana cabin and chose science and technology as his targets – suggesting targets to himself as Mr Vladimir suggests Verloc 'has a go' at astronomy in the form of the Greenwich Observatory.

Gray makes the point that 'In Conrad's time, the sacrosanct science was physics. Today it is economics. Al Qaeda destroyed a building devoted to trade, not one dedicated to the study of the stars. The strategy is the same – to remake the world by spectacular acts of terror.' Once again the scope of Conrad's prophetic vision is clear.

He was clear-eyed about state-sponsored terror, too. In asking Verloc to provoke a 'not especially sanguine' outrage in order to cause the British police to crack down on foreign militants, Mr Vladimir is conducting an episode of what the Assistant Commissioner later in the book calls 'authorized scoundrelism'. It is of a type with which we have become familiar in conspiracy theories since the events of September 11, 2001: the idea that subsequent bombings, even (in the most lurid theory) the attack on the twin towers itself, have been covertly committed by Western and Israeli governments to give them licence to crode civil liberties and abandon international law.

These conspiracy theories cannot be taken seriously in anywise but there is no doubt that the intelligence agencies of democratic Western governments have engaged in countless jobs of 'authorized scoundrelism' since Conrad's time. 'Black ops' as they would now be called, comprise of deniable acts of violence designed for some particular political end, often to call down further violence or legal repression on the potential perpetrators of terror or other political enemies. In such a situation the moral division between the terrorist and the black operator is paper-thin.

To be positively multidimensional is the only viable aesthetic response. Roll up the paper-thin line and you make a circle, the same shape as Adolf and Winnie Verlocs' wedding ring, found stuck to the wood of a steamer bench by one of the ship's hands. Its glitter caught the man's eye, and it remains the only physical sign of Winnie, whom Conrad saw as the true tragic heroine of this tale, with a good deal of, but not total, compassion.

Winnie's fate will haunt her brief, false amour, Tom Ossipon, as he meets with the Professor in the Silenus at the end of the book: 'And Comrade Ossipon raised his bowed head, beloved of various humble women of these isles, Apollo-like in the sunniness of its bush of hair.' So we have come full circle at last, but now hair is covering not secret anti-state political activity nor secret state counter-espionage, nor yet the lie of a domestic situation. Now what the hirsute covering betokens is Ossipon's impoverished inner state as opposed to his outer wealth, which is mostly being used to drown his sorrows. It is as if he is being led, by a long uncrinkling strand of his own yellow hair, into a life of drunkenness and penury in the service of capitalism:

> Already his robust form, with an Embassy's secret-service money (inherited from Mr Verloc) in his pockets, was marching in the gutter as if in training for the task of an inevitable future. Already he bowed his broad shoulders, his head of ambrosial locks, as if ready to receive the leather yoke of the sandwich board.

Ossipon's payback for his betrayal of Winnie is in some ways the most terrible fate of all, Verloc's death by stabbing, Stevie's by explosion, and Winnie's by drowning notwithstanding. For he must continue living in that 'monstrous town' with Winnie's fate on his hands and in his mind. The only person able to explain the 'impenetrable mystery' of her 'act of madness and despair', he remains filled with dread by the reverberations of this 'simple tale', afraid of insanity.

Readers today may approach the story in different guise, appreciative of it as one of Conrad's masterpieces and the first great modern spy novel; which is also to say the first great novel of modernity, since a condition of mixed-up uncertainty, of being double-counter-bluffed till you don't know where or what you are, is emblematic of being modern. As a reading of this book will evidence, it can be exhilarating as well as menacing.

Giles Foden, 2007

AUTHOR'S PREFACE

The origin of 'The Secret Agent': subject, treatment, artistic purpose and every other motive that may induce an author to take up his pen, can, I believe, be traced to a period of mental and emotional reaction.

The actual facts are that I began this book impulsively and wrote it continuously. When in due course it was bound and delivered to the public gaze I found myself reproved for having produced it at all. Some of the admonitions were severe, others had a sorrowful note. I have not got them textually before me but I remember perfectly the general argument, which was very simple; and also my surprise at its nature. All this sounds a very old story now! And yet it is not such a long time ago. I must conclude that I had still preserved much of my pristine innocence in the year 1907. It seems to me now that even an artless person might have foreseen that some criticisms would be based on the ground of sordid surroundings and the moral squalor of the tale.

That of course is a serious objection. It was not universal. In fact it seems ungracious to remember so little reproof amongst so much intelligent and sympathetic appreciation; and I trust that the readers of this Preface will not hasten to put it down to wounded vanity or a natural disposition to ingratitude. I suggest that a charitable heart could very well ascribe my choice to natural modesty. Yet it isn't exactly modesty that makes me select reproof for the illustration of my case. No, it isn't exactly modesty. I am not at all certain that I am modest; but those who have read so far through my work will credit me with enough decency, tact, savoir faire, what you will, to prevent me from making a song for my own glory out of the words of other people. No! The true motive of my selection lies in quite a different trait. I have always had a propensity to justify my action. Not to defend. To justify. Not to insist that I was right but simply to explain that there was no perverse intention, no secret scorn for the natural sensibilities of mankind at the bottom of my impulses.

That kind of weakness is dangerous only so far that it exposes one to the risk of becoming a bore; for the world generally is not interested in the motives of any overt act but in its consequences. Man may smile and smile but he is not an investigating animal. He loves the obvious. He shrinks from explanations. Yet I will go on with mine. It's obvious that I need not have written that book. I was under no necessity to deal with that subject; using the word subject both in the sense of the tale itself and in the larger one of a special manifestation in the life of mankind. This I fully admit. But the thought of elaborating mere ugliness in order to shock, or even simply to surprise my readers by a change of front, has never entered my head. In making this statement I expect to be believed, not only on the evidence of my general character but also for the reason, which anybody can see, that the whole treatment of the tale, its inspiring indignation and underlying pity and contempt, prove my detachment from the squalor and sordidness which lie simply in the outward circumstances of the setting.

The inception of 'The Secret Agent' followed immediately on a two years' period of intense absorption in the task of writing that remote novel, 'Nostromo,' with its far off Latin-American atmosphere; and the profoundly personal 'Mirror of the Sea'. The first an intense creative effort on what I suppose will always remain my largest canvas, the second an unreserved attempt to unveil for a moment the profounder intimacies of the sea and the formative influences of nearly half my life-time. It was a period, too, in which my sense of the truth of things was attended by a very intense imaginative and emotional readiness which, all genuine and faithful to facts as it was, yet made me feel (the task once done) as if I were left behind, aimless amongst mere husks of sensations and lost in a world of other, of inferior, values.

I don't know whether I really felt that I wanted a change, change in my imagination, in my vision and in my mental attitude. I rather think that a change in the fundamental mood had already stolen over me unawares. I don't remember anything definite happening. With 'The Mirror of the Sea' finished in the full consciousness that I had dealt honestly with myself and my readers in every line of that book, I gave myself up to a not unhappy pause. Then, while I was yet standing still, as it were, and certainly not thinking of going out of my way to look for anything ugly, the subject of 'The Secret Agent' – I mean the tale – came to me in the shape of a few words uttered by a friend in a casual conversation about anarchists or rather anarchist activities; how brought about I don't remember now.

I remember, however, remarking on the criminal futility of the whole thing, doctrine, action, mentality; and on the contemptible aspect of the half-crazy pose as of a brazen cheat exploiting the poignant miseries and passionate credulities of a mankind always so tragically eager for self-destruction. That was what made for me its philosophical pretences so unpardonable. Presently, passing to particular instances, we recalled the already old story of the attempt to blow up the Greenwich Observatory; a blood-stained inanity of so fatuous a kind that it was impossible to fathom its origin by any reasonable or even unreasonable process of thought. For perverse unreason has its own logical processes. But that outrage could not be laid hold of mentally in any sort of way, so that one remained faced by the fact of a man blown to bits for nothing even most remotely resembling an idea, anarchistic or other. As to the outer wall of the Observatory it did not show as much as the faintest crack.

I pointed all this out to my friend who remained silent for a while and then remarked in his characteristically casual and omniscient manner: 'Oh, that fellow was half an idiot. His sister committed suicide afterwards.' These were absolutely the only words that passed between us; for extreme surprise at this unexpected piece of information kept me dumb for a moment and he began at once to talk of something else. It never occurred to me later to ask how he arrived at his knowledge. I am sure that if he had seen once in his life the back of an anarchist that must have been the whole extent of his connection with the underworld. He was, however, a man who liked to talk with all sorts of people, and he may have gathered those illuminating facts at second or third hand, from a crossing-sweeper, from a retired police officer, from some vague man in his club, or even, perhaps, from a Minister of State met at some public or private reception.

Of the illuminating quality there could be no doubt whatever. One felt like walking out of a forest on to a plain – there was not much to see but one had plenty of light. No, there was not much to see and, frankly, for a considerable time I didn't even attempt to perceive anything. It was only the illuminating impression that remained. It remained satisfactory but in a passive way. Then, about a week later, I came upon a book which as far as I know had never attained any prominence, the rather summary recollections of an Assistant Commissioner of Police, an obviously able man with a strong religious strain in his character who was appointed to his post at the time of the dynamite outrages in London, away back in the eighties. The book was fairly interesting, very discreet of course; and I have by now forgotten the bulk of its contents. It contained no revelations, it ran over the surface agreeably, and that was all. I won't even try to explain why I should have been arrested by a little passage of about seven lines, in which the author (I believe his name was Anderson) reproduced a short dialogue held in the Lobby of the House of Commons after some unexpected anarchist outrage, with the Home Secretary. I think it was Sir William Harcourt then. He was very much irritated and the official was very apologetic. The phrase, amongst the three which passed between them, that struck me most was Sir W. Harcourt's angry sally: 'All that's very well. But your idea of secrecy over there seems to consist of keeping the Home Secretary in the dark.' Characteristic enough of Sir W. Harcourt's temper but not much in itself. There must have been, however, some sort of atmosphere in the whole incident because all of a sudden I felt myself stimulated. And then ensued in my mind what a student of chemistry would best understand from the analogy of the addition of the tiniest little drop of the right kind, precipitating the process of crystallization in a test tube containing some colourless solution.

It was at first for me a mental change, disturbing a quieted-down imagination, in which strange forms, sharp in outline but imperfectly apprehended, appeared and claimed attention as crystals will do by their bizarre and unexpected shapes. One fell to musing before the phenomenon – even of the past: of South America, a continent of crude sunshine and brutal revolutions, of the sea, the vast expanse of salt waters, the mirror of heaven's frowns and smiles, the reflector of the world's light. Then the vision of an enormous town presented itself, of a monstrous town more populous than some continents and in its man-made might as if indifferent to heaven's frowns and smiles; a cruel devourer of the world's light. There was room enough there to place any story, depth enough there for any passion, variety enough there for any setting, darkness enough to bury five millions of lives.

Irresistibly the town became the background for the ensuing period of deep and tentative meditations. Endless vistas opened before me in various directions. It would take years to find the right way! It seemed to take years! ... Slowly the dawning conviction of Mrs Verloc's maternal passion grew up to a flame between me and that background, tingeing it with its secret ardour and receiving from it in exchange some of its own sombre colouring. At last the story of Winnie Verloc stood out complete from the days of her childhood to the end, unproportioned as yet, with everything still on the first plan, as it were; but ready now to be dealt with. It was a matter of about three days.

This book is *that* story, reduced to manageable proportions, its whole course suggested and centred round the absurd cruelty of the Greenwich Park explosion. I had there a task I will not say arduous but of the most absorbing difficulty. But it had to be done. It was a necessity. The figures grouped about Mrs Verloc and related directly or indirectly to her tragic suspicion that 'life doesn't stand much looking into', are the outcome of that very necessity. Personally I have never had any doubt of the reality of Mrs Verloc's story; but it had to be disengaged from its obscurity in that immense town, it had to be made credible, I don't mean so much as to her soul but as to her surroundings, not so much as to her psychology but as to her humanity. For the surroundings hints were not lacking. I had to fight hard to keep at arm's-length the memories of my solitary and nocturnal walks all over London in my early days, lest they should rush in and overwhelm each page of the story as these emerged one after another from a mood as serious in feeling and thought as any in which I ever wrote a line. In that respect I really think that 'The Secret Agent' is a perfectly genuine piece of work. Even the purely artistic purpose, that of applying an ironic method to a subject of that kind, was formulated with deliberation and in the earnest belief that ironic treatment alone would enable me to say all I felt I would have to say in scorn as well as in pity. It is one of the minor satisfactions of my writing life that having taken that resolve I did manage, it seems to me, to carry it right through to the end. As to the personages whom the absolute necessity of the case – Mrs Verloc's case – brings out in front of the London background, from them, too, I obtained those little satisfactions which really count for so much against the mass of oppressive doubts that haunt so persistently every attempt at creative work. For instance, of Mr Vladimir himself (who was fair game for a caricatural presentation) I was gratified to hear that an experienced man of the world had said 'that Conrad must have been in touch with that sphere or else has an excellent intuition of things', because Mr Vladimir was 'not only possible in detail but quite right in essentials'. Then a visitor from America informed me that all sorts of revolutionary refugees in New York would have it that the book was written by somebody who knew a lot about them. This seemed to me a very high compliment, considering that, as a matter of hard fact, I had seen even less of their kind than the omniscient friend who gave me the first suggestion for the novel. I have no doubt, however, that there had been moments during the writing of the book when I was an extreme revolutionist, I won't say more convinced than they but certainly cherishing a more concentrated purpose than any of them had ever done in the whole course of his life. I don't say this to boast. I was simply attending to my business. In the matter of all my books I have always attended to my business. I have attended to it with complete self-surrender. And this statement, too, is not a boast. I could not have done otherwise. It would have bored me too much to make-believe.

AUTHOR'S PREFACE

The suggestions for certain personages of the tale, both law-abiding and lawless, came from various sources which, perhaps, here and there, some reader may have recognized. They are not very recondite. But I am not concerned here to legitimize any of those people, and even as to my general view of the moral reactions as between the criminal and the police all I will venture to say is that it seems to me to be at least arguable.

The twelve years that have elapsed since the publication of the book have not changed my attitude. I do not regret having written it. Lately, circumstances, which have nothing to do with the general tenor of this preface, have compelled me to strip this tale of the literary robe of indignant scorn it has cost me so much to fit on it decently, years ago. I have been forced, so to speak, to look upon its bare bones. I confess that it makes a grisly skeleton. But still I will submit that telling Winnie Verloc's story to its anarchistic end of utter desolation, madness and despair, and telling it as I have told it here, I have not intended to commit a gratuitous outrage on the feelings of mankind.

J.C.

1920.

THE SECRET AGENT

To
H. G. Wells
The chronicler of Mr. Lewisham's love
the biographer of Kipps and the
historian of the ages to come
this simple tale of the XIX century
is affectionately offered

CHAPTER ONE

M R. VERLOC, going out in the morning, left his
shop nominally in charge of his brother-in-law.
It could be done, because there was very little
business at any time, and practically none at all before
the evening. Mr. Verloc cared but little about his ostensible business. And, moreover, his wife was in charge of
his brother-in-law.

The shop was small, and so was the house. It was one
of those grimy brick houses which existed in large quantities before the era of reconstruction dawned upon London. The shop was a square box of a place, with the front
glazed in small panes. In the daytime the door remained
closed; in the evening it stood discreetly but suspiciously
ajar.

The window contained photographs of more or less
undressed dancing girls; nondescript packages in wrap-
pers like patent medicines; closed yellow paper
envelopes, very flimsy, and marked two-and-six in heavy
black figures; a few numbers of ancient French comic
publications hung across a string as if to dry; a dingy blue
china bowl, a casket of black wood, bottles of marking
ink, and rubber stamps; a few books, with titles hinting
at impropriety; a few apparently old copies of obscure
newspapers, badly printed, with titles like *The Torch, The
Gong* – rousing titles. And the two gas-jets inside the
panes were always turned low, either for economy's sake
or for the sake of the customers.

These customers were either very young men, who

hung about the window for a time before slipping in suddenly; or men of a more mature age, but looking generally as if they were not in funds. Some of that last kind
had the collars of their overcoats turned right up to their
moustaches, and traces of mud on the bottom of their
nether garments, which had the appearance of being
much worn and not very valuable. And the legs inside
them did not, as a general rule, seem of much account
either. With their hands plunged deep in the side pockets of their coats, they dodged in sideways, one shoulder
first, as if afraid to start the bell going.

The bell, hung on the door by means of a curved
ribbon of steel, was difficult to circumvent. It was hopelessly cracked; but of an evening, at the slightest provocation, it clattered behind the customer with impudent
virulence.

It clattered; and at that signal, through the dusty glass
door behind the painted deal counter, Mr. Verloc would
issue hastily from the parlour at the back. His eyes were
naturally heavy; he had an air of having wallowed, fully
dressed, all day on an unmade bed. Another man would
have felt such an appearance a distinct disadvantage. In
a commercial transaction of the retail order much
depends on the seller's engaging and amiable aspect. But
Mr. Verloc knew his business, and remained undisturbed
by any sort of æsthetic doubt about his appearance. With
a firm, steady-eyed impudence, which seemed to hold
back the threat of some abominable menace, he would
proceed to sell over the counter some object looking
obviously and scandalously not worth the money which
passed in the transaction: a small cardboard box with
apparently nothing inside, for instance, or one of those
carefully closed yellow flimsy envelopes, or a soiled volume in paper covers with a promising title. Now and
then it happened that one of the faded, yellow dancing
girls would get sold to an amateur, as though she had
been alive and young.

Sometimes it was Mrs. Verloc who would appear at the call of the cracked bell. Winnie Verloc was a young woman with a full bust, in a tight bodice, and with broad hips. Her hair was very tidy. Steady-eyed like her husband, she preserved an air of unfathomable indifference behind the rampart of the counter. Then the customer of comparatively tender years would get suddenly disconcerted at having to deal with a woman, and with rage in his heart would proffer a request for a bottle of marking ink, retail value sixpence (price in Verloc's shop one-and-sixpence), which, once outside, he would drop stealthily into the gutter.

The evening visitors – the men with collars turned up and soft hats rammed down – nodded familiarly to Mrs. Verloc, and with a muttered greeting, lifted up the flap at the end of the counter in order to pass into the back parlour, which gave access to a passage and to a steep flight of stairs. The door of the shop was the only means of entrance to the house in which Mr. Verloc carried on his business of a seller of shady wares, exercised his vocation of a protector of society, and cultivated his domestic virtues. These last were pronounced. He was thoroughly domesticated. Neither his spiritual, nor his mental, nor his physical needs were of the kind to take him much abroad. He found at home the ease of his body and the peace of his conscience, together with Mrs. Verloc's wifely attentions and Mrs. Verloc's mother's deferential regard.

Winnie's mother was a stout, wheezy woman, with a large brown face. She wore a black wig under a white cap. Her swollen legs rendered her inactive. She considered herself to be of French descent, which might have been true; and after a good many years of married life with a licensed victualler of the more common sort, she provided for the years of widowhood by letting furnished apartments for gentlemen near Vauxhall Bridge Road in a square once of some splendour and still

included in the district of Belgravia. This topographical
fact was of some advantage in advertising her rooms; but
the patrons of the worthy widow were not exactly of the
fashionable kind. Such as they were, her daughter Winnie helped to look after them. Traces of the French
descent which the widow boasted of were apparent in
Winnie, too. They were apparent in the extremely neat
and artistic arrangement of her glossy dark hair. Winnie
had also other charms: her youth; her full, rounded form;
her clear complexion; the provocation of her unfathomable reserve, which never went so far as to prevent conversation, carried on on the lodger's part with animation,
and on hers with an equable amiability. It must be that
Mr. Verloc was susceptible to these fascinations. Mr. Verloc was an intermittent patron. He came and went without any very apparent reason. He generally arrived in
London (like the influenza) from the Continent, only he
arrived unheralded by the Press; and his visitations set in
with great severity. He breakfasted in bed, and remained
wallowing there with an air of quiet enjoyment till noon
every day – and sometimes even to a later hour. But
when he went out he seemed to experience a great difficulty in finding his way back to his temporary home in
the Belgravian square. He left it late, and returned to it
early – as early as three or four in the morning; and on
waking up at ten addressed Winnie, bringing in the
breakfast tray, with jocular, exhausted civility, in the
hoarse, failing tones of a man who had been talking
vehemently for many hours together. His prominent,
heavy-lidded eyes rolled sideways amorously and languidly, the bedclothes were pulled up to his chin, and his
dark smooth moustache covered his thick lips capable of
much honeyed banter.

In Winnie's mother's opinion Mr. Verloc was a very
nice gentleman. From her life's experience gathered in
various 'business houses' the good woman had taken
into her retirement an ideal of gentlemanliness as

exhibited by the patrons of private-saloon bars. Mr. Verloc approached that ideal; he attained it, in fact.

'Of course, we'll take over your furniture, mother,' Winnie had remarked.

The lodging-house was to be given up. It seems it would not answer to carry it on. It would have been too much trouble for Mr. Verloc. It would not have been convenient for his other business. What his business was he did not say; but after his engagement to Winnie he took the trouble to get up before noon, and descending the basement stairs, make himself pleasant to Winnie's mother in the breakfast-room downstairs where she had her motionless being. He stroked the cat, poked the fire, had his lunch served to him there. He left its slightly stuffy cosiness with evident reluctance, but, all the same, remained out till the night was far advanced. He never offered to take Winnie to theatres, as such a nice gentleman ought to have done. His evenings were occupied. His work was in a way political, he told Winnie once. She would have, he warned her, to be very nice to his political friends. And with her straight, unfathomable glance she answered that she would be so, of course.

How much more he told her as to his occupation it was impossible for Winnie's mother to discover. The married couple took her over with the furniture. The mean aspect of the shop surprised her. The change from the Belgravian square to the narrow street in Soho affected her legs adversely. They became of an enormous size. On the other hand, she experienced a complete relief from material cares. Her son-in-law's heavy good nature inspired her with a sense of absolute safety. Her daughter's future was obviously assured, and even as to her son Stevie she need have no anxiety. She had not been able to conceal from herself that he was a terrible encumbrance, that poor Stevie. But in view of Winnie's fondness for her delicate brother, and of Mr. Verloc's kind and generous disposition, she felt that the poor boy

was pretty safe in this rough world. And in her heart of
hearts she was not perhaps displeased that the Verlocs
had no children. As that circumstance seemed perfectly
indifferent to Mr. Verloc, and as Winnie found an object
of quasi-maternal affection in her brother, perhaps this
was just as well for poor Stevie.

For he was difficult to dispose of, that boy. He was
delicate and, in a frail way, good-looking, too, except for
the vacant droop of his lower lip. Under our excellent
system of compulsory education he had learned to read
and write, notwithstanding the unfavourable aspect of
the lower lip. But as errand-boy he did not turn out a
great success. He forgot his messages; he was easily
diverted from the straight path of duty by the attractions
of stray cats and dogs, which he followed down narrow
alleys into unsavoury courts; by the comedies of the
streets, which he contemplated open-mouthed, to the
detriment of his employer's interests; or by the dramas of
fallen horses, whose pathos and violence induced him
sometimes to shriek piercingly in a crowd, which disliked to be disturbed by sounds of distress in its quiet
enjoyment of the national spectacle. When led away by a
grave and protecting policeman, it would often become
apparent that poor Stevie had forgotten his address – at
least for a time. A brusque question caused him to stutter
to the point of suffocation. When startled by anything
perplexing he used to squint horribly. However, he never
had any fits (which was encouraging); and before the
natural outbursts of impatience on the part of his father
he could always, in his childhood's days, run for protection behind the short skirts of his sister Winnie. On the
other hand, he might have been suspected of hiding a
fund of reckless naughtiness. When he had reached the
age of fourteen a friend of his late father, an agent for a
foreign preserved milk firm, having given him an opening as office-boy, he was discovered one foggy afternoon,
in his chief's absence, busy letting off fireworks on the

staircase. He touched off in quick succession a set of
fierce rockets, angry catherine wheels, loudly exploding
squibs – and the matter might have turned out very serious. An awful panic spread through the whole building.
Wild-eyed, choking clerks stampeded through the pass-
ages full of smoke, silk hats and elderly business men
could be seen rolling independently down the stairs.
Stevie did not seem to derive any personal gratification
from what he had done. His motives for this stroke of
originality were difficult to discover. It was only later on
that Winnie obtained from him a misty and confused
confession. It seems that two other office-boys in the
building had worked upon his feelings by tales of injustice and oppression till they had wrought his compassion
to the pitch of that frenzy. But his father's friend, of
course, dismissed him summarily as likely to ruin his
business. After that altruistic exploit Stevie was put to
help wash the dishes in the basement kitchen, and to
black the boots of the gentlemen patronizing the Belgravian mansion. There was obviously no future in such
work. The gentlemen tipped him a shilling now and
then. Mr. Verloc showed himself the most generous of
lodgers. But altogether all that did not amount to much
either in the way of gain or prospects; so that when Winnie announced her engagement to Mr. Verloc her mother
could not help wondering, with a sigh and a glance
towards the scullery, what would become of poor
Stephen now.

It appeared that Mr. Verloc was ready to take him over
together with his wife's mother and with the furniture,
which was the whole visible fortune of the family. Mr.
Verloc gathered everything as it came to his broad, good-
natured breast. The furniture was disposed to the best
advantage all over the house, but Mrs. Verloc's mother
was confined to two back rooms on the first floor. The
luckless Stevie slept in one of them. By this time a
growth of thin fluffy hair had come to blur, like a golden

mist, the sharp line of his small lower jaw. He helped his
sister with blind love and docility in her household
duties. Mr. Verloc thought that some occupation would
be good for him. His spare time he occupied by drawing
circles with compass and pencil on a piece of paper. He
applied himself to that pastime with great industry, with
his elbows spread out and bowed low over the kitchen
table. Through the open door of the parlour at the back
of the shop Winnie, his sister, glanced at him from time
to time with maternal vigilance.

CHAPTER TWO

S UCH was the house, the household, and the business Mr. Verloc left behind him on his way westward at the hour of half-past ten in the morning. It was unusually early for him; his whole person exhaled the charm of almost dewy freshness; he wore his blue cloth overcoat unbuttoned; his boots were shiny; his cheeks, freshly shaven, had a sort of gloss; and even his heavy-lidded eyes, refreshed by a night of peaceful slumber, sent out glances of comparative alertness. Through the park railings these glances beheld men and women riding in the Row, couples cantering past harmoniously, others advancing sedately at a walk, loitering groups of three or four, solitary horsemen looking unsociable, and solitary women followed at a long distance by a groom with a cockade to his hat and a leather belt over his tight-fitting coat. Carriages went bowling by, mostly two-horse broughams, with here and there a victoria with the skin of some wild beast inside and a woman's face and hat emerging above the folded hood. And a peculiarly London sun – against which nothing could be said except that it looked bloodshot – glorified all this by its stare. It hung at a moderate elevation above Hyde Park Corner with an air of punctual and benign vigilance. The very pavement under Mr. Verloc's feet had an old-gold tinge in that diffused light, in which neither wall, nor tree, nor beast, nor man cast a shadow. Mr. Verloc was going westward through a town without shadows in an

atmosphere of powdered old gold. There were red, cop-
pery gleams on the roofs of houses, on the corners of
walls, on the panels of carriages, on the very coats of the
horses, and on the broad back of Mr. Verloc's overcoat,
where they produced a dull effect of rustiness. But Mr.
Verloc was not in the least conscious of having got rusty.
He surveyed through the park railings the evidences of
the town's opulence and luxury with an approving eye.
All these people had to be protected. Protection is the
first necessity of opulence and luxury. They had to be
protected; and their horses, carriages, houses, servants
had to be protected; and the source of their wealth had to
be protected in the heart of the city and the heart of the
country; the whole social order favourable to their
hygienic idleness had to be protected against the shallow
enviousness of unhygienic labour. It had to – and Mr.
Verloc would have rubbed his hands with satisfaction
had he not been constitutionally averse from every
superfluous exertion. His idleness was not hygienic, but
it suited him very well. He was in a manner devoted to it
with a sort of inert fanaticism, or perhaps rather with a
fanatical inertness. Born of industrious parents for a life
of toil, he had embraced indolence from an impulse as
profound, as inexplicable and as imperious as the impulse which directs a man's preference for one particular
woman in a given thousand. He was too lazy even for a
mere demagogue, for a workman orator, for a leader of
labour. It was too much trouble. He required a more perfect form of ease; or it might have been that he was
the victim of a philosophical unbelief in the effective-
ness of every human effort. Such a form of indolence
requires, implies, a certain amount of intelligence. Mr.
Verloc was not devoid of intelligence – and at the
notion of a menaced social order he would perhaps have
winked to himself if there had not been an effort to
make in that sign of scepticism. His big, prominent eyes
were not well adapted to winking. They were rather of

the sort that closes solemnly in slumber with majestic effect.

Undemonstrative and burly in a fat-pig style, Mr. Verloc, without either rubbing his hands with satisfaction or winking sceptically at his thoughts, proceeded on his way. He trod the pavement heavily with his shiny boots, and his general get-up was that of a well-to-do mechanic in business for himself. He might have been anything from a picture-frame maker to a locksmith; an employer of labour in a small way. But there was also about him an indescribable air which no mechanic could have acquired in the practice of his handicraft however dishonestly exercised: the air common to men who live on the vices, the follies, or the baser fears of mankind; the air of moral nihilism common to keepers of gambling hells and disorderly houses; to private detectives and inquiry agents; to drink sellers and, I should say, to the sellers of invigorating electric belts and to the inventors of patent medicines. But of that last I am not sure, not having carried my investigations so far into the depths. For all I know, the expression of these last may be perfectly diabolic. I shouldn't be surprised. What I want to affirm is that Mr. Verloc's expression was by no means diabolic.

Before reaching Knightsbridge, Mr. Verloc took a turn to the left out of the busy main thoroughfare, uproarious with the traffic of swaying omnibuses and trotting vans, in the almost silent, swift flow of hansoms. Under his hat, worn with a slight backward tilt, his hair had been carefully brushed into respectful sleekness; for his business was with an Embassy. And Mr. Verloc, steady like a rock – a soft kind of rock – marched now along a street which could with every propriety be described as private. In its breadth, emptiness, and extent it had the majesty of inorganic nature, of matter that never dies. The only reminder of mortality was a doctor's brougham arrested in august solitude close to the curbstone. The polished knockers of the doors gleamed as far as the eye

could reach, the clean windows shone with a dark
opaque lustre. And all was still. But a milk cart rattled
noisily across the distant perspective; a butcher boy, driving with the noble recklessness of a charioteer at Olym-
pic Games, dashed round the corner sitting high above a
pair of red wheels. A guilty-looking cat issuing from
under the stones ran for a while in front of Mr. Verloc,
then dived into another basement; and a thick police
constable, looking a stranger to every emotion, as if he,
too, were part of inorganic nature, surging apparently out
of a lamp-post, took not the slightest notice of Mr. Verloc. With a turn to the left Mr. Verloc pursued his way
along a narrow street by the side of a yellow wall which,
for some inscrutable reason, had No. 1 Chesham Square
written on it in black letters. Chesham Square was at
least sixty yards away, and Mr. Verloc, cosmopolitan
enough not to be deceived by London's topographical
mysteries, held on steadily, without a sign of surprise or
indignation. At last, with businesslike persistency, he
reached the Square, and made diagonally for the number
10. This belonged to an imposing carriage gate in a high,
clean wall between two houses, of which one rationally
enough bore the number 9 and the other was numbered
37; but the fact that this last belonged to Porthill Street,
a street well known in the neighbourhood, was pro-
claimed by an inscription placed above the ground-floor
windows by whatever highly efficient authority is
charged with the duty of keeping track of London's
strayed houses. Why powers are not asked of Parliament
(a short act would do) for compelling those edifices to
return where they belong is one of the mysteries of
municipal administration. Mr. Verloc did not trouble his
head about it, his mission in life being the protection of
the social mechanism, not its perfectionment or even its
criticism.

It was so early that the porter of the Embassy issued
hurriedly out of his lodge still struggling with the left

sleeve of his livery coat. His waistcoat was red, and he wore knee-breeches, but his aspect was flustered. Mr. Verloc, aware of the rush on his flank, drove it off by simply holding out an envelope stamped with the arms of the Embassy, and passed on. He produced the same talisman also to the footman who opened the door, and stood back to let him enter the hall.

A clear fire burned in a tall fireplace, and an elderly man standing with his back to it, in evening dress and with a chain round his neck, glanced up from the newspaper he was holding spread out in both hands before his calm and severe face. He didn't move; but another lackey, in brown trousers and clawhammer coat edged with thin yellow cord, approaching Mr. Verloc listened to the murmur of his name, and turning round on his heel in silence, began to walk, without looking back once. Mr. Verloc, thus led along a ground-floor passage to the left of the great carpeted staircase, was suddenly motioned to enter a quite small room furnished with a heavy writing-table and a few chairs. The servant shut the door, and Mr. Verloc remained alone. He did not take a seat. With his hat and stick held in one hand he glanced about, passing his other podgy hand over his uncovered sleek head.

Another door opened noiselessly, and Mr. Verloc immobilizing his glance in that direction saw at first only black clothes, the bald top of a head, and a drooping dark grey whisker on each side of a pair of wrinkled hands. The person who had entered was holding a batch of papers before his eyes and walked up to the table with a rather mincing step, turning the papers over the while. Privy Councillor Wurmt, Chancelier d'Ambassade, was rather shortsighted. This meritorious official, laying the papers on the table, disclosed a face of pasty complexion and of melancholy ugliness surrounded by a lot of fine, long dark grey hairs, barred heavily by thick and bushy eyebrows. He put on a black-framed pince-nez upon a blunt and shapeless nose, and seemed struck by Mr. Verloc's appearance. Under the enormous eye-brows his weak eyes blinked pathetically through the glasses.

He made no sign of greeting; neither did Mr. Verloc who certainly knew his place; but a subtle change about the general outlines of his shoulders and back suggested a slight bending of Mr. Verloc's spine under the vast surface of his overcoat. The effect was of unobtrusive deference.

'I have here some of your reports,' said the bureaucrat in an unexpectedly soft and weary voice, and pressing the tip of his forefinger on the papers with force. He paused; and Mr. Verloc, who had recognized his own handwriting very well, waited in an almost breathless silence. 'We are not very satisfied with the attitude of the police here,' the other continued, with every appearance of mental fatigue.

The shoulders of Mr. Verloc, without actually moving, suggested a shrug. And for the first time since he left his home that morning his lips opened.

'Every country has its police,' he said, philosophically. But as the official of the Embassy went on blinking at him steadily he felt constrained to add: 'Allow me to observe that I have no means of action upon the police here.'

'What is desired,' said the man of papers, 'is the occurrence of something definite which should stimulate their vigilance. That is within your province – is it not so?'

Mr. Verloc made no answer except by a sigh, which escaped him involuntarily, for instantly he tried to give his face a cheerful expression. The official blinked doubtfully, as if affected by the dim light of the room. He repeated vaguely:

'The vigilance of the police – and the severity of the magistrates. The general leniency of the judicial procedure here, and the utter absence of all repressive measures, are a scandal to Europe. What is wished for just now is the accentuation of the unrest – of the fermentation which undoubtedly exists —'

'Undoubtedly, undoubtedly,' broke in Mr. Verloc in a deep, deferential bass of an oratorical quality, so utterly different from the tone in which he had spoken before that his interlocutor remained profoundly surprised. 'It exists to a dangerous degree. My reports for the last twelve months make it sufficiently clear.'

'Your reports for the last twelve months,' State Councillor Wurmt began in his gentle and dispassionate tone, 'have been read by me. I failed to discover why you wrote them at all.'

A sad silence reigned for a time. Mr. Verloc seemed to have swallowed his tongue, and the other gazed at the papers on the table fixedly. At last he gave them a slight push.

'The state of affairs you expose there is assumed to exist as the first condition of your employment. What is required at present is not writing, but the bringing to light of a distinct, significant fact – I would almost say of an alarming fact.'

'I need not say that all my endeavours shall be directed to that end,' Mr. Verloc said, with convinced modulations in his conversational husky tone. But the sense of being blinked at watchfully behind the blind glitter of these eyeglasses on the other side of the table disconcerted him. He stopped short with a gesture of absolute devotion. The useful hard-working, if obscure member of the Embassy had an air of being impressed by some newly-born thought.

'You are very corpulent,' he said.

This observation, really of a psychological nature, and advanced with the modest hesitation of an office-man more familiar with ink and paper than with the requirements of active life, stung Mr. Verloc in the manner of a rude personal remark. He stepped back a pace.

'Eh? What were you pleased to say?' he exclaimed, with husky resentment.

The Chancelier d'Ambassade, entrusted with the conduct of this interview, seemed to find it too much for him.

'I think,' he said, 'that you had better see Mr. Vladimir. Yes, decidedly I think you ought to see Mr. Vladimir. Be good enough to wait here,' he added, and went out with mincing steps.

At once Mr. Verloc passed his hand over his hair. A slight perspiration had broken out on his forehead. He let the air escape from his pursed-up lips like a man blowing at a spoonful of hot soup. But when the servant in brown appeared at the door silently, Mr. Verloc had not moved an inch from the place he had occupied throughout the interview. He had remained motionless, as if feeling himself surrounded by pitfalls.

He walked along a passage lighted by a lonely gas-jet, then up a flight of winding stairs, and through a glazed and cheerful corridor on the first floor. The footman threw open a door, and stood aside. The feet of Mr. Verloc felt a thick carpet. The room was large, with three windows; and a young man with a shaven, big face, sitting in a roomy armchair before a vast mahogany writing-table, said in French to the Chancelier d'Ambassade, who was going out with the papers in his hand:

'You are quite right, mon cher. He's fat – the animal.'

Mr. Vladimir, First Secretary, had a drawing-room reputation as an agreeable and entertaining man. He was something of a favourite in society. His wit consisted in discovering droll connections between incongruous ideas; and when talking in that strain he sat well forward on his seat, with his left hand raised, as if exhibiting his funny demonstrations between the thumb and forefinger, while his round and clean-shaven face wore an expression of merry perplexity.

But there was no trace of merriment or perplexity in the way he looked at Mr. Verloc. Lying far back in the deep armchair, with squarely spread elbows, and throwing one leg over a thick knee, he had with his smooth and rosy countenance the air of a preternaturally thriving baby that will not stand nonsense from anybody.

'You understand French, I suppose?' he said.

Mr. Verloc stated huskily that he did. His whole vast bulk had a forward inclination. He stood on the carpet in the middle of the room, clutching his hat and stick in one hand; the other hung lifelessly by his side. He muttered unobtrusively somewhere deep down in his throat something about having done his military service in the French artillery. At once, with contemptuous perversity, Mr. Vladimir changed the language, and began to speak idiomatic English without the slightest trace of a foreign accent.

'Ah! Yes. Of course. Let's see. How much did you get for obtaining the design of the improved breech-block of their new field-gun?'

'Five years' rigorous confinement in a fortress,' Mr. Verloc answered, unexpectedly, but without any sign of feeling.

'You got off easily,' was Mr. Vladimir's comment. 'And, anyhow, it served you right for letting yourself get caught. What made you go in for that sort of thing – eh?'

Mr. Verloc's husky conversational voice was heard speaking of youth, of a fatal infatuation for an unworthy —

'Aha! Cherchez la femme,' Mr. Vladimir deigned to interrupt, unbending, but without affability; there was, on the contrary, a touch of grimness in his condescension. 'How long have you been employed by the Embassy here?' he asked.

'Ever since the time of the late Baron Stott-Wartenheim,' Mr. Verloc answered in subdued tones, and protruding his lips sadly, in sign of sorrow for the deceased diplomat. The First Secretary observed this play of physiognomy steadily.

'Ah! ever since. . . . Well! What have you got to say for yourself?' he asked, sharply.

Mr. Verloc answered with some surprise that he was not aware of having anything special to say. He had been summoned by a letter — And he plunged his hand busily into the side pocket of his overcoat, but before the mocking, cynical watchfulness of Mr. Vladimir, concluded to leave it there.

'Bah!' said the latter. 'What do you mean by getting out of condition like this? You haven't got even the physique of your profession. You – a member of a starving proletariat – never! You – a desperate socialist or anarchist – which is it?'

'Anarchist,' stated Mr. Verloc in a deadened tone.

'Bosh!' went on Mr. Vladimir, without raising his voice. 'You startled old Wurmt himself. You wouldn't deceive an idiot. They all are that by-the-by, but you seem to me simply impossible. So you began your connection with us by stealing the French gun designs. And you got yourself caught. That must have been very disagreeable to our Government. You don't seem to be very smart.'

Mr. Verloc tried to exculpate himself huskily.

'As I've had occasion to observe before, a fatal infatuation for an unworthy —'

Mr. Vladimir raised a large, white, plump hand.

'Ah, yes. The unlucky attachment – of your youth. She got hold of the money, and then sold you to the police – eh?'

The doleful change in Mr. Verloc's physiognomy, the momentary drooping of his whole person, confessed that such was the regrettable case. Mr. Vladimir's hand clasped the ankle reposing on his knee. The sock was of dark blue silk.

'You see, that was not very clever of you. Perhaps you are too susceptible.'

Mr. Verloc intimated in a throaty, veiled murmur that he was no longer young.

'Oh! That's a failing which age does not cure,' Mr. Vladimir remarked, with sinister familiarity. 'But no! You are too fat for that. You could not have come to look like this if you had been at all susceptible. I'll tell you what I think is the matter: you are a lazy fellow. How long have you been drawing pay from this Embassy?'

'Eleven years,' was the answer, after a moment of sulky hesitation. 'I've been charged with several missions to London while His Excellency Baron Stott-Wartenheim was still Ambassador in Paris. Then by his Excellency's instructions I settled down in London. I am English.'

'You are! Are you? Eh?'

'A natural-born British subject,' Mr. Verloc said, stolidly. 'But my father was French, and so —'

'Never mind explaining,' interrupted the other. 'I daresay you could have been legally a Marshal of France and a Member of Parliament in England – and then, indeed, you would have been of some use to our Embassy.'

This flight of fancy provoked something like a faint smile on Mr. Verloc's face. Mr. Vladimir retained an imperturbable gravity.

'But, as I've said, you are a lazy fellow; you don't use your opportunities. In the time of Baron Stott-Wartenheim we had a lot of soft-headed people running this Embassy. They caused fellows of your sort to form a false conception of the nature of a secret service fund. It is my business to correct this misapprehension by telling you what the secret service is not. It is not a philanthropic institution. I've had you called here on purpose to tell you this.'

Mr. Vladimir observed the forced expression of bewilderment on Verloc's face, and smiled sarcastically.

'I see that you understand me perfectly. I daresay you are intelligent enough for your work. What we want now is activity – activity.'

On repeating this last word Mr. Vladimir laid a long white forefinger on the edge of the desk. Every trace of huskiness disappeared from Verloc's voice. The nape of his gross neck became crimson above the velvet collar of his overcoat. His lips quivered before they came widely open.

'If you'll only be good enough to look up my record,' he boomed out in his great, clear, oratorical bass, 'you'll see I gave a warning only three months ago on the occasion of the Grand Duke Romuald's visit to Paris, which was telegraphed from here to the French police, and —'

'Tut, tut!' broke out Mr. Vladimir, with a frowning grimace. 'The French police had no use for your warning. Don't roar like this. What the devil do you mean?'

With a note of proud humility Mr. Verloc apologized for forgetting himself. His voice, famous for years at open-air meetings and at workmen's assemblies in large halls, had contributed, he said, to his reputation of a good and trustworthy comrade. It was, therefore, a part of his usefulness. It had inspired confidence in his principles. 'I was always put up to speak by the leaders at a critical moment,' Mr. Verloc declared, with obvious satisfaction. There was no uproar above which he could not make himself heard, he added; and suddenly he made a demonstration.

'Allow me,' he said. With lowered forehead, without looking up, swiftly and ponderously, he crossed the room to one of the French windows. As if giving way to an uncontrollable impulse, he opened it a little. Mr. Vladimir, jumping up amazed from the depths of the armchair, looked over his shoulder; and below, across the courtyard of the Embassy, well beyond the open gate, could be seen the broad back of a policeman watching idly the gorgeous perambulator of a wealthy baby being wheeled in state across the Square.

'Constable!' said Mr. Verloc, with no more effort than if he were whispering; and Mr. Vladimir burst into a laugh on seeing the policeman spin round as if prodded by a sharp instrument. Mr. Verloc shut the window quietly, and returned to the middle of the room.

'With a voice like that,' he said, putting on the husky conversational pedal, 'I was naturally trusted. And I knew what to say, too.'

Mr. Vladimir, arranging his cravat, observed him in the glass over the mantelpiece.

'I daresay you have the social revolutionary jargon by heart well enough,' he said, contemptuously. 'Vox et. . . . You haven't ever studied Latin – have you?'

'No,' growled Mr. Verloc. 'You did not expect me to know it. I belong to the million. Who knows Latin? Only a few hundred imbeciles who aren't fit to take care of themselves.'

For some thirty seconds longer Mr. Vladimir studied in the mirror the fleshy profile, the gross bulk, of the man behind him. And at the same time he had the advantage of seeing his own face, clean-shaved and round, rosy about the gills, and with the thin, sensitive lips formed exactly for the utterance of those delicate witticisms which had made him such a favourite in the very highest society. Then he turned, and advanced into the room with such determination that the very ends of his quaintly old-fashioned bow necktie seemed to bristle with unspeakable menaces. The movement was so swift and fierce that Mr. Verloc, casting an oblique glance, quailed inwardly.

'Aha! You dare be impudent,' Mr. Vladimir began, with an amazingly guttural intonation not only utterly un-English, but absolutely un-European, and startling even to Mr. Verloc's experience of cosmopolitan slums. 'You dare! Well, I am going to speak plain English to you. Voice won't do. We have no use for your voice. We don't want a voice. We want facts – startling facts – damn you,' he added, with a sort of ferocious discretion, right into Mr. Verloc's face.

'Don't you try to come over me with your Hyperborean manners,' Mr. Verloc defended himself, huskily, looking at the carpet. At this his interlocutor, smiling mockingly above the bristling bow of his necktie, switched the conversation into French.

'You give yourself for an "agent provocateur". The proper business of an "agent provocateur" is to provoke. As far as I can judge from your record kept here, you have done nothing to earn your money for the last three years.'

'Nothing!' exclaimed Verloc, stirring not a limb, and not raising his eyes, but with the note of sincere feeling in his tone. 'I have several times prevented what might have been —'

'There is a proverb in this country which says prevention is better than cure,' interrupted Mr. Vladimir, throwing himself into the armchair. 'It is stupid in a general way. There is no end to prevention. But it is characteristic. They dislike finality in this country. Don't you be too English. And in this particular instance, don't be absurd. The evil is already here. We don't want prevention – we want cure.'

He paused, turned to the desk, and turning over some papers lying there, spoke in a changed, businesslike tone, without looking at Mr. Verloc.

'You know, of course, of the International Conference assembled in Milan?'

Mr. Verloc intimated hoarsely that he was in the habit of reading the daily papers. To a further question his answer was that, of course, he understood what he read. At this Mr. Vladimir, smiling faintly at the documents he was still scanning one after another, murmured 'As long as it is not written in Latin, I suppose.'

'Or Chinese,' added Mr. Verloc, stolidly.

'H'm. Some of your revolutionary friends' effusions are written in a *charabia* every bit as incomprehensible as Chinese —' Mr. Vladimir let fall disdainfully a grey sheet of printed matter. 'What are all these leaflets headed F. P., with a hammer, pen, and torch crossed? What does it mean, this F. P.?' Mr. Verloc approached the imposing writing-table.

'The Future of the Proletariat. It's a society,' he explained, standing ponderously by the side of the arm-chair, 'not anarchist in principle, but open to all shades of revolutionary opinion.'

'Are you in it?'

'One of the Vice-Presidents,' Mr. Verloc breathed out heavily; and the First Secretary of the Embassy raised his head to look at him.

'Then you ought to be ashamed of yourself,' he said, incisively. 'Isn't your society capable of anything else but printing this prophetic bosh in blunt type on this filthy paper – eh? Why don't you do something? Look here. I've this matter in hand now, and I tell you plainly that you will have to earn your money. The good old Stott-Wartenheim times are over. No work, no pay.'

Mr. Verloc felt a queer sensation of faintness in his stout legs. He stepped back one pace, and blew his nose loudly.

He was, in truth, startled and alarmed. The rusty London sunshine struggling clear of the London mist shed a lukewarm brightness into the First Secretary's private room: and in the silence Mr. Verloc heard against a window-pane the faint buzzing of a fly – his first fly of the year – heralding better than any number of swallows the approach of spring. The useless fussing of that tiny, energetic organism affected unpleasantly this big man threatened in his indolence.

In the pause Mr. Vladimir formulated in his mind a series of disparaging remarks concerning Mr. Verloc's face and figure. The fellow was unexpectedly vulgar, heavy, and impudently unintelligent. He looked uncommonly like a master plumber come to present his bill. The First Secretary of the Embassy, from his occasional

excursions into the field of American humour, had
formed a special notion of that class of mechanic as the
embodiment of fraudulent laziness and incompetency.

This was then the famous and trusty secret agent, so
secret that he was never designated otherwise but by the
symbol Δ. in the late Baron Stott-Wartenheim's official,
semi-official, and confidential correspondence; the celebrated agent Δ. whose warnings had the power to
change the schemes and the dates of royal, imperial,
grand-ducal journeys, and sometimes cause them to be
put off altogether! This fellow! And Mr. Vladimir
indulged mentally in an enormous and derisive fit of merriment, partly at his own astonishment, which he judged
naïve, but mostly at the expense of the universally
regretted Baron Stott-Wartenheim. His late Excellency,
whom the august favour of his Imperial master had
imposed as Ambassador upon several reluctant Ministers
of Foreign Affairs, had enjoyed in his lifetime a fame for
an owlish, pessimistic gullibility. His Excellency had the
social revolution on the brain. He imagined himself to be
a diplomatist set apart by a special dispensation to watch
the end of diplomacy, and pretty nearly the end of the
world, in a horrid, democratic upheaval. His prophetic
and doleful despatches had been for years the joke of
Foreign Offices. He was said to have exclaimed on his
deathbed (visited by his Imperial friend and master):
'Unhappy Europe! Thou shalt perish by the moral
insanity of thy children!' He was fated to be the victim of
the first humbugging rascal that came along, thought Mr.
Vladimir, smiling vaguely at Mr. Verloc.

'You ought to venerate the memory of Baron Stott-
Wartenheim,' he exclaimed, suddenly.

The lowered physiognomy of Mr. Verloc expressed a
sombre and weary annoyance.

'Permit me to observe to you,' he said, 'that I came
here because I was summoned by a peremptory letter. I
have been here only twice before in the last eleven

years, and certainly never at eleven in the morning.
It isn't very wise to call me up like this. There is just
a chance of being seen. And that would be no joke for
me.'

Mr. Vladimir shrugged his shoulders.

'It would destroy my usefulness,' continued the other
hotly.

'That's your affair,' murmured Mr. Vladimir, with soft
brutality. 'When you cease to be useful you shall cease to
be employed. Yes. Right off. Cut short. You shall —' Mr.
Vladimir, frowning, paused, at a loss for a sufficiently
idiomatic expression, and instantly brightened up, with a
grin of beautifully white teeth. 'You shall be chucked,'
he brought out, ferociously.

Once more Mr. Verloc had to react with all the force of
his will against that sensation of faintness running down
one's legs which once upon a time had inspired some
poor devil with the felicitous expression: 'My heart went
down into my boots.' Mr. Verloc, aware of the sensation,
raised his head bravely.

Mr. Vladimir bore the look of heavy inquiry with perfect serenity.

'What we want is to administer a tonic to the Conference in Milan,' he said, airily. 'Its deliberations upon
international action for the suppression of political crime
don't seem to get anywhere. England lags. This country
is absurd with its sentimental regard for individual
liberty. It's intolerable to think that all your friends have
got only to come over to —'

'In that way I have them all under my eye,' Mr. Verloc
interrupted, huskily.

'It would be much more to the point to have them all
under lock and key. England must be brought into line.
The imbecile bourgeoisie of this country make themselves the accomplices of the very people whose aim is
to drive them out of their houses to starve in ditches.
And they have the political power still, if they only had

the sense to use it for their preservation. I suppose you agree that the middle classes are stupid?'

Mr. Verloc agreed hoarsely.

'They are.'

'They have no imagination. They are blinded by an idiotic vanity. What they want just now is a jolly good scare. This is the psychological moment to set your friends to work. I have had you called here to develop to you my idea.'

And Mr. Vladimir developed his idea from on high, with scorn and condescension, displaying at the same time an amount of ignorance as to the real aims, thoughts, and methods of the revolutionary world which filled the silent Mr. Verloc with inward consternation. He confounded causes with effects more than was excusable; the most distinguished propagandists with impulsive bomb throwers; assumed organization where in the nature of things it could not exist; spoke of the social revolutionary party one moment as of a perfectly disciplined army, where the word of chiefs was supreme, and at another as if it had been the loosest association of desperate brigands that ever camped in a mountain gorge. Once Mr. Verloc had opened his mouth for a protest, but the raising of a shapely, large white hand arrested him. Very soon he became too appalled to even try to protest. He listened in a stillness of dread which resembled the immobility of profound attention.

'A series of outrages,' Mr. Vladimir continued, calmly, 'executed here in this country; not only *planned* here – that would not do – they would not mind. Your friends could set half the Continent on fire without influencing the public opinion here in favour of a universal repressive legislation. They will not look outside their backyard here.'

Mr. Verloc cleared his throat, but his heart failed him, and he said nothing.

'These outrages need not be especially sanguinary,'

Mr. Vladimir went on, as if delivering a scientific lecture, 'but they must be sufficiently startling – effective. Let them be directed against buildings, for instance. What is the fetish of the hour that all the bourgeoisie recognize – eh, Mr. Verloc?'

Mr. Verloc opened his hands and shrugged his shoulders slightly.

'You are too lazy to think,' was Mr. Vladimir's comment upon that gesture. 'Pay attention to what I say. The fetish of to-day is neither royalty nor religion. Therefore the palace and the church should be left alone. You understand what I mean, Mr. Verloc?'

The dismay and the scorn of Mr. Verloc found vent in an attempt at levity.

'Perfectly. But what of the Embassies? A series of attacks on the various Embassies,' he began; but he could not withstand the cold, watchful stare of the First Secretary.

'You can be facetious, I see,' the latter observed, carelessly. "That's all right. It may enliven your oratory at socialistic congresses. But this room is no place for it. It would be infinitely safer for you to follow carefully what I am saying. As you are being called upon to furnish facts instead of cock-and-bull stories, you had better try to make your profit off what I am taking the trouble to explain to you. The sacrosanct fetish of to-day is science. Why don't you get some of your friends to go for that wooden-faced panjandrum – eh? Is it not part of these institutions which must be swept away before the F. P. comes along?'

Mr. Verloc said nothing. He was afraid to open his lips lest a groan should escape him.

'This is what you should try for. An attempt upon a crowned head or on a president is sensational enough in a way, but not so much as it used to be. It has entered into the general conception of the existence of all chiefs of state. It's almost conventional – especially since so

many presidents have been assassinated. Now let us
take an outrage upon – say a church. Horrible enough at
first sight, no doubt, and yet not so effective as a person
of an ordinary mind might think. No matter how revolutionary and anarchist in inception, there would be fools
enough to give such an outrage the character of a religious manifestation. And that would detract from the
especial alarming significance we wish to give to the act.
A murderous attempt on a restaurant or a theatre would
suffer in the same way from the suggestion of non-
political passion; the exasperation of a hungry man, an
act of social revenge. All this is used up; it is no longer
instructive as an object lesson in revolutionary anarchism. Every newspaper has ready-made phrases to
explain such manifestations away. I am about to give you
the philosophy of bomb throwing from my point of view;
from the point of view you pretend to have been serving
for the last eleven years. I will try not to talk above your
head. The sensibilities of the class you are attacking are
soon blunted. Property seems to them an indestructible
thing. You can't count upon their emotions either of pity
or fear for very long. A bomb outrage to have any
influence on public opinion now must go beyond the
intention of vengeance or terrorism. It must be purely
destructive. It must be that, and only that, beyond the
faintest suspicion of any other object. You anarchists
should make it clear that you are perfectly determined to
make a clean sweep of the whole social creation. But
how to get that appallingly absurd notion into the heads
of the middle classes so that there should be no mistake?
That's the question. By directing your blows at something outside the ordinary passions of humanity is the
answer. Of course, there is art. A bomb in the National
Gallery would make some noise. But it would not be
serious enough. Art has never been their fetish. It's like
breaking a few back windows in a man's house; whereas,
if you want to make him really sit up, you must try at

least to raise the roof. There would be some screaming of
course, but from whom? Artists – art critics and such like
– people of no account. Nobody minds what they say.
But there is learning – science. Any imbecile that has got
an income believes in that. He does not know why, but
he believes it matters somehow. It is the sacrosanct fetish. All the damned professors are radicals at heart. Let
them know that their great panjandrum has got to go,
too, to make room for the Future of the Proletariat. A
howl from all these intellectual idiots is bound to help
forward the labours of the Milan Conference. They will
be writing to the papers. Their indignation would be
above suspicion, no material interests being openly at
stake, and it will alarm every selfishness of the class
which should be impressed. They believe that in some
mysterious way science is at the source of their material
prosperity. They do. And the absurd ferocity of such a
demonstration will affect them more profoundly than
the mangling of a whole street – or theatre – full of their
own kind. To that last they can always say: "Oh! it's mere
class hate." But what is one to say to an act of destructive
ferocity so absurd as to be incomprehensible, inexplicable, almost unthinkable; in fact, mad? Madness alone is
truly terrifying, inasmuch as you cannot placate it either
by threats, persuasion, or bribes. Moreover, I am a civilized man. I would never dream of directing you to
organize a mere butchery, even if I expected the best
results from it. But I wouldn't expect from a butchery
the result I want. Murder is always with us. It is almost
an institution. The demonstration must be against learning – science. But not every science will do. The attack
must have all the shocking senselessness of gratuitous
blasphemy. Since bombs are your means of expression, it
would be really telling if one could throw a bomb into
pure mathematics. But that is impossible. I have been
trying to educate you; I have expounded to you the
higher philosophy of your usefulness, and suggested to

you some serviceable arguments. The practical application of my teaching interests *you* mostly. But from the
moment I have undertaken to interview you I have also
given some attention to the practical aspect of the question. What do you think of having a go at astronomy?'

For some time already Mr. Verloc's immobility by the
side of the armchair resembled a state of collapsed coma
– a sort of passive insensibility interrupted by slight convulsive starts, such as may be observed in the domestic
dog having a nightmare on the hearthrug. And it was in
an uneasy, doglike growl that he repeated the word:

'Astronomy.'

He had not recovered thoroughly as yet from the
state of bewilderment brought about by the effort to
follow Mr. Vladimir's rapid, incisive utterance. It had
overcome his power of assimilation. It had made him
angry. This anger was complicated by incredulity. And
suddenly it dawned upon him that all this was an elaborate joke. Mr. Vladimir exhibited his white teeth in a
smile, with dimples on his round, full face posed with a
complacent inclination above the bristling bow of his
necktie. The favourite of intelligent society women had
assumed his drawing-room attitude accompanying the
delivery of delicate witticisms. Sitting well forward, his
white hand upraised, he seemed to hold delicately
between his thumb and forefinger the subtlety of his
suggestion.

'There could be nothing better. Such an outrage com-
bines the greatest possible regard for humanity with the
most alarming display of ferocious imbecility. I defy the
ingenuity of journalists to persuade their public that any
given member of the proletariat can have a personal griev-
ance against astronomy. Starvation itself could hardly be
dragged in there – eh? And there are other advantages.
The whole civilized world has heard of Greenwich. The
very boot-blacks in the basement of Charing Cross Station know something of it. See?'

The features of Mr. Vladimir, so well known in the best society by their humorous urbanity, beamed with cynical self-satisfaction, which would have astonished the intelligent women his wit entertained so exquisitely. 'Yes,' he continued, with a contemptuous smile, 'the blowing up of the first meridian is bound to raise a howl of execration.'

'A difficult business,' Mr. Verloc mumbled, feeling that this was the only safe thing to say.

'What is the matter? Haven't you the whole gang under your hand? The very pick of the basket? That old terrorist Yundt is here. I see him walking about Piccadilly in his green havelock almost every day. And Michaelis, the ticket-of-leave apostle – you don't mean to say you don't know where he is? Because if you don't, I can tell you,' Mr. Vladimir went on menacingly. 'If you imagine that you are the only one on the secret fund list, you are mistaken.'

This perfectly gratuitous suggestion caused Mr. Verloc to shuffle his feet slightly.

'And the whole Lausanne lot – eh? Haven't they been flocking over here at the first hint of the Milan Conference? This is an absurd country.'

'It will cost money,' Mr. Verloc said, by a sort of instinct.

'That cock won't fight,' Mr. Vladimir retorted, with an amazingly genuine English accent. 'You'll get your screw every month, and no more till something happens. And if nothing happens very soon you won't get even that. What's your ostensible occupation? What are you supposed to live by?'

'I keep a shop,' answered Mr. Verloc.

'A shop! What sort of shop?'

'Stationery, newspapers. My wife —'

'Your what?' interrupted Mr. Vladimir in his guttural Central Asian tones.

'My wife.' Mr. Verloc raised his husky voice slightly. 'I am married.'

'That be damned for a yarn,' exclaimed the other in unfeigned astonishment. 'Married! And you a professed anarchist, too! What is this confounded nonsense? But I suppose it's merely a manner of speaking. Anarchists don't marry. It's well known. They can't. It would be apostasy.'

'My wife isn't one,' Mr. Verloc mumbled, sulkily. 'Moreover, it's no concern of yours.'

'Oh, yes, it is,' snapped Mr. Vladimir. 'I am beginning to be convinced that you are not at all the man for the work you've been employed on. Why you must have discredited yourself completely in your own world by your marriage. Couldn't you have managed without? This is your virtuous attachment – eh? What with one sort of attachment and another you are doing away with your usefulness.'

Mr. Verloc, puffing out his cheeks, let the air escape violently, and that was all. He had armed himself with patience. It was not to be tried much longer. The First Secretary became suddenly very curt, detached, final.

'You may go now,' he said. 'A dynamite outrage must be provoked. I give you a month. The sittings of the Conference are suspended. Before it reassembles again something must have happened here, or your connection with us ceases.'

He changed the note once more with an unprincipled versatility.

'Think over my philosophy, Mr. – Mr. – Verloc,' he said, with a sort of chaffing condescension, waving his hand towards the door. 'Go for the first meridian. You don't know the middle classes as well as I do. Their sensibilities are jaded. The first meridian. Nothing better, and nothing easier, I should think.'

He had got up, and with his thin sensitive lips twitching humorously, watched in the glass over the mantelpiece Mr. Verloc backing out of the room heavily, hat and stick in hand. The door closed.

The footman in trousers, appearing suddenly in the corridor, let Mr. Verloc another way out and through a small door in the corner of the courtyard. The porter standing at the gate ignored his exit completely; and Mr. Verloc retraced the path of his morning's pilgrimage as if in a dream – an angry dream. This detachment from the material world was so complete that, though the mortal envelope of Mr. Verloc had not hastened unduly along the streets, that part of him to which it would be unwarrantably rude to refuse immortality found itself at the shop door all at once, as borne from west to east on the wings of a great wind. He walked straight behind the counter, and sat down on a wooden chair that stood there. No one appeared to disturb his solitude. Stevie, put into a green baize apron, was now sweeping and dusting upstairs, intent and conscientious, as though he were playing at it; and Mrs. Verloc, warned in the kitchen by the clatter of the cracked bell, had merely come to the glazed door of the parlour, and putting the curtain aside a little, had peered into the dim shop. Seeing her husband sitting there shadowy and bulky, with his hat tilted far back on his head, she had at once returned to her stove. An hour or more later she took the green baize apron off her brother Stevie, and instructed him to wash his hands and face in the peremptory tone she had used in that connection for fifteen years or so – ever since she had, in fact, ceased to attend to the boy's hands and face herself. She spared presently a glance away from her dishing-up for the inspection of that face and those hands which Stevie, approaching the kitchen table, offered for her approval with an air of self-assurance hiding a perpetual residue of anxiety. Formerly the anger of the father was the supremely effective sanction of these rites, but Mr. Verloc's placidity in domestic life would have made all mention of anger incredible – even to poor Stevie's nervousness. The theory was that Mr. Verloc would have been inexpressibly pained and shocked by any deficiency of cleanliness at meal times. Winnie after the death of her father found considerable consolation in the feeling that she need no longer tremble for poor Stevie. She could not bear to see the boy hurt. It maddened her. As a little girl she had often faced with blazing eyes the irascible licensed victualler in defence of her brother. Nothing now in Mrs. Verloc's appearance could lead one to suppose that she was capable of a passionate demonstration.

She finished her dishing-up. The table was laid in the parlour. Going to the foot of the stairs she screamed out 'Mother!' Then opening the glazed door leading to the shop, she said quietly 'Adolf!' Mr. Verloc had not changed his position; he had not apparently stirred a limb for an hour and a half. He got up heavily, and came to his dinner in his overcoat and with his hat on, without uttering a word. His silence in itself had nothing startlingly unusual in this household, hidden in the shades of the sordid street seldom touched by the sun, behind the dim shop with its wares of disreputable rubbish. Only that day Mr. Verloc's taciturnity was so obviously thoughtful that the two women were impressed by it. They sat silent themselves, keeping a watchful eye on poor Stevie, lest he should break out into one of his fits of loquacity. He faced Mr. Verloc across the table, and remained very good and quiet, staring vacantly. The endeavour to keep him from making himself objectionable in any way to the master of the house put no inconsiderable anxiety into these two women's lives. 'That boy,' as they alluded to him softly between themselves, had been a source of that sort of anxiety almost from the very day of his birth. The late licensed victualler's humiliation at having such a very peculiar boy for a son manifested itself by a propensity to brutal treatment; for he was a person of fine sensibilities, and his sufferings as a man and a father were perfectly genuine. Afterwards Stevie had to be kept from making himself a nuisance to

the single gentlemen lodgers, who are themselves a
queer lot, and are easily aggrieved. And there was always
the anxiety of his mere existence to face. Visions of a
workhouse infirmary for her child had haunted the old
woman in the basement breakfast-room of the decayed
Belgravian house. 'If you had not found such a good husband, my dear,' she used to say to her daughter, 'I don't
know what would have become of that poor boy.'

Mr. Verloc extended as much recognition to Stevie as
a man not particularly fond of animals may give to his
wife's beloved cat; and this recognition, benevolent and
perfunctory, was essentially of the same quality. Both
women admitted to themselves that not much more
could be reasonably expected. It was enough to earn for
Mr. Verloc the old woman's reverential gratitude. In the
early days, made sceptical by the trials of friendless life,
she used sometimes to ask anxiously: 'You don't think,
my dear, that Mr. Verloc is getting tired of seeing Stevie
about?' To this Winnie replied habitually by a slight toss
of her head. Once, however, she retorted, with a rather
grim pertness: 'He'll have to get tired of me first.' A long
silence ensued. The mother, with her feet propped up
on a stool, seemed to be trying to get to the bottom of
that answer, whose feminine profundity had struck her
all of a heap. She had never really understood why Winnie had married Mr. Verloc. It was very sensible of her,
and evidently had turned out for the best, but her girl
might have naturally hoped to find somebody of a more
suitable age. There had been a steady young fellow, only
son of a butcher in the next street, helping his father in
business, with whom Winnie had been walking out with
obvious gusto. He was dependent on his father, it is true;
but the business was good, and his prospects excellent.
He took her girl to the theatre on several evenings. Then
just as she began to dread to hear of their engagement
(for what could she have done with that big house alone,
with Stevie on her hands), that romance came to an

abrupt end, and Winnie went about looking very dull.
But Mr. Verloc, turning up providentially to occupy the
first-floor front bedroom, there had been no more question of the young butcher. It was clearly providential.

CHAPTER THREE

'...ALL idealization makes life poorer. To beautify it is to take away its character of complexity – it is to destroy it. Leave that to the moralists, my boy. History is made by men, but they do not make it in their heads. The ideas that are born in their consciousness play an insignificant part in the march of events. History is dominated and determined by the tool and the production – by force of economic conditions. Capitalism has made socialism, and the laws made by capitalism for the protection of property are responsible for anarchism. No one can tell what form the social organization may take in the future. Then why indulge in prophetic phantasies? At best they can only interpret the mind of the prophet, and can have no objective value. Leave that pastime to the moralists, my boy.'

Michaelis, the ticket-of-leave apostle, was speaking in an even voice, a voice that wheezed as if deadened and oppressed by the layer of fat on his chest. He had come out of a highly hygienic prison round like a tub, with an enormous stomach and distended cheeks of a pale, semi-transparent complexion, as though for fifteen years the servants of an outraged society had made a point of stuffing him with fattening foods in a damp and lightless cellar. And ever since he had never managed to get his weight down as much as an ounce.

It was said that for three seasons running a very wealthy old lady had sent him for a cure to Marienbad – where he was about to share the public curiosity once with a crowned head – but the police on that occasion ordered him to leave within twelve hours. His martyrdom was continued by forbidding him all access to the healing waters. But he was resigned now.

With his elbow presenting no appearance of a joint, but more like a bend in a dummy's limb, thrown over the back of a chair, he leaned forward slightly over his short and enormous thighs to spit into the grate.

'Yes! I had the time to think things out a little,' he added without emphasis. 'Society has given me plenty of time for meditation.'

On the other side of the fireplace, in the horsehair armchair where Mrs. Verloc's mother was generally privileged to sit, Karl Yundt giggled grimly, with a faint black grimace of a toothless mouth. The terrorist, as he called himself, was old and bald, with a narrow, snow-white wisp of a goatee hanging limply from his chin. An extraordinary expression of underhand malevolence survived in his extinguished eyes. When he rose painfully the thrusting forward of a skinny groping hand deformed by gouty swellings suggested the effort of a moribund murderer summoning all his remaining strength for a last stab. He leaned on a thick stick, which trembled under his other hand.

'I have always dreamed,' he mouthed, fiercely, 'of a band of men absolute in their resolve to discard all scruples in the choice of means, strong enough to give themselves frankly the name of destroyers, and free from the taint of that resigned pessimism which rots the world. No pity for anything on earth, including themselves, and death enlisted for good and all in the service of humanity – that's what I would have liked to see.'

His little bald head quivered, imparting a comical vibration to the wisp of white goatee. His enunciation would have been almost totally unintelligible to a stranger. His worn-out passion, resembling in its impotent fierceness the excitement of a senile sensualist, was badly served by a dried throat and toothless gums which seemed to catch the tip of his tongue. Mr. Verloc, established in the corner of the sofa at the other end of the room, emitted two hearty grunts of assent.

The old terrorist turned slowly his head on his skinny neck from side to side.

'And I could never get as many as three such men together. So much for your rotten pessimism,' he snarled at Michaelis, who uncrossed his thick legs similar to bolsters, and slid his feet abruptly under his chair in sign of exasperation.

He a pessimist! Preposterous! He cried out that the charge was outrageous. He was so far from pessimism that he saw already the end of all private property coming along logically, unavoidably, by the mere development of its inherent viciousness. The possessors of property had not only to face the awakened proletariat, but they had also to fight amongst themselves. Yes. Struggle, warfare, was the condition of private ownership. It was fatal. Ah! he did not depend upon emotional excitement to keep up his belief, no declamations, no anger, no visions of blood-red flags waving, or metaphorical lurid suns of vengeance rising above the horizon of a doomed society. Not he! Cold reason, he boasted, was the basis of his optimism. Yes, optimism —

His laborious wheezing stopped, then, after a gasp or two, he added:

'Don't you think that, if I had not been the optimist I am, I could not have found in fifteen years some means to cut my throat? And, in the last instance, there were always the walls of my cell to dash my head against.'

The shortness of breath took all fire, all animation out of his voice; his great, pale cheeks hung like filled pouches, motionless, without a quiver; but in his blue eyes, narrowed as if peering, there was the same look of confident shrewdness, a little crazy in its fixity, they must have had while the indomitable optimist sat

thinking at night in his cell. Before him, Karl Yundt
remained standing, one wing of his faded greenish havelock thrown back cavalierly over his shoulder. Seated in
front of the fireplace, Comrade Ossipon, ex-medical student, the principal writer of the F. P. leaflets, stretched
out his robust legs, keeping the soles of his boots turned
up to the glow in the grate. A bush of crinkly yellow hair
topped his red, freckled face, with a flattened nose and
prominent mouth cast in the rough mould of the negro
type. His almond-shaped eyes leered languidly over the
high cheekbones. He wore a grey flannel shirt, the loose
ends of a black silk tie hung down the buttoned breast of
his serge coat; and his head resting on the back of his
chair, his throat largely exposed, he raised to his lips a
cigarette in a long wooden tube, puffing jets of smoke
straight up at the ceiling.

Michaelis pursued his idea – *the* idea of his solitary
reclusion – the thought vouchsafed to his captivity and
growing like a faith revealed in visions. He talked to
himself, indifferent to the sympathy or hostility of his
hearers, indifferent indeed to their presence, from the
habit he had acquired of thinking aloud hopefully in
the solitude of the four whitewashed walls of his cell,
in the sepulchral silence of the great blind pile of bricks
near a river, sinister and ugly like a colossal mortuary for
the socially drowned.

He was no good in discussion, not because any
amount of argument could shake his faith, but because
the mere fact of hearing another voice disconcerted him
painfully, confusing his thoughts at once – these
thoughts that for so many years, in a mental solitude
more barren than a waterless desert, no living voice had
ever combated, commented, or approved.

No one interrupted him now, and he made again the
confession of his faith, mastering him irresistible and
complete like an act of grace: the secret of fate discovered in the material side of life; the economic condi-

tion of the world responsible for the past and shaping the future; the source of all history, of all ideas, guiding the mental development of mankind and the very impulses of their passion —

A harsh laugh from Comrade Ossipon cut the tirade dead short in a sudden faltering of the tongue and a bewildered unsteadiness of the apostle's mildly exalted eyes. He closed them slowly for a moment, as if to collect his routed thoughts. A silence fell; but what with the two gas-jets over the table and the glowing grate the little parlour behind Mr. Verloc's shop had become frightfully hot. Mr. Verloc, getting off the sofa with ponderous reluctance, opened the door leading into the kitchen to get more air, and thus disclosed the innocent Stevie, seated very good and quiet at a deal table, drawing circles, circles, circles; innumerable circles, concentric, eccentric; a coruscating whirl of circles that by their tangled multitude of repeated curves, uniformity of form, and confusion of intersecting lines suggested a rendering of cosmic chaos, the symbolism of a mad art attempting the inconceivable. The artist never turned his head; and in all his soul's application to the task his back quivered, his thin neck, sunk into a deep hollow at the base of the skull, seemed ready to snap.

Mr. Verloc, after a grunt of disapproving surprise, returned to the sofa. Alexander Ossipon got up, tall in his threadbare blue serge suit under the low ceiling, shook off the stiffness of long immobility, and strolled away into the kitchen (down two steps) to look over Stevie's shoulder. He came back, pronouncing oracularly: 'Very good. Very characteristic, perfectly typical.'

'What's very good?' grunted, inquiringly, Mr. Verloc, settled again in the corner of the sofa. The other explained his meaning negligently, with a shade of condescension and a toss of his head towards the kitchen:

'Typical of this form of degeneracy – these drawings, I mean.'

'You would call that lad a degenerate, would you?' mumbled Mr. Verloc.

Comrade Alexander Ossipon – nicknamed the Doctor, ex-medical student without a degree; afterwards wandering lecturer to working-men's associations upon the socialistic aspects of hygiene; author of a popular quasi-medical study (in the form of a cheap pamphlet seized promptly by the police) entitled 'The Corroding Vices of the Middle Classes'; special delegate of the more or less mysterious Red Committee, together with Karl Yundt and Michaelis for the work of literary propaganda – turned upon the obscure familiar of at least two Embassies that glance of insufferable, hopelessly dense sufficiency which nothing but the frequentation of science can give to the dulness of common mortals.

'That's what he may be called scientifically. Very good type, too, altogether, of that sort of degenerate. It's enough to glance at the lobes of his ears. If you read Lombroso —'

Mr. Verloc, moody and spread largely on the sofa, continued to look down the row of his waistcoat buttons; but his cheeks became tinged by a faint blush. Of late even the merest derivative of the word science (a term in itself inoffensive and of indefinite meaning) had the curious power of evoking a definitely offensive mental vision of Mr. Vladimir, in his body as he lived, with an almost supernatural clearness. And this phenomenon, deserving justly to be classed amongst the marvels of science, induced in Mr. Verloc an emotional state of dread and exasperation tending to express itself in violent swearing. But he said nothing. It was Karl Yundt who was heard, implacable to his last breath.

'Lombroso is an ass.'

Comrade Ossipon met the shock of this blasphemy by an awful, vacant stare. And the other, his extinguished

eyes without gleams blackening the deep shadows under
the great, bony forehead, mumbled, catching the tip of
his tongue between his lips at every second word as
though he were chewing it angrily:

'Did you ever see such an idiot? For him the criminal
is the prisoner. Simple, is it not? What about those who
shut him up there – forced him in there? Exactly. Forced
him in there. And what is crime? Does he know that, this
imbecile who has made his way in this world of gorged
fools by looking at the ears and teeth of a lot of poor,
luckless devils? Teeth and ears mark the criminal? Do
they? And what about the law that marks him still better
– the pretty branding instrument invented by the
overfed to protect themselves against the hungry? Red-
hot applications on their vile skins – hey? Can't you
smell and hear from here the thick hide of the people
burn and sizzle? That's how criminals are made for your
Lombrosos to write their silly stuff about.'

The knob of his stick and his legs shook together with
passion, whilst the trunk, draped in the wings of the
havelock, preserved his historic attitude of defiance. He
seemed to sniff the tainted air of social cruelty, to strain
his ear for its atrocious sounds. There was an extraordinary force of suggestion in this posturing. The all but
moribund veteran of dynamite wars had been a great
actor in his time – actor on platforms, in secret assemblies, in private interviews. The famous terrorist had
never in his life raised personally as much as his little
finger against the social edifice. He was no man of
action; he was not even an orator of torrential eloquence,
sweeping the masses along in the rushing noise and foam
of a great enthusiasm. With a more subtle intention, he
took the part of an insolent and venomous evoker of sinister impulses which lurk in the blind envy and exasperated vanity of ignorance, in the suffering and misery of
poverty, in all the hopeful and noble illusions of right-
eous anger, pity, and revolt. The shadow of his evil gift

clung to him yet like the smell of a deadly drug in an old vial of poison, emptied now, useless, ready to be thrown away upon the rubbish-heap of things that had served their time.

Michaelis, the ticket-of-leave apostle, smiled vaguely with his glued lips; his pasty moon face drooped under the weight of melancholy assent. He had been a prisoner himself. His own skin had sizzled under the red-hot brand, he murmured softly. But Comrade Ossipon, nicknamed the Doctor, had got over the shock by that time.

'You don't understand,' he began, disdainfully, but stopped short, intimidated by the dead blackness of the cavernous eyes in the face turned slowly towards him with a blind stare, as if guided only by the sound. He gave the discussion up, with a slight shrug of the shoulders.

Stevie, accustomed to move about disregarded, had got up from the kitchen table, carrying off his drawing to bed with him. He had reached the parlour door in time to receive in full the shock of Karl Yundt's eloquent imagery. The sheet of paper covered with circles dropped out of his fingers, and he remained staring at the old terrorist, as if rooted suddenly to the spot by his morbid horror and dread of physical pain. Stevie knew very well that hot iron applied to one's skin hurt very much. His scared eyes blazed with indignation: it would hurt terribly. His mouth dropped open.

Michaelis by staring unwinkingly at the fire had regained that sentiment of isolation necessary for the continuity of his thought. His optimism had begun to flow from his lips. He saw Capitalism doomed in its cradle, born with the poison of the principle of competition in its system. The great capitalists devouring the little capitalists, concentrating the power and the tools of production in great masses, perfecting industrial processes, and in the madness of self-aggrandizement only preparing, organizing, enriching, making ready the law-

ful inheritance of the suffering proletariat. Michaelis pronounced the great word 'Patience' – and his clear blue
glance, raised to the low ceiling of Mr. Verloc's parlour,
had a character of seraphic trustfulness. In the doorway
Stevie, calmed, seemed sunk in hebetude.

Comrade Ossipon's face twitched with exasperation.

'Then it's no use doing anything – no use whatever.'

'I don't say that,' protested Michaelis, gently. His
vision of truth had grown so intense that the sound of a
strange voice failed to rout it this time. He continued to
look down at the red coals. Preparation for the future was
necessary, and he was willing to admit that the great
change would perhaps come in the upheaval of a revolution. But he argued that revolutionary propaganda was a
delicate work of high conscience. It was the education of
the masters of the world. It should be as careful as the
education given to kings. He would have it advance its
tenets cautiously, even timidly, in our ignorance of the
effect that may be produced by any given economic
change upon the happiness, the morals, the intellect, the
history of mankind. For history is made with tools, not
with ideas; and everything is changed by economic conditions – art, philosophy, love, virtue – truth itself!

The coals in the grate settled down with a slight crash;
and Michaelis, the hermit of visions in the desert of a
penitentiary, got up impetuously. Round like a distended balloon, he opened his short, thick arms, as if in a
pathetically hopeless attempt to embrace and hug to his
breast a self-regenerated universe. He gasped with
ardour.

'The future is as certain as the past – slavery, feudal-
ism, individualism, collectivism. This is the statement of
a law, not an empty prophecy.'

The disdainful pout of Comrade Ossipon's thick lips
accentuated the negro type of his face.

'Nonsense,' he said, calmly enough. 'There is no law
and no certainty. The teaching propaganda be hanged.

What the people knows does not matter, were its knowledge ever so accurate. The only thing that matters to us is the emotional state of the masses. Without emotion there is no action.'

He paused, then added with modest firmness:

'I am speaking now to you scientifically – scientifically — Eh? What did you say, Verloc?'

'Nothing,' growled from the sofa Mr. Verloc, who, provoked by the abhorrent sound, had merely muttered a 'Damn.'

The venomous spluttering of the old terrorist without teeth was heard.

'Do you know how I would call the nature of the present economic conditions? I would call it cannibalistic. That's what it is! They are nourishing their greed on the quivering flesh and the warm blood of the people – nothing else.'

Stevie swallowed the terrifying statement with an audible gulp, and at once, as though it had been swift poison, sank limply in a sitting posture on the steps of the kitchen door.

Michaelis gave no signs of having heard anything. His lips seemed glued together for good; not a quiver passed over his heavy cheeks. With troubled eyes he looked for his round, hard hat, and put it on his round head. His round and obese body seemed to float low between the chairs under the sharp elbow of Karl Yundt. The old terrorist, raising an uncertain and clawlike hand, gave a swaggering tilt to a black felt sombrero shading the hollows and ridges of his wasted face. He got in motion slowly, striking the floor with his stick at every step. It was rather an affair to get him out of the house because, now and then, he would stop, as if to think, and did not offer to move again till impelled forward by Michaelis. The gentle apostle grasped his arm with brotherly care; and behind them, his hands in his pockets, the robust Ossipon yawned vaguely. A blue cap with a patent leather peak set well at the back of his yellow bush of hair gave him the aspect of a Norwegian sailor bored with the world after a thundering spree. Mr. Verloc saw his guests off the premises, attending them bareheaded, his heavy overcoat hanging open, his eyes on the ground.

He closed the door behind their backs with restrained violence, turned the key, shot the bolt. He was not satisfied with his friends. In the light of Mr. Vladimir's philosophy of bomb throwing they appeared hopelessly futile. The part of Mr. Verloc in revolutionary politics having been to observe, he could not all at once, either in his own home or in larger assemblies, take the initiative of action. He had to be cautious. Moved by the just indignation of a man well over forty, menaced in what is dearest to him – his repose and his security – he asked himself scornfully what else could have been expected from such a lot, this Karl Yundt, this Michaelis – this Ossipon.

Pausing in his intention to turn off the gas burning in the middle of the shop, Mr. Verloc descended into the abyss of moral reflections. With the insight of a kindred temperament he pronounced his verdict. A lazy lot – this Karl Yundt, nursed by a blear-eyed old woman, a woman he had years ago enticed away from a friend, and afterwards had tried more than once to shake off into the gutter. Jolly lucky for Yundt that she had persisted in coming up time after time, or else there would have been no one now to help him out of the 'bus by the Green Park railings, where that spectre took its constitutional crawl every fine morning. When that indomitable snarling old witch died the swaggering spectre would have to vanish, too – there would be an end to fiery Karl Yundt. And Mr. Verloc's morality was offended also by the optimism of Michaelis, annexed by his wealthy old lady, who had taken lately to sending him to a cottage she had in the country. The ex-prisoner could moon about the shady lanes for days together in a delicious and humanitarian idleness. As to Ossipon, that beggar was sure to want for nothing as long as there were silly girls with savings-bank books in the world. And Mr. Verloc, temperamentally identical with his associates, drew fine distinctions in his mind on the strength of insignificant differences. He drew them with a certain complacency, because the instinct of conventional respectability was strong within him, being only overcome by his dislike of all kinds of recognized labour – a temperamental defect which he shared with a large proportion of revolutionary reformers of a given social state. For obviously one does not revolt against the advantages and opportunities of that state, but against the price which must be paid for the same in the coin of accepted morality, self-restraint, and toil. The majority of revolutionists are the enemies of discipline and fatigue mostly. There are natures, too, to whose sense of justice the price exacted looms up monstrously enormous, odious, oppressive, worrying, humiliating, extortionate, intolerable. Those are the fanatics. The remaining portion of social rebels is accounted for by vanity, the mother of all noble and vile illusions, the companion of poets, reformers, charlatans, prophets, and incendiaries.

Lost for a whole minute in the abyss of meditation, Mr. Verloc did not reach the depth of these abstract considerations. Perhaps he was not able. In any case he had not the time. He was pulled up painfully by the sudden recollection of Mr. Vladimir, another of his associates, whom in virtue of subtle moral affinities he was capable of judging correctly. He considered him as dangerous. A shade of envy crept into his thoughts. Loafing was all very well for these fellows, who knew not Mr. Vladimir, and had women to fall back upon; whereas he had a woman to provide for —

At this point, by a simple association of ideas, Mr. Verloc was brought face to face with the necessity of going to bed some time or other that evening. Then why not go now – at once? He sighed. The necessity was not so normally pleasurable as it ought to have been for a man of his age and temperament. He dreaded the demon of sleeplessness, which he felt had marked him for its own. He raised his arm, and turned off the flaring gas-jet above his head.

A bright band of light fell through the parlour door into the part of the shop behind the counter. It enabled Mr. Verloc to ascertain at a glance the number of silver coins in the till. These were but few; and for the first time since he opened his shop he took a commercial survey of its value. This survey was unfavourable. He had gone into trade for no commercial reasons. He had been guided in the selection of this peculiar line of business by an instinctive leaning towards shady transactions, where money is picked up easily. Moreover, it did not take him out of his own sphere – the sphere which is watched by the police. On the contrary, it gave him a publicly confessed standing in that sphere, and as Mr. Verloc had unconfessed relations which made him familiar with yet careless of the police, there was a distinct advantage in such a situation. But as a means of livelihood it was by itself insufficient.

He took the cash-box out of the drawer, and turning to leave the shop, became aware that Stevie was still downstairs.

What on earth is he doing there? Mr. Verloc asked himself. What's the meaning of these antics? He looked dubiously at his brother-in-law, but he did not ask him for information. Mr. Verloc's intercourse with Stevie was limited to the casual mutter of a morning, after breakfast, 'My boots,' and even that was more a communication at large of a need than a direct order or request. Mr. Verloc perceived with some surprise that he did not know really what to say to Stevie. He stood still in the middle of the parlour, and looked into the kitchen in silence. Nor yet did he know what would happen if he did say anything.

And this appeared very queer to Mr. Verloc in view of the fact, borne upon him suddenly, that he had to provide for this fellow, too. He had never given a moment's thought till then to that aspect of Stevie's existence.

Positively he did not know how to speak to the lad. He watched him gesticulating and murmuring in the kitchen. Stevie prowled round the table like an excited animal in a cage. A tentative 'Hadn't you better go to bed now?' produced no effect whatever; and Mr. Verloc, abandoning the stony contemplation of his brother-in-law's behaviour, crossed the parlour wearily, cash-box in hand. The cause of the general lassitude he felt while climbing the stairs being purely mental, he became alarmed by its inexplicable character. He hoped he was not sickening for anything. He stopped on the dark landing to examine his sensations. But a slight and continuous sound of snoring pervading the obscurity interfered with their clearness. The sound came from his mother-in-law's room. Another one to provide for, he thought – and on this thought walked into the bedroom.

Mrs. Verloc had fallen asleep with the lamp (no gas was laid upstairs) turned up full on the table by the side of the bed. The light thrown down by the shade fell dazzlingly on the white pillow sunk by the weight of her head reposing with closed eyes and dark hair done up in several plaits for the night. She woke up with the sound of her name in her ears, and saw her husband standing over her.

'Winnie! Winnie!'

At first she did not stir, lying very quiet and looking at the cash-box in Mr. Verloc's hand. But when she understood that her brother was 'capering all over the place downstairs' she swung out in one sudden movement on to the edge of the bed. Her bare feet, as if poked through the bottom of an unadorned, sleeved calico sack buttoned tightly at neck and wrists, felt over the rug for the slippers while she looked upward into her husband's face.

'I don't know how to manage him,' Mr. Verloc explained, peevishly. 'Won't do to leave him downstairs alone with the lights.'

She said nothing, glided across the room swiftly, and the door closed upon her white form.

Mr. Verloc deposited the cash-box on the night table, and began the operation of undressing by flinging his overcoat on to a distant chair. His coat and waistcoat followed. He walked about the room in his stockinged feet, and his burly figure, with the hands worrying nervously at his throat, passed and repassed across the long strip of looking-glass in the door of his wife's wardrobe. Then after slipping his braces off his shoulders he pulled up violently the venetian blind, and leaned his forehead against the cold window-pane – a fragile film of glass stretched between him and the enormity of cold, black, wet, muddy, inhospitable accumulation of bricks, slates, and stones, things in themselves unlovely and unfriendly to man.

Mr. Verloc felt the latent unfriendliness of all out of doors with a force approaching to positive bodily anguish. There is no occupation that fails a man more completely than that of a secret agent of police. It's like your horse suddenly falling dead under you in the midst of an uninhabited and thirsty plain. The comparison occurred to Mr. Verloc because he had sat astride various army horses in his time, and had now the sensation of an incipient fall. The prospect was as black as the window-pane against which he was leaning his forehead. And suddenly the face of Mr. Vladimir, clean-shaved and witty, appeared enhaloed in the glow of its rosy complexion like a sort of pink seal impressed on the fatal darkness.

This luminous and mutilated vision was so ghastly physically that Mr. Verloc started away from the window, letting down the venetian blind with a great rattle. Discomposed and speechless with the apprehension of more such visions, he beheld his wife re-enter the room and get into bed in a calm, businesslike manner which made him feel hopelessly lonely in the world. Mrs. Verloc expressed her surprise at seeing him up yet.

'I don't feel very well,' he muttered, passing his hands over his moist brow.

'Giddiness?'

'Yes. Not at all well.'

Mrs. Verloc, with all the placidity of an experienced wife, expressed a confident opinion as to the cause, and suggested the usual remedies; but her husband, rooted in the middle of the room, shook his lowered head sadly.

'You'll catch cold standing there,' she observed.

Mr. Verloc made an effort, finished undressing, and got into bed. Down below in the quiet, narrow street measured footsteps approached the house, then died away, unhurried and firm, as if the passer-by had started to pace out all eternity, from gas-lamp to gas-lamp in a night without end; and the drowsy ticking of the old clock on the landing became distinctly audible in the bedroom.

Mrs. Verloc, on her back, and staring at the ceiling, made a remark.

'Takings very small to-day.'

Mr. Verloc, in the same position, cleared his throat as if for an important statement, but merely inquired:

'Did you turn off the gas downstairs?'

'Yes; I did,' answered Mrs. Verloc, conscientiously. 'That poor boy is in a very excited state to-night,' she murmured, after a pause which lasted for three ticks of the clock.

Mr. Verloc cared nothing for Stevie's excitement, but he felt horribly wakeful, and dreaded facing the darkness and silence that would follow the extinguishing of the lamp. This dread led him to make the remark that Stevie had disregarded his suggestion to go to bed. Mrs. Verloc, falling into the trap, started to demonstrate at length to her husband that this was not 'impudence' of any sort, but simply 'excitement'. There was no young man of his age in London more willing and docile than Stephen, she affirmed; none more affectionate and ready to please, and even useful, as long as people did not upset his poor head. Mrs. Verloc, turning towards her recumbent husband, raised herself on her elbow, and hung over him in her anxiety that he should believe Stevie to be a useful member of the family. That ardour of protecting compassion exalted morbidly in her childhood by the misery of another child tinged her sallow cheeks with a faint dusky blush, made her big eyes gleam under the dark lids. Mrs. Verloc then looked younger; she looked as young as Winnie used to look, and much more animated than the Winnie of the Belgravian mansion days had ever allowed herself to appear to gentlemen lodgers. Mr. Verloc's anxieties had prevented him from attaching any sense to what his wife was saying. It was as if her voice was talking on the other side of a very thick wall. It was her aspect that recalled him to himself.

He appreciated this woman, and the sentiment of this appreciation, stirred by a display of something resembling emotion, only added another pang to his mental anguish. When her voice ceased he moved uneasily, and said:

'I haven't been feeling well for the last few days.'

He might have meant this as an opening to a complete confidence; but Mrs. Verloc laid her head on the pillow again, and staring upward, went on:

'That boy hears too much of what is talked about here. If I had known they were coming to-night I would have seen to it that he went to bed at the same time I did. He was out of his mind with something he overheard about eating people's flesh and drinking blood. What's the good of talking like that?'

There was a note of indignant scorn in her voice. Mr. Verloc was fully responsive now.

'Ask Karl Yundt,' he growled, savagely.

Mrs. Verloc, with great decision, pronounced Karl Yundt 'a disgusting old man'. She declared openly her affection for Michaelis. Of the robust Ossipon, in whose presence she always felt uneasy behind an attitude of stony reserve, she said nothing whatever. And continuing to talk of that brother, who had been for so many years an object of care and fears:

'He isn't fit to hear what's said here. He believes it's all true. He knows no better. He gets into his passions over it.'

Mr. Verloc made no comment.

'He glared at me, as if he didn't know who I was, when I went downstairs. His heart was going like a hammer. He can't help being excitable. I woke mother up, and asked her to sit with him till he went to sleep. It isn't his fault. He's no trouble when he's left alone.'

Mr. Verloc made no comment.

'I wish he had never been to school,' Mrs. Verloc began again, brusquely. 'He's always taking away those newspapers from the window to read. He gets a red face poring over them. We don't get rid of a dozen numbers in a month. They only take up room in the front window. And Mr. Ossipon brings every week a pile of these F. P. tracts to sell at a halfpenny each. I wouldn't give a halfpenny for the whole lot. It's silly reading – that's what it is. There's no sale for it. The other day Stevie got hold of one, and there was a story in it of a German soldier officer tearing half-off the ear of a recruit, and nothing was done to him for it. The brute! I couldn't do anything with Stevie that afternoon. The story was enough, too, to make one's blood boil. But what's the use of printing things like that? We aren't German slaves here, thank God. It's not our business – is it?'

Mr. Verloc made no reply.

'I had to take the carving knife from the boy,' Mrs. Verloc continued, a little sleepily now. 'He was shouting and stamping and sobbing. He can't stand the notion of any cruelty. He would have stuck that officer like a pig if he had seen him then. It's true, too! Some people don't deserve much mercy.' Mrs. Verloc's voice ceased, and the expression of her motionless eyes became more and more contemplative and veiled during the long pause. 'Comfortable, dear?' she asked in a faint, far-away voice. 'Shall I put out the light now?'

The dreary conviction that there was no sleep for him held Mr. Verloc mute and hopelessly inert in his fear of darkness. He made a great effort.

'Yes. Put it out,' he said at last in a hollow tone.

CHAPTER FOUR

MOST of the thirty or so little tables covered by red cloths with a white design stood ranged at right angles to the deep brown wainscoting of the underground hall. Bronze chandeliers with many globes depended from the low, slightly vaulted ceiling, and the fresco paintings ran flat and dull all round the walls without windows, representing scenes of the chase and of outdoor revelry in mediæval costumes. Varlets in green jerkins brandished hunting knives and raised on high tankards of foaming beer.

'Unless I am very much mistaken, you are the man who would know the inside of this confounded affair,' said the robust Ossipon, leaning over, his elbows far out on the table and his feet tucked back completely under his chair. His eyes stared with wild eagerness.

An upright semi-grand piano near the door, flanked by two palms in pots, executed suddenly all by itself a valse tune with aggressive virtuosity. The din it raised was deafening. When it ceased, as abruptly as it had started, the be-spectacled, dingy little man who faced Ossipon behind a heavy glass mug full of beer emitted calmly what had the sound of a general proposition.

'In principle what one of us may or may not know as to any given fact can't be a matter for inquiry to the others.'

'Certainly not,' Comrade Ossipon agreed in a quiet undertone. 'In principle.'

With his big florid face held between his hands he continued to stare hard, while the dingy little man in spectacles coolly took a drink of beer and stood the glass mug back on the table. His flat, large ears departed widely from the sides of his skull, which looked frail enough for Ossipon to crush between thumb and forefinger; the dome of the forehead seemed to rest on the rim of the spectacles; the flat cheeks, of a greasy, unhealthy complexion, were merely smudged by the miserable poverty of a thin dark whisker. The lamentable inferiority of the whole physique was made ludicrous by the supremely self-confident bearing of the individual. His speech was curt, and he had a particularly impressive manner of keeping silent.

Ossipon spoke again from between his hands in a mutter.

'Have you been out much to-day?'

'No. I stayed in bed all the morning,' answered the other. 'Why?'

'Oh! Nothing,' said Ossipon, gazing earnestly and quivering inwardly with the desire to find out something, but obviously intimidated by the little man's overwhelming air of unconcern. When talking with this comrade – which happened but rarely – the big Ossipon suffered from a sense of moral and even physical insignificance. However, he ventured another question. 'Did you walk down here?'

'No; omnibus,' the little man answered, readily enough. He lived far away in Islington, in a small house down a shabby street, littered with straw and dirty paper, where out of school hours a troop of assorted children ran and squabbled with a shrill, joyless, rowdy clamour. His single back room, remarkable for having an extremely large cupboard, he rented furnished from two elderly spinsters, dressmakers in a humble way with a clientele of servant girls mostly. He had a heavy padlock put on the cupboard, but otherwise he was a model lodger, giving no trouble, and requiring practically no attendance. His oddities were that he insisted on being present when

his room was being swept, and that when he went out he
locked his door, and took the key away with him.

Ossipon had a vision of these round black-rimmed
spectacles progressing along the streets on the top of an
omnibus, their self-confident glitter falling here and
there on the walls of houses or lowered upon the heads
of the unconscious stream of people on the pavements.
The ghost of a sickly smile altered the set of Ossipon's
thick lips at the thought of the walls nodding, of people
running for life at the sight of those spectacles. If they
had only known! What a panic! He murmured interroga-
tively: 'Been sitting long here?'

'An hour or more,' answered the other, negligently,
and took a pull at the dark beer. All his movements – the
way he grasped the mug, the act of drinking, the way he
set the heavy glass down and folded his arms – had a
firmness, an assured precision which made the big and
muscular Ossipon, leaning forward with staring eyes and
protruding lips, look the picture of eager indecision.

'An hour,' he said. 'Then it may be you haven't heard
yet the news I've heard just now – in the street. Have
you?'

The little man shook his head negatively the least bit.
But as he gave no indication of curiosity Ossipon ventured to add that he had heard it just outside the place. A
newspaper boy had yelled the thing under his very nose,
and not being prepared for anything of that sort, he was
very much startled and upset. He had to come in there
with a dry mouth. 'I never thought of finding you here,'
he added, murmuring steadily, with his elbows planted
on the table.

'I come here sometimes,' said the other, preserving
his provoking coolness of demeanour.

'It's wonderful that you of all people should have
heard nothing of it,' the big Ossipon continued. His
eyelids snapped nervously upon the shining eyes. 'You
of all people,' he repeated, tentatively. This obvious

restraint argued an incredible and inexplicable timidity of the big fellow before the calm little man, who again lifted the glass mug, drank, and put it down with brusque and assured movements. And that was all.

Ossipon, after waiting for something, word or sign, that did not come, made an effort to assume a sort of indifference.

'Do you,' he said, deadening his voice still more, 'give your stuff to anybody who's up to asking you for it?'

'My absolute rule is never to refuse anybody – as long as I have a pinch by me,' answered the little man with decision.

'That's a principle?' commented Ossipon.

'It's a principle.'

'And you think it's sound?'

The large round spectacles, which gave a look of staring self-confidence to the sallow face, confronted Ossipon like sleepless, unwinking orbs flashing a cold fire.

'Perfectly. Always. Under every circumstance. What could stop me? Why should I not? Why should I think twice about it?'

Ossipon gasped, as it were, discreetly.

'Do you mean to say you would hand it over to a "tec" if one came to ask you for your wares?'

The other smiled faintly.

'Let them come and try it on, and you will see,' he said. 'They know me, but I know also every one of them. They won't come near me – not they.'

His thin, livid lips snapped together firmly. Ossipon began to argue.

'But they could send someone – rig a plant on you. Don't you see? Get the stuff from you in that way, and then arrest you with the proof in their hands.'

'Proof of what? Dealing in explosives without a licence perhaps.' This was meant for a contemptuous jeer, though the expression of the thin, sickly face remained unchanged, and the utterance was negligent. 'I

don't think there's one of them anxious to make that
arrest. I don't think they could get one of them to apply
for a warrant. I mean one of the best. Not one.'

'Why?' Ossipon asked.

'Because they know very well I take care never to part
with the last handful of my wares. I've it always by me.'
He touched the breast of his coat lightly. 'In a thick glass
flask,' he added.

'So I have been told,' said Ossipon, with a shade of
wonder in his voice. 'But I didn't know if —'

'They know,' interrupted the little man, crisply, leaning against the straight chair back, which rose higher
than his fragile head. 'I shall never be arrested. The
game isn't good enough for any policeman of them all.
To deal with a man like me you require sheer, naked,
inglorious heroism.'

Again his lips closed with a self-confident snap. Ossipon repressed a movement of impatience.

'Or recklessness – or simply ignorance,' he retorted.
'They've only to get somebody for the job who does not
know you carry enough stuff in your pocket to blow
yourself and everything within sixty yards of you to
pieces.'

'I never affirmed I could not be eliminated,' rejoined
the other. 'But that wouldn't be an arrest. Moreover, it's
not so easy as it looks.'

'Bah!' Ossipon contradicted. 'Don't be too sure of
that. What's to prevent half-a-dozen of them jumping upon you from behind in the street? With your
arms pinned to your sides you could do nothing – could
you?'

'Yes; I could. I am seldom out in the streets after dark,'
said the little man, impassively, 'and never very late. I
walk always with my right hand closed round the india-
rubber ball which I have in my trouser pocket. The
pressing of this ball actuates a detonator inside the flask
I carry in my pocket. It's the principle of the pneumatic

instantaneous shutter for a camera lens. The tube leads
up —'

With a swift, disclosing gesture he gave Ossipon a
glimpse of an india-rubber tube, resembling a slender
brown worm, issuing from the armhole of his waistcoat
and plunging into the inner breast pocket of his jacket.
His clothes, of a nondescript brown mixture, were
threadbare and marked with stains, dusty in the folds,
with ragged button-holes. 'The detonator is partly
mechanical, partly chemical,' he explained, with casual
condescension.

'It is instantaneous, of course?' murmured Ossipon,
with a slight shudder.

'Far from it,' confessed the other, with a reluctance
which seemed to twist his mouth dolorously. 'A full
twenty seconds must elapse from the moment I press
the ball till the explosion takes place.'

'Phew!' whistled Ossipon, completely appalled.
'Twenty seconds! Horrors! You mean to say that you
could face that? I should go crazy —'

'Wouldn't matter if you did. Of course, it's the weak
point of this special system, which is only for my own
use. The worst is that the manner of exploding is always
the weak point with us. I am trying to invent a detonator
that would adjust itself to all conditions of action, and
even to unexpected changes of conditions. A variable
and yet perfectly precise mechanism. A really intelligent
detonator.'

'Twenty seconds,' muttered Ossipon again. 'Ough!
And then —'

With a slight turn of the head the glitter of the spectacles seemed to gauge the size of the beer saloon in the
basement of the renowned Silenus Restaurant.

'Nobody in this room could hope to escape,' was the
verdict of that survey. 'Nor yet this couple going up the
stairs now.'

The piano at the foot of the staircase clanged through

a mazurka with brazen impetuosity, as though a vulgar and impudent ghost were showing off. The keys sank and rose mysteriously. Then all became still. For a moment Ossipon imagined the overlighted place changed into a dreadful black hole belching horrible fumes choked with ghastly rubbish of smashed brick-work and mutilated corpses. He had such a distinct per-ception of ruin and death that he shuddered again. The other observed, with an air of calm sufficiency:

'In the last instance it is character alone that makes for one's safety. There are very few people in the world whose character is as well established as mine.'

'I wonder how you managed it,' growled Ossipon.

'Force of personality,' said the other, without raising his voice; and coming from the mouth of that obviously miserable organism the assertion caused the robust Ossi-pon to bite his lower lip. 'Force of personality,' he repeated, with ostentatious calm.

'I have the means to make myself deadly, but that by itself, you understand, is absolutely nothing in the way of protection. What is effective is the belief those people have in my will to use the means. That's their impres-sion. It is absolute. Therefore I am deadly.'

'There are individuals of character amongst that lot, too,' muttered Ossipon ominously.

'Possibly. But it is a matter of degree obviously, since, for instance, I am not impressed by them. Therefore they are inferior. They cannot be otherwise. Their char-acter is built upon conventional morality. It leans on the social order. Mine stands free from everything artificial. They are bound in all sorts of conventions. They depend on life, which, in this connection, is a historical fact sur-rounded by all sorts of restraints and considerations, a complex, organized fact open to attack at every point; whereas I depend on death, which knows no restraint and cannot be attacked. My superiority is evident.'

'This is a transcendental way of putting it,' said

Ossipon, watching the cold glitter of the round spectacles. 'I've heard Karl Yundt say much the same thing
not very long ago.'

'Karl Yundt,' mumbled the other, contemptuously,
'the delegate of the International Red Committee, has
been a posturing shadow all his life. There are three of
you delegates, aren't there? I won't define the other two,
as you are one of them. But what you say means nothing.
You are the worthy delegates for revolutionary propaganda, but the trouble is not only that you are as unable to
think independently as any respectable grocer or jour-
nalist of them all, but that you have no character whatever.'

Ossipon could not restrain a start of indignation.

'But what do you want from us?' he exclaimed in a
deadened voice. 'What is it you are after yourself?'

'A perfect detonator,' was the peremptory answer.
'What are you making that face for? You see, you can't
even bear the mention of something conclusive.'

'I am not making a face,' growled the annoyed Ossipon, bearishly.

'You revolutionists,' the other continued, with leisurely
self-confidence, 'are the slaves of the social convention,
which is afraid of you; slaves of it as much as the very
police that stands up in the defence of that convention.
Clearly you are, since you want to revolutionize it. It gov-
erns your thought, of course, and your action, too, and
thus neither your thought nor your action can ever be
conclusive.' He paused, tranquil, with that air of close,
endless silence, then almost immediately went on: 'You
are not a bit better than the forces arrayed against you –
than the police, for instance. The other day I came suddenly upon Chief Inspector Heat at the corner of Totten-
ham Court Road. He looked at me very steadily. But I did
not look at him. Why should I give him more than a
glance? He was thinking of many things – of his superiors, of his reputation, of the law courts, of his salary, of

newspapers – of a hundred things. But I was thinking of
my perfect detonator only. He meant nothing to me. He
was as insignificant as – I can't call to mind anything
insignificant enough to compare him with – except Karl
Yundt perhaps. Like to like. The terrorist and the policeman both come from the same basket. Revolution,
legality – counter moves in the same game; forms of idleness at bottom identical. He plays his little game – so do
you propagandists. But I don't play; I work fourteen
hours a day, and go hungry sometimes. My experiments
cost money now and again, and then I must do without
food for a day or two. You're looking at my beer. Yes. I
have had two glasses already, and shall have another
presently. This is a little holiday, and I celebrate it alone.
Why not? I've the grit to work alone, quite alone, absolutely alone. I've worked alone for years.'

Ossipon's face had turned dusky red.

'At the perfect detonator – eh?' he sneered, very low.

'Yes,' retorted the other. 'It is a good definition. You
couldn't find anything half so precise to define the
nature of your activity with all your committees and
delegations. It is I who am the true propagandist.'

'We won't discuss that point,' said Ossipon, with an air
of rising above personal considerations. 'I am afraid I'll
have to spoil your holiday for you, though. There's a man
blown up in Greenwich Park this morning.'

'How do you know?'

'They have been yelling the news in the streets since
two o'clock. I bought the paper, and just ran in here.
Then I saw you sitting at this table. I've got it in my
pocket now.'

He pulled the newspaper out. It was a good-sized,
rosy sheet, as if flushed by the warmth of its own convictions, which were optimistic. He scanned the pages
rapidly.

'Ah! Here it is. Bomb in Greenwich Park. There isn't
much so far. Half-past eleven. Foggy morning. Effects of

explosion felt as far as Romney Road and Park Place. Enormous hole in the ground under a tree filled with smashed roots and broken branches. All round fragments of a man's body blown to pieces. That's all. The rest's mere newspaper gup. No doubt a wicked attempt to blow up the Observatory, they say. H'm. That's hardly credible.'

He looked at the paper for a while longer in silence then passed it to the other, who after gazing abstractedly at the print laid it down without comment.

It was Ossipon who spoke first – still resentful.

'The fragments of only *one* man, you note. Ergo: blew *himself* up. That spoils your day off for you – don't it? Were you expecting that sort of move? I hadn't the slightest idea – not the ghost of a notion of anything of the sort being planned to come off here – in this country. Under the present circumstances it's nothing short of criminal.'

The little man lifted his thin black eyebrows with dispassionate scorn.

'Criminal! What is that? What *is* crime? What can be the meaning of such an assertion?'

'How am I to express myself? One must use the current words,' said Ossipon, impatiently. 'The meaning of this assertion is that this business may affect our position very adversely in this country. Isn't that crime enough for you? I am convinced you have been giving away some of your stuff lately.'

Ossipon stared hard. The other, without flinching, lowered and raised his head slowly.

'You have!' burst out the editor of the F. P. leaflets in an intense whisper. 'No! And are you really handing it over at large like this, for the asking, to the first fool that comes along?'

'Just so! The condemned social order has not been built up on paper and ink, and I don't fancy that a combination of paper and ink will ever put an end to it, whatever you may think. Yes, I would give the stuff with both hands to every man, woman, or fool that likes to come along. I know what you are thinking about. But I am not taking my cue from the Red Committee. I would see you all hounded out of here, or arrested – or beheaded for that matter – without turning a hair. What happens to us as individuals is not of the least consequence.'

He spoke carelessly, without heat, almost without feeling, and Ossipon, secretly much affected, tried to copy this detachment.

'If the police here knew their business they would shoot you full of holes with revolvers, or else try to sand-bag you from behind in broad daylight.'

The little man seemed already to have considered that point of view in his dispassionate, self-confident manner.

'Yes,' he assented with the utmost readiness. 'But for that they would have to face their own institutions. Do you see? That requires uncommon grit. Grit of a special kind.'

Ossipon blinked.

'I fancy that's exactly what would happen to you if you were to set up your laboratory in the States. They don't stand on ceremony with their institutions there.'

'I am not likely to go and see. Otherwise your remark is just,' admitted the other. 'They have more character over there, and their character is essentially anarchistic. Fertile ground for us, the States – very good ground. The great Republic has the root of the destructive matter in her. The collective temperament is lawless. Excellent. They may shoot us down, but —'

'You are too transcendental for me,' growled Ossipon, with moody concern.

'Logical,' protested the other. 'There are several kinds of logic. This is the enlightened kind. America is all right. It is this country that is dangerous, with her idealistic conception of legality. The social spirit of this

people is wrapped up in scrupulous prejudices, and that
is fatal to our work. You talk of England being our only
refuge! So much the worse. Capua! What do we want
with refuges? Here you talk print, plot, and do nothing. I
daresay it's very convenient for such Karl Yundts.'

He shrugged his shoulders slightly, then added with
the same leisurely assurance: 'To break up the superstition and worship of legality should be our aim. Nothing
would please me more than to see Inspector Heat and
his likes take to shooting us down in broad daylight with
the approval of the public. Half our battle would be won
then; the disintegration of the old morality would have
set in in its very temple. That is what you ought to aim
at. But you revolutionists will never understand that. You
plan the future, you lose yourselves in reveries of economical systems derived from what is; whereas what's
wanted is a clean sweep and a clear start for a new conception of life. That sort of future will take care of itself
if you will only make room for it. Therefore I would
shovel my stuff in heaps at the corners of the streets if I
had enough for that; and as I haven't, I do my best by
perfecting a really dependable detonator.'

Ossipon, who had been mentally swimming in deep
waters, seized upon the last word as if it were a saving
plank.

'Yes. Your detonators. I shouldn't wonder if it weren't
one of your detonators that made a clean sweep of the
man in the park.'

A shade of vexation darkened the determined, sallow
face confronting Ossipon.

'My difficulty consists precisely in experimenting
practically with the various kinds. They must be tried,
after all. Besides —'

Ossipon interrupted.

'Who could that fellow be? I assure you that we in
London had no knowledge — Couldn't you describe the
person you gave the stuff to?'

The other turned his spectacles upon Ossipon like a
pair of searchlights.

'Describe him,' he repeated, slowly. 'I don't think
there can be the slightest objection now. I will describe
him to you in one word – Verloc.'

Ossipon, whom curiosity had lifted a few inches off
his seat, dropped back, as if hit in the face.

'Verloc! Impossible.'

The self-possessed little man nodded slightly once.

'Yes. He's the person. You can't say that in this case I
was giving my stuff to the first fool that came along. He
was a prominent member of the group as far as I understand.'

'Yes,' said Ossipon. 'Prominent. No, not exactly. He
was the centre for general intelligence, and usually
received comrades coming over here. More useful than
important. Man of no ideas. Years ago he used to speak at
meetings – in France, I believe. Not very well, though.
He was trusted by such men as Latorre, Moser, and all
that old lot. The only talent he showed really was his
ability to elude the attentions of the police somehow.
Here, for instance, he did not seem to be looked after
very closely. He was regularly married, you know. I suppose it's with her money that he started that shop.
Seemed to make it pay, too.'

Ossipon paused abruptly, muttered to himself 'I wonder what that woman will do now?' and fell into thought.

The other waited with ostentatious indifference. His
parentage was obscure, and he was generally known only
by his nickname of Professor. His title to that designa-
tion consisted in his having been once assistant demon-
strator in chemistry at some technical institute. He
quarrelled with the authorities upon a question of unfair
treatment. Afterwards he obtained a post in the laboratory of a manufactory of dyes. There, too, he had been
treated with revolting injustice. His struggles, his privations, his hard work to raise himself in the social scale,

had filled him with such an exalted conviction of his merits that it was extremely difficult for the world to treat him with justice – the standard of that notion depending so much upon the patience of the individual. The Professor had genius, but lacked the great social virtue of resignation.

'Intellectually a nonentity,' Ossipon pronounced aloud, abandoning suddenly the inward contemplation of Mrs. Verloc's bereaved person and business. 'Quite an ordinary personality. You are wrong in not keeping more in touch with the comrades, Professor,' he added in a reproving tone. 'Did he say anything to you – give you some idea of his intentions? I hadn't seen him for a month. It seems impossible that he should be gone.'

'He told me it was going to be a demonstration against a building,' said the Professor. 'I had to know that much to prepare the missile. I pointed out to him that I had hardly a sufficient quantity for a completely destructive result, but he pressed me very earnestly to do my best. As he wanted something that could be carried openly in the hand, I proposed to make use of an old one-gallon copal varnish can I happened to have by me. He was pleased at the idea. It gave me some trouble, because I had to cut out the bottom first and solder it on again afterwards. When prepared for use, the can enclosed a wide-mouthed, well-corked jar of thick glass packed around with some wet clay and containing sixteen ounces of X2 green powder. The detonator was connected with the screw top of the can. It was ingenious – a combination of time and shock. I explained the system to him. It was a thin tube of tin enclosing a —'

Ossipon's attention had wandered.

'What do you think has happened?' he interrupted.

'Can't tell. Screwed the top on tight, which would make the connection, and then forgot the time. It was set for twenty minutes. On the other hand, the time contact being made, a sharp shock would bring about the explosion at once. He either ran the time too close, or simply let the thing fall. The contact was made all right – that's clear to me at any rate. The system's worked perfectly. And yet you would think that a common fool in a hurry would be much more likely to forget to make the contact altogether. I was worrying myself about that sort of failure mostly. But there are more kinds of fools than one can guard against. You can't expect a detonator to be absolutely foolproof.'

He beckoned to a waiter. Ossipon sat rigid, with the abstracted gaze of mental travail. After the man had gone away with the money he roused himself, with an air of profound dissatisfaction.

'It's extremely unpleasant for me,' he mused. 'Karl has been in bed with bronchitis for a week. There's an even chance that he will never get up again. Michaelis is luxuriating in the country somewhere. A fashionable publisher has offered him five hundred pounds for a book. It will be a ghastly failure. He has lost the habit of consecutive thinking in prison, you know.'

The Professor on his feet, now buttoning his coat, looked about him with perfect indifference.

'What are you going to do?' asked Ossipon, wearily. He dreaded the blame of the Central Red Committee, a body which had no permanent place of abode, and of whose membership he was not exactly informed. If this affair eventuated in the stoppage of the modest subsidy allotted to the publication of the F. P. pamphlets, then indeed he would have to regret Verloc's inexplicable folly.

'Solidarity with the extremest form of action is one thing, and silly recklessness is another,' he said, with a sort of moody brutality. 'I don't know what came to Verloc. There's some mystery there. However, he's gone. You may take it as you like, but under the circumstances the only policy for the militant revolutionary group is to disclaim all connection with this damned freak of yours.

How to make the disclaimer convincing enough is what bothers me.'

The little man on his feet, buttoned up and ready to go, was no taller than the seated Ossipon. He levelled his spectacles at the latter's face point-blank.

'You might ask the police for a testimonial of good conduct. They know where every one of you slept last night. Perhaps if you asked them they would consent to publish some sort of official statement.'

'No doubt they are aware well enough that we had nothing to do with this,' mumbled Ossipon, bitterly. 'What they will say is another thing.' He remained thoughtful, disregarding the short, owlish, shabby figure standing by his side. 'I must lay hands on Michaelis at once, and get him to speak from his heart at one of our gatherings. The public has a sort of sentimental regard for that fellow. His name is known. And I am in touch with a few reporters on the big dailies. What he would say would be utter bosh, but he has a turn of talk that makes it go down all the same.'

'Like treacle,' interjected the Professor, rather low, keeping an impassive expression.

The perplexed Ossipon went on communing with himself half audibly, after the manner of a man reflecting in perfect solitude.

'Confounded ass! To leave such an imbecile business on my hands. And I don't even know if —'

He sat with compressed lips. The idea of going for news straight to the shop lacked charm. His notion was that Verloc's shop might have been turned already into a police trap. They will be bound to make some arrests, he thought, with something resembling virtuous indignation, for the even tenor of his revolutionary life was menaced by no fault of his. And yet unless he went there he ran the risk of remaining in ignorance of what perhaps it would be very material for him to know. Then he reflected that, if the man in the park had been so very

much blown to pieces as the evening papers said, he
could not have been identified. And if so, the police
could have no special reason for watching Verloc's shop
more closely than any other place known to be fre-
quented by marked anarchists – no more reason, in fact,
than for watching the doors of the Silenus. There would
be a lot of watching all round, no matter where he went.
Still —

'I wonder what I had better do now?' he muttered,
taking counsel with himself.

A rasping voice at his elbow said, with sedate scorn:

'Fasten yourself upon the woman for all she's worth.'

After uttering these words the Professor walked away
from the table. Ossipon, whom that piece of insight
had taken unawares, gave one ineffectual start, and
remained still, with a helpless gaze, as though nailed fast
to the seat of his chair. The lonely piano, without as
much as a music stool to help it, struck a few chords
courageously, and beginning a selection of national airs,
played him out at last to the tune of 'Blue Bells of Scotland'. The painfully detached notes grew faint behind
his back while he went slowly upstairs, across the hall,
and into the street.

In front of the great doorway a dismal row of newspaper sellers standing clear of the pavement dealt out
their wares from the gutter. It was a raw, gloomy day of
the early spring; and the grimy sky, the mud of the
streets, the rags of the dirty men harmonized excellently
with the eruption of the damp, rubbishy sheets of paper
soiled with printers' ink. The posters, maculated with
filth, garnished like tapestry the sweep of the curbstone.
The trade in afternoon papers was brisk, yet, in comparison with the swift, constant march of foot traffic, the
effect was of indifference, of a disregarded distribution.
Ossipon looked hurriedly both ways before stepping out
into the cross-currents, but the Professor was already out
of sight.

CHAPTER FIVE

THE Professor had turned into a street to the left, and walked along, with his head carried rigidly erect, in a crowd whose every individual almost overtopped his stunted stature. It was vain to pretend to himself that he was not disappointed. But that was mere feeling; the stoicism of his thought could not be disturbed by this or any other failure. Next time, or the time after next, a telling stroke would be delivered – something really startling – a blow fit to open the first crack in the imposing front of the great edifice of legal conceptions sheltering the atrocious injustice of society. Of humble origin, and with an appearance really so mean as to stand in the way of his considerable natural abilities, his imagination had been fired early by the tales of men rising from the depths of poverty to positions of authority and affluence. The extreme, almost ascetic purity of his thought, combined with an astounding ignorance of worldly conditions, had set before him a goal of power and prestige to be attained without the medium of arts, graces, tact, wealth – by sheer weight of merit alone. On that view he considered himself entitled to undisputed success. His father, a delicate dark enthusiast with a sloping forehead, had been an itinerant and rousing preacher of some obscure but rigid Christian sect – a man supremely confident in the privileges of his righteousness. In the son, individualist by temperament, once the science of colleges had replaced thoroughly the faith of conventicles, this moral attitude translated itself

into a frenzied puritanism of ambition. He nursed it as
something secularly holy. To see it thwarted opened his
eyes to the true nature of the world, whose morality was
artificial, corrupt, and blasphemous. The way of even the
most justifiable revolutions is prepared by personal impulses disguised into creeds. The Professor's indignation
found in itself a final cause that absolved him from the
sin of turning to destruction as the agent of his ambition.
To destroy public faith in legality was the imperfect for-
mula of his pedantic fanaticism; but the subconscious
conviction that the framework of an established social
order cannot be effectually shattered except by some
form of collective or individual violence was precise and
correct. He was a moral agent – that was settled in his
mind. By exercising his agency with ruthless defiance he
procured for himself the appearances of power and personal prestige. That was undeniable to his vengeful bitterness. It pacified its unrest; and in their own way the
most ardent of revolutionaries are perhaps doing no more
but seeking for peace in common with the rest of mankind – the peace of soothed vanity, of satisfied appetites,
or perhaps of appeased conscience.

Lost in the crowd, miserable and undersized, he
meditated confidently on his power, keeping his hand in
the left pocket of his trousers, grasping lightly the india-
rubber ball, the supreme guarantee of his sinister freedom; but after a while he became disagreeably affected
by the sight of the roadway thronged with vehicles and
of the pavement crowded with men and women. He was
in a long, straight street, peopled by a mere fraction of an
immense multitude; but all round him, on and on, even
to the limits of the horizon hidden by the enormous piles
of bricks, he felt the mass of mankind mighty in its numbers. They swarmed numerous like locusts, industrious
like ants, thoughtless like a natural force, pushing on
blind and orderly and absorbed, impervious to sentiment, to logic, to terror, too, perhaps.

That was the form of doubt he feared most. Impervious to fear! Often while walking abroad, when he happened also to come out of himself, he had such moments of dreadful and sane mistrust of mankind. What if nothing could move them? Such moments come to all men whose ambition aims at a direct grasp upon humanity – to artists, politicians, thinkers, reformers, or saints. A despicable emotional state this, against which solitude fortifies a superior character; and with severe exultation the Professor thought of the refuge of his room, with its padlocked cupboard, lost in a wilderness of poor houses, the hermitage of the perfect anarchist. In order to reach sooner the point where he could take his omnibus, he turned brusquely out of the populous street into a narrow and dusky alley paved with flagstones. On one side the low brick houses had in their dusty windows the sightless, moribund look of incurable decay – empty shells awaiting demolition. From the other side life had not departed wholly as yet. Facing the only gas-lamp yawned the cavern of a second-hand furniture dealer, where, deep in the gloom of a sort of narrow avenue winding through a bizarre forest of wardrobes, with an undergrowth tangle of table legs, a tall pier-glass glimmered like a pool of water in a wood. An unhappy, homeless couch, accompanied by two unrelated chairs, stood in the open. The only human being making use of the alley besides the Professor, coming stalwart and erect from the opposite direction, checked his swinging pace suddenly.

'Hallo!' he said, and stood a little on one side watchfully.

The Professor had already stopped, with a ready half turn which brought his shoulders very near the other wall. His right hand fell lightly on the back of the outcast couch, the left remained purposefully plunged deep in the trousers pocket, and the roundness of the heavy rimmed spectacles imparted an owlish character to his moody, unperturbed face.

It was like a meeting in a side corridor of a mansion full of life. The stalwart man was buttoned up in a dark overcoat, and carried an umbrella. His hat, tilted back, uncovered a good deal of forehead, which appeared very white in the dusk. In the dark patches of the orbits the eyeballs glimmered piercingly. Long, drooping moustaches, the colour of ripe corn, framed with their points the square block of his shaved chin.

'I am not looking for you,' he said, curtly.

The Professor did not stir an inch. The blended noises of the enormous town sank down to an inarticulate low murmur. Chief Inspector Heat of the Special Crimes Department changed his tone.

'Not in a hurry to get home?' he asked, with mocking simplicity.

The unwholesome-looking little moral agent of destruction exulted silently in the possession of personal prestige, keeping in check this man armed with the defensive mandate of a menaced society. More fortunate than Caligula, who wished that the Roman Senate had only one head for the better satisfaction of his cruel lust, he beheld in that one man all the forces he had set at defiance: the force of law, property, oppression, and injustice. He beheld all his enemies and fearlessly confronted them all in a supreme satisfaction of his vanity. They stood perplexed before him as if before a dreadful portent. He gloated inwardly over the chance of this meeting affirming his superiority over all the multitude of mankind.

It was in reality a chance meeting. Chief Inspector Heat had had a disagreeably busy day since his department received the first telegram from Greenwich a little before eleven in the morning. First of all, the fact of the outrage being attempted less than a week after he had assured a high official that no outbreak of anarchist activity was to be apprehended was sufficiently annoying. If he ever thought himself safe in making a statement, it was then. He had made that statement with infinite satisfaction to himself, because it was clear that the high official desired greatly to hear that very thing. He had affirmed that nothing of the sort could even be thought of without the department being aware of it within twenty-four hours; and he had spoken thus in his consciousness of being the great expert of his department. He had gone even so far as to utter words which true wisdom would have kept back. But Chief Inspector Heat was not very wise – at least not truly so. True wisdom, which is not certain of anything in this world of contradictions, would have prevented him from attaining his present position. It would have alarmed his superiors, and done away with his chances of promotion. His promotion had been very rapid.

'There isn't one of them, sir, that we couldn't lay our hands on at any time of night and day. We know what each of them is doing hour by hour,' he had declared. And the high official had deigned to smile. This was so obviously the right thing to say for an officer of Chief Inspector Heat's reputation that it was perfectly delightful. The high official believed the declaration, which chimed in with his idea of the fitness of things. His wisdom was of an official kind, or else he might have reflected upon a matter not of theory but of experience that in the close-woven stuff of relations between conspirator and police there occur unexpected solutions of continuity, sudden holes in space and time. A given anarchist may be watched inch by inch and minute by minute, but a moment always comes when somehow all sight and touch of him are lost for a few hours, during which something (generally an explosion) more or less deplorable does happen. But the high official, carried away by his sense of the fitness of things, had smiled, and now the recollection of that smile was very annoying to Chief Inspector Heat, principal expert in anarchist procedure.

This was not the only circumstance whose recollec-

tion depressed the usual serenity of the eminent special-
ist. There was another dating back only to that very
morning. The thought that when called urgently to
his Assistant Commissioner's private room he had been
unable to conceal his astonishment was distinctly
vexing. His instinct of a successful man had taught him
long ago that, as a general rule, a reputation is built
on manner as much as on achievement. And he felt that
his manner when confronted with the telegram had
not been impressive. He had opened his eyes widely, and
had exclaimed 'Impossible!' exposing himself thereby
to the unanswerable retort of a finger-tip laid forcibly
on the telegram which the Assistant Commissioner,
after reading it aloud, had flung on the desk. To be
crushed, as it were, under the tip of a forefinger was an
unpleasant experience. Very damaging, too! Further-
more, Chief Inspector Heat was conscious of not having
mended matters by allowing himself to express a conviction.

'One thing I can tell you at once: none of our lot had
anything to do with this.'

He was strong in his integrity of a good detective, but
he saw now that an impenetrably attentive reserve
towards this incident would have served his reputation
better. On the other hand, he admitted to himself that it
was difficult to preserve one's reputation if rank out-
siders were going to take a hand in the business. Out-
siders are the bane of the police as of other professions.
The tone of the Assistant Commissioner's remarks had
been sour enough to set one's teeth on edge.

And since breakfast Chief Inspector Heat had not
managed to get anything to eat.

Starting immediately to begin his investigation on the
spot, he had swallowed a good deal of raw, unwholesome
fog in the park. Then he had walked over to the hospital;
and when the investigation in Greenwich was concluded at last he had lost his inclination for food. Not

accustomed, as the doctors are, to examine closely the mangled remains of human beings, he had been shocked by the sight disclosed to his view when a waterproof sheet had been lifted off a table in a certain apartment of the hospital.

Another waterproof sheet was spread over that table in the manner of a tablecloth, with the corners turned up over a sort of mound – a heap of rags, scorched and bloodstained, half concealing what might have been an accumulation of raw material for a cannibal feast. It required considerable firmness of mind not to recoil before that sight. Chief Inspector Heat, an efficient officer of his department, stood his ground, but for a whole minute he did not advance. A local constable in uniform cast a sidelong glance, and said with stolid simplicity:

'He's all there. Every bit of him. It was a job.'

He had been the first man on the spot after the explosion. He mentioned the fact again. He had seen something like a heavy flash of lightning in the fog. At that time he was standing at the door of the King William Street Lodge talking to the keeper. The concussion made him tingle all over. He ran between the trees towards the Observatory. 'As fast as my legs would carry me,' he repeated twice.

Chief Inspector Heat, bending forward over the table in a gingerly and horrified manner, let him run on. The hospital porter and another man turned down the corners of the cloth, and stepped aside. The Chief Inspector's eyes searched the gruesome detail of that heap of mixed things, which seemed to have been collected in shambles and rag shops.

'You used a shovel,' he remarked, observing a sprinkling of small gravel, tiny brown bits of bark, and particles of splintered wood as fine as needles.

'Had to in one place,' said the stolid constable. 'I sent a keeper to fetch a spade. When he heard me scraping the ground with it he leaned his forehead against a tree, and was as sick as a dog.'

The Chief Inspector, stooping guardedly over the table, fought down the unpleasant sensation in his throat. The shattering violence of destruction which had made of that body a heap of nameless fragments affected his feelings with a sense of ruthless cruelty, though his reason told him the effect must have been as swift as a flash of lightning. The man, whoever he was, had died instantaneously; and yet it seemed impossible to believe that a human body could have reached that state of disintegration without passing through the pangs of inconceivable agony. No physiologist, and still less of a metaphysician, Chief Inspector Heat rose by the force of sympathy, which is a form of fear, above the vulgar conception of time. Instantaneous! He remembered all he had ever read in popular publications of long and terrifying dreams dreamed in the instant of waking; of the whole past life lived with frightful intensity by a drowning man as his doomed head bobs up, streaming, for the last time. The inexplicable mysteries of conscious existence beset Chief Inspector Heat till he evolved a horrible notion that ages of atrocious pain and mental torture could be contained between two successive winks of an eye. And meantime the Chief Inspector went on peering at the table with a calm face and the slightly anxious attention of an indigent customer bending over what may be called the by-products of a butcher's shop with a view to an inexpensive Sunday dinner. All the time his trained faculties of an excellent investigator, who scorns no chance of information, followed the self-satisfied, disjointed loquacity of the constable.

'A fair-haired fellow,' the last observed in a placid tone, and paused. 'The old woman who spoke to the sergeant noticed a fair-haired fellow coming out of Maze Hill Station.' He paused. 'And he was a fair-haired fellow. She noticed two men coming out of the station after the uptrain had gone on,' he continued, slowly. 'She couldn't tell if they were together. She took no particular notice of the big one, but the other was a fair, slight chap, carrying a tin varnish can in one hand.' The constable ceased.

'Know the woman?' muttered the Chief Inspector, with his eyes fixed on the table, and a vague notion in his mind of an inquest to be held presently upon a person likely to remain for ever unknown.

'Yes. She's housekeeper to a retired publican, and attends the chapel in Park Place sometimes,' the constable uttered weightily, and paused, with another oblique glance at the table. Then suddenly: 'Well, here he is – all of him I could see. Fair. Slight – slight enough. Look at that foot there. I picked up the legs first, one after another. He was that scattered you didn't know where to begin.'

The constable paused; the least flicker of an innocent, self-laudatory smile invested his round face with an infantile expression.

'Stumbled,' he announced, positively. 'I stumbled once myself, and pitched on my head, too, while running up. Them roots do stick out all about the place. Stumbled against the root of a tree and fell, and that thing he was carrying must have gone off right under his chest, I expect.'

The echo of the words 'Person unknown' repeating itself in his inner consciousness bothered the Chief Inspector considerably. He would have liked to trace this affair back to its mysterious origin for his own information. He was professionally curious. Before the public he would have liked to vindicate the efficiency of his department by establishing the identity of that man. He was a loyal servant. That, however, appeared impossible. The first term of the problem was unreadable – lacked all suggestion but that of atrocious cruelty.

Overcoming his physical repugnance, Chief Inspector Heat stretched out his hand without conviction for the

salving of his conscience, and took up the least soiled of
the rags. It was a narrow strip of velvet with a larger triangular piece of dark blue cloth hanging from it. He held it
up to his eyes; and the police constable spoke.

'Velvet collar. Funny the old woman should have
noticed the velvet collar, Dark blue overcoat with a velvet collar, she has told us. He was the chap she saw, and
no mistake. And here he is all complete, velvet collar and
all. I don't think I missed a single piece as big as a post-
age stamp.'

At this point the trained faculties of the Chief Inspector ceased to hear the voice of the constable. He moved
to one of the windows for better light. His face, averted
from the room, expressed a startled, intense interest
while he examined closely the triangular piece of broad-
cloth. By a sudden jerk he detached it, and only after
stuffing it into his pocket turned round to the room, and
flung the velvet collar back on the table.

'Cover up,' he directed the attendants, curtly, without
another look, and, saluted by the constable, carried off
his spoil hastily.

A convenient train whirled him up to town, alone and
pondering deeply, in a third-class compartment. That
singed piece of cloth was incredibly valuable, and he
could not defend himself from astonishment at the
casual manner it had come into his possession. It was as
if Fate had thrust that clue into his hands. And after the
manner of the average man, whose ambition is to command events, he began to mistrust such a gratuitous and
accidental success – just because it seemed forced upon
him. The practical value of success depends not a little
on the way you look at it. But Fate looks at nothing. It
has no discretion. He no longer considered it eminently
desirable all round to establish publicly the identity of
the man who had blown himself up that morning with
such horrible completeness. But he was not certain of
the view his department would take. A department is to

those it employs a complex personality with ideas and
even fads of its own. It depends on the loyal devotion of
its servants, and the devoted loyalty of trusted servants is
associated with a certain amount of affectionate contempt, which keeps it sweet, as it were. By a benevolent
provision of Nature no man is a hero to his valet, or else
the heroes would have to brush their own clothes. Like-
wise no department appears perfectly wise to the intimacy of its workers. A department does not know so
much as some of its servants. Being a dispassionate
organism, it can never be perfectly informed. It would
not be good for its efficiency to know too much. Chief
Inspector Heat got out of the train in a state of thoughtfulness entirely untainted with disloyalty, but not quite
free of that jealous mistrust which so often springs on the
ground of perfect devotion, whether to women or to
institutions.

It was in this mental disposition, physically very
empty, but still nauseated by what he had seen, that he
had come upon the Professor. Under these conditions
which make for irascibility in a sound, normal man, this
meeting was specially unwelcome to Chief Inspector
Heat. He had not been thinking of the Professor; he had
not been thinking of any individual anarchist at all. The
complexion of that case had somehow forced upon him
the general idea of the absurdity of things human, which
in the abstract is sufficiently annoying to an unphiloso-
phical temperament, and in concrete instances becomes
exasperating beyond endurance. At the beginning of his
career Chief Inspector Heat had been concerned with
the more energetic forms of thieving. He had gained his
spurs in that sphere, and naturally enough had kept for
it, after his promotion to another department, a feeling
not very far removed from affection. Thieving was not a
sheer absurdity. It was a form of human industry, perverse indeed, but still an industry exercised in an industrious world; it was work undertaken for the same reason

as the work in potteries, in coal mines, in fields, in tool-grinding shops. It was labour, whose practical difference from the other forms of labour consisted in the nature of its risk, which did not lie in ankylosis, or lead poisoning, or fire-damp, or gritty dust, but in what may be briefly defined in its own special phraseology as 'Seven years hard.' Chief Inspector Heat was, of course, not insensible to the gravity of moral differences. But neither were the thieves he had been looking after. They submitted to the severe sanctions of a morality familiar to Chief Inspector Heat with a certain resignation. They were his fellow-citizens gone wrong because of imperfect education, Chief Inspector Heat believed; but allowing for that difference, he could understand the mind of a burglar, because, as a matter of fact, the mind and the instincts of a burglar are of the same kind as the mind and the instincts of a police officer. Both recognize the same conventions, and have a working knowledge of each other's methods and of the routine of their respective trades. They understand each other, which is advantageous to both, and establishes a sort of amenity in their relations. Products of the same machine, one classed as useful and the other as noxious, they take the machine for granted in different ways, but with a seriousness essentially the same. The mind of Chief Inspector Heat was inaccessible to ideas of revolt. But his thieves were not rebels. His bodily vigour, his cool, inflexible manner, his courage, and his fairness, had secured for him much respect and some adulation in the sphere of his early successes. He had felt himself revered and admired. And Chief Inspector Heat, arrested within six paces of the anarchist nicknamed the Professor, gave a thought of regret to the world of thieves – sane, without morbid ideals, working by routine, respectful of constituted authorities, free from all taint of hate and despair.

After paying this tribute to what is normal in the constitution of society (for the idea of thieving appeared to his instinct as normal as the idea of property), Chief Inspector Heat felt very angry with himself for having stopped, for having spoken, for having taken that way at all on the ground of it being a short cut from the station to the headquarters. And he spoke again in his big, authoritative voice, which, being moderated, had a threatening character.

'You are not wanted, I tell you,' he repeated.

The anarchist did not stir. An inward laugh of derision uncovered not only his teeth but his gums as well, shook him all over, without the slightest sound. Chief Inspector Heat was led to add, against his better judgment:

'Not yet. When I want you I will know where to find you.'

Those were perfectly proper words, within the tradition and suitable to his character of a police officer addressing one of his special flock. But the reception they got departed from tradition and propriety. It was outrageous. The stunted, weakly figure before him spoke at last.

'I've no doubt the papers would give you an obituary notice then. You know best what that would be worth to you. I should think you can imagine easily the sort of stuff that would be printed. But you may be exposed to the unpleasantness of being buried together with me, though I suppose your friends would make an effort to sort us out as much as possible.'

With all his healthy contempt for the spirit dictating such speeches, the atrocious allusiveness of the words had its effect on Chief Inspector Heat. He had too much insight, and too much exact information as well, to dismiss them as rot. The dusk of this narrow lane took on a sinister tint from the dark, frail little figure, its back to the wall, and speaking with a weak, self-confident voice. To the vigorous, tenacious vitality of the Chief Inspector, the physical wretchedness of that being, so obviously not fit to live, was ominous; for it seemed to him that if he had the misfortune to be such a miserable object he would not have cared how soon he died. Life had such a strong hold upon him that a fresh wave of nausea broke out in slight perspiration upon his brow. The murmur of town life, the subdued rumble of wheels in the two invisible streets to the right and left, came through the curve of the sordid lane to his ears with a precious familiarity and an appealing sweetness. He was human. But Chief Inspector Heat was also a man, and he could not let such words pass.

'All this is good to frighten children with,' he said. 'I'll have you yet.'

It was very well said, without scorn, with an almost austere quietness.

'Doubtless,' was the answer; 'but there's no time like the present, believe me. For a man of real convictions this is a fine opportunity of self-sacrifice. You may not find another so favourable, so humane. There isn't even a cat near us, and these condemned old houses would make a good heap of bricks where you stand. You'll never get me at so little cost to life and property, which you are paid to protect.'

'You don't know who you're speaking to,' said Chief Inspector Heat, firmly. 'If I were to lay my hands on you now I would be no better than yourself.'

'Ah! The game!'

'You may be sure our side will win in the end. It may yet be necessary to make people believe that some of you ought to be shot at sight like mad dogs. Then that will be the game. But I'll be damned if I know what yours is. I don't believe you know yourselves. You'll never get anything by it.'

'Meantime, it's you who get something from it – so far. And you get it easily, too. I won't speak of your salary, but haven't you made your name simply by not understanding what we are after?'

'What are you after, then?' asked Chief Inspector

Heat, with scornful haste, like a man in a hurry who perceives he is wasting his time.

The perfect anarchist answered by a smile which did not part his thin, colourless lips; and the celebrated Chief Inspector felt a sense of superiority which induced him to raise a warning finger.

'Give it up – whatever it is,' he said in an admonishing tone, but not so kindly as if he were condescending to give good advice to a cracksman of repute. 'Give it up. You'll find we are too many for you.'

The fixed smile on the Professor's lips wavered, as if the mocking spirit within had lost its assurance. Chief Inspector Heat went on:

'Don't you believe me – eh? Well, you've only got to look about you. We are. And anyway, you're not doing it well. You're always making a mess of it. Why, if the thieves didn't know their work better they would starve.'

The hint of an invincible multitude behind that man's back roused a sombre indignation in the breast of the Professor. He smiled no longer his enigmatic and mocking smile. The resisting power of numbers, the unattackable stolidity of a great multitude, was the haunting fear of his sinister loneliness. His lips trembled for some time before he managed to say in a strangled voice:

'I am doing my work better than you're doing yours.'

'That'll do now,' interrupted Chief Inspector Heat, hurriedly; and the Professor laughed right out this time. While still laughing he moved on; but he did not laugh long. It was a sad-faced, miserable little man who emerged from the narrow passage into the bustle of the broad thoroughfare. He walked with the nerveless gait of a tramp going on, still going on, indifferent to rain or sun in a sinister detachment from the aspects of sky and earth. Chief Inspector Heat, on the other hand, after watching him for a while, stepped out with the purposeful briskness of a man disregarding indeed the inclemencies of the weather, but conscious of having an

authorized mission on this earth and the moral support of
his kind. All the inhabitants of the immense town, the
population of the whole country, and even the teeming
millions struggling upon the planet, were with him –
down to the very thieves and mendicants. Yes, the
thieves themselves were sure to be with him in his present work. The consciousness of universal support in his
general activity heartened him to grapple with the particular problem.

The problem immediately before the Chief Inspector
was that of managing the Assistant Commissioner of his
department, his immediate superior. This is the peren-
nial problem of trusty and loyal servants; anarchism gave
it its particular complexion, but nothing more. Truth to
say, Chief Inspector Heat thought but little of anarchism.
He did not attach undue importance to it, and could
never bring himself to consider it seriously. It had more
the character of disorderly conduct; disorderly without the human excuse of drunkenness, which at any
rate implies good feeling and an amiable leaning
towards festivity. As criminals, anarchists were distinctly
no class – no class at all. And recalling the Professor,
Chief Inspector Heat, without checking his swinging
pace, muttered through his teeth:

'Lunatic.'

Catching thieves was another matter altogether. It had
that quality of seriousness belonging to every form of
open sport where the best man wins under perfectly
comprehensible rules. There were no rules for dealing
with anarchists. And that was distasteful to the Chief
Inspector. It was all foolishness, but that foolishness
excited the public mind, affected persons in high places,
and touched upon international relations. A hard, merci-
less contempt settled rigidly on the Chief Inspector's
face as he walked on. His mind ran over all the anarchists
of his flock. Not one of them had half the spunk of this or
that burglar he had known. Not half – not one tenth.

At headquarters the Chief Inspector was admitted at once to the Assistant Commissioner's private room. He found him, pen in hand, bent over a great table bestrewn with papers, as if worshipping an enormous double ink-stand of bronze and crystal. Speaking tubes resembling snakes were tied by the heads to the back of the Assistant Commissioner's wooden armchair, and their gaping mouths seemed ready to bite his elbows. And in this attitude he raised only his eyes, whose lids were darker than his face and very much creased. The reports had come in: every anarchist had been exactly accounted for.

After saying this he lowered his eyes, signed rapidly two single sheets of paper, and only then laid down his pen, and sat well back, directing an inquiring gaze at his renowned subordinate. The Chief Inspector stood it well, deferential but inscrutable.

'I daresay you were right,' said the Assistant Commissioner, 'in telling me at first that the London anarchists had nothing to do with this. I quite appreciate the excellent watch kept on them by your men. On the other hand, this, for the public, does not amount to more than a confession of ignorance.'

The Assistant Commissioner's delivery was leisurely, as it were cautious. His thought seemed to rest poised on a word before passing to another, as though words had been the stepping-stones for his intellect picking its way across the waters of error. 'Unless you have brought something useful from Greenwich,' he added.

The Chief Inspector began at once the account of his investigation in a clear, matter-of-fact manner. His superior turning his chair a little, and crossing his thin legs, leaned sideways on his elbow, with one hand shading his eyes. His listening attitude had a sort of angular and sorrowful grace. Gleams as of highly burnished silver played on the sides of his ebony black head when he inclined it slowly at the end.

Chief Inspector Heat waited with the appearance of

turning over in his mind all he had just said, but, as a matter of fact, considering the advisability of saying something more. The Assistant Commissioner cut his hesitation short.

'You believe there were two men?' he asked, without uncovering his eyes.

The Chief Inspector thought it more than probable. In his opinion, the two men had parted from each other within a hundred yards from the Observatory walls. He explained also how the other man could have got out of the park speedily without being observed. The fog, though not very dense, was in his favour. He seemed to have escorted the other to the spot, and then to have left him there to do the job single-handed. Taking the time those two were seen coming out of Maze Hill Station by the old woman, and the time when the explosion was heard, the Chief Inspector thought that the other man might have been actually at the Greenwich Park Station, ready to catch the next train up, at the moment his comrade was destroying himself so thoroughly.

'Very thoroughly – eh?' murmured the Assistant Commissioner from under the shadow of his hand.

The Chief Inspector in a few vigorous words described the aspect of the remains. 'The coroner's jury will have a treat,' he added, grimly.

The Assistant Commissioner uncovered his eyes.

'We shall have nothing to tell them,' he remarked, languidly.

He looked up, and for a time watched the markedly non-committal attitude of his Chief Inspector. His nature was one that is not easily accessible to illusions. He knew that a department is at the mercy of its subordinate officers, who have their own conceptions of loyalty. His career had begun in a tropical colony. He had liked his work there. It was police work. He had been very successful in tracking and breaking up certain nefarious secret societies amongst the natives. Then he took his long leave, and got married rather impulsively. It was a good match from a worldly point of view, but his wife formed an unfavourable opinion of the colonial climate on hearsay evidence. On the other hand, she had influential connections. It was an excellent match. But he did not like the work he had to do now. He felt himself dependent on too many subordinates and too many masters. The near presence of that strange emotional phenomenon called public opinion weighed upon his spirits, and alarmed him by its irrational nature. No doubt that from ignorance he exaggerated to himself its power for good and evil – especially for evil; and the rough east winds of the English spring (which agreed with his wife) augmented his general mistrust of men's motives and of the efficiency of their organization. The futility of office work especially appalled him on those days so trying to his sensitive liver.

He got up, unfolding himself to his full height, and with a heaviness of step remarkable in so slender a man, moved across the room to the window. The panes streamed with rain, and the short street he looked down into lay wet and empty, as if swept clear suddenly by a great flood. It was a very trying day, choked in raw fog to begin with, and now drowned in cold rain. The flickering, blurred flames of gas-lamps seemed to be dissolving in a watery atmosphere. And the lofty pretensions of a mankind oppressed by the miserable indignities of the weather appeared as a colossal and hopeless vanity deserving of scorn, wonder, and compassion.

'Horrible, horrible!' thought the Assistant Commissioner to himself, with his face near the window-pane. 'We have been having this sort of thing now for ten days; no, a fortnight – a fortnight.' He ceased to think completely for a time. That utter stillness of his brain lasted about three seconds. Then he said, perfunctorily: 'You have set inquiries on foot for tracing that other man up and down the line?'

He had no doubt that everything needful had been done. Chief Inspector Heat knew, of course, thoroughly the business of man-hunting. And these were the routine steps, too, that would be taken as a matter of course by the merest beginner. A few inquiries amongst the ticket collectors and the porters of the two small railway stations would give additional details as to the appearance of the two men; the inspection of the collected tickets would show at once where they came from that morning. It was elementary, and could not have been neglected. Accordingly, the Chief Inspector answered that all this had been done directly the old woman had come forward with her deposition. And he mentioned the name of a station. 'That's where they came from, sir,' he went on. 'The porter who took the tickets at Maze Hill remembers two chaps answering to the description passing the barrier. They seemed to him two respectable working-men of a superior sort – sign painters or house decorators. The big man got out of a third-class compartment backward, with a bright tin can in his hand. On the platform he gave it to carry to the fair young fellow who followed him. All this agrees exactly with what the old woman told the police sergeant in Greenwich.'

The Assistant Commissioner, still with his face turned to the window, expressed his doubt as to these two men having had anything to do with the outrage. All this theory rested upon the utterances of an old charwoman who had been nearly knocked down by a man in a hurry. Not a very substantial authority indeed, unless on the ground of sudden inspiration, which was hardly tenable.

'Frankly now, could she have been really inspired?' he queried, with grave irony, keeping his back to the room, as if entranced by the contemplation of the town's colossal forms half lost in the night. He did not even look round when he heard the mutter of the word 'Providential' from the principal subordinate of his department, whose name, printed sometimes in the papers, was familiar to the great public as that of one of its zealous and hard-working protectors. Chief Inspector Heat raised his voice a little.

'Strips and bits of bright tin were quite visible to me,' he said. 'That's a pretty good corroboration.'

'And these men came from that little country station,' the Assistant Commissioner mused aloud, wondering. He was told that such was the name on two tickets out of three given up out of that train at Maze Hill. The third person who got out was a hawker from Gravesend well known to the porters. The Chief Inspector imparted that information in a tone of finality with some ill humour, as loyal servants will do in the consciousness of their fidelity and with the sense of the value of their loyal exertions. And still the Assistant Commissioner did not turn away from the darkness outside, as vast as a sea.

'Two foreign anarchists coming from that place,' he said, apparently to the window-pane. 'It's rather unaccountable.'

'Yes, sir. But it would be still more unaccountable if that Michaelis weren't staying in a cottage in the neighbourhood.'

At the sound of that name, falling unexpectedly into this annoying affair, the Assistant Commissioner dismissed brusquely the vague remembrance of his daily whist party at his club. It was the most comforting habit of his life, in a mainly successful display of his skill without the assistance of any subordinate. He entered his club to play from five to seven, before going home to dinner, forgetting for those two hours whatever was distasteful in his life, as though the game were a beneficent drug for allaying the pangs of moral discontent. His partners were the gloomily humorous editor of a celebrated magazine; a silent, elderly barrister with malicious little eyes; and a highly martial, simple-minded old Colonel with nervous brown hands. They were his club acquaintances merely. He never met them elsewhere except at

the card-table. But they all seemed to approach the game
in the spirit of co-sufferers, as if it were indeed a drug
against the secret ills of existence; and every day as the
sun declined over the countless roofs of the town, a mel-
low, pleasurable impatience, resembling the impulse of a
sure and profound friendship, lightened his professional
labours. And now this pleasurable sensation went out of
him with something resembling a physical shock, and
was replaced by a special kind of interest in his work of
social protection – an improper sort of interest, which
may be defined best as a sudden and alert mistrust of the
weapon in his hand.

CHAPTER SIX

THE lady patroness of Michaelis, the ticket-of-leave apostle of humanitarian hopes, was one of the most influential and distinguished connections of the Assistant Commissioner's wife, whom she called Annie, and treated still rather as a not very wise and utterly inexperienced young girl. But she had consented to accept him on a friendly footing, which was by no means the case with all of his wife's influential connections. Married young and splendidly at some remote epoch of the past, she had had for a time a close view of great affairs and even of some great men. She herself was a great lady. Old now in the number of her years, she had that sort of exceptional temperament which defies time with scornful disregard, as if it were a rather vulgar convention submitted to by the mass of inferior mankind. Many other conventions easier to set aside, alas! failed to obtain her recognition, also on temperamental grounds – either because they bored her, or else because they stood in the way of her scorns and sympathies. Admiration was a sentiment unknown to her (it was one of the secret griefs of her most noble husband against her) – first, as always more or less tainted with mediocrity, and next as being in a way an admission of inferiority. And both were frankly inconceivable to her nature. To be fearlessly outspoken in her opinions came easily to her, since she judged solely from the standpoint of her social position. She was equally untrammelled in her actions; and as her tactfulness proceeded from genuine humanity, her bod-

ily vigour remained remarkable and her superiority was
serene and cordial, three generations had admired her
infinitely, and the last she was likely to see had pronounced her a wonderful woman. Meantime, intelligent,
with a sort of lofty simplicity, and curious at heart, but not
like many women merely of social gossip, she amused her
age by attracting within her ken through the power of her
great, almost historical, social prestige everything that
rose above the dead level of mankind, lawfully or unlaw-
fully, by position, wit, audacity, fortune or misfortune.
Royal Highnesses, artists, men of science, young states-
men, and charlatans of all ages and conditions, who,
unsubstantial and light, bobbing up like corks, show best
the direction of the surface currents, had been welcomed
in that house, listened to, penetrated, understood,
appraised, for her own edification. In her own words, she
liked to watch what the world was coming to. And as she
had a practical mind her judgment of men and things,
though based on special prejudices, was seldom totally
wrong, and almost never wrong-headed. Her drawing-
room was probably the only place in the wide world
where an Assistant Commissioner of Police could meet a
convict liberated on a ticket-of-leave on other than professional and official ground. Who had brought Michaelis
there one afternoon the Assistant Commissioner did not
remember very well. He had a notion it must have been a
certain Member of Parliament of illustrious parentage
and unconventional sympathies, which were the standing
joke of the comic papers. The notabilities and even the
simple notorieties of the day brought each other freely to
that temple of an old woman's not ignoble curiosity. You
never could guess whom you were likely to come upon
being received in semi-privacy within the faded blue silk
and gilt frame screen, making a cosy nook for a couch and
a few armchairs in the great drawing-room, with its hum
of voices and the groups of people seated or standing in
the light of six tall windows.

Michaelis had been the object of a revulsion of popular sentiment, the same sentiment which years ago had
applauded the ferocity of the life sentence passed upon
him for complicity in a rather mad attempt to rescue
some prisoners from a police van. The plan of the conspirators had been to shoot down the horses and over-
power the escort. Unfortunately, one of the police
constables got shot, too. He left a wife and three small
children, and the death of that man aroused through the
length and breadth of a realm for whose defence, welfare, and glory men die every day as matter of duty, an
outburst of furious indignation, of a raging, implacable
pity for the victim. Three ring-leaders got hanged.
Michaelis, young and slim, locksmith by trade, and great
frequenter of evening schools, did not even know that
anybody had been killed, his part with a few others
being to force open the door at the back of the special
conveyance. When arrested he had a bunch of skeleton
keys in one pocket, a heavy chisel in another, and a short
crowbar in his hand: neither more nor less than a burglar.
But no burglar would have received such a heavy sentence. The death of the constable had made him miserable at heart, but the failure of the plot also. He did not
conceal either of these sentiments from his empanelled
countrymen, and that sort of compunction appeared
shockingly imperfect to the crammed court. The judge
on passing sentence commented feelingly upon the
depravity and callousness of the young prisoner.

That made the groundless fame of his condemnation;
the fame of his release was made for him on no better
grounds by people who wished to exploit the sentimental aspect of his imprisonment either for purposes of
their own or for no intelligible purpose. He let them do
so in the innocence of his heart and the simplicity of his
mind. Nothing that happened to him individually had
any importance. He was like those saintly men whose
personality is lost in the contemplation of their faith. His

ideas were not in the nature of convictions. They were inaccessible to reasoning. They formed in all their contradictions and obscurities an invincible and humanitarian creed, which he confessed rather than preached, with an obstinate gentleness, a smile of pacific assurance on his lips, and his candid blue eyes cast down because the sight of faces troubled his inspiration developed in solitude. In that characteristic attitude, pathetic in his grotesque and incurable obesity which he had to drag like a galley slave's bullet to the end of his days, the Assistant Commissioner of Police beheld the ticket-of-leave apostle filling a privileged armchair within the screen. He sat there by the head of the old lady's couch, mild-voiced and quiet, with no more self-consciousness than a very small child, and with something of a child's charm – the appealing charm of trustfulness. Confident of the future, whose secret ways had been revealed to him within the four walls of a well-known penitentiary, he had no reason to look with suspicion upon anybody. If he could not give the great and curious lady a very definite idea as to what the world was coming to, he had managed without effort to impress her by his unembittered faith, by the sterling quality of his optimism.

A certain simplicity of thought is common to serene souls at both ends of the social scale. The great lady was simple in her own way. His views and beliefs had nothing in them to shock or startle her, since she judged them from the standpoint of her lofty position. Indeed, her sympathies were easily accessible to a man of that sort. She was not an exploiting capitalist herself; she was, as it were, above the play of economic conditions. And she had a great capacity of pity for the more obvious forms of common human miseries, precisely because she was such a complete stranger to them that she had to translate her conception into terms of mental suffering before she could grasp the notion of their cruelty. The Assistant Commissioner remembered very well the conversation

between these two. He had listened in silence. It was
something as exciting in a way, and even touching in its
foredoomed futility, as the efforts at moral intercourse
between the inhabitants of remote planets. But this grotesque incarnation of humanitarian passion appealed,
somehow, to one's imagination. At last Michaelis rose,
and taking the great lady's extended hand, shook it,
retained it for a moment in his great cushioned palm
with unembarrassed friendliness, and turned upon the
semi-private nook of the drawing-room his back, vast
and square, and as if distended under the short tweed
jacket. Glancing about in serene benevolence, he wad-
dled along to the distant door between the knots of other
visitors. The murmur of conversations paused on his
passage. He smiled innocently at a tall, brilliant girl,
whose eyes met his accidentally, and went out unconscious of the glances following him across the room.
Michaelis' first appearance in the world was a success – a
success of esteem unmarred by a single murmur of derision. The interrupted conversations were resumed in
their proper tone, grave or light. Only a well-set-up,
long-limbed, active-looking man of forty talking with
two ladies near a window remarked aloud, with an unexpected depth of feeling: 'Eighteen stone, I should say,
and not five foot six. Poor fellow! It's terrible – terrible.'

The lady of the house, gazing absently at the Assistant
Commissioner, left alone with her on the private side of
the screen, seemed to be rearranging her mental
impressions behind her thoughtful immobility of a hand-
some old face. Men with grey moustaches and full,
healthy, vaguely smiling countenances approached, circ-
ling round the screen; two mature women with a
matronly air of gracious resolution; a clean-shaved individual with sunken cheeks, and dangling a gold-
mounted eyeglass on a broad black ribbon with an
old-world, dandified effect. A silence deferential, but
full of reserves, reigned for a moment, and then the great

lady exclaimed, not with resentment, but with a sort of protesting indignation:

'And that officially is supposed to be a revolutionist! What nonsense.' She looked hard at the Assistant Commissioner, who murmured, apologetically:

'Not a dangerous one perhaps.'

'Not dangerous – I should think not indeed. He is a mere believer. It's the temperament of a saint,' declared the great lady in a firm tone. 'And they kept him shut up for twenty years. One shudders at the stupidity of it. And now they have let him out everybody belonging to him is gone away somewhere or dead. His parents are dead; the girl he was to marry has died while he was in prison; he has lost the skill necessary for his manual occupation. He told me all this himself with the sweetest patience; but then, he said, he had had plenty of time to think out things for himself. A pretty compensation! If that's the stuff revolutionists are made of some of us may well go on their knees to them,' she continued in a slightly bantering voice, while the banal society smiles hardened on the worldly faces turned towards her with conventional deference. 'The poor creature is obviously no longer in a position to take care of himself. Somebody will have to look after him a little.'

'He should be recommended to follow a treatment of some sort,' the soldierly voice of the active-looking man was heard advising earnestly from a distance. He was in the pink of condition for his age, and even the texture of his long frock coat had a character of elastic soundness, as if it were a living tissue. 'The man is virtually a cripple,' he added with unmistakable feeling.

Other voices, as if glad of the opening, murmured hasty compassion. 'Quite startling,' 'Monstrous,' 'Most painful to see.' The lank man, with the eyeglass on a broad ribbon, pronounced mincingly the word 'Grotesque,' whose justness was appreciated by those standing near him. They smiled at each other.

The Assistant Commissioner had expressed no opinion either then or later, his position making it impossible for him to ventilate any independent view of a ticket-of-leave convict. But, in truth, he shared the view of his wife's friend and patron that Michaelis was a humanitarian sentimentalist, a little mad, but upon the whole incapable of hurting a fly intentionally. So when that name cropped up suddenly in this vexing bomb affair he realized all the danger of it for the ticket-of-leave apostle, and his mind reverted at once to the old lady's well-established infatuation. Her arbitrary kindness would not brook patiently any interference with Michaelis' freedom. It was a deep, calm, convinced infatuation. She had not only felt him to be inoffensive, but she had said so, which last by a confusion of her absolutist mind became a sort of incontrovertible demonstration. It was as if the monstrosity of the man, with his candid infant's eyes and a fat angelic smile, had fascinated her. She had come to believe almost his theory of the future, since it was not repugnant to her prejudices. She disliked the new element of plutocracy in the social compound, and industrialism as a method of human development appeared to her singularly repulsive in its mechanical and unfeeling character. The humanitarian hopes of the mild Michaelis tended not towards utter destruction, but merely towards the complete economic ruin of the system. And she did not really see where was the moral harm of it. It would do away with all the multitude of the 'parvenus', whom she disliked and mistrusted, not because they had arrived anywhere (she denied that), but because of their profound unintelligence of the world, which was the primary cause of the crudity of their perceptions and the aridity of their hearts. With the annihilation of all capital they would vanish, too; but universal ruin (providing it was universal, as it was revealed to Michaelis) would leave the social values untouched. The disappearance of the last piece of money could not affect people of posi-

tion. She could not conceive how it could affect her position, for instance. She had developed these discoveries
to the Assistant Commissioner with all the serene fear-
lessness of an old woman who had escaped the blight of
indifference. He had made for himself the rule to receive
everything of that sort in a silence which he took care
from policy and inclination not to make offensive. He
had an affection for the aged disciple of Michaelis, a
complex sentiment depending a little on her prestige, on
her personality, but most of all on the instinct of flattered
gratitude. He felt himself really liked in her house. She
was kindness personified. And she was practically wise,
too, after the manner of experienced women. She made
his married life much easier than it would have been
without her generously full recognition of his rights as
Annie's husband. Her influence upon his wife, a
woman devoured by all sorts of small selfishnesses, small
envies, small jealousies, was excellent. Unfortunately,
both her kindness and her wisdom were of unreasonable
complexion, distinctly feminine, and difficult to deal
with. She remained a perfect woman all along her full
tale of years, and not as some of them do become – a sort
of slippery, pestilential old man in petticoats. And it was
as of a woman that he thought of her – the specially
choice incarnation of the feminine, wherein is recruited
the tender, ingenuous, and fierce bodyguard for all sorts
of men who talk under the influence of an emotion, true
or fraudulent; for preachers, seers, prophets, or reformers.

Appreciating the distinguished and good friend of his
wife, and himself, in that way, the Assistant Commissioner became alarmed at the convict Michaelis' possible
fate. Once arrested on suspicion of being in some way,
however remote, a party to this outrage, the man could
hardly escape being sent back to finish his sentence at
least. And that would kill him; he would never come out
alive. The Assistant Commissioner made a reflection

extremely unbecoming his official position without being really creditable to his humanity.

'If the fellow is laid hold of again,' he thought, 'she will never forgive me.'

The frankness of such a secretly outspoken thought could not go without some derisive self-criticism. No man engaged in a work he does not like can preserve many saving illusions about himself. The distaste, the absence of glamour, extend from the occupation to the personality. It is only when our appointed activities seem by a lucky accident to obey the particular earnestness of our temperament that we can taste the comfort of complete self-deception. The Assistant Commissioner did not like his work at home. The police work he had been engaged on in a distant part of the globe had the saving character of an irregular sort of warfare or at least the risk and excitement of open-air sport. His real abilities, which were mainly of an administrative order, were combined with an adventurous disposition. Chained to a desk in the thick of four millions of men, he considered himself the victim of an ironic fate – the same, no doubt, which had brought about his marriage with a woman exceptionally sensitive in the matter of colonial climate, besides other limitations testifying to the delicacy of her nature – and her tastes. Though he judged his alarm sardonically he did not dismiss the improper thought from his mind. The instinct of self-preservation was strong within him. On the contrary, he repeated it mentally with profane emphasis and a fuller precision: 'Damn it! If that infernal Heat has his way the fellow'll die in prison smothered in his fat, and she'll never forgive me.'

His black, narrow figure, with the white band of the collar under the silvery gleams on the close-cropped hair at the back of the head, remained motionless. The silence had lasted such a long time that Chief Inspector Heat ventured to clear his throat. This noise produced its effect. The zealous and intelligent officer was asked by his superior, whose back remained turned to him immovably:

'You connect Michaelis with this affair?'

Chief Inspector Heat was very positive, but cautious.

'Well, sir,' he said, 'we have enough to go upon. A man like that has no business to be at large, anyhow.'

'You will want some conclusive evidence,' came the observation in a murmur.

Chief Inspector Heat raised his eyebrows at the black, narrow back, which remained obstinately presented to his intelligence and his zeal.

'There will be no difficulty in getting up sufficient evidence against *him*,' he said, with virtuous complacency. 'You may trust me for that, sir,' he added, quite unnecessarily, out of the fullness of his heart; for it seemed to him an excellent thing to have that man in hand to be thrown down to the public should it think fit to roar with any special indignation in this case. It was impossible to say yet whether it would roar or not. That in the last instance depended, of course, on the newspaper press. But in any case, Chief Inspector Heat, purveyor of prisons by trade, and a man of legal instincts, did logically believe that incarceration was the proper fate for every declared enemy of the law. In the strength of that conviction he committed a fault of tact. He allowed himself a little conceited laugh, and repeated:

'Trust me for that, sir.'

This was too much for the forced calmness under which the Assistant Commissioner had for upwards of eighteen months concealed his irritation with the system and the subordinates of his office. A square peg forced into a round hole, he had felt like a daily outrage that long-established smooth roundness into which a man of less sharply angular shape would have fitted himself, with voluptuous acquiescence, after a shrug or two. What he resented most was just the necessity of taking so much on trust. At the little laugh of Chief Inspector

Heat's he spun swiftly on his heels, as if whirled away from the window-pane by an electric shock. He caught on the latter's face not only the complacency proper to the occasion lurking under the moustache, but the vestiges of experimental watchfulness in the round eyes, which had been, no doubt, fastened on his back, and now met his glance for a second before the intent character of their stare had the time to change to a merely startled appearance.

The Assistant Commissioner of Police had really some qualifications for his post. Suddenly his suspicion was awakened. It is but fair to say that his suspicions of the police methods (unless the police happened to be a semi-military body organized by himself) was not difficult to arouse. If it ever slumbered from sheer weariness, it was but lightly; and his appreciation of Chief Inspector Heat's zeal and ability, moderate in itself, excluded all notion of moral confidence. 'He's up to something,' he exclaimed, mentally, and at once became angry. Crossing over to his desk with headlong strides, he sat down violently. 'Here I am stuck in a litter of paper,' he reflected, with unreasonable resentment, 'supposed to hold all the threads in my hands, and yet I can but hold what is put in my hand, and nothing else. And they can fasten the other ends of the threads where they please.'

He raised his head, and turned towards his subordinate a long, meagre face with the accentuated features of an energetic Don Quixote.

'Now what is it you've got up your sleeve?'

The other stared. He stared without winking in a perfect immobility of his round eyes, as he was used to stare at the various members of the criminal class when, after being duly cautioned, they made their statements in the tones of injured innocence, or false simplicity, or sullen resignation. But behind that professional and stony fixity there was some surprise, too, for in such a tone, combining nicely the note of contempt and impatience, Chief

Inspector Heat, the right-hand man of the department, was not used to be addressed. He began in a procrastinating manner, like a man taken unawares by a new and unexpected experience.

'What I've got against that man Michaelis you mean, sir?'

The Assistant Commissioner watched the bullet head; the points of that Norse rover's moustache, falling below the line of the heavy jaw; the whole full and pale physiognomy, whose determined character was marred by too much flesh; at the cunning wrinkles radiating from the outer corners of the eyes – and in that purposeful contemplation of the valuable and trusted officer he drew a conviction so sudden that it moved him like an inspiration.

'I have reason to think that when you came into this room,' he said in measured tones, 'it was not Michaelis who was in your mind; not principally – perhaps not at all.'

'You have reason to think, sir?' muttered Chief Inspector Heat, with every appearance of astonishment, which up to a certain point was genuine enough. He had discovered in this affair a delicate and perplexing side, forcing upon the discoverer a certain amount of insincerity – that sort of insincerity which, under the names of skill, prudence, discretion, turns up at one point or another in most human affairs. He felt at the moment like a tight-rope artist might feel if suddenly, in the middle of the performance, the manager of the Music Hall were to rush out of the proper managerial seclusion and begin to shake the rope. Indignation, the sense of moral insecurity engendered by such a treacherous proceeding joined to the immediate apprehension of a broken neck, would, in the colloquial phrase, put him in a state. And there would be also some scandalized concern for his art, too, since a man must identify himself with something more tangible than his own personality,

and establish his pride somewhere, either in his social
position, or in the quality of the work he is obliged to do,
or simply in the superiority of the idleness he may be fortunate enough to enjoy.

'Yes,' said the Assistant Commissioner; 'I have. I do
not mean to say that you have not thought of Michaelis
at all. But you are giving the fact you've mentioned a
prominence which strikes me as not quite candid,
Inspector Heat. If that is really the track of discovery,
why haven't you followed it up at once, either personally
or by sending one of your men to that village?'

'Do you think, sir, I have failed in my duty there?' the
Chief Inspector asked, in a tone which he sought to
make simply reflective. Forced unexpectedly to concen-
trate his faculties upon the task of preserving his bal-
ance, he had seized upon that point, and exposed
himself to a rebuke; for the Assistant Commissioner,
frowning slightly, observed that this was a very improper
remark to make.

'But since you've made it,' he continued, coldly, 'I'll
tell you that this is not my meaning.'

He paused, with a straight glance of his sunken eyes
which was a full equivalent of the unspoken termination
'and you know it.' The head of the so-called Special
Crimes Department, debarred by his position from going
out of doors personally in quest of secrets locked up in
guilty breasts, had a propensity to exercise his considerable gifts for the detection of incriminating truth upon
his own subordinates. That peculiar instinct could hardly
be called a weakness. It was natural. He was a born
detective. It had unconsciously governed his choice of a
career, and if it ever failed him in life it was perhaps in
the one exceptional circumstance of his marriage –
which was also natural. It fed, since it could not roam
abroad, upon the human material which was brought to
it in its official seclusion. We can never cease to be ourselves.

His elbow on the desk, his thin legs crossed and nursing his cheek in the palm of his meagre hand, the Assistant Commissioner in charge of the Special Crimes branch was getting hold of the case with growing interest. His Chief Inspector, if not an absolutely worthy foeman of his penetration, was at any rate the most worthy of all within his reach. A mistrust of established reputations was strictly in character with the Assistant Commissioner's ability as detector. His memory evoked a certain old fat and wealthy native chief in the distant colony whom it was a tradition for the successive Colonial Governors to trust and make much of as a firm friend and supporter of the order and legality established by white men; whereas, when examined sceptically, he was found out to be principally his own good friend, and nobody else's. Not precisely a traitor, but still a man of many dangerous reservations in his fidelity, caused by a due regard for his own advantage, comfort, and safety. A fellow of some innocence in his naïve duplicity, but none the less dangerous. He took some finding out. He was physically a big man, too, and (allowing for the difference of colour, of course) Chief Inspector Heat's appearance recalled him to the memory of his superior. It was not the eyes nor yet the lips exactly. It was bizarre. But does not Alfred Wallace relate in his famous book on the Malay Archipelago how, amongst the Aru Islanders, he discovered in an old and naked savage with a sooty skin a peculiar resemblance to a dear friend at home?

For the first time since he took up his appointment the Assistant Commissioner felt as if he were going to do some real work for his salary. And that was a pleasurable sensation. 'I'll turn him inside out like an old glove,' thought the Assistant Commissioner, with his eyes resting pensively upon Chief Inspector Heat.

'No, that was not my thought,' he began again. 'There is no doubt about you knowing your business – no doubt at all; and that's precisely why I —' He stopped short, and changing his tone: 'What could you bring up against Michaelis of a definite nature? I mean apart from the fact that the two men under suspicion – you're certain there were two of them – came last from a railway station within three miles of the village where Michaelis is living now.'

'This by itself is enough for us to go upon, sir, with that sort of man,' said the Chief Inspector, with returning composure. The slight, approving movement of the Assistant Commissioner's head went far to pacify the resentful astonishment of the renowned officer. For Chief Inspector Heat was a kind man, an excellent husband, a devoted father; and the public and departmental confidence he enjoyed, acting favourably upon an amiable nature, disposed him to feel friendly towards the successive Assistant Commissioners he had seen pass through that very room. There had been three in his time. The first one, a soldierly, abrupt, red-faced person, with white eyebrows and an explosive temper, could be managed with a silken thread. He left on reaching the age limit. The second, a perfect gentleman, knowing his own and everybody else's place to a nicety, on resigning to take up a higher appointment out of England got decorated for (really) Inspector Heat's services. To work with him had been a pride and a pleasure. The third, a bit of a dark horse from the first, was at the end of eighteen months something of a dark horse still to the department. Upon the whole Chief Inspector Heat believed him to be in the main harmless – odd-looking, but harmless. He was speaking now, and the Chief Inspector listened with outward deference (which means nothing, being a matter of duty) and inwardly with benevolent toleration.

'Michaelis reported himself before leaving London for the country?'

'Yes, sir. He did.'

'And what may he be doing there?' continued the Assistant Commissioner, who was perfectly informed on that point. Fitted with painful tightness into an old wooden armchair, before a worm-eaten oak table in an upstairs room of a four-roomed cottage with a roof of moss-grown tiles, Michaelis was writing night and day in a shaky, slanting hand that 'Autobiography of a Prisoner' which was to be like a book of Revelation in the history of mankind. The conditions of confined space, seclusion, and solitude in a small four-roomed cottage were favourable to his inspiration. It was like being in prison, except that one was never disturbed for the odious purpose of taking exercise according to the tyrannical regulations of his old home in the penitentiary. He could not tell whether the sun still shone on the earth or not. The perspiration of the literary labour dropped from his brow. A delightful enthusiasm urged him on. It was the liberation of his inner life, the letting out of his soul into the wide world. And the zeal of his guileless vanity (first awakened by the offer of five hundred pounds from a publisher) seemed something predestined and holy.

'It would be, of course, most desirable to be informed exactly,' insisted the Assistant Commissioner, uncandidly.

Chief Inspector Heat, conscious of renewed irritation at this display of scrupulousness, said that the county police had been notified from the first of Michaelis' arrival, and that a full report could be obtained in a few hours. A wire to the superintendent —

Thus he spoke, rather slowly, while his mind seemed already to be weighing the consequences. A slight knitting of the brow was the outward sign of this. But he was interrupted by a question.

'You've sent that wire already?'

'No, sir,' he answered, as if surprised.

The Assistant Commissioner uncrossed his legs suddenly. The briskness of that movement contrasted with the casual way in which he threw out a suggestion.

'Would you think that Michaelis had anything to do
with the preparation of that bomb, for instance?'

The Chief Inspector assumed a reflective manner.

'I wouldn't say so. There's no necessity to say anything at present. He associates with men who are classed
as dangerous. He was made a delegate of the Red Committee less than a year after his release on licence. A sort
of compliment, I suppose.'

And the Chief Inspector laughed a little angrily, a
little scornfully. With a man of that sort scrupulousness
was a misplaced and even an illegal sentiment. The celebrity bestowed upon Michaelis on his release two years
ago by some emotional journalists in want of special copy
had rankled ever since in his breast. It was perfectly legal
to arrest that man on the barest suspicion. It was legal
and expedient on the face of it. His two former chiefs
would have seen the point at once; whereas this one,
without saying either yes or no, sat there, as if lost in a
dream. Moreover, besides being legal and expedient, the
arrest of Michaelis solved a little personal difficulty
which worried Chief Inspector Heat somewhat. This difficulty had its bearing upon his reputation, upon his
comfort, and even upon the efficient performance of his
duties. For, if Michaelis no doubt knew something about
this outrage, the Chief Inspector was fairly certain that
he did not know too much. This was just as well. He
knew much less – the Chief Inspector was positive –
than certain other individuals he had in his mind, but
whose arrest seemed to him inexpedient, besides being a
more complicated matter, on account of the rules of the
game. The rules of the game did not protect so much
Michaelis, who was an ex-convict. It would be stupid not
to take advantage of legal facilities, and the journalists
who had written him up with emotional gush would be
ready to write him down with emotional indignation.

This prospect, viewed with confidence, had the
attraction of a personal triumph for Chief Inspector

Heat. And deep down in his blameless bosom of an average married citizen, almost unconscious but potent nevertheless, the dislike of being compelled by events to meddle with the desperate ferocity of the Professor had its say. This dislike had been strengthened by the chance meeting in the lane. The encounter did not leave behind with Chief Inspector Heat that satisfactory sense of superiority the members of the police force get from the unofficial but intimate side of their intercourse with the criminal classes, by which the vanity of power is soothed, and the vulgar love of domination over our fellow-creatures is flattered as worthily as it deserves.

The perfect anarchist was not recognized as a fellow-creature by Chief Inspector Heat. He was impossible – a mad dog to be left alone. Not that the Chief Inspector was afraid of him; on the contrary, he meant to have him some day. But not yet: he meant to get hold of him in his own time, properly and effectively, according to the rules of the game. The present was not the right time for attempting that feat, not the right time for many reasons, personal and of public service. This being the strong feeling of Inspector Heat, it appeared to him just and proper that this affair should be shunted off its obscure and inconvenient track, leading goodness knows where, into a quiet (and lawful) siding called Michaelis. And he repeated, as if reconsidering the suggestion conscientiously:

'The bomb. No, I would not say that exactly. We may never find that out. But it's clear that he is connected with this in some way, which we can find out without much trouble.'

His countenance had that look of grave, overbearing indifference once well known and much dreaded by the better sort of thieves. Chief Inspector Heat, though what is called a man, was not a smiling animal. But his inward state was that of satisfaction at the passively receptive attitude of the Assistant Commissioner, who murmured gently:

'And you really think that the investigation should be made in that direction?'

'I do, sir.'

'Quite convinced?'

'I am, sir. That's the true line for us to take.'

The Assistant Commissioner withdrew the support of his hand from his reclining head with a suddenness that, considering his languid attitude, seemed to menace his whole person with collapse. But, on the contrary, he sat up, extremely alert, behind the great writing-table on which his hand had fallen with the sound of a sharp blow.

'What I want to know is what put it out of your head till now.'

'Put it out of my head,' repeated the Chief Inspector very slowly.

'Yes. Till you were called into this room – you know.'

The Chief Inspector felt as if the air between his clothing and his skin had become unpleasantly hot. It was the sensation of an unprecedented and incredible experience.

'Of course,' he said, exaggerating the deliberation of his utterance to the utmost limits of possibility, 'if there is a reason, of which I know nothing, for not interfering with the convict Michaelis, perhaps it's just as well I didn't start the county police after him.'

This took such a long time to say that the unflagging attention of the Assistant Commissioner seemed a wonderful feat of endurance. His retort came without delay.

'No reason whatever that I know of. Come, Chief Inspector, this finessing with me is highly improper on your part – highly improper. And it's also unfair, you know. You shouldn't leave me to puzzle things out for myself like this. Really, I am surprised.'

He paused, then added smoothly: 'I need scarcely tell you that this conversation is altogether unofficial.'

These words were far from pacifying the Chief Inspector. The indignation of a betrayed tight-rope performer was strong within him. In his pride of a trusted servant he was affected by the assurance that the rope was not shaken for the purpose of breaking his neck, as by an exhibition of impudence. As if anybody were afraid! Assistant Commissioners come and go, but a valuable Chief Inspector is not an ephemeral office phenomenon. He was not afraid of getting a broken neck. To have his performance spoiled was more than enough to account for the glow of honest indignation. And as thought is no respecter of persons, the thought of Chief Inspector Heat took a threatening and prophetic shape. 'You, my boy,' he said to himself, keeping his round and habitually roving eyes fastened upon the Assistant Commissioner's face – 'you, my boy, you don't know your place, and your place won't know you very long either, I bet.'

As if in provoking answer to that thought, something like the ghost of an amiable smile passed on the lips of the Assistant Commissioner. His manner was easy and businesslike while he persisted in administering another shake to the tight-rope.

'Let us come now to what you have discovered on the spot, Chief Inspector,' he said.

'A fool and his job are soon parted,' went on the train of prophetic thought in Chief Inspector Heat's head. But it was immediately followed by the reflection that a higher official, even when 'fired out' (this was the precise image), has still the time as he flies through the door to launch a nasty kick at the shinbones of a subordinate. Without softening very much the basilisk nature of his stare, he said, impassively:

'We are coming to that part of my investigation, sir,'

'That's right. Well, what have you brought away from it?'

The Chief Inspector, who had made up his mind to jump off the rope, came to the ground with gloomy frankness.

'I've brought away an address,' he said, pulling out of his pocket without haste a singed rag of dark blue cloth. 'This belongs to the overcoat the fellow who got himself blown to pieces was wearing. Of course, the overcoat may not have been his, and may even have been stolen. But that's not at all probable if you look at this.'

The Chief Inspector, stepping up to the table, smoothed out carefully the rag of blue cloth. He had picked it up from the repulsive heap in the mortuary, because a tailor's name is found sometimes under the collar. It is not often of much use, but still — He only half expected to find anything useful, but certainly he did not expect to find – not under the collar at all, but stitched carefully on the under side of the lapel – a square piece of calico with an address written on it in marking ink.

The Chief Inspector removed his smoothing hand.

'I carried it off with me without anybody taking notice,' he said. 'I thought it best. It can always be produced if required.'

The Assistant Commissioner, rising a little in his chair, pulled the cloth over to his side of the table. He sat looking at it in silence. Only the number 32 and the name of Brett Street were written in marking ink on a piece of calico slightly larger than an ordinary cigarette paper. He was genuinely surprised.

'Can't understand why he should have gone about labelled like this,' he said, looking up at Chief Inspector Heat. 'It's a most extraordinary thing.'

'I met once in the smoking-room of a hotel an old gentleman who went about with his name and address sewn on in all his coats in case of an accident or sudden illness,' said the Chief Inspector. 'He professed to be eighty-four years old, but he didn't look his age. He told me he was also afraid of losing his memory suddenly, like those people he had been reading of in the papers.'

A question from the Assistant Commissioner, who wanted to know what was No. 32 Brett Street, interrupted that reminiscence abruptly. The Chief Inspector, driven down to the ground by unfair artifices, had elected to walk the path of unreserved openness. If he believed firmly that to know too much was not good for the department, the judicious holding back of knowledge was as far as his loyalty dared to go for the good of the service. If the Assistant Commissioner wanted to mismanage this affair nothing, of course, could prevent him. But, on his own part, he now saw no reason for a display of alacrity. So he answered concisely:

'It's a shop, sir.'

The Assistant Commissioner, with his eyes lowered on the rag of blue cloth, waited for more information. As that did not come he proceeded to obtain it by a series of questions propounded with gentle patience. Thus he acquired an idea of the nature of Mr. Verloc's commerce, of his personal appearance, and heard at last his name. In a pause the Assistant Commissioner raised his eyes, and discovered some animation on the Chief Inspector's face. They looked at each other in silence.

'Of course,' said the latter, 'the department has no record of that man.'

'Did any of my predecessors have any knowledge of what you have told me now?' asked the Assistant Commissioner, putting his elbows on the table and raising his joined hands before his face, as if about to offer prayer, only that his eyes had not a pious expression.

'No, sir; certainly not. What would have been the object? That sort of man could never be produced publicly to any good purpose. It was sufficient for me to know who he was, and to make use of him in a way that could be used publicly.'

'And do you think that sort of private knowledge consistent with the official position you occupy?'

'Perfectly, sir. I think it's quite proper. I will take the liberty to tell you, sir, that it makes me what I am – and I am looked upon as a man who knows his work. It's a private affair of my own. A personal friend of mine in the French police gave me the hint that the fellow was an Embassy spy. Private friendship, private information, private use of it – that's how I look upon it.'

The Assistant Commissioner, after remarking to himself that the mental state of the renowned Chief Inspector seemed to affect the outline of his lower jaw, as if the lively sense of his high professional distinction had been located in that part of his anatomy, dismissed the point for the moment with a calm 'I see.' Then leaning his cheek on his joined hands:

'Well, then – speaking privately if you like – how long have you been in private touch with this Embassy spy?'

To this inquiry the private answer of the Chief Inspector, so private that it was never shaped into audible words, was:

'Long before you were even thought of for your place here.'

The so-to-speak public utterance was much more precise.

'I saw him for the first time in my life a little more than seven years ago, when two Imperial Highnesses and the Imperial Chancellor were on a visit here. I was put in charge of all the arrangements for looking after them. Baron Stott-Wartenheim was Ambassador then. He was a very nervous old gentleman. One evening, three days before the Guildhall Banquet, he sent word that he wanted to see me for a moment. I was downstairs, and the carriages were at the door to take the Imperial Highnesses and the Chancellor to the opera. I went up at once. I found the Baron walking up and down his bedroom in a pitiable state of distress, squeezing his hands

together. He assured me he had the fullest confidence in
our police and in my abilities, but he had there a man
just come over from Paris whose information could be
trusted implicitly. He wanted me to hear what that man
had to say. He took me at once into a dressing-room next
door, where I saw a big fellow in a heavy overcoat sitting
all alone on a chair, and holding his hat and stick in one
hand. The Baron said to him in French "Speak, my
friend." The light in that room was not very good. I
talked with him for some five minutes perhaps. He
certainly gave me a piece of very startling news. Then
the Baron took me aside nervously to praise him up
to me, and when I turned round again I discovered that
the fellow had vanished like a ghost. Got up and sneaked
out down some back stairs, I suppose. There was no time
to run after him, as I had to hurry off after the Ambassador down the great staircase, and see the party started
safe for the opera. However, I acted upon the information that very night. Whether it was perfectly correct or
not, it did look serious enough. Very likely it saved us
from an ugly trouble on the day of the Imperial visit to
the City.

    'Some time later, a month or so after my promotion to
Chief Inspector, my attention was attracted to a big burly
man, I thought I had seen somewhere before, coming
out in a hurry from a jeweller's shop in the Strand. I went
after him, as it was on my way towards Charing Cross,
and there seeing one of our detectives across the road, I
beckoned him over, and pointed out the fellow to him,
with instructions to watch his movements for a couple of
days, and then report to me. No later than next afternoon
my man turned up to tell me that the fellow had married
his landlady's daughter at a registrar's office that very day
at 11.30 A.M., and had gone off with her to Margate for a
week. Our man had seen the luggage being put on the
cab. There were some old Paris labels on one of the bags.
Somehow I couldn't get the fellow out of my head, and

the very next time I had to go to Paris on service I spoke
about him to that friend of mine in the Paris police. My
friend said: "From what you tell me I think you must
mean a rather well-known hanger-on and emissary of the
Revolutionary Red Committee. He says he is an Eng-
lishman by birth. We have an idea that he has been for a
good few years now a secret agent of one of the foreign
Embassies in London." This woke up my memory completely. He was the vanishing fellow I saw sitting on a
chair in Baron Stott-Wartenheim's bathroom. I told my
friend that he was quite right. The fellow was a secret
agent to my certain knowledge. Afterwards my friend
took the trouble to ferret out the complete record of that
man for me. I thought I had better know all there was to
know; but I don't suppose you want to hear his history
now, sir?'

The Assistant Commissioner shook his supported
head. 'The history of your relations with that useful personage is the only thing that matters just now,' he said,
closing slowly his weary, deep-set eyes, and then opening them swiftly with a greatly refreshed glance.

'There's nothing official about them,' said the Chief
Inspector, bitterly. 'I went into his shop one evening,
told him who I was, and reminded him of our first meeting. He didn't as much as twitch an eyebrow. He said
that he was married and settled now, and that all he
wanted was not to be interfered with in his little business. I took it upon myself to promise him that, as long as
he didn't go in for anything obviously outrageous, he
would be left alone by the police. That was worth something to him, because a word from us to the Custom-
House people would have been enough to get some of
these packages he gets from Paris and Brussels opened
in Dover, with confiscation to follow for certain, and perhaps a prosecution as well at the end of it.'

'That's a very precarious trade,' murmured the Assistant Commissioner. 'Why did he go in for that?'

The Chief Inspector raised scornful eyebrows dispassionately.

'Most likely got a connection – friends on the Continent – amongst people who deal in such wares. They would be just the sort he would consort with. He's a lazy dog, too – like the rest of them.'

'What do you get from him in exchange for your protection?'

The Chief Inspector was not inclined to enlarge on the value of Mr. Verloc's services.

'He would not be much good to anybody but myself. One has got to know a good deal beforehand to make use of a man like that. I can understand the sort of hint he can give. And when I want a hint he can generally furnish it to me.'

The Chief Inspector lost himself suddenly in a discreet reflective mood; and the Assistant Commissioner repressed a smile at the fleeting thought that the reputation of Chief Inspector Heat might possibly have been made in a great part by the Secret Agent Verloc.

'In a more general way of being of use, all our men of the Special Crimes section on duty at Charing Cross and Victoria have orders to take careful notice of anybody they may see with him. He meets the new arrivals frequently, and afterwards keeps track of them. He seems to have been told off for that sort of duty. When I want an address in a hurry, I can always get it from him. Of course, I know how to manage our relations. I haven't seen him to speak to three times in the last two years. I drop him a line, unsigned, and he answers me in the same way at my private address.'

From time to time the Assistant Commissioner gave an almost imperceptible nod. The Chief Inspector added that he did not suppose Mr. Verloc to be deep in the confidence of the prominent members of the Revolutionary International Council, but that he was generally trusted of that there could be no doubt. 'Whenever I've had reason to think there was something in the wind,' he concluded, 'I've always found he could tell me something worth knowing.'

The Assistant Commissioner made a significant remark.

'He failed you this time.'

'Neither had I wind of anything in any other way,' retorted Chief Inspector Heat. 'I asked him nothing so he could tell me nothing. He isn't one of our men. It isn't as if he were in our pay.'

'No,' muttered the Assistant Commissioner. 'He's a spy in the pay of a foreign government. We could never confess to him.'

'I must do my work in my own way,' declared the Chief Inspector. 'When it comes to that I would deal with the devil himself, and take the consequences. There are things not fit for everybody to know.'

'Your idea of secrecy seems to consist in keeping the chief of your department in the dark. That's stretching it perhaps a little too far, isn't it? He lives over his shop?'

'Who – Verloc? Oh, yes. He lives over his shop. The wife's mother, I fancy, lives with them.'

'Is the house watched?'

'Oh, dear, no. It wouldn't do. Certain people who come there are watched. My opinion is that he knows nothing of this affair.'

'How do you account for this?' The Assistant Commissioner nodded at the cloth rag lying before him on the table.

'I don't account for it at all, sir. It's simply unaccountable. It can't be explained by what I know.' The Chief Inspector made those admissions with the frankness of a man whose reputation is established as if on a rock. 'At any rate not at this present moment. I think that the man who had most to do with it will turn out to be Michaelis.'

'You do?'

'Yes, sir; because I can answer for all the others.'

'What about that other man supposed to have escaped from the park?'

'I should think he's far away by this time,' opined the Chief Inspector.

The Assistant Commissioner looked hard at him, and rose suddenly, as though having made up his mind to some course of action. As a matter of fact, he had that very moment succumbed to a fascinating temptation. The Chief Inspector heard himself dismissed with instructions to meet his superior early next morning for further consultation upon the case. He listened with an impenetrable face, and walked out of the room with measured steps.

Whatever might have been the plans of the Assistant Commissioner they had nothing to do with that desk work, which was the bane of his existence because of its confined nature and apparent lack of reality. It could not have had, or else the general air of alacrity that came upon the Assistant Commissioner would have been inexplicable. As soon as he was left alone he looked for his hat impulsively, and put it on his head. Having done that, he sat down again to reconsider the whole matter. But as his mind was already made up, this did not take long. And before Chief Inspector Heat had gone very far on the way home, he also left the building.

CHAPTER SEVEN

THE Assistant Commissioner walked along a short
and narrow street like a wet, muddy trench, then
crossing a very broad thoroughfare entered a public edifice, and sought speech with a young private secretary (unpaid) of a great personage.

This fair, smooth-faced young man, whose symmet-
rically arranged hair gave him the air of a large and neat
schoolboy, met the Assistant Commissioner's request
with a doubtful look, and spoke with bated breath.

'Would he see you? I don't know about that. He has
walked over from the House an hour ago to talk with the
permanent Under-Secretary, and now he's ready to walk
back again. He might have sent for him; but he does it
for the sake of a little exercise, I suppose. It's all the
exercise he can find time for while this session lasts. I
don't complain; I rather enjoy these little strolls. He
leans on my arm, and doesn't open his lips. But, I say,
he's very tired, and – well – not in the sweetest of tem-
pers just now.'

'It's in connection with that Greenwich affair.'

'Oh! I say! He's very bitter against you people. But I
will go and see, if you insist.'

'Do. That's a good fellow,' said the Assistant Commissioner.

The unpaid secretary admired this pluck. Composing
for himself an innocent face, he opened a door, and went
in with the assurance of a nice and privileged child. And
presently he reappeared, with a nod to the Assistant

Commissioner, who passing through the same door left open for him, found himself with the great personage in a large room.

Vast in bulk and stature, with a long white face, which, broadened at the base by a big double chin, appeared egg-shaped in the fringe of thin greyish whisker, the great personage seemed an expanding man. Unfortunate from a tailoring point of view, the cross-folds in the middle of a buttoned black coat added to the impression, as if the fastenings of the garment were tried to the utmost. From the head, set upward on a thick neck, the eyes, with puffy lower lids, stared with a haughty droop on each side of a hooked, aggressive nose, nobly salient in the vast pale circumference of the face. A shiny silk hat and a pair of worn gloves lying ready on the end of a long table looked expanded, too, enormous.

He stood on the hearthrug in big, roomy boots, and uttered no word of greeting.

'I would like to know if this is the beginning of another dynamite campaign,' he asked at once in a deep, very smooth voice. 'Don't go into details. I have no time for that.'

The Assistant Commissioner's figure before this big and rustic Presence had the frail slenderness of a reed addressing an oak. And indeed the unbroken record of that man's descent surpassed in the number of centuries the age of the oldest oak in the country.

'No. As far as one can be positive about anything I can assure you that it is not.'

'Yes. But your idea of assurances over there,' said the great man, with a contemptuous wave of his hand towards a window giving on the broad thoroughfare, 'seems to consist mainly in making the Secretary of State look a fool. I have been told positively in this very room less than a month ago that nothing of the sort was even possible.'

The Assistant Commissioner glanced in the direction of the window calmly.

'You will allow me to remark, Sir Ethelred, that so far I have had no opportunity to give you assurances of any kind.'

The haughty droop of the eyes was focussed now upon the Assistant Commissioner.

'True,' confessed the deep, smooth voice. 'I sent for Heat. You are still rather a novice in your new berth. And how are you getting on over there?'

'I believe I am learning something every day.'

'Of course, of course. I hope you will get on.'

'Thank you, Sir Ethelred. I've learned something to-day, and even within the last hour or so. There is much in this affair of a kind that does not meet the eye in a usual anarchist outrage, even if one looked into it as deep as can be. That's why I am here.'

The great man put his arms akimbo, the backs of his big hands resting on his hips.

'Very well. Go on. Only no details, pray. Spare me the details.'

'You shall not be troubled with them, Sir Ethelred,' the Assistant Commissioner began, with a calm and untroubled assurance. While he was speaking the hands on the face of the clock behind the great man's back – a heavy, glistening affair of massive scrolls in the same dark marble as the mantelpiece, and with a ghostly, evanescent tick – had moved through the space of seven minutes. He spoke with a studious fidelity to a parenthetical manner, into which every little fact – that is, every detail – fitted with delightful ease. Not a murmur nor even a movement hinted at interruption. The great Personage might have been the statue of one of his own princely ancestors stripped of a crusader's war harness, and put into an ill-fitting frock coat. The Assistant Commissioner felt as though he were at liberty to talk for an hour. But he kept his head, and at the end of the time mentioned above he broke off with a sudden conclusion, which, reproducing the opening statement, pleasantly surprised Sir Ethelred by its apparent swiftness and force.

'The kind of thing which meets us under the surface of this affair, otherwise without gravity, is unusual – in this precise form at least – and requires special treatment.'

The tone of Sir Ethelred was deepened, full of conviction.

'I should think so – involving the Ambassador of a foreign power!'

'Oh! The Ambassador!' protested the other, erect and slender, allowing himself a mere half smile. 'It would be stupid of me to advance anything of the kind. And it is absolutely unnecessary, because if I am right in my surmises, whether ambassador or hall porter it's a mere detail.'

Sir Ethelred opened a wide mouth, like a cavern, into which the hooked nose seemed anxious to peer; there came from it a subdued rolling sound, as from a distant organ with the scornful indignation stop.

'No! These people are too impossible. What do they mean by importing their methods of Crim-Tartary here? A Turk would have more decency.'

'You forget, Sir Ethelred, that strictly speaking we know nothing positively – as yet.'

'No! But how would you define it? Shortly?'

'Barefaced audacity amounting to childishness of a peculiar sort.'

'We can't put up with the innocence of nasty little children,' said the great and expanded personage, expanding a little more, as it were. The haughty, drooping glance struck crushingly the carpet at the Assistant Commissioner's feet. 'They'll have to get a hard rap on the knuckles over this affair. We must be in a position to — What is your general idea, stated shortly? No need to go into details.'

'No, Sir Ethelred. In principle, I should lay it down

that the existence of secret agents should not be tol-
erated, as tending to augment the positive dangers of the
evil against which they are used. That the spy will fabri-
cate his information is a mere commonplace. But in the
sphere of political and revolutionary action, relying partly
on violence, the professional spy has every facility to fab-
ricate the very facts themselves, and will spread the
double evil of emulation in one direction, and of panic,
hasty legislation, unreflecting hate, on the other. However, this is an imperfect world —'

The deep-voiced Presence on the hearthrug, motionless, with big elbows stuck out, said hastily:

'Be lucid, please.'

'Yes, Sir Ethelred — An imperfect world. Therefore
directly the character of this affair suggested itself to me,
I thought it should be dealt with with special secrecy,
and ventured to come over here.'

'That's right,' approved the great Personage, glancing
down complacently over his double chin. 'I am glad
there's somebody over at your shop who thinks that the
Secretary of State may be trusted now and then.'

The Assistant Commissioner had an amused smile.

'I was really thinking that it might be better at this
stage for Heat to be replaced by —'

'What! Heat? An ass – eh?' exclaimed the great man,
with distinct animosity.

'Not at all. Pray, Sir Ethelred, don't put that unjust
interpretation on my remarks.'

'Then what? Too clever by half?'

'Neither – at least not as a rule. All the grounds of my
surmises I have from him. The only thing I've discovered by myself is that he has been making use of that
man privately. Who could blame him? He's an old police
hand. He told me virtually that he must have tools to
work with. It occurred to me that this tool should be sur-
rendered to the Special Crimes division as a whole,
instead of remaining the private property of Chief

Inspector Heat. I extended my conception of our departmental duties to the suppression of the secret agent. But
Chief Inspector Heat is an old departmental hand. He
would accuse me of perverting its morality and attacking
its efficiency. He would define it bitterly as protection
extended to the criminal class of revolutionists. It would
mean just that to him.'

'Yes. But what do you mean?'

'I mean to say, first, that there's but poor comfort in
being able to declare that any given act of violence –
damaging property or destroying life – is not the work of
anarchism at all, but of something else altogether – some
species of authorized scoundrelism. This, I fancy, is
much more frequent than we suppose. Next, it's obvious
that the existence of these people in the pay of foreign
governments destroys in a measure the efficiency of our
supervision. A spy of that sort can afford to be more reckless than the most reckless of conspirators. His occupation is free from all restraint. He's without as much faith
as is necessary for complete negation, and without that
much law as is implied in lawlessness. Thirdly, the existence of these spies amongst the revolutionary groups,
which we are reproached for harbouring here, does away
with all certitude. You have received a reassuring statement from Chief Inspector Heat some time ago. It was
by no means groundless – and yet this episode happens.
I call it an episode, because this affair, I make bold to say,
is episodic; it is no part of any general scheme, however
wild. The very peculiarities which surprise and perplex
Chief Inspector Heat establish its character in my eyes. I
am keeping clear of details, Sir Ethelred.'

The Personage on the hearthrug had been listening
with profound attention.

'Just so. Be as concise as you can.'

The Assistant Commissioner intimated by an earnest,
deferential gesture that he was anxious to be concise.

'There is a peculiar stupidity and feebleness in the

THE SECRET AGENT 129

conduct of this affair which gives me excellent hopes of
getting behind it and finding there something else than
an individual freak of fanaticism. For it is a planned
thing, undoubtedly. The actual perpetrator seems to
have been led by the hand to the spot, and then abandoned hurriedly to his own devices. The inference is
that he was imported from abroad for the purpose of
committing this outrage. At the same time one is forced
to the conclusion that he did not know enough English
to ask his way, unless one were to accept the fantastic
theory that he was a deaf mute. I wonder now — But this
is idle. He has destroyed himself by an accident,
obviously. Not an extraordinary accident. But an extraordinary little fact remains: the address on his clothing
discovered by the merest accident, too. It is an incredible little fact, so incredible that the explanation which
will account for it is bound to touch the bottom of this
affair. Instead of instructing Heat to go on with this case,
my intention is to seek this explanation personally – by
myself, I mean – where it may be picked up. That is in a
certain shop in Brett Street, and on the lips of a certain
secret agent once upon a time the confidential and
trusted spy of the late Baron Stott-Wartenheim, Ambassador of a Great Power to the Court of St. James.'

The Assistant Commissioner paused, then added:
'Those fellows are a perfect pest.' In order to raise his
drooping glance to the speaker's face, the Personage on
the hearthrug had gradually tilted his head farther back,
which gave him an aspect of extraordinary haughtiness.

'Why not leave it to Heat?'

'Because he is an old departmental hand. They have
their own morality. My line of inquiry would appear to
him an awful perversion of duty. For him the plain duty
is to fasten the guilt upon as many prominent anarchists
as he can on some slight indications he had picked up in
the course of his investigation on the spot; whereas I, he
would say, am bent upon vindicating their innocence. I

am trying to be as lucid as I can in presenting this obscure matter to you without details.'

'He would, would he?' muttered the proud head of Sir Ethelred from its lofty elevation.

'I am afraid so – with an indignation and disgust of which you or I can have no idea. He's an excellent servant. We must not put an undue strain on his loyalty. That's always a mistake. Besides, I want a free hand – a freer hand than it would be perhaps advisable to give Chief Inspector Heat. I haven't the slightest wish to spare this man Verloc. He will, I imagine, be extremely startled to find his connection with this affair, whatever it may be, brought home to him so quickly. Frightening him will not be very difficult. But our true objective lies behind him somewhere. I want your authority to give him such assurances of personal safety as I may think proper.'

'Certainly,' said the Personage on the hearthrug. 'Find out as much as you can; find it out in your own way.'

'I must set about it without loss of time, this very evening,' said the Assistant Commissioner.

Sir Ethelred shifted one hand under his coat tails, and tilting back his head, looked at him steadily.

'We'll have a late sitting to-night,' he said. 'Come to the House with your discoveries if we are not gone home. I'll warn Toodles to look out for you. He'll take you into my room.'

The numerous family and the wide connections of the youthful-looking Private Secretary cherished for him the hope of an austere and exalted destiny. Meantime, the social sphere he adorned in his hours of idleness chose to pet him under the above nickname. And Sir Ethelred, hearing it on the lips of his wife and girls every day (mostly at breakfast-time), had conferred upon it the dignity of unsmiling adoption.

The Assistant Commissioner was surprised and gratified extremely.

'I shall certainly bring my discoveries to the House on the chance of you having the time to —'

'I won't have the time,' interrupted the great Personage. 'But I will see you. I haven't the time now — And you are going yourself?'

'Yes, Sir Ethelred. I think it the best way.'

The Personage had tilted his head so far back that, in order to keep the Assistant Commissioner under his observation, he had to nearly close his eyes.

'H'm. Ha! And how do you propose — Will you assume a disguise?'

'Hardly a disguise! I'll change my clothes, of course.'

'Of course,' repeated the great man, with a sort of absent-minded loftiness. He turned his big head slowly, and over his shoulder gave a haughty, oblique stare to the ponderous marble timepiece with the sly, feeble tick. The gilt hands had taken the opportunity to steal through no less than five and twenty minutes behind his back.

The Assistant Commissioner, who could not see them, grew a little nervous in the interval. But the great man presented to him a calm and undismayed face.

'Very well,' he said, and paused, as if in deliberate contempt of the official clock. 'But what first put you in motion in this direction?'

'I have been always of opinion,' began the Assistant Commissioner.

'Ah. Yes! Opinion. That's of course. But the immediate motive?'

'What shall I say, Sir Ethelred? A new man's antagonism to old methods. A desire to know something at first hand. Some impatience. It's my old work, but the harness is different. It has been chafing me a little in one or two tender places.'

'I hope you'll get on over there,' said the great man, kindly, extending his hand, soft to the touch, but broad and powerful like the hand of a glorified farmer. The Assistant Commissioner shook it, and withdrew.

In the outer room Toodles, who had been waiting perched on the edge of a table, advanced to meet him, subduing his natural buoyancy.

'Well? Satisfactory?' he asked, with airy importance.

'Perfectly. You've earned my undying gratitude,' answered the Assistant Commissioner, whose long face looked wooden in contrast with the peculiar character of the other's gravity, which seemed perpetually ready to break into ripples and chuckles.

'That's all right. But, seriously, you can't imagine how irritated he is by the attacks on his Bill for the Nationalization of Fisheries. They call it the beginning of social revolution. Of course, it is a revolutionary measure. But these fellows have no decency. The personal attacks —'

'I read the papers,' remarked the Assistant Commissioner.

'Odious? Eh? And you have no notion what a mass of work he has got to get through every day. He does it all himself. Seems unable to trust any one with these Fisheries.'

'And yet he's given a whole half hour to the consideration of my very small sprat,' interjected the Assistant Commissioner.

'Small! Is it? I'm glad to hear that. But it's a pity you didn't keep away, then. This fight takes it out of him frightfully. The man's getting exhausted. I feel it by the way he leans on my arm as we walk over. And, I say, is he safe in the streets? Mullins has been marching his men up here this afternoon. There's a constable stuck by every lamp-post, and every second person we meet between this and Palace Yard is an obvious "tec". It will get on his nerves presently. I say, these foreign scoundrels aren't likely to throw something at him – are they? It would be a national calamity. The country can't spare him.'

'Not to mention yourself. He leans on your arm,' suggested the Assistant Commissioner, soberly. 'You would both go.'

'It would be an easy way for a young man to go down into history? Not so many British Ministers have been assassinated as to make it a minor incident. But seriously now —'

'I am afraid that if you want to go down into history you'll have to do something for it. Seriously, there's no danger whatever for both of you but from overwork.'

The sympathetic Toodles welcomed this opening for a chuckle.

'The Fisheries won't kill me. I am used to late hours,' he declared, with ingenuous levity. But, feeling an instant compunction, he began to assume an air of states-manlike moodiness, as one draws on a glove. 'His massive intellect will stand any amount of work. It's his nerves that I am afraid of. The reactionary gang, with that abusive brute Cheeseman at their head, insult him every night.'

'If he will insist on beginning a revolution!' mur-mured the Assistant Commissioner.

'The time has come, and he is the only man great enough for the work,' protested the revolutionary Tood-les, flaring up under the calm, speculative gaze of the Assistant Commissioner. Somewhere in a corridor a dis-tant bell tinkled urgently, and with devoted vigilance the young man pricked up his ears at the sound. 'He's ready to go now,' he exclaimed in a whisper, snatched up his hat, and vanished from the room.

The Assistant Commissioner went out by another door in a less elastic manner. Again he crossed the wide thoroughfare, walked along a narrow street, and re-entered hastily his own departmental buildings. He kept up this accelerated pace to the door of his private room. Before he had closed it fairly his eyes sought his desk. He stood still for a moment, then walked up, looked all round on the floor, sat down in his chair, rang a bell, and waited.

'Chief Inspector Heat gone yet?'

'Yes, sir. Went away half-an-hour ago.'

He nodded. 'That will do.' And sitting still, with his hat pushed off his forehead, he thought that it was just like Heat's confounded cheek to carry off quietly the only piece of material evidence. But he thought this without animosity. Old and valued servants will take liberties. The piece of overcoat with the address sewn on was certainly not a thing to leave about. Dismissing from his mind this manifestation of Chief Inspector Heat's mistrust, he wrote and despatched a note to his wife, charging her to make his apologies to Michaelis' great lady, with whom they were engaged to dine that evening.

The short jacket and the low, round hat he assumed in a sort of curtained alcove containing a washstand, a row of wooden pegs and a shelf, brought out wonderfully the length of his grave, brown face. He stepped back into the full light of the room, looking like the vision of a cool, reflective Don Quixote, with the sunken eyes of a dark enthusiast and a very deliberate manner. He left the scene of his daily labours quickly like an unobtrusive shadow. His descent into the street was like the descent into a slimy aquarium from which the water had been run off. A murky, gloomy dampness enveloped him. The walls of the houses were wet, the mud of the roadway glistened with an effect of phosphorescence, and when he emerged into the Strand out of a narrow street by the side of Charing Cross Station the genius of the locality assimilated him. He might have been but one more of the queer foreign fish that can be seen of an evening about there flitting round the dark corners.

He came to a stand on the very edge of the pavement, and waited. His exercised eyes had made out in the confused movements of lights and shadows thronging the roadway the crawling approach of a hansom. He gave no sign; but when the low step gliding along the curbstone came to his feet he dodged in skilfully in front of the big turning wheel, and spoke up through the little trap door almost before the man gazing supinely ahead from his perch was aware of having been boarded by a fare.

It was not a long drive. It ended by signal abruptly, nowhere in particular, between two lamp-posts before a large drapery establishment – a long range of shops already lapped up in sheets of corrugated iron for the night. Tendering a coin through the trap door the fare slipped out and away, leaving an effect of uncanny, eccentric ghostliness upon the driver's mind. But the size of the coin was satisfactory to his touch, and his education not being literary, he remained untroubled by the fear of finding it presently turned to a dead leaf in his pocket. Raised above the world of fares by the nature of his calling, he contemplated their action with a limited interest. The sharp pulling of his horse right round expressed his philosophy.

Meantime, the Assistant Commissioner was already giving his order to a waiter in a little Italian restaurant round the corner – one of those traps for the hungry, long and narrow, baited with a perspective of mirrors and white napery; without air, but with an atmosphere of their own – an atmosphere of fraudulent cookery mocking an abject mankind in the most pressing of its miserable necessities. In this immoral atmosphere the Assistant Commissioner, reflecting upon his enterprise, seemed to lose some more of his identity. He had a sense of loneliness, of evil freedom. It was rather pleasant. When, after paying for his short meal, he stood up and waited for his change, he saw himself in the sheet of glass, and was struck by his foreign appearance. He contemplated his own image with a melancholy and inquisitive gaze, then by sudden inspiration raised the collar of his jacket. This arrangement appeared to him commendable, and he completed it by giving an upward twist to the ends of his black moustache. He was satisfied by the subtle modification of his personal aspect caused by

these small changes. 'That'll do very well,' he thought.
'I'll get a little wet, a little splashed —'

He became aware of the waiter at his elbow and of a
small pile of silver coins on the edge of the table before
him. The waiter kept one eye on it, while his other eye
followed the long back of a tall, not very young girl, who
passed up to a distant table looking perfectly sightless
and altogether unapproachable. She seemed to be an
habitual customer.

On going out the Assistant Commissioner made to
himself the observation that the patrons of the place had
lost in the frequentation of fraudulent cookery all their
national and private characteristics. And this was strange,
since the Italian restaurant is such a peculiarly British
institution. But these people were as denationalized as
the dishes set before them with every circumstance of
unstamped respectability. Neither was their personality
stamped in any way, professionally, socially, or racially.
They seemed created for the Italian restaurant, unless
the Italian restaurant had been perchance created for
them. But that last hypothesis was unthinkable, since
one could not place them anywhere outside those special
establishments. One never met these enigmatical persons elsewhere. It was impossible to form a precise idea
what occupations they followed by day and where they
went to bed at night. And he himself had become
unplaced. It would have been impossible for anybody to
guess his occupation. As to going to bed, there was a
doubt even in his own mind. Not indeed in regard to
his domicile itself, but very much so in respect of the
time when he would be able to return there. A pleasurable feeling of independence possessed him when
he heard the glass doors swing to behind his back with a
sort of imperfect baffled thud. He advanced at once into
an immensity of greasy slime and damp plaster interspersed with lamps, and enveloped, oppressed, penetrated, choked, and suffocated by the blackness of a wet

London night, which is composed of soot and drops
of water.

Brett Street was not very far away. It branched off, narrow, from the side of an open triangular space surrounded by dark and mysterious houses, temples of
petty commerce emptied of traders for the night. Only a
fruiterer's stall at the corner made a violent blaze of light
and colour. Beyond all was black, and the few people
passing in that direction vanished at one stride beyond
the glowing heaps of oranges and lemons. No footsteps
echoed. They would never be heard of again. The
adventurous head of the Special Crimes Department
watched these disappearances from a distance with an
interested eye. He felt light-hearted, as though he had
been ambushed all alone in a jungle many thousands of
miles away from departmental desks and official ink-
stands. This joyousness and dispersion of thought before
a task of some importance seems to prove that this
world of ours is not such a very serious affair after all. For
the Assistant Commissioner was not constitutionally
inclined to levity.

The policeman on the beat projected his sombre and
moving form against the luminous glory of oranges and
lemons, and entered Brett Street without haste. The
Assistant Commissioner, as though he were a member of
the criminal classes, lingered out of sight, awaiting his
return. But this constable seemed to be lost for ever to
the force. He never returned: must have gone out at the
other end of Brett Street.

The Assistant Commissioner, reaching this conclusion, entered the street in his turn, and came upon a
large van arrested in front of the dimly lit window-panes
of a carters' eating-house. The man was refreshing himself inside, and the horses, their big heads lowered to the
ground, fed out of nose-bags steadily. Farther on, on the
opposite side of the street, another suspect patch of dim
light issued from Mr. Verloc's shop front, hung with

papers, heaving with vague piles of cardboard boxes and the shapes of books. The Assistant Commissioner stood observing it across the roadway. There could be no mistake. By the side of the front window, encumbered by the shadows of nondescript things, the door, standing ajar, let escape on the pavement a narrow, clear streak of gaslight within.

Behind the Assistant Commissioner the van and horses, merged into one mass, seemed something alive – a square-backed black monster blocking half the street, with sudden iron-shod stampings, fierce jingles, and heavy, blowing sighs. The harshly festive, ill-omened glare of a large and prosperous public-house faced the other end of Brett Street across a wide road. This barrier of blazing lights, opposing the shadows gathered about the humble abode of Mr. Verloc's domestic happiness, seemed to drive the obscurity of the street back upon itself, make it more sullen, brooding, and sinister.

CHAPTER EIGHT

HAVING infused by persistent importunities some sort of heat into the chilly interest of several licensed victuallers (the acquaintances once upon a time of her late unlucky husband), Mrs. Verloc's mother had at last secured her admission to certain almshouses founded by a wealthy innkeeper for the destitute widows of the trade.

This end, conceived in the astuteness of her uneasy heart, the old woman had pursued with secrecy and determination. That was the time when her daughter Winnie could not help passing a remark to Mr. Verloc that 'mother has been spending half-crowns and five shillings almost every day this last week in cab fares.' But the remark was not made grudgingly. Winnie respected her mother's infirmities. She was only a little surprised at this sudden mania for locomotion. Mr. Verloc, who was sufficiently magnificent in his way, had grunted the remark impatiently aside as interfering with his meditations. These were frequent, deep, and prolonged; they bore upon a matter more important than five shillings. Distinctly more important, and beyond all comparison more difficult to consider in all its aspects with philosophical serenity.

Her object attained in astute secrecy, the heroic old woman had made a clean breast of it to Mrs. Verloc. Her soul was triumphant and her heart tremulous. Inwardly she quaked, because she dreaded and admired the calm, self-contained character of her daughter Winnie, whose

displeasure was made redoubtable by a diversity of
dreadful silences. But she did not allow her inward
apprehensions to rob her of the advantage of venerable
placidity conferred upon her outward person by her
triple chin, the floating ampleness of her ancient form,
and the impotent condition of her legs.

The shock of the information was so unexpected that
Mrs. Verloc, against her usual practice when addressed,
interrupted the domestic occupation she was engaged
upon. It was the dusting of the furniture in the parlour
behind the shop. She turned her head towards her
mother.

'Whatever did you want to do that for?' she exclaimed,
in scandalized astonishment.

The shock must have been severe to make her depart
from that distant and uninquiring acceptance of facts
which was her force and her safeguard in life.

'Weren't you made comfortable enough here?'

She had lapsed into these inquiries, but next moment
she saved the consistency of her conduct by resuming
her dusting, while the old woman sat scared and dumb
under her dingy white cap and lustreless dark wig.

Winnie finished the chair, and ran the duster along
the mahogany at the back of the horsehair sofa on which
Mr. Verloc loved to take his ease in hat and overcoat. She
was intent on her work, but presently she permitted herself another question.

'How in the world did you manage it, mother?'

As not affecting the inwardness of things, which it was
Mrs. Verloc's principle to ignore, this curiosity was excusable. It bore merely on the methods. The old woman
welcomed it eagerly as bringing forward something that
could be talked about with much sincerity.

She favoured her daughter by an exhaustive answer
full of names and enriched by side comments upon the
ravages of time as observed in the alteration of human
countenances. The names were principally the names of

licensed victuallers – 'poor daddy's friends, my dear.'
She enlarged with special appreciation on the kindness
and condescension of a large brewer, a Baronet and an
M.P., the Chairman of the Governors of the Charity. She
expressed herself thus warmly because she had been
allowed to interview by appointment his Private Secretary – 'a very polite gentleman, all in black, with a gentle,
sad voice, but so very, very thin and quiet. He was like a
shadow, my dear.'

Winnie, prolonging her dusting operations till the tale
was told to the end, walked out of the parlour into the
kitchen (down two steps) in her usual manner, without
the slightest comment.

Shedding a few tears in sign of rejoicing at her
daughter's mansuetude in this terrible affair, Mrs. Verloc's mother gave play to her astuteness in the direction
of her furniture, because it was her own; and sometimes
she wished it hadn't been. Heroism is all very well, but
there are circumstances when the disposal of a few tables
and chairs, brass bedsteads, and so on, may be big with
remote and disastrous consequences. She required a few
pieces herself, the Foundation which, after many importunities, had gathered her to its charitable breast, giving nothing but bare planks and cheaply papered bricks
to the objects of its solicitude. The delicacy guiding
her choice to the least valuable and most dilapidated
articles passed unacknowledged, because Winnie's
philosophy consisted in not taking notice of the inside of
facts; she assumed that mother took what suited her
best. As to Mr. Verloc, his intense meditation, like a sort
of Chinese wall, isolated him completely from the phenomena of this world of vain effort and illusory appearances.

Her selection made, the disposal of the rest became a
perplexing question in a particular way. She was leaving
it in Brett Street, of course. But she had two children.
Winnie was provided for by her sensible union with that

excellent husband, Mr. Verloc. Stevie was destitute –
and a little peculiar. His position had to be considered
before the claims of legal justice and even the promptings of partiality. The possession of the furniture would
not be in any sense a provision. He ought to have it – the
poor boy. But to give it to him would be like tampering
with his position of complete dependence. It was a sort
of claim which she feared to weaken. Moreover, the sus-
ceptibilities of Mr. Verloc would perhaps not brook being
beholden to his brother-in-law for the chairs he sat on. In
a long experience of gentlemen lodgers, Mrs. Verloc's
mother had acquired a dismal but resigned notion of the
fantastic side of human nature. What if Mr. Verloc suddenly took it into his head to tell Stevie to take his
blessed sticks somewhere out of that? A division, on the
other hand, however carefully made, might give some
cause of offence to Winnie. No. Stevie must remain destitute and dependent. And at the moment of leaving
Brett Street she had said to her daughter: 'No use waiting till I am dead, is there? Everything I leave here is
altogether your own now, my dear.'

Winnie, with her hat on, silent behind her mother's
back, went on arranging the collar of the old woman's
cloak. She got her handbag, an umbrella, with an
impassive face. The time had come for the expenditure
of the sum of three-and-sixpence on what might well be
supposed the last cab drive of Mrs. Verloc's mother's life.
They went out at the shop door.

The conveyance awaiting them would have illus-
trated the proverb that 'truth can be more cruel than cari-
cature,' if such a proverb existed. Crawling behind an
infirm horse, a metropolitan hackney carriage drew up on
wobbly wheels and with a maimed driver on the box.
This last peculiarity caused some embarrassment.
Catching sight of a hooked iron contrivance protruding
from the left sleeve of the man's coat, Mrs. Verloc's
mother lost suddenly the heroic courage of these days.

She really couldn't trust herself. 'What do you think, Winnie?' She hung back. The passionate expostulations of the big-faced cabman seemed to be squeezed out of a blocked throat. Leaning over from his box, he whispered with mysterious indignation. What was the matter now? Was it possible to treat a man so? His enormous and unwashed countenance flamed red in the muddy stretch of the street. Was it likely they would have given him a licence, he inquired desperately, if —

The police constable of the locality quieted him by a friendly glance; then addressing himself to the two women without marked consideration, said:

'He's been driving a cab for twenty years. I never knew him to have an accident.'

'Accident!' shouted the driver in a scornful whisper.

The policeman's testimony settled it. The modest assemblage of seven people, mostly under age, dispersed. Winnie followed her mother into the cab. Stevie climbed on the box. His vacant mouth and distressed eyes depicted the state of his mind in regard to the transactions which were taking place. In the narrow streets the progress of the journey was made sensible to those within by the near fronts of the houses gliding past slowly and shakily, with a great rattle and jingling of glass, as if about to collapse behind the cab; and the infirm horse, with the harness hung over his sharp backbone flapping very loose about his thighs, appeared to be dancing mincingly on his toes with infinite patience. Later on, in the wider space of Whitehall, all visual evidences of motion became imperceptible. The rattle and jingle of glass went on indefinitely in front of the long Treasury building – and time itself seemed to stand still.

At last Winnie observed: 'This isn't a very good horse.'

Her eyes gleamed in the shadow of the cab straight ahead, immovable. On the box, Stevie shut his vacant mouth first, in order to ejaculate earnestly: 'Don't.'

The driver, holding high the reins twisted around the hook, took no notice. Perhaps he had not heard. Stevie's breast heaved.

'Don't whip.'

The man turned slowly his bloated and sodden face of many colours bristling with white hairs. His little red eyes glistened with moisture. His big lips had a violet tint. They remained closed. With the dirty back of his whip-hand he rubbed the stubble sprouting on his enormous chin.

'You mustn't,' stammered out Stevie, violently, 'it hurts.'

'Mustn't whip,' queried the other in a thoughtful whisper, and immediately whipped. He did this, not because his soul was cruel and his heart evil, but because he had to earn his fare. And for a time the walls of St. Stephen's, with its towers and pinnacles, contemplated in immobility and silence a cab that jingled. It rolled, too, however. But on the bridge there was a commotion. Stevie suddenly proceeded to get down from the box. There were shouts on the pavement, people ran forward, the driver pulled up, whispering curses of indignation and astonishment. Winnie lowered the window, and put her head out, white as a ghost. In the depths of the cab, her mother was exclaiming, in tones of anguish: 'Is that boy hurt? Is that boy hurt?'

Stevie was not hurt, he had not even fallen, but excitement as usual had robbed him of the power of connected speech. He could do no more than stammer at the window: 'Too heavy. Too heavy.' Winnie put out her hand on to his shoulder.

'Stevie! Get up on the box directly, and don't try to get down again.'

'No. No. Walk. Must walk.'

In trying to state the nature of that necessity he stammered himself into utter incoherence. No physical impossibility stood in the way of his whim. Stevie could have managed easily to keep pace with the infirm, dancing horse without getting out of breath. But his sister withheld her consent decisively. 'The idea! Who ever heard of such a thing! Run after a cab!' Her mother, frightened and helpless in the depths of the conveyance, entreated:

'Oh, don't let him, Winnie. He'll get lost. Don't let him.'

'Certainly not. What next! Mr. Verloc will be sorry to hear of this nonsense, Stevie – I can tell you. He won't be happy at all.'

The idea of Mr. Verloc's grief and unhappiness acting as usual powerfully upon Stevie's fundamentally docile disposition, he abandoned all resistance, and climbed up again on the box, with a face of despair.

The cabby turned at him his enormous and inflamed countenance truculently. 'Don't you go for trying this silly game again, young fellow.'

After delivering himself thus in a stern whisper, strained almost to extinction, he drove on, ruminating solemnly. To his mind the incident remained somewhat obscure. But his intellect, though it had lost its pristine vivacity in the benumbing years of sedentary exposure to the weather, lacked not independence or sanity. Gravely he dismissed the hypothesis of Stevie being a drunken young nipper.

Inside the cab the spell of silence, in which the two women had endured shoulder to shoulder the jolting, rattling, and jingling of the journey, had been broken by Stevie's outbreak. Winnie raised her voice.

'You've done what you wanted, mother. You'll have only yourself to thank for it if you aren't happy afterwards. And I don't think you'll be. That I don't. Weren't you comfortable enough in the house? Whatever people'll think of us – you throwing yourself like this on a Charity?'

'My dear,' screamed the old woman earnestly above

the noise, 'you've been the best of daughters to me. As to Mr. Verloc – there —'

Words failing her on the subject of Mr. Verloc's excellence, she turned her old tearful eyes to the roof of the cab. Then she averted her head on the pretence of looking out of the window, as if to judge of their progress. It was insignificant, and went on close to the curbstone. Night, the early dirty night, the sinister, noisy, hopeless, and rowdy night of South London, had overtaken her on her last cab drive. In the gas-light of the low-fronted shops her big cheeks glowed with an orange hue under a black and mauve bonnet.

Mrs. Verloc's mother's complexion had become yellow by the effect of age and from a natural predisposition to biliousness, favoured by the trials of a difficult and worried existence, first as wife, then as widow. It was a complexion that under the influence of a blush would take on an orange tint. And this woman, modest indeed but hardened in the fires of adversity, of an age, moreover, when blushes are not expected, had positively blushed before her daughter. In the privacy of a four-wheeler, on her way to a charity cottage (one of a row) which by the exiguity of its dimensions and the simplicity of its accommodation, might well have been devised in kindness as a place of training for the still more straitened circumstances of the grave, she was forced to hide from her own child a blush of remorse and shame.

Whatever people will think? She knew very well what they did think, the people Winnie had in her mind – the old friends of her husband, and others too, whose interest she had solicited with such flattering success. She had not known before what a good beggar she could be. But she guessed very well what inference was drawn from her application. On account of that shrinking delicacy, which exists side by side with aggressive brutality in masculine nature, the inquiries into her circumstances had not been pushed very far. She had checked them by

a visible compression of the lips and some display of an
emotion determined to be eloquently silent. And the
men would become suddenly incurious, after the manner of their kind. She congratulated herself more than
once on having nothing to do with women, who being
naturally more callous and avid of details, would have
been anxious to be exactly informed by what sort of
unkind conduct her daughter and son-in-law had driven
her to that sad extremity. It was only before the Secretary
of the great brewer M.P. and Chairman of the Charity,
who, acting for his principal, felt bound to be conscientiously inquisitive as to the real circumstances of the
applicant, that she had burst into tears outright and
aloud, as a cornered woman will weep. The thin and polite gentleman, after contemplating her with an air of
being 'struck all of a heap', abandoned his position under
the cover of soothing remarks. She must not distress herself. The deed of the Charity did not absolutely specify
'childless widows'. In fact, it did not by any means dis-
qualify her. But the discretion of the Committee must be
an informed discretion. One could understand very well
her unwillingness to be a burden, etc., etc. Thereupon, to
his profound disappointment, Mrs. Verloc's mother wept
some more with an augmented vehemence.

The tears of that large female in a dark, dusty wig, and
ancient silk dress festooned with dingy white cotton
lace, were the tears of genuine distress. She had wept
because she was heroic and unscrupulous and full of love
for both her children. Girls frequently get sacrificed to
the welfare of the boys. In this case she was sacrificing
Winnie. By the suppression of truth she was slandering
her. Of course, Winnie was independent, and need not
care for the opinion of people that she would never see
and who would never see her; whereas poor Stevie had
nothing in the world he could call his own except his
mother's heroism and unscrupulousness.

The first sense of security following on Winnie's mar-

riage wore off in time (for nothing lasts), and Mrs. Verloc's mother, in the seclusion of the back bedroom, had
recalled the teaching of that experience which the world
impresses upon a widowed woman. But she had recalled
it without vain bitterness; her store of resignation
amounted almost to dignity. She reflected stoically that
everything decays, wears out, in this world; that the way
of kindness should be made easy to the well disposed;
that her daughter Winnie was a most devoted sister, and
a very self-confident wife indeed. As regards Winnie's
sisterly devotion, her stoicism flinched. She excepted
that sentiment from the rule of decay affecting all things
human and some things divine. She could not help it;
not to do so would have frightened her too much. But in
considering the conditions of her daughter's married
state, she rejected firmly all flattering illusions. She took
the cold and reasonable view that the less strain put on
Mr. Verloc's kindness the longer its effects were likely to
last. That excellent man loved his wife, of course, but he
would, no doubt, prefer to keep as few of her relations as
was consistent with the proper display of that sentiment.
It would be better if its whole effect were concentrated
on poor Stevie. And the heroic old woman resolved on
going away from her children as an act of devotion and as
a move of deep policy.

   The 'virtue' of this policy consisted in this (Mrs. Verloc's mother was subtle in her way), that Stevie's moral
claim would be strengthened. The poor boy – a good,
useful boy, if a little peculiar – had not a sufficient standing. He had been taken over with his mother, somewhat
in the same way as the furniture of the Belgravian mansion had been taken over, as if on the ground of belonging to her exclusively. What will happen, she asked
herself (for Mrs. Verloc's mother was in a measure
imaginative), when I die? And when she asked herself that question it was with dread. It was also terrible
to think that she would not then have the means of

knowing what happened to the poor boy. But by making him over to his sister, by going thus away, she gave him the advantage of a directly dependent position. This was the more subtle sanction of Mrs. Verloc's mother's heroism and unscrupulousness. Her act of abandonment was really an arrangement for settling her son permanently in life. Other people made material sacrifices for such an object, she in that way. It was the only way. Moreover, she would be able to see how it worked. Ill or well she would avoid the horrible incertitude on the death-bed. But it was hard, hard, cruelly hard.

The cab rattled, jingled, jolted; in fact, the last was quite extraordinary. By its disproportionate violence and magnitude it obliterated every sensation of onward movement; and the effect was of being shaken in a stationary apparatus like a mediæval device for the punishment of crime, or some very new-fangled invention for the cure of a sluggish liver. It was extremely distressing; and the raising of Mrs. Verloc's mother's voice sounded like a wail of pain.

'I know, my dear, you'll come to see me as often as you can spare the time. Won't you?'

'Of course,' answered Winnie, shortly, staring straight before her.

And the cab jolted in front of a steamy, greasy shop in a blaze of gas and in the smell of fried fish.

The old woman raised a wail again.

'And, my dear, I must see that poor boy every Sunday. He won't mind spending the day with his old mother —'

Winnie screamed out stolidly:

'Mind! I should think not. That poor boy will miss you something cruel. I wish you had thought a little of that, mother.'

Not think of it! The heroic woman swallowed a playful and inconvenient object like a billiard ball, which had tried to jump out of her throat. Winnie sat mute for a

while, pouting at the front of the cab, then snapped out,
which was an unusual tone with her:

'I expect I'll have a job with him at first, he'll be that
restless —'

'Whatever you do, don't let him worry your husband,
my dear.'

Thus they discussed on familiar lines the bearings of a
new situation. And the cab jolted. Mrs. Verloc's mother
expressed some misgivings. Could Stevie be trusted to
come all that way alone? Winnie maintained that he was
much less 'absent-minded' now. They agreed as to that.
It could not be denied. Much less – hardly at all. They
shouted at each other in the jingle with comparative
cheerfulness. But suddenly the maternal anxiety broke
out afresh. There were two omnibuses to take, and a
short walk between. It was too difficult! The old woman
gave way to grief and consternation.

Winnie stared forward.

'Don't you upset yourself like this, mother. You must
see him, of course.'

'No, my dear. I'll try not to.'

She mopped her streaming eyes.

'But you can't spare the time to come with him, and if
he should forget himself and lose his way and somebody
spoke to him sharply, his name and address may slip his
memory, and he'll remain lost for days and days —'

The vision of a workhouse infirmary for poor Stevie –
if only during inquiries – wrung her heart. For she was a
proud woman. Winnie's stare had grown hard, intent,
inventive.

'I can't bring him to you myself every week,' she
cried. 'But don't you worry, mother. I'll see to it that he
don't get lost for long.'

They felt a peculiar bump; a vision of brick pillars
lingered before the rattling windows of the cab; a sudden
cessation of atrocious jolting and uproarious jingling
dazed the two women. What had happened? They sat

motionless and scared in the profound stillness, till the
door came open, and a rough, strained whispering was
heard:

' 'Ere you are!'

A range of gabled little houses, each with one dim yellow window, on the ground floor, surrounded the dark
open space of a grass plot planted with shrubs and railed
off from the patchwork of lights and shadows in the wide
road, resounding with the dull rumble of traffic. Before
the door of one of these tiny houses — one without a light
in the little downstairs window – the cab had come to a
standstill. Mrs. Verloc's mother got out first, backwards,
with a key in her hand. Winnie lingered on the flagstone
path to pay the cabman. Stevie, after helping to carry
inside a lot of small parcels, came out and stood under
the light of a gas-lamp belonging to the Charity. The
cabman looked at the pieces of silver, which, appearing
very minute in his big, grimy palm, symbolized the insignificant results which reward the ambitious courage and
toil of a mankind whose day is short on this earth of evil.

He had been paid decently – four one-shilling pieces
– and he contemplated them in perfect stillness, as if
they had been the surprising terms of a melancholy
problem. The slow transfer of that treasure to an inner
pocket demanded much laborious groping in the depths
of decayed clothing. His form was squat and without
flexibility. Stevie, slender, his shoulders a little up, and
his hands thrust deep in the side pockets of his warm
overcoat, stood at the edge of the path, pouting.

The cabman, pausing in his deliberate movements,
seemed struck by some misty recollection.

'Oh! 'Ere you are, young fellow,' he whispered. 'You'll
know him again – won't you?'

Stevie was staring at the horse, whose hind quarters
appeared unduly elevated by the effect of emancipation.
The little stiff tail seemed to have been fitted in for a
heartless joke; and at the other end the thin, flat neck,

like a plank covered with old horse-hide, drooped to the ground under the weight of an enormous bony head. The ears hung at different angles, negligently; and the macabre figure of that mute dweller on the earth steamed straight up from ribs and backbone in the muggy stillness of the air.

The cabman struck lightly Stevie's breast with the iron hook protruding from a ragged, greasy sleeve.

'Look 'ere, young feller. 'Ow'd *you* like to sit behind this 'oss up to two o'clock in the morning p'raps?'

Stevie looked vacantly into the fierce little eyes with red-edged lids.

'He ain't lame,' pursued the other, whispering with energy. 'He ain't got no sore places on 'im. 'Ere he is. 'Ow would *you* like —'

His strained, extinct voice invested his utterance with a character of vehement secrecy. Stevie's vacant gaze was changing slowly into dread.

'You may well look! Till three and four o'clock in the morning. Cold and 'ungry. Looking for fares. Drunks.'

His jovial purple cheeks bristled with white hairs; and like Virgil's Silenus, who, his face smeared with the juice of berries, discoursed of Olympian Gods to the innocent shepherds of Sicily, he talked to Stevie of domestic matters and the affairs of men whose sufferings are great and immortality by no means assured.

'I am a night cabby, I am,' he whispered, with a sort of boastful exasperation. 'I've got to take out what they will blooming well give me at the yard. I've got my missus and four kids at 'ome.'

The monstrous nature of that declaration of paternity seemed to strike the world dumb. A silence reigned, during which the flanks of the old horse, the steed of apocalyptic misery, smoked upwards in the light of the charitable gas-lamp.

The cabman grunted, then added in his mysterious whisper:

'This ain't an easy world.'

Stevie's face had been twitching for some time and at last his feelings burst out in their usual concise form.

'Bad! Bad!'

His gaze remained fixed on the ribs of the horse, self-conscious and sombre, as though he were afraid to look about him at the badness of the world. And his slenderness, his rosy lips and pale, clear complexion, gave him the aspect of a delicate boy, notwithstanding the fluffy growth of golden hair on his cheeks. He pouted in a scared way like a child. The cabman, short and broad, eyed him with his fierce little eyes that seemed to smart in a clear and corroding liquid.

' 'Ard on 'osses, but dam' sight 'arder on poor chaps like me,' he wheezed just audibly.

'Poor! Poor!' stammered out Stevie, pushing his hands deeper into his pocket with convulsive sympathy. He could say nothing; for the tenderness to all pain and all misery, the desire to make the horse happy and the cabman happy, had reached the point of a bizarre longing to take them to bed with him. And that, he knew, was impossible. For Stevie was not mad. It was, as it were, a symbolic longing; and at the same time it was very distinct, because springing from experience, the mother of wisdom. Thus when as a child he cowered in a dark corner scared, wretched, sore, and miserable with the black, black misery of the soul, his sister Winnie used to come along, and carry him off to bed with her, as into a heaven of consoling peace. Stevie, though apt to forget mere facts, such as his name and address for instance, had a faithful memory of sensations. To be taken into a bed of compassion was the supreme remedy, with the only one disadvantage of being difficult of application on a large scale. And looking at the cabman, Stevie perceived this clearly, because he was reasonable.

The cabman went on with his leisurely preparations as if Stevie had not existed. He made as if to hoist himself on the box, but at the last moment, from some obscure motive, perhaps merely from disgust with carriage exercise, desisted. He approached instead the motionless partner of his labours, and stooping to seize the bridle, lifted up the big, weary head to the height of his shoulder with one effort of his right arm, like a feat of strength.

'Come on,' he whispered, secretly.

Limping, he led the cab away. There was an air of austerity in this departure, the scrunched gravel of the drive crying out under the slowly turning wheels, the horse's lean thighs moving with ascetic deliberation away from the light into the obscurity of the open space bordered dimly by the pointed roofs and the feebly shining windows of the little almshouses. The plaint of the gravel travelled slowly all round the drive. Between the lamps of the charitable gateway the slow cortège reappeared, lighted up for a moment, the short, thick man limping busily, with the horse's head held aloft in his fist, the lank animal walking in stiff and forlorn dignity, the dark, low box on wheels rolling behind comically with an air of waddling. They turned to the left. There was a pub down the street, within fifty yards of the gate.

Stevie left alone beside the private lamp-post of the Charity, his hands thrust deep into his pockets, glared with vacant sulkiness. At the bottom of his pockets his incapable, weak hands were clinched hard into a pair of angry fists. In the face of anything which affected directly or indirectly his morbid dread of pain, Stevie ended by turning vicious. A magnanimous indignation swelled his frail chest to bursting, and caused his candid eyes to squint. Supremely wise in knowing his own powerlessness, Stevie was not wise enough to restrain his passions. The tenderness of his universal charity had two phases as indissolubly joined and connected as the reverse and obverse sides of a medal. The anguish of immoderate compassion was succeeded by the pain of an innocent but pitiless rage. Those two states expressing themselves outwardly by the same signs of futile bodily agitation, his sister Winnie soothed his excitement without ever fathoming its twofold character. Mrs. Verloc wasted no portion of this transient life in seeking for fundamental information. This is a sort of economy having all the appearances and some of the advantages of prudence. Obviously it may be good for one not to know too much. And such a view accords very well with constitutional indolence.

On that evening on which it may be said that Mrs. Verloc's mother having parted for good from her children had also departed this life, Winnie Verloc did not investigate her bother's psychology. The poor boy was excited, of course. After once more assuring the old woman on the threshold that she would know how to guard against the risk of Stevie losing himself for very long on his pilgrimages of filial piety, she took her brother's arm to walk away. Stevie did not even mutter to himself, but with the special sense of sisterly devotion developed in her earliest infancy, she felt that the boy was very much excited indeed. Holding tight to his arm, under the appearance of leaning on it, she thought of some words suitable to the occasion.

'Now, Stevie, you must look well after me at the crossings, and get first into the 'bus, like a good brother.'

This appeal to manly protection was received by Stevie with his usual docility. It flattered him. He raised his head and threw out his chest.

'Don't be nervous, Winnie. Mustn't be nervous! 'Bus all right,' he answered in a brusque, slurring stammer partaking of the timorousness of a child and the resolution of a man. He advanced fearlessly with the woman on his arm, but his lower lip dropped. Nevertheless, on the pavement of the squalid and wide thoroughfare, whose poverty in all the amenities of life stood foolishly exposed by a mad profusion of gas-lights, their resem-

blance to each other was so pronounced as to strike the
casual passers-by.

Before the doors of the public-house at the corner,
where the profusion of gas-light reached the height of
positive wickedness, a four-wheeled cab standing by the
curbstone, with no one on the box, seemed cast out into
the gutter on account of irremediable decay. Mrs. Verloc
recognized the conveyance. Its aspect was so profoundly
lamentable, with such a perfection of grotesque misery
and weirdness of macabre detail, as if it were the Cab of
Death itself, that Mrs. Verloc, with that ready compassion of a woman for a horse (when she is not sitting
behind him), exclaimed vaguely:

'Poor brute.'

Hanging back suddenly, Stevie inflicted an arresting
jerk upon his sister.

'Poor! Poor!' he ejaculated, appreciatively. 'Cabman
poor, too. He told me himself.'

The contemplation of the infirm and lonely steed
overcame him. Jostled, but obstinate, he would remain
there, trying to express the view newly opened to his
sympathies of the human and equine misery in close
association. But it was very difficult. 'Poor brute, poor
people!' was all he could repeat. It did not seem forcible
enough, and he came to a stop with an angry splutter:
'Shame!' Stevie was no master of phrases, and perhaps
for that very reason his thoughts lacked clearness and
precision. But he felt with greater completeness and
some profundity. That little word contained all his sense
of indignation and horror at one sort of wretchedness
having to feed upon the anguish of the other – at the
poor cabman beating the poor horse in the name, as it
were, of his poor kids at home. And Stevie knew what it
was to be beaten. He knew it from experience. It was a
bad world. Bad! Bad!

Mrs. Verloc, his only sister, guardian, and protector,
could not pretend to such depths of insight. Moreover,

she had not experienced the magic of the cabman's eloquence. She was in the dark as to the inwardness of the
word 'Shame.' And she said placidly:

'Come along, Stevie. You can't help that.'

The docile Stevie went along; but now he went along
without pride, shamblingly, and muttering half words,
and even words that would have been whole if they had
not been made up of halves that did not belong to each
other. It was as though he had been trying to fit all the
words he could remember to his sentiments in order to
get some sort of corresponding idea. And, as a matter of
fact, he got it at last. He hung back to utter it at once.

'Bad world for poor people.'

Directly he had expressed that thought he became
aware that it was familiar to him already in all its consequences. This circumstance strengthened his conviction
immensely, but also augmented his indignation.
Somebody, he felt, ought to be punished for it – punished with great severity. Being no sceptic, but a moral
creature, he was in a manner at the mercy of his right-
eous passions.

'Beastly!' he added, concisely.

It was clear to Mrs. Verloc that he was greatly excited.

'Nobody can help that,' she said. 'Do come along. Is
that the way you're taking care of me?'

Stevie mended his pace obediently. He prided himself on being a good brother. His morality, which was
very complete, demanded that from him. Yet he was
pained at the information imparted by his sister Winnie –
who was good. Nobody could help that! He came along
gloomily, but presently he brightened up. Like the rest
of mankind, perplexed by the mystery of the universe,
he had his moments of consoling trust in the organized
powers of the earth.

'Police,' he suggested, confidently.

'The police aren't for that,' observed Mrs. Verloc,
cursorily, hurrying on her way.

Stevie's face lengthened considerably. He was thinking. The more intense his thinking, the slacker was the
droop of his lower jaw. And it was with an aspect of hopeless vacancy that he gave up his intellectual enterprise.

'Not for that?' he mumbled, resigned but surprised.
'Not for that?' He had formed for himself an ideal conception of the metropolitan police as a sort of benevolent
institution for the suppression of evil. The notion of
benevolence especially was very closely associated with
his sense of the power of the men in blue. He had liked
all police constables tenderly, with a guileless trustfulness. And he was pained. He was irritated, too, by a suspicion of duplicity in the members of the force. For
Stevie was frank and as open as the day himself. What
did they mean by pretending then? Unlike his sister,
who put her trust in face values, he wished to go to the
bottom of the matter. He carried on his inquiry by means
of an angry challenge.

'What are they for then, Winn? What are they for? Tell
me.'

Winnie disliked controversy. But fearing most a fit of
black depression consequent on Stevie missing his
mother very much at first, she did not altogether decline
the discussion. Guiltless of all irony, she answered yet in
a form which was not perhaps unnatural in the wife of
Mr. Verloc, Delegate of the Central Red Committee,
personal friend of certain anarchists, and a votary of
social revolution.

'Don't you know what the police are for, Stevie? They
are there so that them as have nothing shouldn't take
anything away from them who have.'

She avoided using the verb 'to steal', because it
always made her brother uncomfortable. For Stevie was
delicately honest. Certain simple principles had been
instilled into him so anxiously (on account of his 'queer-
ness') that the mere names of certain transgressions
filled him with horror. He had been always easily

impressed by speeches. He was impressed and startled now, and his intelligence was very alert.

'What?' he asked at once, anxiously. 'Not even if they were hungry? Mustn't they?'

The two had paused in their walk.

'Not if they were ever so,' said Mrs. Verloc, with the equanimity of a person untroubled by the problem of the distribution of wealth, and exploring the perspective of the roadway for an omnibus of the right colour. 'Certainly not. But what's the use of talking about all that? You aren't ever hungry.'

She cast a swift glance at the boy, like a young man, by her side. She saw him amiable, attractive, affectionate, and only a little, a very little peculiar. And she could not see him otherwise, for he was connected with what there was of the salt of passion in her tasteless life – the passion of indignation, of courage, of pity, and even of self-sacrifice. She did not add: 'And you aren't likely ever to be as long as I live.' But she might very well have done so, since she had taken effectual steps to that end. Mr. Verloc was a very good husband. It was her honest impression that nobody could help liking the boy. She cried out suddenly:

'Quick, Stevie. Stop that green 'bus.'

And Stevie, tremulous and important with his sister Winnie on his arm, flung up the other high above his head at the approaching 'bus, with complete success.

An hour afterwards Mr. Verloc raised his eyes from a newspaper he was reading, or at any rate looking at, behind the counter, and in the expiring clatter of the door-bell beheld Winnie, his wife, enter and cross the shop on her way upstairs, followed by Stevie, his brother-in-law. The sight of his wife was agreeable to Mr. Verloc. It was his idiosyncrasy. The figure of his brother-in-law remained imperceptible to him because of the morose thoughtfulness that lately had fallen like a veil between Mr. Verloc and the appearances of the world of senses.

He looked after his wife fixedly, without a word, as
though she had been a phantom. His voice for home use
was husky and placid, but now it was heard not at all. It
was not heard at supper, to which he was called by his
wife in the usual brief manner: 'Adolf.' He sat down to
consume it without conviction, wearing his hat pushed
far back on his head. It was not devotion to an outdoor
life, but the frequentation of foreign cafés which was
responsible for that habit, investing with a character of
unceremonious impermanency Mr. Verloc's steady
fidelity to his own fireside. Twice at the clatter of the
cracked bell he arose without a word, disappeared into
the shop, and came back silently. During these absences
Mrs. Verloc, becoming acutely aware of the vacant place
at her right hand, missed her mother very much, and
stared stonily; while Stevie, from the same reason, kept
on shuffling his feet, as though the floor under the table
were uncomfortably hot. When Mr. Verloc returned to sit
in his place, like the very embodiment of silence, the
character of Mrs. Verloc's stare underwent a subtle
change, and Stevie ceased to fidget with his feet,
because of his great and awed regard for his sister's husband. He directed at him glances of respectful compassion. Mr. Verloc was sorry. His sister Winnie had
impressed upon him (in the omnibus) that Mr. Verloc
would be found at home in a state of sorrow, and must
not be worried. His father's anger, the irritability of
gentlemen lodgers, and Mr. Verloc's predisposition to
immoderate grief, had been the main sanctions of
Stevie's self-restraint. Of these sentiments, all easily provoked, but not always easy to understand, the last had
the greatest moral efficiency – because Mr. Verloc was
good. His mother and his sister had established that ethical fact on an unshakable foundation. They had established, erected, consecrated it behind Mr. Verloc's back,
for reasons that had nothing to do with abstract morality.
And Mr. Verloc was not aware of it. It is but bare justice

to him to say that he had no notion of appearing good to
Stevie. Yet so it was. He was even the only man so quali-
fied in Stevie's knowledge, because the gentlemen lodgers had been too transient and too remote to have
anything very distinct about them but perhaps their
boots; and as regards the disciplinary measures of his
father, the desolation of his mother and sister shrank from
setting up a theory of goodness before the victim. It
would have been too cruel. And it was even possible that
Stevie would not have believed them. As far as Mr. Verloc
was concerned, nothing could stand in the way of Stevie's
belief. Mr. Verloc was obviously yet mysteriously *good*.
And the grief of a good man is august.

Stevie gave glances of reverential compassion to his
brother-in-law. Mr. Verloc was sorry. The brother of Winnie had never before felt himself in such close commu-
nion with the mystery of that man's goodness. It was an
understandable sorrow. And Stevie himself was sorry. He
was very sorry. The same sort of sorrow. And his attention being drawn to this unpleasant state, Stevie shuffled
his feet. His feelings were habitually manifested by the
agitation of his limbs.

'Keep your feet quiet, dear,' said Mrs. Verloc, with
authority and tenderness; then turning towards her husband in an indifferent voice, the masterly achievement
of instinctive tact: 'Are you going out to-night?' she
asked.

The mere suggestion seemed repugnant to Mr. Verloc. He shook his head moodily, and then sat still with
downcast eyes, looking at the piece of cheese on his
plate for a whole minute. At the end of that time he got
up, and went out – went right out in the clatter of the
shop-door bell. He acted thus inconsistently, not from
any desire to make himself unpleasant, but because of an
unconquerable restlessness. It was no earthly good going
out. He could not find anywhere in London what he
wanted. But he went out. He led a cortège of dismal

thoughts along dark streets, through lighted streets, in and out of two flash bars, as if in a half-hearted attempt to make a night of it, and finally back again to his menaced home, where he sat down fatigued behind the counter, and they crowded urgently round him, like a pack of hungry black hounds. After locking up the house and putting out the gas he took them upstairs with him – a dreadful escort for a man going to bed. His wife had preceded him some time before, and with her ample form defined vaguely under the counterpane, her head on the pillow, and a hand under the cheek, offered to his distraction the view of early drowsiness arguing the possession of an equable soul. Her big eyes stared wide open, inert and dark against the snowy whiteness of the linen. She did not move.

She had an equable soul. She felt profoundly that things do not stand much looking into. She made her force and her wisdom of that instinct. But the taciturnity of Mr. Verloc had been lying heavily upon her for a good many days. It was, as a matter of fact, affecting her nerves. Recumbent and motionless, she said placidly:

'You'll catch cold walking about in your socks like this.'

This speech, becoming the solicitude of the wife and the prudence of the woman, took Mr. Verloc unawares. He had left his boots downstairs, but he had forgotten to put on his slippers, and he had been turning about the bedroom on noiseless pads like a bear in a cage. At the sound of his wife's voice he stopped and stared at her with a somnambulistic, expressionless gaze so long that Mrs. Verloc moved her limbs slightly under the bedclothes. But she did not move her black head sunk in the white pillow, one hand under her cheek and the big, dark, unwinking eyes.

Under her husband's expressionless stare, and remembering her mother's empty room across the landing, she felt an acute pang of loneliness. She had never been parted from her mother before. They had stood by each other. She felt that they had, and she said to herself that now mother was gone – gone for good. Mrs. Verloc had no illusions. Stevie remained, however. And she said:

'Mother's done what she wanted to do. There's no sense in it that I can see. I'm sure she couldn't have thought you had enough of her. It's perfectly wicked, leaving us like that.'

Mr. Verloc was not a well-read person; his range of allusive phrases was limited, but there was a peculiar aptness in circumstances which made him think of rats leaving a doomed ship. He very nearly said so. He had grown suspicious and embittered. Could it be that the old woman had such an excellent nose? But the unreasonableness of such a suspicion was patent, and Mr. Verloc held his tongue. Not altogether, however. He muttered, heavily:

'Perhaps it's just as well.'

He began to undress. Mrs. Verloc kept very still, perfectly still, with her eyes fixed in a dreamy, quiet stare. And her heart for the fraction of a second seemed to stand still, too. That night she was 'not quite herself', as the saying is, and it was borne upon her with some force that a simple sentence may hold several diverse meanings – mostly disagreeable. *How* was it just as well? And why? But she did not allow herself to fall into the idleness of barren speculation. She was rather confirmed in her belief that things did not stand being looked into. Practical and subtle in her way, she brought Stevie to the front without loss of time, because in her the singleness of purpose had the unerring nature and the force of an instinct.

'What I am going to do to cheer up that boy for the first few days I'm sure I don't know. He'll be worrying himself from morning till night before he gets used to mother being away. And he's such a good boy. I couldn't do without him.'

Mr. Verloc went on divesting himself of his clothing with the unnoticing inward concentration of a man undressing in the solitude of a vast and hopeless desert. For thus inhospitably did this fair earth, our common inheritance, present itself to the mental vision of Mr. Verloc. All was so still without and within that the lonely ticking of the clock on the landing stole into the room as if for the sake of company.

Mr. Verloc, getting into bed on his own side, remained prone and mute behind Mrs. Verloc's back. His thick arms rested abandoned on the outside of the counterpane like dropped weapons, like discarded tools. At that moment he was within a hair's breadth of making a clean breast of it all to his wife. The moment seemed propitious. Looking out of the corners of his eyes, he saw her ample shoulders draped in white, the back of her head, with the hair done for the night in three plaits tied up with black tapes at the ends. And he forbore. Mr. Verloc loved his wife as a wife should be loved – that is, maritally, with the regard one has for one's chief possession. This head arranged for the night, those ample shoulders, had an aspect of familiar sacredness – the sacredness of domestic peace. She moved not, massive and shapeless like a recumbent statue in the rough; he remembered her wide-open eyes looking into the empty room. She was mysterious, with the mysteriousness of living beings. The far-famed secret agent Δ. of the late Baron Stott-Wartenheim's alarmist despatches was not the man to break into such mysteries. He was easily intimidated. And he was also indolent, with the indolence which is so often the secret of good nature. He forbore touching that mystery out of love, timidity, and indolence. There would be always time enough. For several minutes he bore his sufferings silently in the drowsy silence of the room. And then he disturbed it by a resolute declaration.

'I am going on the Continent to-morrow.'

His wife might have fallen asleep already. He could
not tell. As a matter of fact, Mrs. Verloc had heard him.
Her eyes remained very wide open, and she lay very still,
confirmed in her instinctive conviction that things don't
bear looking into very much. And yet it was nothing very
unusual for Mr. Verloc to take such a trip. He renewed
his stock from Paris and Brussels. Often he went over to
make his purchases personally. A little select connection
of amateurs was forming around the shop in Brett Street,
a secret connection eminently proper for any business
undertaken by Mr. Verloc, who, by a mystic accord of
temperament and necessity, had been set apart to be a
secret agent all his life.

He waited for a while, then added: 'I'll be away a
week or perhaps a fortnight. Get Mrs. Neale to come for
the day.'

Mrs. Neale was the charwoman of Brett Street. Victim
of her marriage with a debauched joiner, she was
oppressed by the needs of many infant children. Red-
armed, and aproned in coarse sacking up to the arm-pits,
she exhaled the anguish of the poor in a breath of soap-
suds and rum, in the uproar of scrubbing, in the clatter of
tin pails.

Mrs. Verloc, full of deep purpose, spoke in the tone of
the shallowest indifference.

'There is no need to have the woman here all day. I
shall do very well with Stevie.'

She let the lonely clock on the landing count off fifteen ticks into the abyss of eternity, and asked:

'Shall I put the light out?'

Mr. Verloc snapped at his wife huskily.

'Put it out.'

CHAPTER NINE

M R. VERLOC, returning from the Continent at the end of ten days, brought back a mind evidently unrefreshed by the wonders of foreign travel and a countenance unlighted by the joys of homecoming. He entered in the clatter of the shop-bell with an air of sombre and vexed exhaustion. His bag in hand, his head lowered, he strode straight behind the counter, and let himself fall into the chair, as though he had tramped all the way from Dover. It was early morning. Stevie, dusting various objects displayed in the front windows, turned to gape at him with reverence and awe.

'Here!' said Mr. Verloc, giving a slight kick to the gladstone bag on the floor; and Stevie flung himself upon it, seized it, bore it off with triumphant devotion. He was so prompt that Mr. Verloc was distinctly surprised.

Already at the clatter of the shop-bell Mrs. Neale, blackleading the parlour grate, had looked through the door, and rising from her knees had gone, aproned, and grimy with everlasting toil, to tell Mrs. Verloc in the kitchen that 'there was the master come back.'

Winnie came no farther than the inner shop door.

'You'll want some breakfast,' she said from a distance.

Mr. Verloc moved his hands slightly, as if overcome by an impossible suggestion. But once enticed into the parlour he did not reject the food set before him. He ate as if in a public place, his hat pushed off his forehead, the skirts of his heavy overcoat hanging in a triangle on each

166

side of the chair. And across the length of the table
covered with brown oilcloth Winnie, his wife, talked
evenly at him the wifely talk, as artfully adapted, no
doubt, to the circumstances of this return as the talk of
Penelope to the return of the wandering Odysseus. Mrs.
Verloc, however, had done no weaving during her husband's absence. But she had had all the upstairs room
cleaned thoroughly, had sold some wares, had seen Mr.
Michaelis several times. He had told her the last time
that he was going away to live in a cottage in the country,
somewhere on the London, Chatham, and Dover line.
Karl Yundt had come, too, once, led under the arm by
that 'wicked old house-keeper of his'. He was 'a disgusting old man'. Of Comrade Ossipon, whom she had
received curtly, entrenched behind the counter with a
stony face and a far-away gaze, she said nothing, her
mental reference to the robust anarchist being marked
by a short pause, with the faintest possible blush. And
bringing her brother Stevie as soon as she could into the
current of domestic events, she mentioned that the boy
had moped a good deal.

'It's all along of mother leaving us like this.'

Mr. Verloc neither said 'Damn!' nor yet 'Stevie be
hanged!' And Mrs. Verloc, not let into the secret of his
thoughts, failed to appreciate the generosity of this
restraint.

'It isn't that he doesn't work as well as ever,' she continued. 'He's been making himself very useful. You'd
think he couldn't do enough for us.'

Mr. Verloc directed a casual and somnolent glance at
Stevie, who sat on his right, delicate, pale-faced, his rosy
mouth open vacantly. It was not a critical glance. It had
no intention. And if Mr. Verloc thought for a moment
that his wife's brother looked uncommonly useless, it
was only a dull and fleeting thought, devoid of that force
and durability which enables sometimes a thought to
move the world. Leaning back, Mr. Verloc uncovered his

head. Before his extended arm could put down the hat
Stevie pounced upon it, and bore it off reverently into
the kitchen. And again Mr. Verloc was surprised.

'You could do anything with that boy, Adolf', Mrs. Verloc said, with her best air of inflexible calmness. 'He
would go through fire for you. He —'

She paused attentive, her ear turned towards the door
of the kitchen.

There Mrs. Neale was scrubbing the floor. At Stevie's
appearance she groaned lamentably, having observed
that he could be induced easily to bestow for the benefit
of her infant children the shilling his sister Winnie
presented him with from time to time. On all fours
amongst the puddles, wet and begrimed, like a sort of
amphibious and domestic animal living in ashbins and
dirty water, she uttered the usual exordium: 'It's all very
well for you, kept doing nothing like a gentleman.' And
she followed it with the everlasting plaint of the poor,
pathetically mendacious, miserably authenticated by
the horrible breath of cheap rum and soap-suds. She
scrubbed hard, snuffling all the time, and talking
volubly. And she was sincere. And on each side of her
thin red nose her bleared, misty eyes swam in tears,
because she felt really the want of some sort of stimulant
in the morning.

In the parlour Mrs. Verloc observed, with knowledge:

'There's Mrs. Neale at it again with her harrowing
tales about her little children. They can't be all so little
as she makes them out. Some of them must be big
enough by now to try to do something for themselves. It
only makes Stevie angry.'

These words were confirmed by a thud as of a fist
striking the kitchen table. In the normal evolution of his
sympathy Stevie had become angry on discovering that
he had no shilling in his pocket. In his inability to relieve
at once Mrs. Neale's 'little 'uns' privations, he felt that
somebody should be made to suffer for it. Mrs. Verloc

rose, and went into the kitchen to 'stop that nonsense'.
And she did it firmly but gently. She was well aware that
directly Mrs. Neale received her money she went round
the corner to drink ardent spirits in a mean and musty
public-house – the unavoidable station on the *via dolorosa*
of her life. Mrs. Verloc's comment upon this practice had
an unexpected profundity, as coming from a person dis-
inclined to look under the surface of things. 'Of course,
what is she to do to keep up? If I were like Mrs. Neale I
expect I wouldn't act any different.'

In the afternoon of the same day, as Mr. Verloc, coming with a start out of the last of a long series of dozes
before the parlour fire, declared his intention of going
out for a walk, Winnie said from the shop:

'I wish you would take that boy out with you, Adolf.'

For the third time that day Mr. Verloc was surprised.
He stared stupidly at his wife. She continued in her
steady manner. The boy, whenever he was not doing
anything, moped in the house. It made her uneasy; it
made her nervous, she confessed. And that from the
calm Winnie sounded like exaggeration. But, in truth,
Stevie moped in the striking fashion of an unhappy
domestic animal. He would go up on the dark landing, to
sit on the floor at the foot of the tall clock, with his knees
drawn up and his head in his hands. To come upon his
pallid face, with its big eyes gleaming in the dusk, was
discomposing; to think of him up there was uncomfortable.

Mr. Verloc got used to the startling novelty of the idea.
He was fond of his wife as a man should be – that is,
generously. But a weighty objection presented itself to
his mind, and he formulated it.

'He'll lose sight of me perhaps, and get lost in the
street,' he said.

Mrs. Verloc shook her head competently.

'He won't. You don't know him. That boy just wor-
ships you. But if you should miss him —'

Mrs. Verloc paused for a moment, but only for a
moment.

'You just go on, and have your walk out. Don't worry.
He'll be all right. He's sure to turn up safe here before
very long.'

This optimism procured for Mr. Verloc his fourth surprise of the day.

'Is he?' he grunted, doubtfully. But perhaps his
brother-in-law was not such an idiot as he looked. His
wife would know best. He turned away his heavy eyes,
saying huskily: 'Well, let him come along, then,' and
relapsed into the clutches of black care, that perhaps
prefers to sit behind a horseman, but knows also how to
tread close on the heels of people not sufficiently well
off to keep horses – like Mr. Verloc, for instance.

Winnie, at the shop door, did not see this fatal attend-
ant upon Mr. Verloc's walks. She watched the two figures
down the squalid street, one tall and burly, the other
slight and short, with a thin neck, and the peaked shoulders raised slightly under the large semi-transparent ears.
The material of their overcoats was the same, their hats
were black and round in shape. Inspired by the similarity
of wearing apparel, Mrs. Verloc gave rein to her fancy.

'Might be father and son,' she said to herself. She
thought also that Mr. Verloc was as much of a father as
poor Stevie ever had in his life. She was aware also that it
was her work. And with peaceful pride she congratulated
herself on a certain resolution she had taken a few years
before. It had cost her some effort, and even a few tears.

She congratulated herself still more on observing in
the course of days that Mr. Verloc seemed to be taking
kindly to Stevie's companionship. Now, when ready to
go out for his walk, Mr. Verloc called aloud to the boy, in
the spirit, no doubt, in which a man invites the attendance of the household dog, though, of course, in a different manner. In the house Mr. Verloc could be detected
staring curiously at Stevie a good deal. His own

demeanour had changed. Taciturn still, he was not so listless. Mrs. Verloc thought that he was rather jumpy at times. It might have been regarded as an improvement. As to Stevie, he moped no longer at the foot of the clock, but muttered to himself in corners instead in a threatening tone. When asked 'What is it you're saying, Stevie?' he merely opened his mouth, and squinted at his sister. At odd times he clenched his fists without apparent cause, and when discovered in solitude would be scowling at the wall, with the sheet of paper and the pencil given him for drawing circles lying blank and idle on the kitchen table. This was a change, but it was no improvement. Mrs. Verloc, including all these vagaries under the general definition of excitement, began to fear that Stevie was hearing more than was good for him of her husband's conversations with his friends. During his 'walks' Mr. Verloc, of course, met and conversed with various persons. It could hardly be otherwise. His walks were an integral part of his outdoor activities, which his wife had never looked deeply into. Mrs. Verloc felt that the position was delicate, but she faced it with the same impenetrable calmness which impressed and even astonished the customers of the shop and made the other visitors keep their distance a little wonderingly. No! She feared that there were things not good for Stevie to hear of, she told her husband. It only excited the poor boy, because he could not help them being so. Nobody could.

It was in the shop. Mr. Verloc made no comment. He made no retort, and yet the retort was obvious. But he refrained from pointing out to his wife that the idea of making Stevie the companion of his walks was her own, and nobody else's. At that moment, to an impartial observer, Mr. Verloc would have appeared more than human in his magnanimity. He took down a small cardboard box from a shelf, peeped in to see that the contents were all right, and put it down gently on the counter. Not till that was done did he break the silence, to the effect that most likely Stevie would profit greatly by being sent out of town for a while; only he supposed his wife could not get on without him.

'Could not get on without him!' repeated Mrs. Verloc, slowly. 'I couldn't get on without him if it were for his good! The idea! Of course, I can get on without him. But there's nowhere for him to go.'

Mr. Verloc got out some brown paper and a ball of string; and meanwhile he muttered that Michaelis was living in a little cottage in the country. Michaelis wouldn't mind giving Stevie a room to sleep in. There were no visitors and no talk there. Michaelis was writing a book.

Mrs. Verloc declared her affection for Michaelis; mentioned her abhorrence of Karl Yundt, 'nasty old man'; and of Ossipon she said nothing. As to Stevie, he could be no other than very pleased. Mr. Michaelis was always so nice and kind to him. He seemed to like the boy. Well, the boy was a good boy.

'You, too, seem to have grown quite fond of him of late,' she added, after a pause, with her inflexible assurance.

Mr. Verloc, tying up the cardboard box into a parcel for the post, broke the string by an injudicious jerk, and muttered several swear words confidentially to himself. Then raising his tone to the usual husky mutter, he announced his willingness to take Stevie into the country himself, and leave him all safe with Michaelis.

He carried out this scheme on the very next day. Stevie offered no objection. He seemed rather eager, in a bewildered sort of way. He turned his candid gaze inquisitively to Mr. Verloc's heavy countenance at frequent intervals, especially when his sister was not looking at him. His expression was proud, apprehensive, and concentrated, like that of a small child entrusted for the first time with a box of matches and the permission to strike a light. But Mrs. Verloc, gratified by her brother's

docility, recommended him not to dirty his clothes
unduly in the country. At this Stevie gave his sister,
guardian, and protector a look, which for the first time in
his life seemed to lack the quality of perfect childlike
trustfulness. It was haughtily gloomy. Mrs. Verloc smiled.

'Goodness me! You needn't be offended. You know
you do get yourself very untidy when you get a chance,
Stevie.'

Mr. Verloc was already gone some way down the street.

Thus in consequence of her mother's heroic proceedings, and of her brother's absence on this villegiature,
Mrs. Verloc found herself oftener than usual all alone not
only in the shop, but in the house. For Mr. Verloc had to
take his walks. She was alone longer than usual on the
day of the attempted bomb outrage in Greenwich Park,
because Mr. Verloc went out very early that morning and
did not come back till nearly dusk. She did not mind
being alone. She had no desire to go out. The weather
was too bad, and the shop was cosier than the streets. Sitting behind the counter with some sewing, she did not
raise her eyes from her work when Mr. Verloc entered in
the aggressive clatter of the bell. She had recognized his
step on the pavement outside.

She did not raise her eyes, but as Mr. Verloc, silent,
and with his hat rammed down upon his forehead, made
straight for the parlour door, she said, serenely:

'What a wretched day. You've been perhaps to see
Stevie?'

'No! I haven't,' said Mr. Verloc, softly, and slammed
the glazed parlour door behind him with unexpected
energy.

For some time Mrs. Verloc remained quiescent, with
her work dropped in her lap, before she put it away
under the counter and got up to light the gas. This done,
she went into the parlour on her way to the kitchen. Mr.
Verloc would want his tea presently. Confident of the
power of her charms, Winnie did not expect from her

husband in the daily intercourse of their married life a
ceremonious amenity of address and courtliness of manner; vain and antiquated forms at best, probably never
very exactly observed, discarded nowadays even in the
highest spheres, and always foreign to the standards of
her class. She did not look for courtesies from him. But
he was a good husband, and she had a loyal respect for
his rights.

Mrs. Verloc would have gone through the parlour and
on to her domestic duties in the kitchen with the perfect
serenity of a woman sure of the power of her charms. But
a slight, very slight, and rapid rattling sound grew upon
her hearing. Bizarre and incomprehensible, it arrested
Mrs. Verloc's attention. Then as its character became
plain to the ear she stopped short, amazed and concerned. Striking a match on the box she held in her hand,
she turned on and lighted, above the parlour table, one of
the two gas-burners, which being defective, first whistled
as if astonished, and then went on purring comfortably
like a cat.

Mr. Verloc, against his usual practice, had thrown off
his overcoat. It was lying on the sofa. His hat, which he
must also have thrown off, rested overturned under the
edge of the sofa. He had dragged a chair in front of the
fireplace, and his feet planted inside the fender, his head
held between his hands, he was hanging low over the
glowing grate. His teeth rattled with an ungovernable
violence, causing his whole enormous back to tremble at
the same rate. Mrs. Verloc was startled.

'You've been getting wet,' she said.

'Not very,' Mr. Verloc managed to falter out, in a profound shudder. By a great effort he suppressed the rattling of his teeth.

'I'll have you laid up on my hands,' she said, with
genuine uneasiness.

'I don't think so,' remarked Mr. Verloc, snuffling
huskily.

He had certainly contrived somehow to catch an abominable cold between seven in the morning and five in the afternoon. Mrs. Verloc looked at his bowed back.

'Where have you been to-day?' she asked.

'Nowhere,' answered Mr. Verloc in a low, choked nasal tone. His attitude suggested aggrieved sulks or a severe headache. The unsufficiency and uncandidness of his answer became painfully apparent in the dead silence of the room. He snuffled apologetically, and added: 'I've been to the bank.'

Mrs. Verloc became attentive.

'You have!' she said, dispassionately. 'What for?'

Mr. Verloc mumbled, with his nose over the grate, and with marked unwillingness:

'Draw the money out!'

'What do you mean? All of it?'

'Yes. All of it.'

Mrs. Verloc spread out with care the scanty tablecloth, got two knives and two forks out of the table drawer, and suddenly stopped in her methodical proceedings.

'What did you do that for?'

'May want it soon,' snuffled vaguely Mr. Verloc, who was coming to the end of his calculated indiscretions.

'I don't know what you mean,' remarked his wife in a tone perfectly casual, but standing stock still between the table and the cupboard.

'You know you can trust me,' Mr. Verloc remarked to the grate, with hoarse feeling.

Mrs. Verloc turned slowly towards the cupboard, saying with deliberation:

'Oh, yes. I can trust you.'

And she went on with her methodical proceedings. She laid two plates, got the bread, the butter, going to and fro quietly between the table and the cupboard in the peace and silence of her home. On the point of taking out the jam, she reflected practically: 'He will be feeling hungry, having been away all day,' and she

returned to the cupboard once more to get the cold beef.
She set it under the purring gas-jet, and with a passing
glance at her motionless husband hugging the fire, she
went (down two steps) into the kitchen. It was only
when coming back, carving knife and fork in hand, that
she spoke again.

'If I hadn't trusted you I wouldn't have married you.'

Bowed under the overmantel, Mr. Verloc, holding his
head in both hands, seemed to have gone to sleep. Winnie made the tea, and called out in an undertone:

'Adolf.'

Mr. Verloc got up at once, and staggered a little before
he sat down at the table. His wife, examining the sharp
edge of the carving knife, placed it on the dish, and
called his attention to the cold beef. He remained insensible to the suggestion, with his chin on his breast.

'You should feed your cold,' Mrs. Verloc said, dog-
matically.

He looked up, and shook his head. His eyes were
bloodshot and his face red. His fingers had ruffled his
hair into a dissipated untidiness. Altogether he had a
disreputable aspect, expressive of the discomfort, the
irritation, and the gloom following a heavy debauch. But
Mr. Verloc was not a debauched man. In his conduct he
was respectable. His appearance might have been the
effect of a feverish cold. He drank three cups of tea, but
abstained from food entirely. He recoiled from it with
sombre aversion when urged by Mrs. Verloc, who said at
last:

'Aren't your feet wet? You had better put on your slippers. You aren't going out any more this evening.'

Mr. Verloc intimated by morose grunts and signs that
his feet were not wet, and that anyhow he did not care.
The proposal as to slippers was disregarded as beneath
his notice. But the question of going out in the evening
received an unexpected development. It was not of
going out in the evening that Mr. Verloc was thinking.

His thoughts embraced a vaster scheme. From moody and incomplete phrases it became apparent that Mr. Verloc had been considering the expediency of emigrating. It was not very clear whether he had in his mind France or California.

The utter unexpectedness, improbability, and inconceivableness of such an event robbed this vague declaration of all its effect. Mrs. Verloc, as placidly as if her husband had been threatening her with the end of the world, said:

'The idea!'

Mr. Verloc declared himself sick and tired of everything, and besides — She interrupted him.

'You've a bad cold.'

It was indeed obvious that Mr. Verloc was not in his usual state, physically and even mentally. A sombre irresolution held him silent for a while. Then he murmured a few ominous generalities on the theme of necessity.

'Will have to,' repeated Winnie, sitting calmly back, with folded arms, opposite her husband. 'I should like to know who's to make you. You ain't a slave. No one need be a slave in this country – and don't you make yourself one.' She paused, and with invincible and steady candour: 'The business isn't so bad,' she went on. 'You've a comfortable home.'

She glanced all round the parlour, from the corner cupboard to the good fire in the grate. Ensconced cosily behind the shop of doubtful wares, with the mysteriously dim window, and its door suspiciously ajar in the obscure and narrow street, it was in all essentials of domestic propriety and domestic comfort a respectable home. Her devoted affection missed out of it her brother Stevie, now enjoying a damp villegiature in the Kentish lanes under the care of Mr. Michaelis. She missed him poignantly, with all the force of her protecting passion. This was the boy's home, too – the roof, the cupboard, the stoked grate. On this thought Mrs. Verloc rose, and

walking to the other end of the table, said in the fullness
of her heart:

'And you are not tired of me.'

Mr. Verloc made no sound. Winnie leaned on his
shoulder from behind, and pressed her lips to his forehead. Thus she lingered. Not a whisper reached them
from the outside world. The sound of footsteps on the
pavement died out in the discreet dimness of the shop.
Only the gas-jet above the table went on purring equably
in the brooding silence of the parlour.

During the contact of that unexpected and lingering
kiss Mr. Verloc, gripping with both hands the edges of
his chair, preserved a hieratic immobility. When the
pressure was removed he let go the chair, rose, and went
to stand before the fireplace. He turned no longer his
back to the room. With his features swollen and an air of
being drugged, he followed his wife's movements with
his eyes.

Mrs. Verloc went about serenely, clearing up the table.
Her tranquil voice commented on the idea thrown out in
a reasonable and domestic tone. It wouldn't stand exam-
ination. She condemned it from every point of view. But
her only real concern was Stevie's welfare. He appeared
to her thought in that connection as sufficiently 'peculiar' not to be taken rashly abroad. And that was all. But
talking round that vital point, she approached absolute
vehemence in her delivery. Meanwhile, with brusque
movements, she arrayed herself in an apron for the washing up of cups. And as if excited by the sound of her
uncontradicted voice, she went so far as to say in a tone
almost tart:

'If you go abroad you'll have to go without me.'

'You know I wouldn't,' said Mr. Verloc, huskily, and
the unresonant voice of his private life trembled with an
enigmatical emotion.

Already Mrs. Verloc was regretting her words. They
had sounded more unkind than she meant them to be.

They had also the unwisdom of unnecessary things. In fact, she had not meant them at all. It was a sort of phrase that is suggested by the demon of perverse inspiration. But she knew a way to make it as if it had not been.

She turned her head over her shoulder and gave that man planted heavily in front of the fireplace a glance, half arch, half cruel, out of her large eyes – a glance of which the Winnie of the Belgravian mansion days would have been incapable, because of her respectability and her ignorance. But the man was her husband now, and she was no longer ignorant. She kept it on him for a whole second, with her grave face motionless like a mask, while she said playfully:

'You couldn't. You would miss me too much.'

Mr. Verloc started forward.

'Exactly,' he said in a louder tone, throwing his arms out and making a step towards her. Something wild and doubtful in his expression made it appear uncertain whether he meant to strangle or to embrace his wife. But Mrs. Verloc's attention was called away from that manifestation by the clatter of the shop-bell.

'Shop, Adolf. You go.'

He stopped, his arms came down slowly.

'You go,' repeated Mrs. Verloc. 'I've got my apron on.'

Mr. Verloc obeyed woodenly, stony-eyed, and like an automaton whose face had been painted red. And this resemblance to a mechanical figure went so far that he had an automaton's absurd air of being aware of the machinery inside of him.

He closed the parlour door, and Mrs. Verloc, moving briskly, carried the tray into the kitchen. She washed the cups and some other things before she stopped in her work to listen. No sound reached her. The customer was a long time in the shop. It was a customer, because if he had not been Mr. Verloc would have taken him inside. Undoing the strings of her apron with a jerk, she threw it on a chair, and walked back to the parlour slowly.

At that precise moment Mr. Verloc entered from the shop.

He had gone in red. He came out a strange papery white. His face, losing its drugged, feverish stupor, had in that short time acquired a bewildered and harassed expression. He walked straight to the sofa, and stood looking down at his overcoat lying there, as though he were afraid to touch it.

'What's the matter?' asked Mrs. Verloc in a subdued voice. Through the door left ajar she could see that the customer was not gone yet.

'I find I'll have to go out this evening,' said Mr. Verloc. He did not attempt to pick up his outer garment.

Without a word Winnie made for the shop, and shutting the door after her, walked in behind the counter. She did not look overtly at the customer till she had established herself comfortably on the chair. But by that time she had noted that he was tall and thin, and wore his moustaches twisted up. In fact, he gave the sharp points a twist just then. His long, bony face rose out of a turned-up collar. He was a little splashed, a little wet. A dark man, with the ridge of the cheekbone well defined under the slightly hollow temple. A complete stranger. Not a customer, either.

Mrs. Verloc looked at him placidly.

'You came over from the Continent?' she said after a time.

The long, thin stranger, without exactly looking at Mrs. Verloc, answered only by a faint and peculiar smile.

Mrs. Verloc's steady, incurious gaze rested on him.

'You understand English, don't you?'

'Oh, yes. I understand English.'

There was nothing foreign in his accent, except that he seemed in his slow enunciation to be taking pains with it. And Mrs. Verloc, in her varied experience, had come to the conclusion that some foreigners could speak

better English than the natives. She said, looking at the
door of the parlour fixedly:

'You don't think perhaps of staying in England for
good?'

The stranger gave her again a silent smile. He had a
kindly mouth and probing eyes. And he shook his head a
little sadly, it seemed.

'My husband will see you through all right. Meantime, for a few days you couldn't do better than
take lodgings with Mr. Guigliani. Continental Hotel it's
called. Private. It's quiet. My husband will take you
there.'

'A good idea,' said the thin, dark man, whose glance
had hardened suddenly.

'You knew Mr. Verloc before – didn't you? Perhaps in
France?'

'I have heard of him,' admitted the visitor in his slow,
painstaking tone, which yet had a certain curtness of
intention.

There was a pause. Then he spoke again, in a far less
elaborate manner.

'Your husband has not gone out to wait for me in the
street by chance?'

'In the street!' repeated Mrs. Verloc, surprised. 'He
couldn't. There's no other door to the house.'

For a moment she sat impassive, then left her seat to
go and peep through the glazed door. Suddenly she
opened it, and disappeared into the parlour.

Mr. Verloc had done no more than put on his overcoat. But why he should remain afterwards leaning over
the table propped up on his two arms as though he were
feeling giddy or sick, she could not understand. 'Adolf,'
she called out half aloud; and when he had raised himself:

'Do you know that man?' she asked, rapidly.

'I've heard of him,' whispered uneasily Mr. Verloc,
darting a wild glance at the door.

Mrs. Verloc's fine, incurious eyes lighted up with a flash of abhorrence.

'One of Karl Yundt's friends – beastly old man.'

'No! No!' protested Mr. Verloc, busy fishing for his hat. But when he got it from under the sofa he held it as if he did not know the use of a hat.

'Well – he's waiting for you,' said Mrs. Verloc at last. 'I say, Adolf, he ain't one of them Embassy people you have been bothered with of late?'

'Bothered with Embassy people,' repeated Mr. Verloc, with a heavy start of surprise and fear. 'Who's been talking to you of the Embassy people?'

'Yourself.'

'I! I! Talked of the Embassy to you!'

Mr. Verloc seemed scared and bewildered beyond measure. His wife explained:

'You've been talking a little in your sleep of late, Adolf.'

'What – what did I say? What do you know?'

'Nothing much. It seemed mostly nonsense. Enough to let me guess that something worried you.'

Mr. Verloc rammed his hat on his head. A crimson flood of anger ran over his face.

'Nonsense – eh? The Embassy people! I would cut their hearts out one after another. But let them look out. I've got a tongue in my head.'

He fumed, pacing up and down between the table and the sofa, his open overcoat catching against the angles. The red flood of anger ebbed out, and left his face all white, with quivering nostrils. Mrs. Verloc, for the purposes of practical existence, put down these appearances to the cold.

'Well,' she said, 'get rid of the man whoever he is, as soon as you can, and come back home to me. You want looking after for a day or two.'

Mr. Verloc calmed down, and, with resolution

imprinted on his pale face, had already opened the door, when his wife called him back in a whisper:

'Adolf! Adolf!' He came back, startled. 'What about that money you drew out?' she asked. 'You've got it in your pocket? Hadn't you better —'

Mr. Verloc gazed stupidly into the palm of his wife's extended hand for some time before he slapped his brow.

'Money! Yes! Yes! I didn't know what you meant.'

He drew out of his breast pocket a new pigskin pocket-book. Mrs. Verloc received it without another word, and stood still till the bell, clattering after Mr. Verloc and Mr. Verloc's visitor, had quieted down. Only then she peeped in at the amount, drawing the notes out for the purpose. After this inspection she looked round thoughtfully, with an air of mistrust in the silence and solitude of the house. This abode of her married life appeared to her as lonely and unsafe as though it had been situated in the midst of a forest. No receptacle she could think of amongst the solid, heavy furniture seemed other but flimsy and particularly tempting to her conception of a house-breaker. It was an ideal conception, endowed with sublime faculties and a miraculous insight. The till was not to be thought of. It was the first spot a thief would make for. Mrs. Verloc, unfastening hastily a couple of hooks, slipped the pocket-book under the bodice of her dress. Having thus disposed of her husband's capital, she was rather glad to hear the clatter of the door-bell, announcing an arrival. Assuming the fixed, unabashed stare and the stony expression reserved for the casual customer, she walked in behind the counter.

A man standing in the middle of the shop was inspecting it with a swift, cool, all-round glance. His eyes ran over the walls, took in the ceiling, noted the floor – all in a moment. The points of a long fair moustache fell below the line of the jaw. He smiled the smile of an old if dis-

tant acquaintance, and Mrs. Verloc remembered having
seen him before. Not a customer. She softened her 'customer stare' to mere indifference, and faced him across
the counter.

He approached, on his side, confidentially, but not too
markedly so.

'Husband at home, Mrs. Verloc?' he asked in an easy,
full tone.

'No. He's gone out.'

'I am sorry for that. I've called to get from him a little
private information.'

This was the exact truth. Chief Inspector Heat had
been all the way home and had even gone so far as to
think of getting into his slippers, since practically he was,
he told himself, chucked out of that case. He indulged in
some scornful and in a few angry thoughts, and found
the occupation so unsatisfactory that he resolved to seek
relief out of doors. Nothing prevented him paying a
friendly call on Mr. Verloc, casually as it were. It was in
the character of a private citizen that walking out privately he made use of his customary conveyances. Their
general direction was towards Mr. Verloc's home. Chief
Inspector Heat respected his own private character so
consistently that he took especial pains to avoid all the
police constables on point and patrol duty in the vicinity
of Brett Street. This precaution was much more necessary for a man of his standing than for an obscure Assistant
Commissioner. Private Citizen Heat entered the street,
manœuvring in a way which in a member of the criminal
classes would have been stigmatized as slinking. The
piece of cloth picked up in Greenwich was in his pocket.
Not that he had the slightest intention of producing it in
his private capacity. On the contrary, he wanted to know
just what Mr. Verloc would be disposed to say voluntarily.
He hoped Mr. Verloc's talk would be of a nature to in-
criminate Michaelis. It was a conscientiously professional
hope in the main, but not without its moral value. For

Chief Inspector Heat was a servant of justice. Finding Mr. Verloc from home, he felt disappointed.

'I would wait for him a little if I were sure he wouldn't be long,' he said.

Mrs. Verloc volunteered no assurance of any kind.

'The information I need is quite private,' he repeated. 'You understand what I mean? I wonder if you could give me a notion where he's gone to?'

Mrs. Verloc shook her head.

'Can't say.'

She turned away to range some boxes on the shelves behind the counter. Chief Inspector Heat looked at her thoughtfully for a time.

'I suppose you know who I am?' he said.

Mrs. Verloc glanced over her shoulder. Chief Inspector Heat was amazed at her coolness.

'Come! You know I am in the police,' he said, sharply.

'I don't trouble my head much about it,' Mrs. Verloc remarked, returning to the ranging of her boxes.

'My name is Heat. Chief Inspector Heat of the Special Crimes section.'

Mrs. Verloc adjusted nicely in its place a small cardboard box, and turning round, faced him again, heavy-eyed, with idle hands hanging down. A silence reigned for a time.

'So your husband went out a quarter of an hour ago! And he didn't say when he would be back?'

'He didn't go out alone,' Mrs. Verloc let fall negligently.

'A friend?'

Mrs. Verloc touched the back of her hair. It was in perfect order.

'A stranger who called.'

'I see. What sort of man was that stranger? Would you mind telling me?'

Mrs. Verloc did not mind. And when Chief Inspector Heat heard of a man dark, thin, with a long face and turned-up moustaches, he gave signs of perturbation, and exclaimed:

'Dash me if I didn't think so! He hasn't lost any time.'

He was intensely disgusted in the secrecy of his heart at the unofficial conduct of his immediate chief. But he was not quixotic. He lost all desire to await Mr. Verloc's return. What they had gone out for he did not know, but he imagined it possible that they would return together. The case is not followed properly, it's being tampered with, he thought, bitterly.

'I am afraid I haven't time to wait for your husband,' he said.

Mrs. Verloc received this declaration listlessly. Her detachment had impressed Chief Inspector Heat all along. At this precise moment it whetted his curiosity. Chief Inspector Heat hung in the wind, swayed by his passions like the most private of citizens.

'I think,' he said, looking at her steadily, 'that you could give me a pretty good notion of what's going on if you liked.'

Forcing her fine, inert eyes to return his gaze, Mrs. Verloc murmured:

'Going on! What *is* going on?'

'Why, the affair I came to talk about a little with your husband.'

That day Mrs. Verloc had glanced at a morning paper as usual. But she had not stirred out of doors. The newsboys never invaded Brett Street. It was not a street for their business. And the echo of their cries, drifting along the populous thoroughfares, expired between the dirty brick walls without reaching the threshold of the shop. Her husband had not brought an evening paper home. At any rate she had not seen it. Mrs. Verloc knew nothing whatever of any affair. And she said so, with a genuine note of wonder in her quiet voice.

Chief Inspector Heat did not believe for a moment in

so much ignorance. Curtly, without amiability, he stated the bare fact.

Mrs. Verloc turned away her eyes.

'I call it silly,' she pronounced, slowly. She paused. 'We ain't downtrodden slaves here.'

The Chief Inspector waited watchfully. Nothing more came.

'And your husband didn't mention anything to you when he came home?'

Mrs. Verloc simply turned her face from right to left in sign of negation. A languid, baffling silence reigned in the shop. Chief Inspector Heat felt provoked beyond endurance.

'There was another small matter,' he began in a detached tone, 'which I wanted to speak to your husband about. There came into our hands a – a – what we believe is – a stolen overcoat.'

Mrs. Verloc, with her mind specially aware of thieves that evening, touched lightly the bosom of her dress.

'We have lost no overcoat,' she said, calmly.

'That's funny,' continued Private Citizen Heat. 'I see you keep a lot of marking ink here —'

He took up a small bottle, and looked at it against the gas-jet in the middle of the shop.

'Purple – isn't it?' he remarked, setting it down again. 'As I said, it's strange. Because the overcoat has got a label sewn on the inside with your address written in marking ink.'

Mrs. Verloc leaned over the counter with a low exclamation.

'That's my brother's, then.'

'Where's your brother? Can I see him?' asked the Chief Inspector, briskly. Mrs. Verloc leaned a little more over the counter.

'No. He isn't here. I wrote that label myself.'

'Where's your brother now?'

'He's been away living with – a friend – in the country.'

'The overcoat comes from the country. And what's the name of the friend?'

'Michaelis,' confessed Mrs. Verloc in an awed whisper.

The Chief Inspector let out a whistle. His eyes snapped.

'Just so. Capital. And your brother now, what's he like – a sturdy, darkish chap – eh?'

'Oh, no,' exclaimed Mrs. Verloc, fervently. 'That must be the thief. Stevie's slight and fair.'

'Good,' said the Chief Inspector in an approving tone. And while Mrs. Verloc, wavering between alarm and wonder, stared at him, he sought for information. Why have the address sewn like this inside the coat? And he heard that the mangled remains he had inspected that morning with extreme repugnance were those of a youth, nervous, absent-minded, peculiar, and also that the woman who was speaking to him had had the charge of that boy since he was a baby.

'Easily excitable?' he suggested.

'Oh, yes. He is. But how did he come to lose his coat —'

Chief Inspector Heat suddenly pulled out a pink newspaper he had bought less than half-an-hour ago. He was interested in horses. Forced by his calling into an attitude of doubt and suspicion towards his fellow-citizens, Chief Inspector Heat relieved the instinct of credulity implanted in the human breast by putting unbounded faith in the sporting prophets of that particular evening publication. Dropping the extra special on to the counter, he plunged his hand again into his pocket, and pulling out the piece of cloth fate had presented him with out of a heap of things that seemed to have been collected in shambles and rag shops, he offered it to Mrs. Verloc for inspection.

'I suppose you recognize this?'

She took it mechanically in both her hands. Her eyes seemed to grow bigger as she looked.

'Yes,' she whispered, then raised her head, and staggered backward a little.

'Whatever for is it torn out like this?'

The Chief Inspector snatched across the counter the cloth out of her hands, and she sat heavily on the chair. He thought: identification's perfect. And in that moment he had a glimpse into the whole amazing truth. Verloc was the 'other man'.

'Mrs. Verloc,' he said, 'it strikes me that you know more of this bomb affair than even you yourself are aware of.'

Mrs. Verloc sat still, amazed, lost in boundless astonishment. What was the connection? And she became so rigid all over that she was not able to turn her head at the clatter of the bell, which caused the private investigator Heat to spin round on his heel. Mr. Verloc had shut the door, and for a moment the two men looked at each other.

Mr. Verloc, without looking at his wife, walked up to the Chief Inspector, who was relieved to see him return alone.

'You here!' muttered Mr. Verloc, heavily. 'Who are you after?'

'No one,' said Chief Inspector Heat in a low tone. 'Look here, I would like a word or two with you.'

Mr. Verloc, still pale, had brought an air of resolution with him. Still he didn't look at his wife. He said:

'Come in here, then.' And he led the way into the parlour.

The door was hardly shut when Mrs. Verloc, jumping up from the chair, ran to it as if to fling it open, but instead of doing so fell on her knees, with her ear to the keyhole. The two men must have stopped directly they were through, because she heard plainly the Chief

Inspector's voice, though she could not see his finger pressed against her husband's breast emphatically.

'You are the other man, Verloc. Two men were seen entering the park.'

And the voice of Mr. Verloc said:

'Well, take me now. What's to prevent you? You have the right.'

'Oh, no! I know too well who you have been giving yourself away to. He'll have to manage this little affair all by himself. But don't you make a mistake, it's I who found you out.'

Then she heard only muttering. Inspector Heat must have been showing to Mr. Verloc the piece of Stevie's overcoat, because Stevie's sister, guardian, and protector heard her husband a little louder.

'I never noticed that she had hit upon that dodge.'

Again for a time Mrs. Verloc heard nothing but murmurs, whose mysteriousness was less nightmarish to her brain than the horrible suggestions of shaped words. Then Chief Inspector Heat, on the other side of the door, raised his voice:

'You must have been mad.'

And Mr. Verloc's voice answered, with a sort of gloomy fury:

'I have been mad for a month or more, but I am not mad now. It's all over. It shall all come out of my head, and hang the consequences.'

There was a silence, and then Private Citizen Heat murmured:

'What's coming out?'

'Everything,' exclaimed the voice of Mr. Verloc, and then sank very low.

After a while it rose again.

'You have known me for several years now, and you've found me useful, too. You know I was a straight man. Yes, straight.'

This appeal to old acquaintance must have been extremely distasteful to the Chief Inspector.

His voice took on a warning note.

'Don't you trust so much to what you have been promised. If I were you I would clear out. I don't think we will run after you.'

Mr. Verloc was heard to laugh a little.

'Oh, yes; you hope the others will get rid of me for you – don't you? No, no; you don't shake me off now. I have been a straight man to those people too long, and now everything must come out.'

'Let it come out, then,' the indifferent voice of Chief Inspector Heat assented. 'But tell me now how did you get away?'

'I was making for Chesterfield Walk,' Mrs. Verloc heard her husband's voice, 'when I heard the bang. I started running then. Fog. I saw no one till I was past the end of George Street. Don't think I met any one till then.'

'So easy as that!' marvelled the voice of Chief Inspector Heat. 'The bang startled you, eh?'

'Yes; it came too soon,' confessed the gloomy, husky voice of Mr. Verloc.

Mrs. Verloc pressed her ear to the keyhole; her lips were blue, her hands cold as ice, and her pale face, in which the two eyes seemed like two black holes, felt to her as if it were enveloped in flames.

On the other side of the door the voices sank very low. She caught words now and then, sometimes in her husband's voice, sometimes in the smooth tones of the Chief Inspector. She heard this last say:

'We believe he stumbled against the root of a tree?'

There was a husky, voluble murmur, which lasted for some time, and then the Chief Inspector, as if answering some inquiry, spoke emphatically:

'Of course. Blown to small bits: limbs, gravel, clothing, bones, splinters – all mixed up together. I tell you they had to fetch a shovel to gather him up with.'

Mrs. Verloc sprang up suddenly from her crouching position, and stopping her ears, reeled to and fro between the counter and the shelves on the wall towards the chair. Her crazed eyes noted the sporting sheet left by the Chief Inspector, and as she knocked herself against the counter she snatched it up, fell into the chair, tore the optimistic, rosy sheet right across in trying to open it, then flung it on the floor. On the other side of the door, Chief Inspector Heat was saying to Mr. Verloc, the secret agent:

'So your defence will be practically a full confession?'

'It will. I am going to tell the whole story.'

'You won't be believed as much as you fancy you will.'

And the Chief Inspector remained thoughtful. The turn this affair was taking meant the disclosure of many things – the laying waste of fields of knowledge, which, cultivated by a capable man, had a distinct value for the individual and for the society. It was sorry, sorry meddling. It would leave Michaelis unscathed; it would drag to light the Professor's home industry; disorganize the whole system of supervision; make no end of a row in the papers, which, from that point of view, appeared to him by a sudden illumination as invariably written by fools for the reading of imbeciles. Mentally he agreed with the words Mr. Verloc let fall at last in answer to his last remark.

'Perhaps not. But it will upset many things. I have been a straight man, and I shall keep straight in this —'

'If they let you,' said the Chief Inspector, cynically. 'You will be preached to, no doubt, before they put you into the dock. And in the end you may yet get let in for a sentence that will surprise you. I wouldn't trust too much the gentleman who's been talking to you.'

Mr. Verloc listened, frowning.

'My advice to you is to clear out while you may. I have no instructions. There are some of them,' continued Chief Inspector Heat, laying a peculiar stress on the word 'them', 'who think you are already out of the world.'

'Indeed!' Mr. Verloc was moved to say. Though since his return from Greenwich he had spent most of his time sitting in the tap-room of an obscure little public-house, he could hardly have hoped for such favourable news.

'That's the impression about you.' The Chief Inspector nodded at him. 'Vanish. Clear out.'

'Where to?' snarled Mr. Verloc. He raised his head, and gazing at the closed door of the parlour, muttered feelingly: 'I only wish you would take me away to-night. I would go quietly.'

'I daresay,' assented sardonically the Chief Inspector, following the direction of his glance.

The brow of Mr. Verloc broke into slight moisture. He lowered his husky voice confidentially before the unmoved Chief Inspector.

'The lad was half-witted, irresponsible. Any court would have seen that at once. Only fit for the asylum. And that was the worst that would've happened to him if —'

The Chief Inspector, his hand on the door handle, whispered into Mr. Verloc's face:

'He may've been half-witted, but you must have been crazy. What drove you off your head like this?'

Mr. Verloc, thinking of Mr. Vladimir, did not hesitate in the choice of words.

'A Hyperborean swine,' he hissed, forcibly. 'A what you might call a – a gentleman.'

The Chief Inspector, steady-eyed, nodded briefly his comprehension, and opened the door. Mrs. Verloc, behind the counter, might have heard but did not see his departure, pursued by the aggressive clatter of the bell. She sat at her post of duty behind the counter. She sat rigidly erect in the chair with two dirty pink pieces of paper lying spread out at her feet. The palms of her hands were pressed convulsively to her face, with the

tips of the fingers contracted against the forehead, as
though the skin had been a mask which she was ready to
tear off violently. The perfect immobility of her pose
expressed the agitation of rage and despair, all the potential violence of tragic passions, better than any shallow
display of shrieks, with the beating of a distracted head
against the walls, could have done. Chief Inspector Heat,
crossing the shop at his busy, swinging pace, gave her
only a cursory glance. And when the cracked bell ceased
to tremble on its curved ribbon of steel nothing stirred
near Mrs. Verloc, as if her attitude had the locking power
of a spell. Even the butterfly-shaped gas flames posed on
the ends of the suspended T-bracket burned without a
quiver. In that shop of shady wares fitted with deal
shelves painted a dull brown, which seemed to devour
the sheen of the light, the gold circlet of the wedding
ring on Mrs. Verloc's left hand glittered exceedingly with
the untarnished glory of a piece from some splendid
treasure of jewels, dropped in a dust-bin.

CHAPTER TEN

THE Assistant Commissioner, driven rapidly in a hansom from the neighbourhood of Soho in the direction of Westminster, got out at the very centre of the Empire on which the sun never sets. Some stalwart constables, who did not seem particularly impressed by the duty of watching the august spot, saluted him. Penetrating through a portal by no means lofty into the precincts of the House which is *the* House, *par excellence*, in the minds of many millions of men, he was met at last by the volatile and revolutionary Toodles.

That neat and nice young man concealed his astonishment at the early appearance of the Assistant Commissioner, whom he had been told to look out for some time about midnight. His turning up so early he concluded to be the sign that things, whatever they were, had gone wrong. With an extremely ready sympathy, which in nice youngsters goes often with a joyous temperament, he felt sorry for the great Presence he called 'The Chief', and also for the Assistant Commissioner, whose face appeared to him more ominously wooden than ever before, and quite wonderfully long. 'What a queer, foreign-looking chap he is,' he thought to himself, smiling from a distance with friendly buoyancy. And directly they came together he began to talk with the kind intention of burying the awkwardness of failure under a heap of words. It looked as if the great assault threatened for that night were going to fizzle out. An inferior henchman of 'that brute Cheeseman' was up

195

boring mercilessly a very thin House with some shamelessly cooked statistics. He, Toodles, hoped he would
bore them into a count out every minute. But then he
might be only marking time to let that guzzling Cheeseman dine at his leisure. Anyway, the Chief could not be
persuaded to go home.

'He will see you at once, I think. He's sitting all alone
in his room thinking of all the fishes of the sea,' concluded Toodles, airily. 'Come along.'

Notwithstanding the kindness of his disposition, the
young private secretary (unpaid) was accessible to the
common failings of humanity. He did not wish to harrow
the feelings of the Assistant Commissioner, who looked
to him uncommonly like a man who has made a mess of
his job. But his curiosity was too strong to be restrained
by mere compassion. He could not help, as they went
along, to throw over his shoulder lightly:

'And your sprat?'

'Got him,' answered the Assistant Commissioner with
a concision which did not mean to be repellent in the
least.

'Good. You've no idea how these great men dislike to
be disappointed in small things.'

After this profound observation the experienced
Toodles seemed to reflect. At any rate he said nothing for
quite two seconds. Then:

'I'm glad. But – I say – is it really such a very small
thing as you make it out?'

'Do you know what may be done with a sprat?' the
Assistant Commissioner asked in his turn.

'He's sometimes put into a sardine box,' chuckled
Toodles, whose erudition on the subject of the fishing
industry was fresh and, in comparison with his ignorance
of all other industrial matters, immense. 'There are
sardine canneries on the Spanish coast which —'

The Assistant Commissioner interrupted the appren-
tice statesman.

'Yes. Yes. But a sprat is also thrown away sometimes in order to catch a whale.'

'A whale. Phew!' exclaimed Toodles, with bated breath. 'You're after a whale, then?'

'Not exactly. What I am after is more like a dog-fish. You don't know perhaps what a dog-fish is like.'

'Yes; I do. We're buried in special books up to our necks – whole shelves full of them – with plates. . . . It's a noxious, rascally-looking, altogether detestable beast, with a sort of smooth face and moustaches.'

'Described to a T,' commended the Assistant Commissioner. 'Only mine is clean-shaven altogether. You've seen him. It's a witty fish.'

'I have seen him!' said Toodles, incredulously. 'I can't conceive where I could have seen him.'

'At the Explorers', I should say,' dropped the Assistant Commissioner, calmly. At the name of that extremely exclusive club Toodles looked scared, and stopped short.

'Nonsense,' he protested, but in an awestruck tone. 'What do you mean? A member?'

'Honorary,' muttered the Assistant Commissioner through his teeth.

'Heavens!'

Toodles looked so thunderstruck that the Assistant Commissioner smiled faintly.

'That's between ourselves strictly,' he said.

'That's the beastliest thing I've ever heard in my life,' declared Toodles, feebly, as if astonishment had robbed him of all his buoyant strength in a second.

The Assistant Commissioner gave him an unsmiling glance. Till they came to the door of the great man's room, Toodles preserved a scandalized and solemn silence, as though he were offended with the Assistant Commissioner for exposing such an unsavoury and disturbing fact. It revolutionized his idea of the Explorers' Club's extreme selectness, of its social purity. Toodles was revolutionary only in politics; his social beliefs and

personal feelings he wished to preserve unchanged
through all the years allotted to him on this earth
which, upon the whole, he believed to be a nice place to
live on.

He stood aside.

'Go in without knocking,' he said.

Shades of green silk fitted low over all the lights
imparted to the room something of a forest's deep gloom.
The haughty eyes were physically the great man's weak
point. This point was wrapped up in secrecy. When an
opportunity offered, he rested them conscientiously.
The Assistant Commissioner entering saw at first only a
big pale hand supporting a big head, and concealing the
upper part of a big pale face. An open despatch-box
stood on the writing-table near a few oblong sheets of
paper and a scattered handful of quill pens. There was
absolutely nothing else on the large flat surface except a
little bronze statuette draped in a toga, mysteriously
watchful in its shadowy immobility. The Assistant Commissioner, invited to take a chair, sat down. In the dim
light, the salient points of his personality, the long face,
the black hair, his lankness, made him look more foreign
than ever.

The great man manifested no surprise, no eagerness,
no sentiment whatever. The attitude in which he rested
his menaced eyes was profoundly meditative. He did not
alter it the least bit. But his tone was not dreamy.

'Well! What is it that you've found out already? You
came upon something unexpected on the first step.'

'Not exactly unexpected, Sir Ethelred. What I mainly
came upon was a psychological state.'

The Great Presence made a slight movement.

'You must be lucid, please.'

'Yes, Sir Ethelred. You know no doubt that most criminals at some time or other feel an irresistible need of con-
fessing – of making a clean breast of it to somebody –
to anybody. And they do it often to the police. In that

Verloc whom Heat wished so much to screen I've found a man in that particular psychological state. The man, figuratively speaking, flung himself on my breast. It was enough on my part to whisper to him who I was and to add "I know that you are at the bottom of this affair." It must have seemed miraculous to him that we should know already, but he took it all in the stride. The wonderfulness of it never checked him for a moment. There remained for me only to put to him the two questions: Who put you up to it? and Who was the man who did it? He answered the first with remarkable emphasis. As to the second question, I gather that the fellow with the bomb was his brother-in-law – quite a lad – a weak-minded creature. . . . It is rather a curious affair – too long perhaps to state fully just now.'

'What then have you learned?' asked the great man.

'First, I've learned that the ex-convict Michaelis had nothing to do with it, though indeed the lad had been living with him temporarily in the country up to eight o'clock this morning. It is more than likely that Michaelis knows nothing of it to this moment.'

'You are positive as to that?' asked the great man.

'Quite certain, Sir Ethelred. This fellow Verloc went there this morning, and took away the lad on the pretence of going out for a walk in the lanes. As it was not the first time that he did this, Michaelis could not have the slightest suspicion of anything unusual. For the rest, Sir Ethelred, the indignation of this man Verloc had left nothing in doubt – nothing whatever. He had been driven out of his mind almost by an extraordinary performance, which for you or me it would be difficult to take as seriously meant, but which produced a great impression obviously on him.'

The Assistant Commissioner then imparted briefly to the great man, who sat still, resting his eyes under the screen of his hand, Mr. Verloc's appreciation of Mr. Vladimir's proceedings and character. The Assistant

Commissioner did not seem to refuse it a certain amount
of competency. But the great personage remarked:

'All this seems very fantastic.'

'Doesn't it? One would think a ferocious joke. But our
man took it seriously, it appears. He felt himself threatened. Formerly, you know, he was in direct communication with old Stott-Wartenheim himself, and had come to
regard his services as indispensable. It was an extremely
rude awakening. I imagine that he lost his head. He
became angry and frightened. Upon my word, my
impression is that he thought these Embassy people
quite capable not only to throw him out but to give him
away, too, in some manner or other —'

'How long were you with him?' interrupted the
Presence from behind his big hand.

'Some forty minutes, Sir Ethelred, in a house of bad
repute called Continental Hotel, closeted in a room
which by-the-by I took for the night. I found him under
the influence of that reaction which follows the effort of
crime. The man cannot be defined as a hardened criminal. It is obvious that he did not plan the death of that
wretched lad – his brother-in-law. That was a shock to
him – I could see that. Perhaps he is a man of strong sensibilities. Perhaps he was even fond of the lad – who
knows? He might have hoped that the fellow would get
clear away; in which case it would have been almost
impossible to bring this thing home to any one. At any rate,
he risked consciously nothing more but arrest for him.'

The Assistant Commissioner paused in his speculations to reflect for a moment.

'Though how, in that last case, he could hope to have
his own share in the business concealed is more than I
can tell,' he continued, in his ignorance of poor Stevie's
devotion to Mr. Verloc (who was *good*), and of his truly
peculiar dumbness, which in the old affair of fireworks
on the stairs had for many years resisted entreaties, coax-
ing, anger, and other means of investigation used by his

beloved sister. For Stevie was loyal. . . . 'No, I can't imagine. It's possible that he never thought of that at all. It sounds an extravagant way of putting it, Sir Ethelred, but his state of dismay suggested to me an impulsive man who, after committing suicide with the notion that it would end all his troubles, had discovered that it did nothing of the kind.'

The Assistant Commissioner gave this definition in an apologetic voice. But in truth there is a sort of lucidity proper to extravagant language, and the great man was not offended. A slight jerky movement of the big body half lost in the gloom of the green silk shades, of the big head leaning on the big hand, accompanied an intermittent stifled but powerful sound. The great man had laughed.

'What have you done with him?'

The Assistant Commissioner answered very readily:

'As he seemed very anxious to get back to his wife in the shop I let him go, Sir Ethelred.'

'You did? But the fellow will disappear.'

'Pardon me. I don't think so. Where could he go to? Moreover, you must remember that he has got to think of the danger from his comrades, too. He's there at his post. How could he explain leaving it? But even if there were no obstacles to his freedom of action he would do nothing. At present he hasn't enough moral energy to take a resolution of any sort. Permit me also to point out that if I had detained him we would have been committed to a course of action on which I wished to know your precise intentions first.'

The great personage rose heavily, an imposing, shadowy form in the greenish gloom of the room.

'I'll see the Attorney-General to-night, and will send for you to-morrow morning. Is there anything more you'd wish to tell me now?'

The Assistant Commissioner had stood up also, slender and flexible.

'I think not, Sir Ethelred, unless I were to enter into details which —'

'No. No details, please.'

The great shadowy form seemed to shrink away as if in physical dread of details; then came forward, expanded, enormous, and weighty, offering a large hand. 'And you say that this man has got a wife?'

'Yes, Sir Ethelred,' said the Assistant Commissioner, pressing deferentially the extended hand. 'A genuine wife and a genuinely, respectably, marital relation. He told me that after his interview at the Embassy he would have thrown everything up, would have tried to sell his shop, and leave the country, only he felt certain that his wife would not even hear of going abroad. Nothing could be more characteristic of the respectable bond than that,' went on, with a touch of grimness, the Assistant Commissioner, whose own wife, too, had refused to hear of going abroad. 'Yes, a genuine wife. And the victim was a genuine brother-in-law. From a certain point of view we are here in the presence of a domestic drama.'

The Assistant Commissioner laughed a little; but the great man's thoughts seemed to have wandered far away, perhaps to the questions of his country's domestic policy, the battle-ground of his crusading valour against the paynim Cheeseman. The Assistant Commissioner withdrew quietly, unnoticed, as if already forgotten.

He had his own crusading instincts. This affair, which, in one way or another, disgusted Chief Inspector Heat, seemed to him a providentially given starting-point for a crusade. He had it much at heart to begin. He walked slowly home, meditating that enterprise on the way, and thinking over Mr. Verloc's psychology in a composite mood of repugnance and satisfaction. He walked all the way home. Finding the drawing-room dark, he went upstairs, and spent some time between the bedroom and the dressing-room, changing his clothes, going to and fro with the air of a thoughtful somnambulist. But he shook it off before going out again to join his wife at the house of the great lady patroness of Michaelis.

He knew he would be welcome there. On entering the smaller of the two drawing-rooms he saw his wife in a small group near the piano. A youngish composer in pass of becoming famous was discoursing from a music stool to two thick men whose backs looked old, and three slender women whose backs looked young. Behind the screen the great lady had only two persons with her: a man and a woman, who sat side by side on armchairs at the foot of her couch. She extended her hand to the Assistant Commissioner.

'I never hoped to see you here to-night. Annie told me —'

'Yes. I had no idea myself that my work would be over so soon.'

The Assistant Commissioner added in a low tone: 'I am glad to tell you that Michaelis is altogether clear of this —'

The patroness of the ex-convict received this assurance indignantly.

'Why? Were your people stupid enough to connect him with —'

'Not stupid,' interrupted the Assistant Commissioner, contradicting deferentially. 'Clever enough – quite clever enough for that.'

A silence fell. The man at the foot of the couch had stopped speaking to the lady, and looked on with a faint smile.

'I don't know whether you ever met before,' said the great lady.

Mr. Vladimir and the Assistant Commissioner, introduced, acknowledged each other's existence with punctilious and guarded courtesy.

'He's been frightening me,' declared suddenly the lady who sat by the side of Mr. Vladimir, with an inclina-

tion of the head towards that gentleman. The Assistant
Commissioner knew the lady.

'You do not look frightened,' he pronounced, after sur-
veying her conscientiously with his tired and equable
gaze. He was thinking meantime to himself that in this
house one met everybody sooner or later. Mr. Vladimir's
rosy countenance was wreathed in smiles, because he
was witty, but his eyes remained serious, like the eyes of
convinced man.

'Well, he tried to at least,' amended the lady.

'Force of habit perhaps,' said the Assistant Commissioner, moved by an irresistible inspiration.

'He has been threatening society with all sorts of horrors,' continued the lady, whose enunciation was caress-
ing and slow, 'apropos of this explosion in Greenwich
Park. It appears we all ought to quake in our shoes at
what's coming if those people are not suppressed all over
the world. I had no idea this was such a grave affair.'

Mr. Vladimir, affecting not to listen, leaned towards
the couch, talking amiably in subdued tones, but he
heard the Assistant Commissioner say:

'I've no doubt that Mr. Vladimir has a very precise
notion of the true importance of this affair.'

Mr. Vladimir asked himself what that confounded and
intrusive policeman was driving at. Descended from
generations victimized by the instruments of an arbitrary
power, he was racially, nationally, and individually afraid
of the police. It was an inherited weakness, altogether
independent of his judgment, of his reason, of his
experience. He was born to it. But that sentiment, which
resembled the irrational horror some people have of cats,
did not stand in the way of his immense contempt for the
English police. He finished the sentence addressed to
the great lady, and turned slightly in his chair.

'You mean that we have a great experience of these
people. Yes; indeed, we suffer greatly from their activity,
while you' – Mr. Vladimir hesitated for a moment, in

smiling perplexity – 'While you suffer their presence gladly in your midst,' he finished, displaying a dimple in each clean-shaven cheek. Then he added more gravely: 'I may even say – because you do.'

When Mr. Vladimir ceased speaking the Assistant Commissioner lowered his glance, and the conversation dropped. Almost immediately afterwards Mr. Vladimir took leave. Directly his back was turned on the couch the Assistant Commissioner rose, too.

'I thought you were going to stay and take Annie home,' said the lady patroness of Michaelis.

'I find that I've yet a little work to do to-night.'

'In connection —?'

'Well, yes – in a way.'

'Tell me, what is it really – this horror?'

'It's difficult to say what it is, but it may yet be a *cause célèbre*,' said the Assistant Commissioner.

He left the drawing-room hurriedly, and found Mr. Vladimir still in the hall, wrapping up his throat carefully in a large silk handkerchief. Behind him a footman waited, holding his overcoat. Another stood ready to open the door. The Assistant Commissioner was duly helped into his coat, and let out at once. After descending the front steps he stopped, as if to consider the way he should take. On seeing this through the door held open, Mr. Vladimir lingered in the hall to get out a cigar and asked for a light. It was furnished to him by an elderly man out of livery with an air of calm solicitude. But the match went out; the footman then closed the door, and Mr. Vladimir lighted his large Havana with leisurely care. When at last he got out of the house, he saw with disgust the 'confounded policeman' still standing on the pavement.

'Can he be waiting for me?' thought Mr. Vladimir, looking up and down for some signs of a hansom. He saw none. A couple of carriages waited by the curbstone, their lamps blazing steadily, the horses standing perfectly still, as if carved in stone, the coachmen sitting motionless under the big fur capes, without as much as a quiver stirring the white thongs of their big whips. Mr. Vladimir walked on, and the 'confounded policeman' fell into step at his elbow. He said nothing. At the end of the fourth stride Mr. Vladimir felt infuriated and uneasy. This could not last.

'Rotten weather,' he growled, savagely.

'Mild,' said the Assistant Commissioner without passion. He remained silent for a little while. 'We've got hold of a man called Verloc,' he announced, casually.

Mr. Vladimir did not stumble, did not stagger back, did not change his stride. But he could not prevent himself from exclaiming: 'What?' The Assistant Commissioner did not repeat his statement. 'You know him,' he went on in the same tone.

Mr. Vladimir stopped, and became guttural.

'What makes you say that?'

'I don't. It's Verloc who says that.'

'A lying dog of some sort,' said Mr. Vladimir in somewhat Oriental phraseology. But in his heart he was almost awed by the miraculous cleverness of the English police. The change of his opinion on the subject was so violent that it made him for a moment feel slightly sick. He threw away his cigar, and moved on.

'What pleased me most in this affair,' the Assistant Commissioner went on, talking slowly, 'is that it makes such an excellent starting-point for a piece of work which I've felt must be taken in hand – that is, the clearing out of this country of all the foreign political spies, police, and that sort of – of – dogs. In my opinion they are a ghastly nuisance; also an element of danger. But we can't very well seek them out individually. The only way is to make their employment unpleasant to their employers. The thing's becoming indecent. And dangerous, too, for us, here.'

Mr. Vladimir stopped again for a moment.

'What do you mean?'

'The prosecution of this Verloc will demonstrate to the public both the danger and the indecency.'

'Nobody will believe what a man of that sort says,' said Mr. Vladimir, contemptuously.

'The wealth and precision of detail will carry conviction to the great mass of the public,' advanced the Assistant Commissioner gently.

'So that is seriously what you mean to do.'

'We've got the man; we have no choice.'

'You will be only feeding up the lying spirit of these revolutionary scoundrels,' Mr. Vladimir protested. 'What do you want to make a scandal for? – from morality – or what?'

Mr. Vladimir's anxiety was obvious. The Assistant Commissioner, having ascertained in this way that there must be some truth in the summary statements of Mr. Verloc, said indifferently:

'There's a practical side, too. We have really enough to do to look after the genuine article. You can't say we are not effective. But we don't intend to let ourselves be bothered by shams under any pretext whatever.'

Mr. Vladimir's tone became lofty.

'For my part, I can't share your view. It is selfish. My sentiments for my own country cannot be doubted; but I've always felt that we ought to be good Europeans besides – I mean governments and men.'

'Yes,' said the Assistant Commissioner simply. 'Only you look at Europe from its other end. But,' he went on in a good-natured tone, 'the foreign governments cannot complain of the inefficiency of our police. Look at this outrage; a case specially difficult to trace inasmuch as it was a sham. In less than twelve hours we have established the identity of a man literally blown to shreds, have found the organizer of the attempt, and have had a glimpse of the inciter behind him. And we could have gone further; only we stopped at the limits of our territory.'

'So this instructive crime was planned abroad,' Mr. Vladimir said, quickly. 'You admit it was planned abroad?'

'Theoretically. Theoretically only, on foreign territory; abroad only by a fiction,' said the Assistant Commissioner, alluding to the character of Embassies which are supposed to be part and parcel of the country to which they belong. 'But that's a detail. I talked to you of this business because it's your government that grumbles most at our police. You see that we are not so bad. I wanted particularly to tell you of our success.'

'I'm sure I'm very grateful,' muttered Mr. Vladimir through his teeth.

'We can put our finger on every anarchist here,' went on the Assistant Commissioner, as though he were quoting Chief Inspector Heat. 'All that's wanted now is to do away with the agent provocateur to make everything safe.'

Mr. Vladimir held up his hand to a passing hansom.

'You're not going in here,' remarked the Assistant Commissioner, looking at a building of noble proportions and hospitable aspect, with the light of a great hall falling through its glass doors on a broad flight of steps.

But Mr. Vladimir, sitting, stony-eyed, inside the hansom, drove off without a word.

The Assistant Commissioner himself did not turn into the noble building. It was the Explorers' Club. The thought passed through his mind that Mr. Vladimir, honorary member, would not be seen very often there in the future. He looked at his watch. It was only half-past ten. He had had a very full evening.

CHAPTER ELEVEN

FTER Chief Inspector Heat had left him Mr. Verloc moved about the parlour. From time to time he eyed his wife through the open door. 'She knows all about it now,' he thought to himself with commiseration for her sorrow and with some satisfaction as regarded himself. Mr. Verloc's soul, if lacking greatness perhaps, was capable of tender sentiments. The prospect of having to break the news to her had put him into a fever. Chief Inspector Heat had relieved him of the task. That was good as far as it went. It remained for him now to face her grief.

Mr. Verloc had never expected to have to face it on account of death, whose catastrophic character cannot be argued away by sophisticated reasoning or persuasive eloquence. Mr. Verloc never meant Stevie to perish with such abrupt violence. He did not mean him to perish at all. Stevie dead was a much greater nuisance than ever he had been when alive. Mr. Verloc had augured a favourable issue to his enterprise, basing himself not on Stevie's intelligence, which sometimes plays queer tricks with a man, but on the blind docility and on the blind devotion of the boy. Though not much of a psychologist, Mr. Verloc had gauged the depth of Stevie's fanaticism. He dared cherish the hope of Stevie walking away from the walls of the Observatory as he had been instructed to do, taking the way shown to him several times previously, and rejoining his brother-in-law, the wise and good Mr. Verloc, outside the precincts of the

park. Fifteen minutes ought to have been enough for the
veriest fool to deposit the engine and walk away. And the
Professor had guaranteed more than fifteen minutes. But
Stevie had stumbled within five minutes of being left to
himself. And Mr. Verloc was shaken morally to pieces.
He had foreseen everything but that. He had foreseen
Stevie distracted and lost – sought for – found in some
police station or provincial workhouse in the end. He
had foreseen Stevie arrested, and was not afraid, because
Mr. Verloc had a great opinion of Stevie's loyalty, which
had been carefully indoctrinated with the necessity of
silence in the course of many walks. Like a peripatetic
philosopher, Mr. Verloc, strolling along the streets of
London, had modified Stevie's view of the police by
conversations full of subtle reasonings. Never had a sage
a more attentive and admiring disciple. The submission
and worship were so apparent that Mr. Verloc had come
to feel something like a liking for the boy. In any case, he
had not foreseen the swift bringing home of his connection. That his wife should hit upon the precaution of
sewing the boy's address inside his overcoat was the last
thing Mr. Verloc would have thought of. One can't think
of everything. That was what she meant when she said
that he need not worry if he lost Stevie during their
walks. She had assured him that the boy would turn up
all right. Well, he had turned up with a vengeance!

'Well, well,' muttered Mr. Verloc in his wonder. What
did she mean by it? Spare him the trouble of keeping an
anxious eye on Stevie? Most likely she had meant well.
Only she ought to have told him of the precaution she
had taken.

Mr. Verloc walked behind the counter of the shop. His
intention was not to overwhelm his wife with bitter
reproaches. Mr. Verloc felt no bitterness. The unexpected march of events had converted him to the doctrine of fatalism. Nothing could be helped now. He said:

'I didn't mean any harm to come to the boy.'

Mrs. Verloc shuddered at the sound of her husband's voice. She did not uncover her face. The trusted secret agent of the late Baron Stott-Wartenheim looked at her for a time with a heavy, persistent, undiscerning glance. The torn evening paper was lying at her feet. It could not have told her much. Mr. Verloc felt the need of talking to his wife.

'It's that damned Heat – eh?' he said. 'He upset you. He's a brute, blurting it out like this to a woman. I made myself ill thinking how to break it to you. I sat for hours in the little parlour of Cheshire Cheese thinking over the best way. You understand I never meant any harm to come to that boy.'

Mr. Verloc, the Secret Agent, was speaking the truth. It was his marital affection that had received the greatest shock from the premature explosion. He added:

'I didn't feel particularly gay sitting there and thinking of you.'

He observed another slight shudder of his wife, which affected his sensibility. As she persisted in hiding her face in her hands, he thought he had better leave her alone for a while. On this delicate impulse Mr. Verloc withdrew into the parlour again, where the gas-jet purred like a contented cat. Mrs. Verloc's wifely forethought had left the cold beef on the table with carving knife and fork and half a loaf of bread for Mr. Verloc's supper. He noticed all these things now for the first time, and cutting himself a piece of bread and meat, began to eat.

His appetite did not proceed from callousness. Mr. Verloc had not eaten any breakfast that day. He had left his home fasting. Not being an energetic man, he found his resolution in nervous excitement, which seemed to hold him mainly by the throat. He could not have swallowed anything solid. Michaelis' cottage was as destitute of provisions as the cell of a prisoner. The ticket-of-leave apostle lived on a little milk and crusts of stale bread. Moreover, when Mr. Verloc arrived he had already gone

upstairs after his frugal meal. Absorbed in the toil and
delight of literary composition, he had not even
answered Mr. Verloc's shout up the little staircase.

'I am taking this young fellow home for a day or two.'

And, in truth, Mr. Verloc did not wait for an answer,
but had marched out of the cottage at once, followed by
the obedient Stevie.

Now that all action was over and his fate taken out of
his hands with unexpected swiftness, Mr. Verloc felt terribly empty physically. He carved the meat, cut the
bread, and devoured his supper standing by the table,
and now and then casting a glance towards his wife. Her
prolonged immobility disturbed the comfort of his refection. He walked again into the shop, and came up very
close to her. This sorrow with a veiled face made Mr.
Verloc uneasy. He expected, of course, his wife to be
very much upset, but he wanted her to pull herself
together. He needed all her assistance and all her loyalty
in these new conjunctures his fatalism had already
accepted.

'Can't be helped,' he said in a tone of gloomy sympathy. 'Come, Winnie, we've got to think of to-morrow.
You'll want all your wits about you after I am taken
away.'

He paused. Mrs. Verloc's breast heaved convulsively.
This was not reassuring to Mr. Verloc, in whose view the
newly created situation required from the two people
most concerned in it calmness, decision, and other
qualities incompatible with the mental disorder of passionate sorrow. Mr. Verloc was a humane man; he had
come home prepared to allow every latitude to his wife's
affection for her brother. Only he did not understand
either the nature or the whole extent of that sentiment.
And in this he was excusable, since it was impossible for
him to understand it without ceasing to be himself. He
was startled and disappointed, and his speech conveyed
it by a certain roughness of tone.

'You might look at a fellow,' he observed after waiting a while.

As if forced through the hands covering Mrs. Verloc's face the answer came, deadened, almost pitiful.

'I don't want to look at you as long as I live.'

'Eh? What!' Mr. Verloc was merely startled by the superficial and literal meaning of this declaration. It was obviously unreasonable, the mere cry of exaggerated grief. He threw over it the mantle of his marital indulgence. The mind of Mr. Verloc lacked profundity. Under the mistaken impression that the value of individuals consists in what they are in themselves, he could not possibly comprehend the value of Stevie in the eyes of Mrs. Verloc. She was taking it confoundedly hard, he thought to himself. It was all the fault of that damned Heat. What did he want to upset the woman for? But she mustn't be allowed, for her own good, to carry on so till she got quite beside herself.

'Look here! You can't sit like this in the shop,' he said with affected severity, in which there was some real annoyance; for urgent practical matters must be talked over if they had to sit up all night. 'Somebody might come in at any minute,' he added, and waited again. No effect was produced, and the idea of the finality of death occurred to Mr. Verloc during the pause. He changed his tone. 'Come. This won't bring him back,' he said, gently, feeling ready to take her in his arms and press her to his breast, where impatience and compassion dwelt side by side. But except for a short shudder Mrs. Verloc remained apparently unaffected by the force of that terrible truism. It was Mr. Verloc himself who was moved. He was moved in his simplicity to urge moderation by asserting the claims of his own personality.

'Do be reasonable, Winnie. What would it have been if you had lost me?'

He had vaguely expected to hear her cry out. But she did not budge. She leaned back a little, quieted down to

a complete, unreadable stillness. Mr. Verloc's heart began
to beat faster with exasperation and something resembling alarm. He laid his hand on her shoulder, saying:
    'Don't be a fool, Winnie.'
    She gave no sign. It was impossible to talk to any pur-
pose with a woman whose face one cannot see. Mr. Verloc caught hold of his wife's wrists. But her hands
seemed glued fast. She swayed forward bodily to his tug,
and nearly went off the chair. Startled to feel her so helplessly limp, he was trying to put her back on the chair
when she stiffened suddenly all over, tore herself out of
his hands, ran out of the shop, across the parlour, and into
the kitchen. This was very swift. He had just a glimpse
of her face and that much of her eyes that he knew she
had not looked at him.
    It all had the appearance of a struggle for the posses-
sion of a chair, because Mr. Verloc instantly took his
wife's place in it. Mr. Verloc did not cover his face with
his hands, but a sombre thoughtfulness veiled his features. A term of imprisonment could not be avoided. He
did not wish now to avoid it. A prison was a place as safe
from certain unlawful vengeances as the grave, with this
advantage, that in a prison there is room for hope. What
he saw before him was a term of imprisonment, an early
release, and then life abroad somewhere, such as he had
contemplated already, in case of failure. Well, it was a
failure, if not exactly the sort of failure he had feared. It
had been so near success that he could have positively
terrified Mr. Vladimir out of his ferocious scoffing with
this proof of occult efficiency. So at least it seemed now
to Mr. Verloc. His prestige with the Embassy would have
been immense if – if his wife had not had the unlucky
notion of sewing on the address inside Stevie's overcoat.
Mr. Verloc, who was no fool, had soon perceived the
extraordinary character of the influence he had over
Stevie, though he did not understand exactly its origin –
the doctrine of his supreme wisdom and goodness

inculcated by two anxious women. In all the eventualities he had foreseen Mr. Verloc had calculated with correct insight on Stevie's instinctive loyalty and blind discretion. The eventuality he had not foreseen had appalled him as a humane man and a fond husband. From every other point of view it was rather advantageous. Nothing can equal the everlasting discretion of death. Mr. Verloc, sitting perplexed and frightened in the small parlour of the Cheshire Cheese, could not help acknowledging that to himself, because his sensibility did not stand in the way of his judgment. Stevie's violent disintegration, however disturbing to think about, only assured the success; for, of course, the knocking down of a wall was not the aim of Mr. Vladimir's menaces, but the production of a moral effect. With much trouble and distress on Mr. Verloc's part the effect might be said to have been produced. When, however, most unexpectedly, it came home to roost in Brett Street, Mr. Verloc, who had been struggling like a man in a nightmare for the preservation of his position, accepted the blow in the spirit of a convinced fatalist. The position was gone through no one's fault really. A small, tiny fact had done it. It was like slipping on a bit of orange peel in the dark and breaking your leg.

Mr. Verloc drew a weary breath. He nourished no resentment against his wife. He thought: She will have to look after the shop while they keep me locked up. And thinking also how cruelly she would miss Stevie at first, he felt greatly concerned about her health and spirits. How would she stand her solitude – absolutely alone in that house? It would not do for her to break down while he was locked up. What would become of the shop then? The shop was an asset. Though Mr. Verloc's fatalism accepted his undoing as a secret agent, he had no mind to be utterly ruined, mostly, it must be owned, from regard for his wife.

Silent, and out of his line of sight in the kitchen, she

frightened him. If only she had her mother with her. But
that silly old woman — An angry dismay possessed Mr.
Verloc. He must talk with his wife. He could tell her certainly that a man does get desperate under certain circumstances. But he did not go incontinently to impart to
her that information. First of all, it was clear to him that
this evening was no time for business. He got up to close
the street door and put the gas out in the shop.

Having thus assured a solitude around his hearthstone
Mr. Verloc walked into the parlour, and glanced down
into the kitchen. Mrs. Verloc was sitting in the place
where poor Stevie usually established himself of an evening with paper and pencil for the pastime of drawing
these coruscations of innumerable circles suggesting
chaos and eternity. Her arms were folded on the table,
and her head was lying on her arms. Mr. Verloc contemplated her back and the arrangement of her hair for a
time, then walked away from the kitchen door. Mrs. Verloc's philosophical, almost disdainful incuriosity, the
foundation of their accord in domestic life, made it
extremely difficult to get into contact with her, now this
tragic necessity had arisen. Mr. Verloc felt this difficulty
acutely. He turned around the table in the parlour with
his usual air of a large animal in a cage.

Curiosity being one of the forms of self-revelation, a
systematically incurious person remains always partly
mysterious. Every time he passed near the door Mr. Verloc glanced at his wife uneasily. It was not that he was
afraid of her. Mr. Verloc imagined himself loved by that
woman. But she had not accustomed him to make con-
fidences. And the confidence he had to make was of a
profound psychological order. How with his want of practice could he tell her what he himself felt but vaguely:
that there are conspiracies of fatal destiny, that a notion
grows in a mind sometimes till it acquires an outward
existence, an independent power of its own, and even a
suggestive voice? He could not inform her that a man

may be haunted by a fat, witty, clean-shaved face till the wildest expedient to get rid of it appears a child of wisdom.

On this mental reference to a First Secretary of a great Embassy, Mr. Verloc stopped in the doorway, and looking down into the kitchen with an angry face and clenched fists, addressed his wife.

'You don't know what a brute I had to deal with.'

He started off to make another perambulation of the table; then when he had come to the door again he stopped, glaring in from the height of two steps.

'A silly, jeering, dangerous brute, with no more sense than — After all these years! A man like me! And I have been playing my head at that game. You didn't know. Quite right, too. What was the good of telling you that I stood the risk of having a knife stuck into me any time these seven years we've been married? I am not a chap to worry a woman that's fond of me. You had no business to know.'

Mr. Verloc took another turn round the parlour, fuming.

'A venomous beast,' he began again from the doorway. 'Drive me out into a ditch to starve for a joke. I could see he thought it was a damned good joke. A man like me! Look here! Some of the highest in the world got to thank me for walking on their two legs to this day. That's the man you've got married to, my girl!'

He perceived that his wife had sat up. Mrs. Verloc's arms remained lying stretched on the table. Mr. Verloc watched her back as if he could read there the effect of his words.

'There isn't a murdering plot for the last eleven years that I hadn't my finger in at the risk of my life. There's scores of these revolutionists I've sent off, with their bombs in their blamed pockets, to get themselves caught on the frontier. The old Baron knew what I was worth to his country. And here suddenly a swine comes along – an ignorant, overbearing swine.'

Mr. Verloc, stepping slowly down two steps, entered the kitchen, took a tumbler off the dresser, and holding it in his hand, approached the sink, without looking at his wife.

'It wasn't the old Baron who would have had the wicked folly of getting me to call on him at eleven in the morning. There are two or three in this town that, if they had seen me going in, would have made no bones about knocking me on the head sooner or later. It was a silly, murderous trick to expose for nothing a man – like me.'

Mr. Verloc, turning on the tap above the sink, poured three glasses of water, one after another, down his throat to quench the fires of his indignation. Mr. Vladimir's conduct was like a hot brand which set his internal economy in a blaze. He could not get over the disloyalty of it. This man, who would not work at the usual hard tasks which society sets to its humbler members, had exercised his secret industry with an indefatigable devotion. There was in Mr. Verloc a fund of loyalty. He had been loyal to his employers, to the cause of social stability – and to his affections, too – as became apparent when, after standing the tumbler in the sink, he turned about, saying:

'If I hadn't thought of you I would have taken the bullying brute by the throat and rammed his head into the fireplace. I'd have been more than a match for that pink-faced, smooth-shaved —'

Mr. Verloc neglected to finish the sentence, as if there could be no doubt of the terminal word. For the first time in his life he was taking that incurious woman into his confidence. The singularity of the event, the force and importance of the personal feelings aroused in the course of this confession, drove Stevie's fate clean out of Mr. Verloc's mind. The boy's stuttering existence of fears and indignations, together with the violence of his end, had passed out of Mr. Verloc's mental sight for a time.

For that reason, when he looked up he was startled by
the inappropriate character of his wife's stare. It was not
a wild stare, and it was not inattentive, but its attention
was peculiar and not satisfactory, inasmuch that it
seemed concentrated upon some point beyond Mr. Verloc's person. The impression was so strong that Mr.
Verloc glanced over his shoulder. There was nothing
behind him: there was just the whitewashed wall. The
excellent husband of Winnie Verloc saw no writing on
the wall. He turned to his wife again, repeating, with
some emphasis:

'I would have taken him by the throat. As true as I
stand here, if I hadn't thought of you then I would have
half choked the life out of the brute before I let him get
up. And don't you think he would have been anxious to
call the police – either. He wouldn't have dared. You
understand why – don't you?'

He blinked at his wife knowingly.

'No,' said Mrs. Verloc in an unresonant voice, and
without looking at him at all. 'What are you talking
about?'

A great discouragement, the result of fatigue, came
upon Mr. Verloc. He had had a very full day, and his
nerves had been tried to the utmost. After a month of
maddening worry, ending in an unexpected catastrophe,
the storm-tossed spirit of Mr. Verloc longed for repose.
His career as a secret agent had come to an end in a way
no one could have foreseen; only, now, perhaps he could
manage to get a night's sleep at last. But looking at his
wife, he doubted it. She was taking it very hard – not at
all like herself, he thought. He made an effort to speak.

'You'll have to pull yourself together, my girl,' he said,
sympathetically. 'What's done can't be undone.'

Mrs. Verloc gave a slight start, though not a muscle of
her white face moved in the least. Mr. Verloc, who was
not looking at her, continued ponderously:

'You go to bed now. What you want is a good cry.'

This opinion had nothing to recommend it but the general consent of mankind. It is universally understood that, as if it were nothing more substantial than vapour floating in the sky, every emotion of a woman is bound to end in a shower. And it is very probable that had Stevie died in his bed under her despairing gaze, in her protecting arms, Mrs. Verloc's grief would have found relief in a flood of bitter and pure tears. Mrs. Verloc, in common with other human beings, was provided with a fund of unconscious resignation sufficient to meet the normal manifestation of human destiny. Without 'troubling her head about it,' she was aware that it 'did not stand looking into very much.' But the lamentable circumstances of Stevie's end, which to Mr. Verloc's mind had only an episodic character, as part of a greater disaster, dried her tears at their very source. It was the effect of a white-hot iron drawn across her eyes; at the same time her heart, hardened and chilled into a lump of ice, kept her body in an inward shudder, set her features into a frozen, contemplative immobility addressed to a whitewashed wall with no writing on it. The exigencies of Mrs. Verloc's temperament, which, when stripped of its philosophical reserve, was maternal and violent, forced her to roll a series of thoughts in her motionless head. These thoughts were rather imagined than expressed. Mrs. Verloc was a woman of singularly few words, either for public or private use. With the rage and dismay of a betrayed woman, she reviewed the tenor of her life in visions concerned mostly with Stevie's difficult existence from its earliest days. It was a life of single purpose and of a noble unity of inspiration, like those rare lives that have left their mark on the thoughts and feelings of mankind. But the visions of Mrs. Verloc lacked nobility and magnificence. She saw herself putting the boy to bed by the light of a single candle on the deserted top floor of a 'business house', dark under the roof and scintillating exceedingly with lights and cut glass at the level of the

street like a fairy palace. That meretricious splendour
was the only one to be met in Mrs. Verloc's visions. She
remembered brushing the boy's hair and tying his pina-
fores – herself in a pinafore still; the consolations admin-
istered to a small and badly scared creature by another
creature nearly as small but not quite so badly scared;
she had the vision of the blows intercepted (often with
her own head), of a door held desperately shut against a
man's rage (not for very long); of a poker flung once (not
very far), which stilled that particular storm into the
dumb and awful silence which follows a thunder-clap.
And all these scenes of violence came and went accompanied by the unrefined noise of deep vociferations proceeding from a man wounded in his paternal pride,
declaring himself obviously accursed since one of his
kids was a 'slobbering idjut and the other a wicked she-
devil.' It was of her that this had been said many years
ago.

Mrs. Verloc heard the words again in a ghostly fashion,
and then the dreary shadow of the Belgravian mansion
descended upon her shoulders. It was a crushing memory, an exhausting vision of countless breakfast trays carried up and down innumerable stairs, of endless haggling
over pence, of the endless drudgery of sweeping, dusting, cleaning, from basement to attics; while the impotent mother, staggering on swollen legs, cooked in a
grimy kitchen, and poor Stevie, the unconscious pre-
siding genius of all their toil, blacked the gentlemen's
boots in the scullery. But this vision had a breath of a hot
London summer in it, and for a central figure a young
man wearing his Sunday best, with a straw hat on his
dark head and a wooden pipe in his mouth. Affectionate
and jolly, he was a fascinating companion for a voyage
down the sparkling stream of life; only his boat was very
small. There was room in it for a girl-partner at the oar,
but no accommodation for passengers. He was allowed
to drift away from the threshold of the Belgravian

mansion while Winnie averted her tearful eyes. He was not a lodger. The lodger was Mr. Verloc, indolent and keeping late hours, sleepily jocular of a morning from under his bedclothes, but with gleams of infatuation in his heavy-lidded eyes, and always with some money in his pockets. There was no sparkle of any kind on the lazy stream of his life. It flowed through secret places. But his barque seemed a roomy craft, and his taciturn magnanimity accepted as a matter of course the presence of passengers.

Mrs. Verloc pursued the visions of seven years' security for Stevie loyally paid for on her part; of security growing into confidence, into a domestic feeling, stagnant and deep like a placid pool, whose guarded surface hardly shuddered on the occasional passage of Comrade Ossipon, the robust anarchist with shamelessly inviting eyes, whose glance had a corrupt clearness sufficient to enlighten any woman not absolutely imbecile.

A few seconds only had elapsed since the last word had been uttered aloud in the kitchen, and Mrs. Verloc was staring already at the vision of an episode not more than a fortnight old. With eyes whose pupils were extremely dilated she stared at the vision of her husband and poor Stevie walking up Brett Street side by side away from the shop. It was the last scene of an existence created by Mrs. Verloc's genius; an existence foreign to all grace and charm, without beauty and almost without decency, but admirable in the continuity of feeling and tenacity of purpose. And this last vision had such plastic relief, such nearness of form, such a fidelity of suggestive detail, that it wrung from Mrs. Verloc an anguished and faint murmur, reproducing the supreme illusion of her life, an appalled murmur that died out on her blanched lips.

'Might have been father and son.'

Mr. Verloc stopped, and raised a careworn face. 'Eh? What did you say?' he asked. Receiving no reply, he resumed his sinister tramping. Then with a menacing flourish of a thick, fleshy fist, he burst out:

'Yes. The Embassy people. A pretty lot, ain't they! Before a week's out I'll make some of them wish themselves twenty feet under ground. Eh? What?'

He glanced sideways, with his head down. Mrs. Verloc gazed at the whitewashed wall. A blank wall – perfectly blank. A blankness to run at and dash your head against. Mrs. Verloc remained immovably seated. She kept still as the population of half the globe would keep still in astonishment and despair, were the sun suddenly put out in the summer sky by the perfidy of a trusted providence.

'The Embassy,' Mr. Verloc began again, after a preliminary grimace which bared his teeth wolfishly. 'I wish I could get loose in there with a cudgel for half-an-hour. I would keep on hitting till there wasn't a single unbroken bone left amongst the whole lot. But never mind, I'll teach them yet what it means trying to throw out a man like me to rot in the streets. I've a tongue in my head. All the world shall know what I've done for them. I am not afraid. I don't care. Everything'll come out. Every damned thing. Let them look out!'

In these terms did Mr. Verloc declare his thirst for revenge. It was a very appropriate revenge. It was in harmony with the promptings of Mr. Verloc's genius. It had also the advantage of being within the range of his powers and of adjusting itself easily to the practice of his life, which had consisted precisely in betraying the secret and unlawful proceedings of his fellow-men. Anarchists or diplomats were all one to him. Mr. Verloc was temperamentally no respecter of persons. His scorn was equally distributed over the whole field of his operations. But as a member of a revolutionary proletariat – which he undoubtedly was – he nourished a rather inimical sentiment against social distinction.

'Nothing on earth can stop me now,' he added, and

paused, looking fixedly at his wife, who was looking fixedly at a blank wall.

The silence in the kitchen was prolonged, and Mr. Verloc felt disappointed. He had expected his wife to say something. But Mrs. Verloc's lips, composed in their usual form, preserved a statuesque immobility like the rest of her face. And Mr. Verloc was disappointed. Yet the occasion did not, he recognized, demand speech from her. She was a woman of very few words. For reasons involved in the very foundation of his psychology, Mr. Verloc was inclined to put his trust in any woman who had given herself to him. Therefore he trusted his wife. Their accord was perfect, but it was not precise. It was a tacit accord, congenial to Mrs. Verloc's incuriosity and to Mr. Verloc's habits of mind, which were indolent and secret. They refrained from going to the bottom of facts and motives.

This reserve, expressing, in a way, their profound confidence in each other, introduced at the same time a certain element of vagueness into their intimacy. No system of conjugal relations is perfect. Mr. Verloc presumed that his wife had understood him but he would have been glad to hear her say what she thought at the moment. It would have been a comfort.

There were several reasons why this comfort was denied him. There was a physical obstacle: Mrs. Verloc had not sufficient command over her voice. She did not see any alternative between screaming and silence, and instinctively she chose the silence. Winnie Verloc was temperamentally a silent person. And there was the paralyzing atrocity of the thought which occupied her. Her cheeks were blanched, her lips ashy, her immobility amazing. And she thought without looking at Mr. Verloc: 'This man took the boy away to murder him. He took the boy away from his home to murder him. He took the boy away from me to murder him!'

Mrs. Verloc's whole being was racked by that

inconclusive and maddening thought. It was in her veins, in her bones, in the roots of her hair. Mentally she assumed the biblical attitude of mourning – the covered face, the rent garments; the sound of wailing and lamentation filled her head. But her teeth were violently clenched, and her tearless eyes were hot with rage, because she was not a submissive creature. The protection she had extended over her brother had been in its origin of a fierce and indignant complexion. She had to love him with a militant love. She had battled for him – even against herself. His loss had the bitterness of defeat, with the anguish of a baffled passion. It was not an ordinary stroke of death. Moreover, it was not death that took Stevie from her. It was Mr. Verloc who took him away. She had seen him. She had watched him, without raising a hand, take the boy away. And she had let him go, like – like a fool – a blind fool. Then after he had murdered the boy he came home to her. Just came home like any other man would come home to his wife. . . .

Through her set teeth Mrs. Verloc muttered at the wall:

'And I thought he had caught a cold.'

Mr. Verloc heard these words and appropriated them.

'It was nothing,' he said, moodily. 'I was upset. I was upset on your account.'

Mrs. Verloc, turning her head slowly, transferred her stare from the wall to her husband's person. Mr. Verloc, with the tips of his fingers between his lips, was looking on the ground.

'Can't be helped,' he mumbled, letting his hand fall. 'You must pull yourself together. You'll want all your wits about you. It is you who brought the police about our ears. Never mind, I won't say anything more about it,' continued Mr. Verloc, magnanimously. 'You couldn't know.'

'I couldn't,' breathed out Mrs. Verloc. It was as if a corpse had spoken. Mr. Verloc took up the thread of his discourse.

'I don't blame you. I'll make them sit up. Once under
lock and key it will be safe enough for me to talk – you
understand. You must reckon on me being two years
away from you,' he continued, in a tone of sincere concern. 'It will be easier for you than for me. You'll have
something to do, while I — Look here, Winnie, what you
must do is to keep this business going for two years. You
know enough for that. You've a good head on you. I'll
send you word when it's time to go about trying to sell.
You'll have to be extra careful. The comrades will be
keeping an eye on you all the time. You'll have to be as
artful as you know how, and as close as the grave. No one
must know what you are going to do. I have no mind to
get a knock on the head or a stab in the back directly I
am let out.'

Thus spoke Mr. Verloc, applying his mind with ingenuity and forethought to the problems of the future. His
voice was sombre, because he had a correct sentiment of
the situation. Everything which he did not wish to pass
had come to pass. The future had become precarious.
His judgment, perhaps, had been momentarily obscured
by his dread of Mr. Vladimir's truculent folly. A man
somewhat over forty may be excusably thrown into considerable disorder by the prospect of losing his employment, especially if the man is a secret agent of political
police, dwelling secure in the consciousness of his high
value and in the esteem of high personages. He was
excusable.

Now the thing had ended in a crash. Mr. Verloc was
cool; but he was not cheerful. A secret agent who throws
his secrecy to the winds from desire of vengeance, and
flaunts his achievements before the public eye, becomes
the mark for desperate and bloodthirsty indignations.
Without unduly exaggerating the danger, Mr. Verloc
tried to bring it clearly before his wife's mind. He repeated that he had no intention of letting the revolutionists do away with him.

He looked straight into his wife's eyes. The enlarged pupils of the woman received his stare into their unfathomable depths.

'I am too fond of you for that,' he said, with a little nervous laugh.

A faint flush coloured Mrs. Verloc's ghastly and motionless face. Having done with the visions of the past, she had not only heard, but had also understood the words uttered by her husband. By their extreme disaccord with her mental condition these words produced on her a slightly suffocating effect. Mrs. Verloc's mental condition had the merit of simplicity; but it was not sound. It was governed too much by a fixed idea. Every nook and cranny of her brain was filled with the thought that this man, with whom she had lived without distaste for seven years, had taken the 'poor boy' away from her in order to kill him – the man to whom she had grown accustomed in body and mind; the man whom she had trusted, took the boy away to kill him! In its form, in its substance, in its effect, which was universal, altering even the aspect of inanimate things, it was a thought to sit still and marvel at for ever and ever. Mrs. Verloc sat still. And across that thought (not across the kitchen) the form of Mr. Verloc went to and fro, familiarly in hat and overcoat, stamping with his boots upon her brain. He was probably talking, too; but Mrs. Verloc's thought for the most part covered the voice.

Now and then, however, the voice would make itself heard. Several connected words emerged at times. Their purport was generally hopeful. On each of these occasions Mrs. Verloc's dilated pupils, losing their far-off fixity, followed her husband's movements with the effect of black care and impenetrable attention. Well informed upon all matters relating to his secret calling, Mr. Verloc augured well for the success of his plans and combinations. He really believed that it would be upon the whole easy for him to escape the knife of infuriated revolution-

ists. He had exaggerated the strength of their fury and
the length of their arm (for professional purposes) too
often to have many illusions one way or the other. For to
exaggerate with judgment one must begin by measuring
with nicety. He knew also how much virtue and how
much infamy is forgotten in two years – two long years.
His first really confidential discourse to his wife was
optimistic from conviction. He also thought it good
policy to display all the assurance he could muster. It
would put heart into the poor woman. On his liberation,
which, harmonizing with the whole tenor of his life,
would be secret, of course, they would vanish together
without loss of time. As to covering up the tracks, he
begged his wife to trust him for that. He knew how it was
to be done so that the devil himself —

He waved his hand. He seemed to boast. He wished
only to put heart into her. It was a benevolent intention,
but Mr. Verloc had the misfortune not to be in accord
with his audience.

The self-confident tone grew upon Mrs. Verloc's ear
which let most of the words go by; for what were words
to her now? What could words do to her for good or evil
in the face of her fixed idea? Her black glance followed
that man who was asserting his impunity – the man who
had taken poor Stevie from home to kill him somewhere.
Mrs. Verloc could not remember exactly where, but her
heart began to beat very perceptibly.

Mr. Verloc, in a soft and conjugal tone, was now
expressing his firm belief that there were yet a good few
years of quiet life before them both. He did not go into
the question of means. A quiet life it must be and, as it
were, nestling in the shade, concealed among men
whose flesh is grass; modest, like the life of violets. The
words used by Mr. Verloc were: 'Lie low for a bit.' And
far from England, of course. It was not clear whether Mr.
Verloc had in his mind Spain or South America; but at
any rate somewhere abroad.

This last word, falling into Mrs. Verloc's ear, produced a definite impression. This man was talking of going abroad. The impression was completely disconnected; and such is the force of mental habit that Mrs. Verloc at once and automatically asked herself: 'And what of Stevie?'

It was a sort of forgetfulness; but instantly she became aware that there was no longer any occasion for anxiety on that score. There would never be any occasion any more. The poor boy had been taken out and killed. The poor boy was dead.

This shaking piece of forgetfulness stimulated Mrs. Verloc's intelligence. She began to perceive certain consequences which would have surprised Mr. Verloc. There was no need for her now to stay there, in that kitchen, in that house, with that man – since the boy was gone for ever. No need whatever. And on that Mrs. Verloc rose as if raised by a spring. But neither could she see what there was to keep her in the world at all. And this inability arrested her. Mr. Verloc watched her with marital solicitude.

'You're looking more like yourself,' he said, uneasily. Something peculiar in the blackness of his wife's eyes disturbed his optimism. At that precise moment Mrs. Verloc began to look upon herself as released from all earthly ties. She had her freedom. Her contract with existence, as represented by that man standing over there, was at an end. She was a free woman. Had this view become in some way perceptible to Mr. Verloc he would have been extremely shocked. In his affairs of the heart Mr. Verloc had been always carelessly generous, yet always with no other idea than that of being loved for himself. Upon this matter, his ethical notions being in agreement with his vanity, he was completely incorrigible. That this should be so in the case of his virtuous and legal connection he was perfectly certain. He had grown older, fatter, heavier, in the belief that he lacked no fascination for being loved for his own sake. When he saw Mrs. Verloc starting to walk out of the kitchen without a word he was disappointed.

'Where are you going to?' he called out rather sharply. 'Upstairs?'

Mrs. Verloc in the doorway turned at the voice. An instinct of prudence born of fear, the excessive fear of being approached and touched by that man, induced her to nod at him slightly (from the height of two steps), with a stir of the lips which the conjugal optimism of Mr. Verloc took for a wan and uncertain smile.

'That's right,' he encouraged her gruffly. 'Rest and quiet's what you want. Go on. It won't be long before I am with you.'

Mrs. Verloc, the free woman who had had really no idea where she was going to, obeyed the suggestion with rigid steadiness.

Mr. Verloc watched her. She disappeared up the stairs. He was disappointed. There was that within him which would have been more satisfied if she had been moved to throw herself upon his breast. But he was generous and indulgent. Winnie was always undemonstrative and silent. Neither was Mr. Verloc himself prodigal of endearments and words as a rule. But this was not an ordinary evening. It was an occasion when a man wants to be fortified and strengthened by open proofs of sympathy and affection. Mr. Verloc sighed, and put out the gas in the kitchen. Mr. Verloc's sympathy with his wife was genuine and intense. It almost brought tears into his eyes as he stood in the parlour reflecting on the loneliness hanging over her head. In this mood Mr. Verloc missed Stevie very much out of a difficult world. He thought mournfully of his end. If only that lad had not stupidly destroyed himself!

The sensation of unappeasable hunger, not unknown after the strain of a hazardous enterprise to adventurers of tougher fibre than Mr. Verloc, overcame him again.

The piece of roast beef, laid out in the likeness of funereal baked meats for Stevie's obsequies, offered itself largely to his notice. And Mr. Verloc again partook. He partook ravenously, without restraint and decency, cutting thick slices with the sharp carving knife, and swallowing them without bread. In the course of that refection it occurred to Mr. Verloc that he was not hearing his wife move about the bedroom as he should have done. The thought of finding her perhaps sitting on the bed in the dark not only cut Mr. Verloc's appetite, but also took from him the inclination to follow her upstairs just yet. Laying down the carving knife, Mr. Verloc listened with careworn attention.

He was comforted by hearing her move at last. She walked suddenly across the room, and threw the window up. After a period of stillness up there, during which he figured her to himself with her head out, he heard the sash being lowered slowly. Then she made a few steps, and sat down. Every resonance of his house was familiar to Mr. Verloc, who was thoroughly domesticated. When next he heard his wife's footsteps overhead he knew, as well as if he had seen her doing it, that she had been putting on her walking shoes. Mr. Verloc wriggled his shoulders slightly at this ominous symptom, and moving away from the table, stood with his back to the fireplace, his head on one side, and gnawing perplexedly at the tips of his fingers. He kept track of her movements by the sound. She walked here and there violently, with abrupt stoppages, now before the chest of drawers, then in front of the wardrobe. An immense load of weariness, the harvest of a day of shocks and surprises, weighed Mr. Verloc's energies to the ground.

He did not raise his eyes till he heard his wife descending the stairs. It was as he had guessed, she was dressed for going out.

Mrs. Verloc was a free woman. She had thrown open the window of the bedroom either with the intention of screaming Murder! Help! or of throwing herself out. For she did not exactly know what use to make of her freedom. Her personality seemed to have been torn into two pieces, whose mental operations did not adjust themselves very well to each other. The street, silent and deserted from end to end, repelled her by taking sides with that man who was so certain of his impunity. She was afraid to shout lest no one should come. Obviously no one would come. Her instinct of self-preservation recoiled from the depth of the fall into that sort of slimy, deep trench. Mrs. Verloc closed the window, and dressed herself to go out into the street by another way. She was a free woman. She had dressed herself thoroughly, down to the tying of a black veil over her face. As she appeared before him in the light of the parlour, Mr. Verloc observed that she had even her little handbag hanging from her left wrist. . . . Flying off to her mother, of course.

The thought that women were wearisome creatures after all presented itself to his fatigued brain. But he was too generous to harbour it for more than an instant. This man, hurt cruelly in his vanity, remained magnanimous in his conduct, allowing himself no satisfaction of a bitter smile or of a contemptuous gesture. With true greatness of soul, he only glanced at the wooden clock on the wall, and said in a perfectly calm but forcible manner:

'Five and twenty minutes past eight, Winnie. There's no sense in going over there so late. You will never manage to get back to-night.'

Before his extended hand Mrs. Verloc had stopped short. He added, heavily: 'Your mother will be gone to bed before you get there. This is the sort of news that can wait.'

Nothing was further from Mrs. Verloc's thoughts than going to her mother. She recoiled at the mere idea, and feeling a chair behind her, she obeyed the suggestion of the touch, and sat down. Her intention had been simply to get outside the door for ever. And if this feeling

was correct, its mental form took an unrefined shape
corresponding to her origin and station. 'I would rather
walk the streets all the days of my life,' she thought. But
this creature, whose moral nature had been subjected to
a shock of which, in the physical order, the most violent
earthquake of history could only be a faint and languid
rendering, was at the mercy of mere trifles, of casual con-
tacts. She sat down. With her hat and veil she had the
air of a visitor, of having looked in on Mr. Verloc for a
moment. Her instant docility encouraged him, whilst her
aspect of only temporary and silent acquiescence provoked him a little.

'Let me tell you, Winnie,' he said with authority, 'that
your place is here this evening. Hang it all! you brought
the damned police high and low about my ears. I don't
blame you – but it's your doing all the same. You'd better
take this confounded hat off. I can't let you go out, old
girl,' he added in a softened voice.

Mrs. Verloc's mind got hold of that declaration with
morbid tenacity. The man who had taken Stevie out
from under her very eyes to murder him in a locality
whose name was at the moment not present to her memory would not allow her to go out. Of course he wouldn't.
Now he had murdered Stevie he would never let her go.
He would want to keep her for nothing. And on this
characteristic reasoning, having all the force of insane
logic, Mrs. Verloc's disconnected wits went to work practically. She could slip by him, open the door, run out. But
he would dash out after her, seize her round the body,
drag her back into the shop. She could scratch, kick, and
bite – and stab, too; but for stabbing she wanted a knife.
Mrs. Verloc sat still under her black veil, in her own
house, like a masked and mysterious visitor of impenetrable intentions.

Mr. Verloc's magnanimity was not more than human.
She had exasperated him at last.

'Can't you say something? You have your own dodges

for vexing a man. Oh, yes! I know your deaf-and-dumb
trick. I've seen you at it before to-day. But just now it
won't do. And to begin with, take this damned thing off.
One can't tell whether one is talking to a dummy or to a
live woman.'

He advanced, and stretching out his hand, dragged
the veil off, unmasking a still unreadable face, against
which his nervous exasperation was shattered like a glass
bubble flung against a rock. 'That's better,' he said, to
cover his momentary uneasiness, and retreated back to
his old station by the mantelpiece. It never entered his
head that his wife could give him up. He felt a little
ashamed of himself, for he was fond and generous. What
could he do? Everything had been said already. He protested vehemently.

'By heavens! You know that I hunted high and low. I
ran the risk of giving myself away to find somebody for
that accursed job. And I tell you again I couldn't find any
one crazy enough or hungry enough. What do you take
me for – a murderer, or what? The boy is gone. Do you
think I wanted him to blow himself up? He's gone. His
troubles are over. Ours are just going to begin, I tell you,
precisely because he did blow himself up. I don't blame
you. But just try to understand that it was a pure accident; as much an accident as if he had been run over by a
'bus while crossing the street.'

His generosity was not infinite, because he was a
human being – and not a monster, as Mrs. Verloc
believed him to be. He paused, and a snarl lifting his
moustaches above a gleam of white teeth gave him the
expression of a reflective beast, not very dangerous – a
slow beast with a sleek head, gloomier than a seal, and
with a husky voice.

'And when it comes to that, it's as much your doing as
mine. That's so. You may glare as much as you like. I
know what you can do in that way. Strike me dead if I
ever would have thought of the lad for that purpose. It

was you who kept on shoving him in my way when I was
half distracted with the worry of keeping the lot of us out
of trouble. What the devil made you? One would think
you were doing it on purpose. And I am damned if I
know that you didn't. There's no saying how much of
what's going on you have got hold of on the sly with your
infernal don't-care-a-damn way of looking nowhere in
particular, and saying nothing at all. . . .'

His husky, domestic voice ceased for a while. Mrs.
Verloc made no reply. Before that silence he felt
ashamed of what he had said. But as often happens to
peaceful men in domestic tiffs, being ashamed he
pushed another point.

'You have a devilish way of holding your tongue sometimes,' he began again, without raising his voice.
'Enough to make some men go mad. It's lucky for you
that I am not so easily put out as some of them would be
by your deaf-and-dumb sulks. I am fond of you. But
don't you go too far. This isn't the time for it. We ought
to be thinking of what we've got to do. And I can't let
you go out to-night, galloping off to your mother with
some crazy tale or other about me. I won't have it. Don't
you make any mistake about it: if you will have it that I
killed the boy, then you've killed him as much as I.'

In sincerity of feeling and openness of statement,
these words went far beyond anything that had ever
been said in this home, kept up on the wages of a secret
industry eked out by the sale of more or less secret
wares: the poor expedients devised by a mediocre mankind for preserving an imperfect society from the dangers of moral and physical corruption, both secret, too, of
their kind. They were spoken because Mr. Verloc had
felt himself really outraged; but the reticent decencies of
this home life, nestling in a shady street behind a shop
where the sun never shone, remained apparently undisturbed. Mrs. Verloc heard him out with perfect propriety,
and then rose from her chair in her hat and jacket like a

visitor at the end of a call. She advanced towards her husband, one arm extended as if for a silent leave-taking.
Her net veil dangling down by one end of the left side of
her face gave an air of disorderly formality to her
restrained movements. But when she arrived as far as the
hearthrug, Mr. Verloc was no longer standing there. He
had moved off in the direction of the sofa, without raising his eyes to watch the effect of his tirade. He was
tired, resigned in a truly marital spirit. But he felt hurt in
the tender spot of his secret weakness. If she would go
on sulking in that dreadful overcharged silence – why
then she must. She was a master in that domestic art. Mr.
Verloc flung himself heavily upon the sofa, disregarding
as usual the fate of his hat, which, as if accustomed to
take care of itself, made for a safe shelter under the table.

He was tired. The last particle of his nervous force
had been expended in the wonders and agonies of this
day full of surprising failures coming at the end of a
harassing month of scheming and insomnia. He was
tired. A man isn't made of stone. Hang everything! Mr.
Verloc reposed characteristically, clad in his outdoor garments. One side of his open overcoat was lying partly on
the ground. Mr. Verloc wallowed on his back. But he
longed for a more perfect rest – for sleep – for a few hours
of delicious forgetfulness. That would come later. Provi-
sionally he rested. And he thought: 'I wish she would
give over this damned nonsense. It's exasperating.'

There must have been something imperfect in Mrs.
Verloc's sentiment of regained freedom. Instead of taking
the way of the door she leaned back, with her shoulders
against the tablet of the mantelpiece, as a wayfarer rests
against a fence. A tinge of wildness in her aspect was
derived from the black veil hanging like a rag against her
cheek, and from the fixity of her black gaze where the
light of the room was absorbed and lost without the trace
of a single gleam. This woman, capable of a bargain the
mere suspicion of which would have been infinitely

shocking to Mr. Verloc's idea of love, remained irresol-
ute, as if scrupulously aware of something wanting on
her part for the formal closing of the transaction.

On the sofa Mr. Verloc wriggled his shoulders into
perfect comfort, and from the fullness of his heart
emitted a wish which was certainly as pious as anything
likely to come from such a source.

'I wish to goodness,' he growled, huskily, 'I had never
seen Greenwich Park or anything belonging to it.'

The veiled sound filled the small room with its
moderate volume, well adapted to the modest nature of
the wish. The waves of air of the proper length, propa-
gated in accordance with correct mathematical formulas,
flowed around all the inanimate things in the room,
lapped against Mrs. Verloc's head as if it had been a head
of stone. And incredible as it may appear, the eyes of
Mrs. Verloc seemed to grow still larger. The audible wish
of Mr. Verloc's overflowing heart flowed into an empty
place in his wife's memory. Greenwich Park. A park!
That's where the boy was killed. A park – smashed branches, torn leaves, gravel, bits of brotherly flesh and bone,
all spouting up together in the manner of a firework. She
remembered now what she had heard, and she remembered it pictorially. They had to gather him up with the
shovel. Trembling all over with irrepressible shudders,
she saw before her the very implement with its ghastly
load scraped up from the ground. Mrs. Verloc closed her
eyes desperately, throwing upon that vision the night of
her eyelids, where after a rainlike fall of mangled limbs
the decapitated head of Stevie lingered suspended
alone, and fading out slowly like the last star of a pyro-
technic display. Mrs. Verloc opened her eyes.

Her face was no longer stony. Anybody could have
noted the subtle change on her features, in the stare of
her eyes, giving her a new and startling expression; an
expression seldom observed by competent persons
under the conditions of leisure and security demanded

for thorough analysis, but whose meaning could not be
mistaken at a glance. Mrs. Verloc's doubts as to the end
of the bargain no longer existed; her wits, no longer disconnected, were working under the control of her will.
But Mr. Verloc observed nothing. He was reposing in
that pathetic condition of optimism induced by excess of
fatigue. He did not want any more trouble – with his
wife, too – of all people in the world. He had been
unanswerable in his vindication. He was loved for himself. The present phase of her silence he interpreted
favourably. This was the time to make it up with her.
The silence had lasted long enough. He broke it by calling to her in an undertone:

'Winnie.'

'Yes,' answered obediently Mrs. Verloc the free
woman. She commanded her wits now, her vocal organs;
she felt herself to be in an almost preternaturally perfect
control of every fibre of her body. It was all her own,
because the bargain was at an end. She was clear sighted.
She had become cunning. She chose to answer him so
readily for a purpose. She did not wish that man to
change his position on the sofa which was very suitable
to the circumstances. She succeeded. The man did not
stir. But after answering him she remained leaning negligently against the mantelpiece in the attitude of a resting wayfarer. She was unhurried. Her brow was smooth.
The head and shoulders of Mr. Verloc were hidden from
her by the high side of the sofa. She kept her eyes fixed
on his feet.

She remained thus mysteriously still and suddenly
collected till Mr. Verloc was heard with an accent of
marital authority, and moving slightly to make room for
her to sit on the edge of the sofa.

'Come here,' he said in a peculiar tone, which might
have been the tone of brutality, but was intimately
known to Mrs. Verloc as the note of wooing.

She started forward at once, as if she were still a loyal

woman bound to that man by an unbroken contract. Her right hand skimmed slightly the end of the table, and when she had passed on towards the sofa the carving knife had vanished without the slightest sound from the side of the dish. Mr. Verloc heard the creaky plank in the floor, and was content. He waited. Mrs. Verloc was coming. As if the homeless soul of Stevie had flown for shelter straight to the breast of his sister, guardian, and protector, the resemblance of her face with that of her brother grew at every step, even to the droop of the lower lip, even to the slight divergence of the eyes. But Mr. Verloc did not see that. He was lying on his back and staring upwards. He saw partly on the ceiling and partly on the wall the moving shadow of an arm with a clenched hand holding a carving knife. It flickered up and down. Its movements were leisurely. They were leisurely enough for Mr. Verloc to recognize the limb and the weapon.

They were leisurely enough for him to take in the full meaning of the portent, and to taste the flavour of death rising in his gorge. His wife had gone raving mad – murdering mad. They were leisurely enough for the first paralyzing effect of this discovery to pass away before a resolute determination to come out victorious from the ghastly struggle with that armed lunatic. They were leisurely enough for Mr. Verloc to elaborate a plan of defence involving a dash behind the table, and the felling of the woman to the ground with a heavy wooden chair. But they were not leisurely enough to allow Mr. Verloc the time to move either hand or foot. The knife was already planted in his breast. It met no resistance on its way. Hazard has such accuracies. Into that plunging blow, delivered over the side of the couch, Mrs. Verloc had put all the inheritance of her immemorial and obscure descent, the simple ferocity of the age of caverns, and the unbalanced nervous fury of the age of bar-rooms. Mr. Verloc, the Secret Agent, turning slightly on his side with the force of the blow, expired without stirring a limb, in the muttered sound of the word 'Don't' by way of protest.

Mrs. Verloc had let go the knife, and her extraordinary resemblance to her late brother had faded, had become very ordinary now. She drew a deep breath, the first easy breath since Chief Inspector Heat had exhibited to her the labelled piece of Stevie's overcoat. She leaned forward on her folded arms over the side of the sofa. She adopted that easy attitude not in order to watch or gloat over the body of Mr. Verloc, but because of the undulatory and swinging movements of the parlour, which for some time behaved as though it were at sea in a tempest. She was giddy but calm. She had become a free woman with a perfection of freedom which left her nothing to desire and absolutely nothing to do, since Stevie's urgent claim on her devotion no longer existed. Mrs. Verloc, who thought in images, was not troubled now by visions, because she did not think at all. And she did not move. She was a woman enjoying her complete irresponsibility and endless leisure, almost in the manner of a corpse. She did not move, she did not think. Neither did the mortal envelope of the late Mr. Verloc reposing on the sofa. Except for the fact that Mrs. Verloc breathed these two would have been perfectly in accord: that accord of prudent reserve without superfluous words, and sparing of signs, which had been the foundation of their respectable home life. For it had been respectable, covering by a decent reticence the problems that may arise in the practice of a secret profession and the commerce of shady wares. To the last its decorum had remained undisturbed by unseemly shrieks and other misplaced sincerities of conduct. And after the striking of the blow, this respectability was continued in immobility and silence.

Nothing moved in the parlour till Mrs. Verloc raised her head slowly and looked at the clock with inquiring mistrust. She had become aware of a ticking sound in the room. It grew upon her ear, while she remembered clearly that the clock on the wall was silent, had no audible tick. What did it mean by beginning to tick so loudly all of a sudden? Its face indicated ten minutes to nine. Mrs. Verloc cared nothing for time, and the ticking went on. She concluded it could not be the clock, and her sullen gaze moved along the walls, wavered, and became vague, while she strained her hearing to locate the sound. Tic, tic, tic.

After listening for some time Mrs. Verloc lowered her gaze deliberately on her husband's body. Its attitude of repose was so homelike and familiar that she could do so without feeling embarrassed by any pronounced novelty in the phenomena of her home life. Mr. Verloc was taking his habitual ease. He looked comfortable.

By the position of the body the face of Mr. Verloc was not visible to Mrs. Verloc, his widow. Her fine, sleepy eyes, travelling downward on the track of the sound, became contemplative on meeting a flat object of bone which protruded a little beyond the edge of the sofa. It was the handle of the domestic carving knife with nothing strange about it but its position at right angles to Mr. Verloc's waistcoat and the fact that something dripped from it. Dark drops fell on the floorcloth one after another, with a sound of ticking growing fast and furious like the pulse of an insane clock. At its highest speed this ticking changed into a continuous sound of trickling. Mrs. Verloc watched that transformation with shadows of anxiety coming and going on her face. It was a trickle, dark, swift, thin. . . . Blood!

At this unforeseen circumstance Mrs. Verloc abandoned her pose of idleness and irresponsibility.

With a sudden snatch at her skirts and a faint shriek she ran to the door, as if the trickle had been the first sign of a destroying flood. Finding the table in her way she gave it a push with both hands as though it had been alive, with such force that it went for some distance on its four legs, making a loud, scraping racket, whilst the big dish with the joint crashed heavily on the floor.

Then all became still. Mrs. Verloc on reaching the door had stopped. A round hat disclosed in the middle of the floor by the moving of the table rocked slightly on its crown in the wind of her flight.

CHAPTER TWELVE

WINNIE VERLOC, the widow of Mr. Verloc, the sister of the late faithful Stevie (blown to fragments in a state of innocence and in the conviction of being engaged in a humanitarian enterprise), did not run beyond the door of the parlour. She had indeed run away so far from a mere trickle of blood, but that was a movement of instinctive repulsion. And there she had paused, with staring eyes and lowered head. As though she had run through long years in her flight across the small parlour, Mrs. Verloc by the door was quite a different person from the woman who had been leaning over the sofa, a little swimmy in her head, but otherwise free to enjoy the profound calm of idleness and irresponsibility. Mrs. Verloc was no longer giddy. Her head was steady. On the other hand, she was no longer calm. She was afraid.

If she avoided looking in the direction of her reposing husband it was not because she was afraid of him. Mr. Verloc was not frightful to behold. He looked comfortable. Moreover, he was dead. Mrs. Verloc entertained no vain delusions on the subject of the dead. Nothing brings them back, neither love nor hate. They can do nothing to you. They are as nothing. Her mental state was tinged by a sort of austere contempt for that man who had let himself be killed so easily. He had been the master of a house, the husband of a woman, and the murderer of her Stevie. And now he was of no account in every respect. He was of less practical account than the

clothing on his body, than his overcoat, than his boots –
than that hat lying on the floor. He was nothing. He was
not worth looking at. He was even no longer the murderer of poor Stevie. The only murderer that would be
found in the room when people came to look for Mr. Verloc would be – herself!

Her hands shook so that she failed twice in the task of
refastening her veil. Mrs. Verloc was no longer a person
of leisure and irresponsibility. She was afraid. The stabbing of Mr. Verloc had been only a blow. It had relieved
the pent-up agony of shrieks strangled in her throat, of
tears dried up in her hot eyes, of the maddening and
indignant rage at the atrocious part played by that man,
who was less than nothing now, in robbing her of the boy.
It had been an obscurely prompted blow. The blood
trickling on the floor off the handle of the knife had
turned it into an extremely plain case of murder. Mrs
Verloc, who always refrained from looking deep into
things, was compelled to look into the very bottom of
this thing. She saw there no haunting face, no reproach-
ful shade, no vision of remorse, no sort of ideal conception. She saw there an object. That object was the
gallows. Mrs. Verloc was afraid of the gallows.

She was terrified of them ideally. Having never set
eyes on that last argument of men's justice except in
illustrative woodcuts to a certain type of tales, she first
saw them erect against a black and stormy background,
festooned with chains and human bones, circled about
by birds that peck at dead men's eyes. This was frightful
enough, but Mrs. Verloc, though not a well-informed
woman, had a sufficient knowledge of the institutions of
her country to know that gallows are no longer erected
romantically on the banks of dismal rivers or on wind-
swept headlands, but in the yards of jails. There within
four high walls, as if into a pit, at dawn of day, the murderer was brought out to be executed, with a horrible
quietness and, as the reports in the newspapers always

said, 'in the presence of the authorities.' With her eyes
staring on the floor, her nostrils quivering with anguish
and shame, she imagined herself all alone amongst a lot
of strange gentlemen in silk hats who were calmly proceeding about the business of hanging her by the neck.
That – never! Never! And how was it done? The
impossibility of imagining the details of such quiet
execution added something maddening to her abstract
terror. The newspapers never gave any details except
one, but that one with some affectation was always there
at the end of a meagre report. Mrs. Verloc remembered
its nature. It came with a cruel burning pain into her
head, as if the words 'The drop given was fourteen feet'
had been scratched on her brain with a hot needle. 'The
drop given was fourteen feet.'

These words affected her physically, too. Her throat
became convulsed in waves to resist strangulation; and
the apprehension of the jerk was so vivid that she seized
her head in both hands as if to save it from being torn off
her shoulders. 'The drop given was fourteen feet.' No!
that must never be. She could not stand *that*. The
thought of it even was not bearable. She could not stand
thinking of it. Therefore Mrs. Verloc formed the resolution to go at once and throw herself into the river off one
of the bridges.

This time she managed to refasten her veil. With her
face as if masked, all black from head to foot except for
some flowers in her hat, she looked up mechanically at
the clock. She thought it must have stopped. She could
not believe that only two minutes had passed since she
had looked at it last. Of course not. It had been stopped
all the time. As a matter of fact, only three minutes had
elapsed from the moment she had drawn the first deep,
easy breath after the blow, to this moment when Mrs.
Verloc formed the resolution to drown herself in the
Thames. But Mrs. Verloc could not believe that. She
seemed to have heard or read that clocks and watches

always stopped at the moment of murder for the undoing
of the murderer. She did not care. 'To the bridge – and
over I go.' . . . But her movements were slow.

She dragged herself painfully across the shop, and had
to hold on to the handle of the door before she found the
necessary fortitude to open it. The street frightened her,
since it led either to the gallows or to the river. She
floundered over the doorstep head forward, arms thrown
out, like a person falling over the parapet of a bridge.
This entrance into the open air had a foretaste of drowning; a slimy dampness enveloped her, entered her nostrils, clung to her hair. It was not actually raining, but
each gas-lamp had a rusty little halo of mist. The van and
horses were gone, and in the black street the curtained
window of the carters' eating-house made a square patch
of soiled blood-red light glowing faintly very near the
level of the pavement. Mrs. Verloc, dragging herself
slowly towards it, thought that she was a very friendless
woman. It was true. It was so true that, in a sudden longing to see some friendly face, she could think of no one
else but of Mrs. Neale, the charwoman. She had no
acquaintances of her own. Nobody would miss her in a
social way. It must not be imagined that the Widow
Verloc had forgotten her mother. This was not so. Winnie
had been a good daughter because she had been a
devoted sister. Her mother had always leaned on her for
support. No consolation or advice could be expected
there. Now that Stevie was dead the bond seemed to be
broken. She could not face the old woman with the
horrible tale. Moreover, it was too far. The river was her
present destination. Mrs. Verloc tried to forget her
mother.

Each step cost her an effort of will which seemed the
last possible. Mrs. Verloc had dragged herself past the
red glow of the eating-house window. 'To the bridge –
and over I go,' she repeated to herself with fierce obsti-
nacy. She put out her hand just in time to steady herself

against a lamp-post. 'I'll never get there before morning,' she thought. The fear of death paralyzed her efforts to escape the gallows. It seemed to her she had been staggering in that street for hours. 'I'll never get there,' she thought. 'They'll find me knocking about the streets. It's too far.' She held on, panting under her black veil.

'The drop given was fourteen feet.'

She pushed the lamp-post away from her violently, and found herself walking. But another wave of faintness overtook her like a great sea, washing away her heart clean out of her breast. 'I will never get there,' she muttered, suddenly arrested, swaying lightly where she stood. 'Never.'

And perceiving the utter impossibility of walking as far as the nearest bridge, Mrs. Verloc thought of a flight abroad.

It came to her suddenly. Murderers escaped. They escaped abroad. Spain or California. Mere names. The vast world created for the glory of man was only a vast blank to Mrs. Verloc. She did not know which way to turn. Murderers had friends, relations, helpers – they had knowledge. She had nothing. She was the most lonely of murderers that ever struck a mortal blow. She was alone in London: and the whole town of marvels and mud, with its maze of streets and its mass of lights, was sunk in a hopeless night, rested at the bottom of a black abyss from which no unaided woman could hope to scramble out.

She swayed forward, and made a fresh start blindly, with an awful dread of falling down; but at the end of a few steps, unexpectedly, she found a sensation of support, of security. Raising her head, she saw a man's face peering closely at her veil. Comrade Ossipon was not afraid of strange women, and no feeling of false delicacy could prevent him from striking an acquaintance with a woman apparently very much intoxicated. Comrade Ossipon was interested in women. He held up this one between his two large palms, peering at her in a business-

like way till he heard her say faintly 'Mr. Ossipon!' and
then he very nearly let her drop to the ground.

'Mrs. Verloc!' he exclaimed. 'You here!'

It seemed impossible to him that she should have
been drinking. But one never knows. He did not go into
that question, but attentive not to discourage kind fate
surrendering to him the widow of Comrade Verloc, he
tried to draw her to his breast. To his astonishment she
came quite easily, and even rested on his arm for a
moment before she attempted to disengage herself.
Comrade Ossipon would not be brusque with kind fate.
He withdrew his arm in a natural way.

'You recognized me,' she faltered out, standing before
him, fairly steady on her legs.

'Of course I did,' said Ossipon with perfect readiness.
'I was afraid you were going to fall. I've thought of you
too often lately not to recognize you anywhere, at any
time. I've always thought of you – ever since I first set
eyes on you.'

Mrs. Verloc seemed not to hear. 'You were coming to
the shop?' she said, nervously.

'Yes; at once,' answered Ossipon. 'Directly I read the
paper.'

In fact, Comrade Ossipon had been skulking for a
good two hours in the neighbourhood of Brett Street,
unable to make up his mind for a bold move. The robust
anarchist was not exactly a bold conqueror. He remembered that Mrs. Verloc had never responded to his glances by the slightest sign of encouragement. Besides, he
thought the shop might be watched by the police, and
Comrade Ossipon did not wish the police to form an
exaggerated notion of his revolutionary sympathies.
Even now he did not know precisely what to do. In comparison with his usual amatory speculations this was a big
and serious undertaking. He ignored how much there
was in it and how far he would have to go in order to get
hold of what there was to get – supposing there was a

THE SECRET AGENT 249

chance at all. These perplexities checking his elation imparted to his tone a soberness well in keeping with the circumstances.

'May I ask you where you were going?' he inquired in a subdued voice.

'Don't ask me!' cried Mrs. Verloc with a shuddering, repressed violence. All her strong vitality recoiled from the idea of death. 'Never mind where I was going. . . .'

Ossipon concluded that she was very much excited but perfectly sober. She remained silent by his side for a moment, then all at once she did something which he did not expect. She slipped her hand under his arm. He was startled by the act itself certainly, and quite as much, too, by the palpably resolute character of this movement. But this being a delicate affair, Comrade Ossipon behaved with delicacy. He contented himself by pressing the hand slightly against his robust ribs. At the same time he felt himself being impelled forward, and yielded to the impulse. At the end of Brett Street he became aware of being directed to the left. He submitted.

The fruiterer at the corner had put out the blazing glory of his oranges and lemons, and Brett Place was all darkness, interspersed with the misty halos of the few lamps defining its triangular shape, with a cluster of three lights on one stand in the middle. The dark forms of the man and woman glided slowly arm in arm along the walls with a loverlike and homeless aspect in the miserable night.

'What would you say if I were to tell you that I was going to find you?' Mrs. Verloc asked, gripping his arm with force.

'I would say that you couldn't find any one more ready to help you in your trouble,' answered Ossipon, with a notion of making tremendous headway. In fact, the progress of this delicate affair was almost taking his breath away.

'In my trouble!' Mrs. Verloc repeated, slowly.

'Yes.'

'And do you know what my trouble is?' she whispered with strange intensity.

'Ten minutes after seeing the evening paper,' explained Ossipon with ardour, 'I met a fellow whom you may have seen once or twice at the shop perhaps, and I had a talk with him which left no doubt whatever in my mind. Then I started for here, wondering whether you — I've been fond of you beyond words ever since I set eyes on your face,' he cried, as if unable to command his feelings.

Comrade Ossipon assumed correctly that no woman was capable of wholly disbelieving such a statement. But he did not know that Mrs. Verloc accepted it with all the fierceness the instinct of self-preservation imparts to the grip of a drowning person. To the widow of Mr. Verloc the robust anarchist was like a radiant messenger of life.

They walked slowly, in step. 'I thought so,' Mrs. Verloc murmured, faintly.

'You've read it in my eyes,' suggested Ossipon with great assurance.

'Yes,' she breathed out into his inclined ear.

'A love like mine could not be concealed from a woman like you,' he went on, trying to detach his mind from material considerations such as the business value of the shop, and the amount of money Mr. Verloc might have left in the bank. He applied himself to the sentimental side of the affair. In his heart of hearts he was a little shocked at his success. Verloc had been a good fellow, and certainly a very decent husband as far as one could see. However, Comrade Ossipon was not going to quarrel with his luck for the sake of a dead man. Resolutely he suppressed his sympathy for the ghost of Comrade Verloc, and went on:

'I could not conceal it. I was too full of you. I daresay you could not help seeing it in my eyes. But I could not guess it. You were always so distant. . . .'

'What else did you expect?' burst out Mrs. Verloc. 'I was a respectable woman —'

She paused, then added, as if speaking to herself, in sinister resentment: 'Till he made me what I am.'

Ossipon let that pass, and took up his running.

'He never did seem to me to be quite worthy of you,' he began, throwing loyalty to the winds. 'You were worthy of a better fate.'

Mrs. Verloc interrupted bitterly:

'Better fate! He cheated me out of seven years of life.'

'You seemed to live so happily with him.' Ossipon tried to exculpate the lukewarmness of his past conduct. 'It's that what's made me timid. You seemed to love him. I was surprised – and jealous,' he added.

'Love him!' Mrs. Verloc cried out in a whisper full of scorn and rage. 'Love him! I was a good wife to him. I am a respectable woman. You thought I loved him! You did! Look here, Tom — '

The sound of this name thrilled Comrade Ossipon with pride. For his name was Alexander, and he was called Tom by arrangement with the most familiar of his intimates. It was a name of friendship – of moments of expansion. He had no idea that she had ever heard it used by anybody. It was apparent that she had not only caught it, but had treasured it in her memory – perhaps in her heart.

'Look here, Tom! I was a young girl. I was done up. I was tired. I had two people depending on what I could do, and it did seem as if I couldn't do any more. Two people – mother and the boy. He was much more mine than mother's. I sat up nights and nights with him on my lap, all alone upstairs, when I wasn't more than eight years old myself. And then — He was mine, I tell you. . . . You can't understand that. No man can understand it. What was I to do? There was a young fellow —'

The memory of the early romance with the young butcher survived, tenacious, like the image of a glimpsed

ideal in that heart quailing before the fear of the gallows
and full of revolt against death.

'That was the man I loved then,' went on the widow of
Mr. Verloc. 'I suppose he could see it in my eyes, too.
Five and twenty shillings a week, and his father threatened to kick him out of the business if he made such a
fool of himself as to marry a girl with a crippled mother
and a crazy idiot of a boy on her hands. But he would
hang about me, till one evening I found the courage to
slam the door in his face. I had to do it. I loved him dearly.
Five and twenty shillings a week! There was that other
man – a good lodger. What is a girl to do? Could I've
gone on the streets? He seemed kind. He wanted me,
anyhow. What was I to do with mother and that poor
boy? Eh? I said yes. He seemed good-natured, he was
freehanded, he had money, he never said anything.
Seven years – seven years a good wife to him, the kind,
the good, the generous, the — And he loved me. Oh, yes.
He loved me till I sometimes wished myself — Seven
years. Seven years a wife to him. And do you know what
he was, that dear friend of yours? Do you know what he
was? . . . He was a devil!'

The superhuman vehemence of that whispered statement completely stunned Comrade Ossipon. Winnie
Verloc turning about held him by both arms, facing him
under the falling mist in the darkness and solitude of
Brett Place, in which all sounds of life seemed lost as if
in a triangular well of asphalt and bricks, of blind houses
and unfeeling stones.

'No; I didn't know,' he declared, with a sort of flabby
stupidity, whose comical aspect was lost upon a woman
haunted by the fear of the gallows, 'but I do now. I – I
understand,' he floundered on, his mind speculating as
to what sort of atrocities Verloc could have practised
under the sleepy, placid appearances of his married estate. It was positively awful. 'I understand,' he
repeated, and then by a sudden inspiration uttered an

'Unhappy woman!' of lofty commiseration instead of the
more familiar 'Poor darling!' of his usual practice. This
was no usual case. He felt conscious of something abnor-
mal going on, while he never lost sight of the greatness
of the stake. 'Unhappy, brave woman!'

He was glad to have discovered that variation; but he
could discover nothing else. 'Ah, but he is dead now,'
was the best he could do. And he put a remarkable
amount of animosity into his guarded exclamation. Mrs.
Verloc caught at his arm with a sort of frenzy. 'You
guessed then he was dead,' she murmured, as if beside
herself. 'You! You guessed what I had to do. Had to!'

There were suggestions of triumph, relief, gratitude in the indefinable tone of these words. It engrossed
the whole attention of Ossipon to the detriment of
mere literal sense. He wondered what was up with her,
why she had worked herself into this state of wild excitement. He even began to wonder whether the hidden
causes of that Greenwich Park affair did not lie deep
in the unhappy circumstances of the Verlocs' married
life. He went so far as to suspect Mr. Verloc of having
selected that extraordinary manner of committing
suicide. By Jove! that would account for the utter inanity
and wrong-headedness of the thing. No anarchist manifestation was required by the circumstances. Quite the
contrary; and Verloc was as well aware of that as any
other revolutionist of his standing. What an immense
joke if Verloc had simply made fools of the whole of
Europe, of the revolutionary world, of the police, of the
press, and of the cocksure Professor as well. Indeed,
thought Ossipon, in astonishment, it seemed almost certain that he did! Poor beggar! It struck him as very
possible that of that household of two it wasn't precisely
the man who was the devil.

Alexander Ossipon, nicknamed the Doctor, was naturally inclined to think indulgently of his men friends. He
eyed Mrs. Verloc hanging on his arm. Of his women

friends he thought in a specially practical way. Why Mrs.
Verloc should exclaim at his knowledge of Mr. Verloc's
death, which was no guess at all, did not disturb him beyond measure. Women often talked like lunatics. But he
was curious to know how she had been informed. The
papers could tell her nothing beyond the mere fact: the
man blown to pieces in Greenwich Park not having been
identified. It was inconceivable on any theory that Verloc
should have given her an inkling of his intention – whatever it was. This problem interested Comrade Ossipon
immensely. He stopped short. They had gone then along
the three sides of Brett Place, and were near the end of
Brett Street again.

'How did you first come to hear of it?' he asked in a
tone he tried to render appropriate to the character of the
revelations which had been made to him by the woman
at his side.

She shook violently for a while before she answered in
a listless voice:

'From the police. A chief inspector came. Chief
Inspector Heat he said he was. He showed me — '

Mrs. Verloc choked. 'Oh, Tom, they had to gather him
up with a shovel.'

Her breast heaved with dry sobs. In a moment Ossipon found his tongue.

'The police! Do you mean to say the police came
already? That Chief Inspector Heat himself actually
came to tell you?'

'Yes,' she confirmed in the same listless tone. 'He
came. Just like this. He came. I didn't know. He showed
me a piece of overcoat, and — Just like that. Do you
know this? he says.'

'Heat! Heat! And what did he do?'

Mrs. Verloc's head dropped. 'Nothing. He did nothing. He went away. The police were on that man's side,'
she murmured, tragically. 'Another one came, too.'

'Another – another inspector, do you mean?' asked

Ossipon, in great excitement, and very much in the tone
of a scared child.

'I don't know. He came. He looked like a foreigner.
He may have been one of them Embassy people.'

Comrade Ossipon nearly collapsed under this new
shock.

'Embassy! Are you aware what you are saying? What
Embassy? What on earth do you mean by Embassy?'

'It's that place in Chesham Square. The people he
cursed so. I don't know. What does it matter!'

'And that fellow, what did he do or say to you?'

'I don't remember. . . . Nothing. . . . I don't care.
Don't ask me,' she pleaded in a weary voice.

'All right. I won't,' assented Ossipon, tenderly. And he
meant it, too, not because he was touched by the pathos
of the pleading voice, but because he felt himself losing
his footing in the depths of this tenebrous affair. Police!
Embassy! Phew! For fear of adventuring his intelligence
into ways where its natural lights might fail to guide it
safely he dismissed resolutely all suppositions, surmises,
and theories out of his mind. He had the woman there,
absolutely flinging herself at him, and that was the principal consideration. But after what he had heard nothing
could astonish him any more. And when Mrs. Verloc, as if
startled suddenly out of a dream of safety, began to urge
upon him wildly the necessity of an immediate flight on
the Continent, he did not exclaim in the least. He simply
said with unaffected regret that there was no train till the
morning, and stood looking thoughtfully at her face,
veiled in black net, in the light of a gas-lamp veiled in a
gauze of mist.

Near him, her black form merged in the night, like a
figure half chiselled out of a block of black stone. It was
impossible to say what she knew, how deep she was
involved with policemen and Embassies. But if she
wanted to get away, it was not for him to object. He was
anxious to be off himself. He felt that the business, the

shop so strangely familiar to chief inspectors and members of foreign Embassies, was not the place for him. That must be dropped. But there was the rest. These savings. The money!

'You must hide me till the morning somewhere,' she said in a dismayed voice.

'Fact is, my dear, I can't take you where I live. I share the room with a friend.'

He was somewhat dismayed himself. In the morning the blessed 'tecs will be out in all the stations, no doubt. And if they once got hold of her, for one reason or another she would be lost to him indeed.

'But you must. Don't you care for me at all – at all? What are you thinking of?'

She said this violently, but she let her clasped hands fall in discouragement. There was a silence, while the mist fell, and darkness reigned undisturbed over Brett Place. Not a soul, not even the vagabond, lawless, and amorous soul of a cat, came near the man and the woman facing each other.

'It would be possible perhaps to find a safe lodging somewhere,' Ossipon spoke at last. 'But the truth is, my dear, I have not enough money to go and try with – only a few pence. We revolutionists are not rich.'

He had fifteen shillings in his pocket. He added:

'And there's the journey before us, too – first thing in the morning at that.'

She did not move, made no sound, and Comrade Ossipon's heart sank a little. Apparently she had no suggestion to offer. Suddenly she clutched at her breast, as if she had felt a sharp pain there.

'But I have,' she gasped. 'I have the money. I have enough money. Tom! Let us go from here.'

'How much have you got?' he inquired, without stirring to her tug; for he was a cautious man.

'I have the money, I tell you. All the money.'

'What do you mean by it? All the money there was in the bank, or what?' he asked, incredulously, but ready not to be surprised at anything in the way of luck.

'Yes, yes!' she said, nervously. 'All there was. I've it all.'

'How on earth did you manage to get hold of it already?' he marvelled.

'He gave it to me,' she murmured, suddenly subdued and trembling. Comrade Ossipon put down his rising surprise with a firm hand.

'Why, then – we are saved,' he uttered, slowly.

She leaned forward, and sank against his breast. He welcomed her there. She had all the money. Her hat was in the way of very marked effusion; her veil, too. He was adequate in his manifestations, but no more. She received them without resistance and without abandonment, passively, as if only half-sensible. She freed herself from his lax embrace without difficulty.

'You will save me, Tom,' she broke out, recoiling, but still keeping her hold on him by the two lapels of his damp coat. 'Save me. Hide me. Don't let them have me. You must kill me first. I couldn't do it myself – I couldn't, I couldn't – not even for what I am afraid of.'

She was confoundedly bizarre, he thought. She was beginning to inspire him with an indefinite uneasiness. He said surlily, for he was busy with important thoughts:

'What the devil *are* you afraid of?'

'Haven't you guessed what I was driven to do!' cried the woman. Distracted by the vividness of her dreadful apprehensions, her head ringing with forceful words, that kept the horror of her position before her mind, she had imagined her incoherence to be clearness itself. She had no conscience of how little she had audibly said in the disjointed phrases completed only in her thought. She had felt the relief of a full confession, and she gave a special meaning to every sentence spoken by Comrade Ossipon, whose knowledge did not in the least resemble

her own. 'Haven't you guessed what I was driven to
do!' Her voice fell. 'You needn't be long in guessing
then what I am afraid of,' she continued, in a bitter and
sombre murmur. 'I won't have it. I won't. I won't. I
won't. You must promise to kill me first!' She shook the
lapels of his coat. 'It must never be!'

He assured her curtly that no promises on his part
were necessary, but he took good care not to contradict
her in set terms, because he had had much to do with
excited women, and he was inclined in general to let his
experience guide his conduct in preference to applying
his sagacity to each special case. His sagacity in this case
was busy in other directions. Women's words fell into
water, but the shortcomings of time-tables remained.
The insular nature of Great Britain obtruded itself upon
his notice in an odious form. 'Might just as well be put
under lock and key every night,' he thought irritably, as
non-plussed as though he had a wall to scale with the
woman on his back. Suddenly he slapped his forehead.
He had by dint of cudgelling his brains just thought of
the Southampton–St. Malo service. The boat left about
midnight. There was a train at 10:30. He became cheery
and ready to act.

'From Waterloo. Plenty of time. We are all right after
all . . . What's the matter now? This isn't the way,' he
protested.

Mrs. Verloc, having hooked her arm into his, was
trying to drag him into Brett Street again.

'I've forgotten to shut the shop door as I went out,'
she whispered, terribly agitated.

The shop and all that was in it had ceased to interest
Comrade Ossipon. He knew how to limit his desires. He
was on the point of saying 'What of that? Let it be,' but
he refrained. He disliked argument about trifles. He
even mended his pace considerably on the thought that
she might have left the money in the drawer. But his
willingness lagged behind her feverish impatience.

The shop seemed to be quite dark at first. The door stood ajar. Mrs. Verloc, leaning against the front, grasped out:

'Nobody has been in. Look! The light – the light in the parlour.'

Ossipon, stretching his head forward, saw a faint gleam in the darkness of the shop.

'There is,' he said.

'I forgot it.' Mrs. Verloc's voice came from behind her veil faintly. And as he stood waiting for her to enter first, she said louder: 'Go in and put it out – or I'll go mad.'

He made no immediate objection to this proposal, so strangely motived. 'Where's all that money?' he asked.

'On me! Go, Tom. Quick! Put it out.... Go in!' she cried, seizing him by both shoulders from behind.

Not prepared for a display of physical force, Comrade Ossipon stumbled far into the shop before her push. He was astonished at the strength of the woman and scandalized by her proceedings. But he did not retrace his steps in order to remonstrate with her severely in the street. He was beginning to be disagreeably impressed by her fantastic behaviour. Moreover, this or never was the time to humour the woman. Comrade Ossipon avoided easily the end of the counter, and approached calmly the glazed door of the parlour. The curtain over the panes being drawn back a little he, by a very natural impulse, looked in, just as he made ready to turn the handle. He looked in without a thought, without intention, without curiosity of any sort. He looked in because he could not help looking in. He looked in, and discovered Mr. Verloc reposing quietly on the sofa.

A yell coming from the innermost depths of his chest died out unheard and transformed into a sort of greasy, sickly taste on his lips. At the same time the mental personality of Comrade Ossipon executed a frantic leap backwards. But his body, left thus without intellectual guidance, held on to the door handle with the unthink-

ing force of an instinct. The robust anarchist did not
even totter. And he stared, his face close to the glass, his
eyes protruding out of his head. He would have given
anything to get away, but his returning reason informed
him that it would not do to let go the door handle. What
was it – madness, a nightmare, or a trap into which he had
been decoyed with fiendish artfulness? Why – what for?
He did not know. Without any sense of guilt in his breast,
in the full peace of his conscience as far as these people
were concerned, the idea that he would be murdered for
mysterious reasons by the couple Verloc passed not so
much across his mind as across the pit of his stomach, and
went out, leaving behind a trail of sickly faintness – an
indisposition. Comrade Ossipon did not feel very well in
a very special way for a moment – a long moment. And he
stared. Mr. Verloc lay very still meanwhile, simulating
sleep for reasons of his own, while that savage woman of
his was guarding the door – invisible and silent in the
dark and deserted street. Was all this some sort of terrifying arrangement invented by the police for his especial
benefit? His modesty shrank from that explanation.

But the true sense of the scene he was beholding
came to Ossipon through the contemplation of the hat. It
seemed an extraordinary thing, an ominous object, a
sign. Black, and rim upward, it lay on the floor before the
couch as if prepared to receive the contributions of
pence from people who would come presently to behold
Mr. Verloc in the fullness of his domestic ease reposing
on a sofa. From the hat the eyes of the robust anarchist
wandered to the displaced table, gazed at the broken
dish for a time, received a kind of optical shock from
observing a white gleam under the imperfectly closed
eyelids of the man on the couch. Mr. Verloc did not seem
so much asleep now as lying down with a bent head and
looking insistently at his left breast. And when Comrade
Ossipon had made out the handle of the knife he turned
away from the glazed door, and retched violently.

The crash of the street door flung to made his very soul leap in a panic. This house with its harmless tenant could still be made a trap of – a trap of a terrible kind. Comrade Ossipon had no settled conception now of what was happening to him. Catching his thigh against the end of the counter, he spun round, staggered with a cry of pain, felt in the distracting clatter of the bell his arms pinned to his sides by a convulsive hug, while the cold lips of a woman moved creepily on his very ear to form the words:

'Policeman! He has seen me!'

He ceased to struggle; she never let him go. Her hands had locked themselves with an inseparable twist of fingers on his robust back. While the footsteps approached, they breathed quickly, breast to breast, with hard, laboured breaths, as if theirs had been the attitude of a deadly struggle, while, in fact, it was the attitude of deadly fear. And the time was long.

The constable on the beat had in truth seen something of Mrs. Verloc; only coming from the lighted thoroughfare at the other end of Brett Street, she had been no more to him than a flutter in the darkness. And he was not even quite sure that there had been a flutter. He had no reason to hurry up. On coming abreast of the shop he observed that it had been closed early. There was nothing very unusual in that. The men on duty had special instructions about that shop: what went on about there was not to be meddled with unless absolutely disorderly, but any observations made were to be reported. There were no observations to make; but from a sense of duty and for the peace of his conscience, owing also to that doubtful flutter of the darkness, the constable crossed the road, and tried the door. The spring latch, whose key was reposing for ever off duty in the late Mr. Verloc's waistcoat pocket, held as well as usual. While the conscientious officer was shaking the handle, Ossi-

pon felt the cold lips of the woman stirring again creepily
against his very ear:

'If he comes in kill me – kill me, Tom.'

The constable moved away, flashing as he passed the
light of his dark lantern, merely for form's sake, at
the shop window. For a moment longer the man and
the woman inside stood motionless, panting, breast to
breast; then her fingers came unlocked, her arms fell by
her sides slowly. Ossipon leaned against the counter.
The robust anarchist wanted support badly. This was
awful. He was almost too disgusted for speech. Yet he
managed to utter a plaintive thought, showing at least
that he realized his position.

'Only a couple of minutes later and you'd have made
me blunder against the fellow poking about here with
his damned dark lantern.'

The widow of Mr. Verloc, motionless in the middle of
the shop, said insistently:

'Go in and put that light out, Tom. It will drive me
crazy.'

She saw vaguely his vehement gesture of refusal.
Nothing in the world would have induced Ossipon to go
into the parlour. He was not superstitious, but there was
too much blood on the floor; a beastly pool of it all round
the hat. He judged he had been already too near that
corpse for his peace of mind – for the safety of his neck,
perhaps!

'At the meter then! There. Look. In that corner.'

The robust form of Comrade Ossipon, striding brusque and shadowy across the shop, squatted in a corner
obediently; but this obedience was without grace. He
fumbled nervously – and suddenly in the sound of a
muttered curse the light behind the glazed door flicked
out to a gasping, hysterical sigh of a woman. Night, the
inevitable reward of men's faithful labours on this earth,
night had fallen on Mr. Verloc, the tried revolutionist –
'one of the old lot' – the humble guardian of society;

the invaluable Secret Agent Δ. of Baron Stott-Wartenheim's despatches; a servant of law and order, faithful, trusted, accurate, admirable, with perhaps one single amiable weakness: the idealistic belief in being loved for himself.

Ossipon groped his way back through the stuffy atmosphere, as black as ink now, to the counter. The voice of Mrs. Verloc, standing in the middle of the shop, vibrated after him in that blackness with a desperate protest.

'I will not be hanged, Tom. I will not —'

She broke off. Ossipon from the counter issued a warning: 'Don't shout like this,' then seemed to reflect profoundly. 'You did this thing quite by yourself?' he inquired in a hollow voice, but with an appearance of masterful calmness which filled Mrs. Verloc's heart with grateful confidence in his protecting strength.

'Yes,' she whispered, invisible.

'I wouldn't have believed it possible,' he muttered. 'Nobody would.' She heard him move about and the snapping of a lock in the parlour door. Comrade Ossipon had turned the key on Mr. Verloc's repose; and this he did not from reverence for its eternal nature or any other obscurely sentimental consideration, but for the precise reason that he was not at all sure that there was not someone else hiding somewhere in the house. He did not believe the woman, or rather he was incapable by now of judging what could be true, possible, or even probable on this astounding universe. He was terrified out of all capacity for belief or disbelief in regard to this extraordinary affair, which began with police inspectors and Embassies and would end goodness knows where – on the scaffold for someone. He was terrified at the thought that he could not prove the use he made of his time ever since seven o'clock, for he had been skulking about Brett Street. He was terrified at this savage woman who had brought him in there, and would probably

saddle him with complicity, at least if he were not careful. He was terrified at the rapidity with which he had
been involved in such danger – decoyed into it. It was
some twenty minutes since he had met her – not more.

The voice of Mrs. Verloc rose subdued, pleading
piteously: 'Don't let them hang me, Tom! Take me out
of the country. I'll work for you. I'll slave for you. I'll love
you. I've no one in the world. . . . Who would look at me
if you don't!' She ceased for a moment; then in the
depths of the loneliness made round her by an insignificant thread of blood trickling off the handle of a knife,
she found a dreadful inspiration to her – who had been
the respectable girl of the Belgravian mansion, the loyal,
respectable wife of Mr. Verloc. 'I won't ask you to marry
me,' she breathed out in shamefaced accents.

She moved a step forward in the darkness. He was terrified at her. He would not have been surprised if she
had suddenly produced another knife destined for his
breast. He certainly would have made no resistance. He
had really not enough fortitude in him just then to tell
her to keep back. But he inquired in a cavernous, strange
tone: 'Was he asleep?'

'No,' she cried, and went on rapidly: 'He wasn't. Not
he. He had been telling me that nothing could touch
him. After taking the boy away from under my very eyes
to kill him – the loving, innocent, harmless lad. My own,
I tell you. He was lying on the couch quite easy – after
killing the boy – my boy. I would have gone on the
streets to get out of his sight. And he says to me like this:
"Come here," after telling me I had helped to kill the
boy. You hear, Tom? He says like this: "Come here,"
after taking my very heart out of me along with the boy
to smash in the dirt.'

She ceased, then dreamily repeated twice: 'Blood and
dirt. Blood and dirt.' A great light broke upon Comrade
Ossipon. It was that half-witted lad then who had
perished in the park. And the fooling of everybody all

round appeared more complete than ever – colossal. He exclaimed scientifically, in the extremity of his astonishment: 'The degenerate – by heavens!'

'Come here.' The voice of Mrs. Verloc rose again. 'What did he think I was made of? Tell me, Tom. Come here! Me! Like this! I had been looking at the knife, and I thought I would come then if he wanted me so much. Oh, yes! I came – for the last time. . . . With the knife.'

He was excessively terrified at her – the sister of the degenerate – a degenerate herself of a murdering type . . . or else of the lying type. Comrade Ossipon might have been said to be terrified scientifically in addition to all other kinds of fear. It was an immeasurable and composite funk, which from its very excess gave him in the dark a false appearance of calm and thoughtful deliberation. For he moved and spoke with difficulty, being as if half frozen in his will and mind – and no one could see his ghastly face. He felt half dead.

He leaped a foot high. Unexpectedly Mrs. Verloc had desecrated the unbroken, reserved decency of her home by a shrill and terrible shriek.

'Help, Tom! Save me. I won't be hanged!'

He rushed forward, groping for her mouth with a silencing hand, and the shriek died out. But in his rush he had knocked her over. He felt her now clinging round his legs, and his terror reached its culminating point, became a sort of intoxication, entertained delusions, acquired the characteristics of delirium tremens. He positively saw snakes now. He saw the woman twined round him like a snake, not to be shaken off. She was not deadly. She was death itself – the companion of life.

Mrs. Verloc, as if relieved by the outburst, was very far from behaving noisily now. She was pitiful.

'Tom, you can't throw me off now,' she murmured from the floor. 'Not unless you crush my head under your heel. I won't leave you.'

'Get up,' said Ossipon.

His face was so pale as to be quite visible in the profound black darkness of the shop; while Mrs. Verloc, veiled, had no face, almost no discernible form. The trembling of something small and white, a flower in her hat, marked her place, her movements.

It rose in the blackness. She had got up from the floor, and Ossipon regretted not having run out at once into the street. But he perceived easily that it would not do. It would not do. She would run after him. She would pursue him shrieking till she sent every policeman within hearing in chase. And then goodness only knew what she would say of him. He was so frightened that for a moment the insane notion of strangling her in the dark passed through his mind. And he became more frightened than ever! She had him. He saw himself living in abject terror in some obscure hamlet in Spain or Italy; till some fine morning they found him dead, too, with a knife in his breast – like Mr. Verloc. He sighed deeply. He dared not move. And Mrs. Verloc waited in silence the good pleasure of her saviour, deriving comfort from his reflective silence.

Suddenly he spoke up in an almost natural voice. His reflections had come to an end.

'Let's get out, or we will lose the train.'

'Where are we going to, Tom?' she asked, timidly. Mrs. Verloc was no longer a free woman.

'Let's get to Paris first, the best way we can. . . . Go out first, and see if the way's clear.'

She obeyed. Her voice came subdued through the cautiously opened door.

'It's all right.'

Ossipon came out. Notwithstanding his endeavours to be gentle, the cracked bell clattered behind the closed door in the empty shop, as if trying in vain to warn the reposing Mr. Verloc of the final departure of his wife – accompanied by his friend.

In the hansom they presently picked up, the robust

anarchist became explanatory. He was still awfully pale, with eyes that seemed to have sunk a whole half-inch into his tense face. But he seemed to have thought of everything with extraordinary method.

'When we arrive,' he discoursed in a queer, monotonous tone, 'you must go into the station ahead of me, as if we did not know each other. I will take the tickets, and slip yours into your hand as I pass you. Then you will go into the first-class ladies' waiting-room, and sit there till ten minutes before the train starts. Then you come out. I will be outside. You go in first on the platform, as if you did not know me. There may be eyes watching there that know what's what. Alone you are only a woman going off by train. I am known. With me, you may be guessed at as Mrs. Verloc running away. Do you understand, my dear?' he added, with an effort.

'Yes,' said Mrs. Verloc, sitting there against him in the hansom all rigid with the dread of the gallows and the fear of death. 'Yes, Tom.' And she added to herself, like an awful refrain: 'The drop given was fourteen feet.'

Ossipon, not looking at her, and with a face like a fresh plaster cast of himself after a wasting illness, said: 'By-the-by, I ought to have the money for the tickets now.'

Mrs. Verloc, undoing some hooks of her bodice, while she went on staring ahead beyond the splashboard, handed over to him the new pigskin pocket-book. He received it without a word, and seemed to plunge it deep somewhere into his very breast. Then he slapped his coat on the outside.

All this was done without the exchange of a single glance; they were like two people looking out for the first sight of a desired goal. It was not till the hansom swung round a corner and towards the bridge that Ossipon opened his lips again.

'Do you know how much money there is in that thing?' he asked, as if addressing slowly some hobgoblin sitting between the ears of the horse.

'No,' said Mrs. Verloc. 'He gave it to me. I didn't count. I thought nothing of it at the time. Afterwards —'

She moved her right hand a little. It was so expressive, that little movement of that right hand which had struck the deadly blow into a man's heart less than an hour before, that Ossipon could not repress a shudder. He exaggerated it then purposely, and muttered:

'I am cold. I got chilled through.'

Mrs. Verloc looked straight ahead at the perspective of her escape. Now and then, like a sable streamer blown across a road, the words 'The drop given was fourteen feet' got in the way of her tense stare. Through her black veil the whites of her big eyes gleamed lustrously like the eyes of a masked woman.

Ossipon's rigidity had something businesslike, a queer official expression. He was heard again all of a sudden, as though he had released a catch in order to speak.

'Look here! Do you know whether your – whether he kept his account at the bank in his own name or in some other name?'

Mrs. Verloc turned upon him her masked face and the big white gleam of her eyes.

'Other name?' she said, thoughtfully.

'Be exact in what you say,' Ossipon lectured in the swift motion of the hansom. 'It's extremely important. I will explain to you. The bank has the numbers of these notes. If they were paid to him in his own name, then when his – his death becomes known, the notes may serve to track us since we have no other money. You have no other money on you?'

She shook her head negatively.

'None whatever?' he insisted.

'A few coppers.'

'It would be dangerous in that case. The money would have then to be dealt specially with. Very specially. We'd have perhaps to lose more than half the amount in order to get these notes changed in a certain

safe place I know of in Paris. In the other case – I mean if
he had his account and got paid out under some other
name – say Smith, for instance – the money is perfectly
safe to use. You understand? The bank has no means of
knowing that Mr. Verloc and, say, Smith are one and the
same person. Do you see how important it is that you
should make no mistake in answering me? Can you
answer that query at all? Perhaps not. Eh?'

She said composedly:

'I remember now! He didn't bank in his own name.
He told me once that it was on deposit in the name of
Prozor.'

'You are sure?'

'Certain.'

'You don't think the bank had any knowledge of his
real name? Or anybody in the bank or —'

She shrugged her shoulders.

'How can I know? Is it likely, Tom?'

'No. I suppose it's not likely. It would have been more
comfortable to know. . . . Here we are. Get out first, and
walk straight in. Move smartly.'

He remained behind, and paid the cabman out of his
own loose silver. The programme traced by his minute
foresight was carried out. When Mrs. Verloc, with her
ticket for St. Malo in her hand, entered the ladies'
waiting-room, Comrade Ossipon walked into the bar,
and in seven minutes absorbed three goes of hot brandy
and water.

'Trying to drive out a cold,' he explained to the bar-
maid, with a friendly nod and a grimacing smile. Then
he came out, bringing out from that festive interlude the
face of a man who had drunk at the very Fountain of Sorrow. He raised his eyes to the clock. It was time. He
waited.

Punctual, Mrs. Verloc came out, with her veil down,
and all black – black as commonplace death itself,
crowned with a few cheap and pale flowers. She passed

close to a little group of men who were laughing, but whose laughter could have been struck dead by a single word. Her walk was indolent, but her back was straight, and Comrade Ossipon looked after it in terror before making a start himself.

The train was drawn up, with hardly anybody about its row of open doors. Owing to the time of the year and to the abominable weather there were but few passengers. Mrs. Verloc walked slowly along the line of empty compartments till Ossipon touched her elbow from behind.

'In here.'

She got in, and he remained on the platform looking about. She bent forward, and in a whisper:

'What is it, Tom? Is there any danger?'

'Wait a moment. There's the guard.'

She saw him accost the man in uniform. They talked for a while. She heard the guard say 'Very well, sir,' and saw him touch his cap. Then Ossipon came back, saying: 'I told him not to let anybody get into our compartment.'

She was leaning forward on her seat. 'You think of everything. . . . You'll get me off, Tom?' she asked in a gust of anguish, lifting her veil brusquely to look at her saviour.

She had uncovered a face like adamant. And out of this face the eyes looked on, big, dry, enlarged, lightless, burnt out like two black holes in the white, shining globes.

'There is no danger,' he said, gazing into them with an earnestness almost rapt, which to Mrs. Verloc, flying from the gallows, seemed to be full of force and tenderness. This devotion deeply moved her – and the adamantine face lost the stern rigidity of its terror. Comrade Ossipon gazed at it as no lover ever gazed at his mistress's face. Alexander Ossipon, anarchist, nicknamed the Doctor, author of a medical (and improper) pamphlet, late lecturer on the social aspects of hygiene to working men's clubs, was free from the trammels of conventional morality – but he submitted to the rule of science. He was scientific, and he gazed scientifically at that woman, the sister of a degenerate, a degenerate herself – of a murdering type. He gazed at her, and invoked Lombroso, as an Italian peasant recommends himself to his favourite saint. He gazed scientifically. He gazed at her cheeks, at her nose, at her eyes, at her ears. . . . Bad! . . . Fatal! Mrs. Verloc's pale lips parting, slightly relaxed under his passionately attentive gaze, he gazed also at her teeth. . . . Not a doubt remained . . . a murdering type. . . . If Comrade Ossipon did not recommend his terrified soul to Lombroso, it was only because on scientific grounds he could not believe that he carried about him such a thing as a soul. But he had in him the scientific spirit, which moved him to testify on the platform of a railway station in nervous, jerky phrases.

'He was an extraordinary lad, that brother of yours. Most interesting to study. A perfect type in a way. Perfect!'

He spoke scientifically in his secret fear. And Mrs. Verloc, hearing these words of commendation vouchsafed to her beloved dead, swayed forward with a flicker of light in her sombre eyes, like a ray of sunshine heralding a tempest of rain.

'He was that indeed,' she whispered, softly, with quivering lips. 'You took a lot of notice of him, Tom. I loved you for it.'

'It's almost incredible the resemblance there was between you two,' pursued Ossipon, giving a voice to his abiding dread, and trying to conceal his nervous, sickening impatience for the train to start. 'Yes, he resembled you.'

These words were not especially touching or sympathetic. But the fact of that resemblance insisted upon was enough in itself to act upon her emotions powerfully. With a little faint cry, and throwing her arms out, Mrs. Verloc burst into tears at last.

Ossipon entered the carriage, hastily closed the door
and looked out to see the time by the station clock.
Eight minutes more. For the first three of these Mrs.
Verloc wept violently and helplessly without pause or
interruption. Then she recovered somewhat, and sobbed
gently in an abundant fall of tears. She tried to talk to her
saviour, to the man who was the messenger of life.

'Oh, Tom! How could I fear to die after he was taken
away from me so cruelly! How could I! How could I be
such a coward!'

She lamented aloud her love of life, that life without
grace or charm, and almost without decency, but of an
exalted faithfulness of purpose, even unto murder. And,
as often happens in the lament of poor humanity rich in
suffering but indigent in words, the truth – the very cry
of truth – was found in a worn and artificial shape
picked up somewhere among the phrases of sham sentiment.

'How could I be so afraid of death! Tom, I tried. But I
am afraid. I tried to do away with myself. And I couldn't.
Am I hard? I suppose the cup of horrors was not full
enough for such as me. Then when you came. . . .'

She paused. Then in a gust of confidence and gratitude, 'I will live all my days for you, Tom!' she sobbed
out.

'Go over into the other corner of the carriage, away
from the platform,' said Ossipon, solicitously. She let her
saviour settle her comfortably, and he watched the coming on of another crisis of weeping, still more violent
than the first. He watched the symptoms with a sort of
medical air, as if counting seconds. He heard the guard's
whistle at last. An involuntary contraction of the upper
lip bared his teeth with all the aspect of savage resolution as he felt the train beginning to move. Mrs. Verloc
heard and felt nothing, and Ossipon, her saviour, stood
still. He felt the train roll quicker, rumbling heavily to
the sound of the woman's loud sobs, and then crossing

the carriage in two long strides he opened the door deliberately, and leaped out.

He had leaped out at the very end of the platform; and such was his determination in sticking to his desperate plan that he managed by a sort of miracle, performed almost in the air, to slam to the door of the carriage. Only then did he find himself rolling head over heels like a shot rabbit. He was bruised, shaken, pale as death, and out of breath when he got up. But he was calm, and perfectly able to meet the excited crowd of railway men who had gathered round him in a moment. He explained, in gentle and convincing tones, that his wife had started at a moment's notice for Brittany to her dying mother; that, of course, she was greatly upset, and he considerably concerned at her state; that he was trying to cheer her up, and had absolutely failed to notice at first that the train was moving out. To the general exclamation 'Why didn't you go on to Southampton, then, sir?' he objected the inexperience of a young sister-in-law left alone in the house with three small children, and her alarm at his absence, the telegraph offices being closed. He had acted on impulse. 'But I don't think I'll ever try that again,' he concluded; smiled all round; distributed some small change, and marched without a limp out of the station.

Outside, Comrade Ossipon, flush of safe banknotes as never before in his life, refused the offer of a cab.

'I can walk,' he said, with a little friendly laugh to the civil driver.

He could walk. He walked. He crossed the bridge. Later on the towers of the Abbey saw in their massive immobility the yellow bush of his hair passing under the lamps. The lights of Victoria saw him, too, and Sloane Square, and the railings of the park. And Comrade Ossipon once more found himself on a bridge. The river, a sinister marvel of still shadows and flowing gleams mingling below in a black silence, arrested his attention. He stood looking over the parapet for a long time. The clock tower boomed a brazen blast above his drooping head. He looked up at the dial. . . . Half-past twelve of a wild night in the Channel.

And again Comrade Ossipon walked. His robust form was seen that night in distant parts of the enormous town slumbering monstrously on a carpet of mud under a veil of raw mist. It was seen crossing the streets without life and sound, or diminishing in the interminable straight perspectives of shadowy houses bordering empty roadways lined by strings of gas-lamps. He walked through Squares, Places, Ovals, Commons, through monotonous streets with unknown names where the dust of humanity settles inert and hopeless out of the stream of life. He walked. And suddenly turning into a strip of a front garden with a mangy grass plot, he let himself into a small grimy house with a latchkey he took out of his pocket.

He threw himself down on his bed all dressed, and lay still for a whole quarter of an hour. Then he sat up suddenly, drawing up his knees, and clasping his legs. The first dawn found him open-eyed, in that same posture. This man who could walk so long, so far, so aimlessly, without showing a sign of fatigue, could also remain sitting still for hours without stirring a limb or an eyelid. But when the late sun sent its rays into the room he unclasped his hands, and fell back on the pillow. His eyes stared at the ceiling. And suddenly they closed. Comrade Ossipon slept in the sunlight.

CHAPTER THIRTEEN

THE enormous iron padlock on the doors of the wall cupboard was the only object in the room on which the eye could rest without becoming afflicted by the miserable unloveliness of forms and the poverty of material. Unsaleable in the ordinary course of business on account of its noble proportions, it had been ceded to the Professor for a few pence by a marine dealer in the east of London. The room was large, clean, respectable, and poor with that poverty suggesting the starvation of every human need except mere bread. There was nothing on the walls but the paper, an expanse of arsenical green, soiled with indelible smudges here and there, and with stains resembling faded maps of uninhabited continents.

At a deal table near a window sat Comrade Ossipon, holding his head between his fists. The Professor, dressed in his only suit of shoddy tweeds, but flapping to and fro on the bare boards a pair of incredibly dilapidated slippers, had thrust his hands deep into the over-strained pockets of his jacket. He was relating to his robust guest a visit he had lately been paying to the Apostle Michaelis. The Perfect Anarchist had even been unbending a little.

'The fellow didn't know anything of Verloc's death. Of course! He never looks at the newspapers. They make him too sad, he says. But never mind. I walked into his cottage. Not a soul anywhere. I had to shout half-a-dozen times before he answered me. I thought he was

fast asleep yet, in bed. But not at all. He had been writing his book for four hours already. He sat in that tiny
cage in a litter of manuscript. There was a half-eaten raw
carrot on the table near him. His breakfast. He lives on a
diet of raw carrots and a little milk now.'

'How does he look on it?' asked Comrade Ossipon,
listlessly.

'Angelic. . . . I picked up a handful of his pages from
the floor. The poverty of reasoning is astonishing. He has
no logic. He can't think consecutively. But that's nothing.
He has divided his biography into three parts, entitled –
"Faith, Hope, Charity." He is elaborating now the idea of
a world planned out like an immense and nice hospital,
with gardens and flowers, in which the strong are to
devote themselves to the nursing of the weak.'

The Professor paused.

'Conceive you this folly, Ossipon? The weak! The
source of all evil on this earth!' he continued with his
grim assurance. 'I told him that I dreamt of a world like
shambles, where the weak would be taken in hand for
utter extermination.

'Do you understand, Ossipon? The source of all evil!
They are our sinister masters – the weak, the flabby, the
silly, the cowardly, the faint of heart, and the slavish of
mind. They have power. They are the multitude. Theirs
is the kingdom of the earth. Exterminate, exterminate!
That is the only way of progress. It is! Follow me, Ossipon. First the great multitude of the weak must go, then
the only relatively strong. You see? First the blind, then
the deaf and the dumb, then the halt and the lame – and
so on. Every taint, every vice, every prejudice, every
convention must meet its doom.'

'And what remains?' asked Ossipon in a stifled voice.

'I remain – if I am strong enough,' asserted the sallow
little Professor, whose large ears, thin like membranes,
and standing far out from the sides of his frail skull, took
on suddenly a deep red tint.

'Haven't I suffered enough from this oppression of the weak?' he continued, forcibly. Then tapping the breast-pocket of his jacket: 'And yet *I am* the force,' he went on. 'But the time! The time! Give me time! Ah! that multitude, too stupid to feel either pity or fear. Sometimes I think they have everything on their side. Everything – even death – my own weapon.'

'Come and drink some beer with me at the Silenus,' said the robust Ossipon after an interval of silence pervaded by the rapid flap, flap of the slippers on the feet of the Perfect Anarchist. This last accepted. He was jovial that day in his own peculiar way. He slapped Ossipon's shoulder.

'Beer! So be it! Let us drink and be merry, for we are strong, and to-morrow we die.'

He busied himself with putting on his boots, and talked meanwhile in his curt, resolute tones.

'What's the matter with you, Ossipon? You look glum and seek even my company. I hear that you are seen constantly in places where men utter foolish things over glasses of liquor. Why? Have you abandoned your collection of women? They are the weak who feed the strong – eh?'

He stamped one foot, and picked up his other laced boot, heavy, thick-soled, unblacked, mended many times. He smiled to himself grimly.

'Tell me, Ossipon, terrible man, has ever one of your victims killed herself for you – or are your triumphs so far incomplete – for blood alone puts a seal on greatness? Blood. Death. Look at history.'

'You be damned,' said Ossipon, without turning his head.

'Why? Let that be the hope of the weak, whose theology has invented hell for the strong. Ossipon, my feeling for you is amicable contempt. You couldn't kill a fly.'

But rolling to the feast on the top of the omnibus the Professor lost his high spirits. The contemplation of the multitudes thronging the pavements extinguished his assurance under a load of doubt and uneasiness which he could shake off after a period of seclusion in the room with the large cupboard closed by an enormous padlock.

'And so,' said over his shoulder Comrade Ossipon, who sat on the seat behind. 'And so Michaelis dreams of a world like a beautiful and cheery hospital.'

'Just so. An immense charity for the healing of the weak,' assented the Professor, sardonically.

'That's silly,' admitted Ossipon. 'You can't heal weakness. But after all Michaelis may not be so far wrong. In two hundred years doctors will rule the world. Science reigns already. It reigns in the shade maybe – but it reigns. And all science must culminate at last in the science of healing – not the weak, but the strong. Mankind wants to live – to live.'

'Mankind,' asserted the Professor with a self-confident glitter of his iron-rimmed spectacles, 'does not know what it wants.'

'But you do,' growled Ossipon. 'Just now you've been crying for time – time. Well, the doctors will serve you out your time – if you are good. You profess yourself to be one of the strong – because you carry in your pocket enough stuff to send yourself and, say, twenty other people into eternity. But eternity is a damned hole. It's time that you need. You – if you met a man who could give you for certain ten years of time, you would call him your master.'

'My device is: No God! No master,' said the Professor, sententiously, as he rose to get off the 'bus.

Ossipon followed. 'Wait till you are lying flat on your back at the end of your time,' he retorted, jumping off the footboard after the other. 'Your scurvy, shabby, mangy little bit of time,' he continued across the street, and hopping on to the curbstone.

'Ossipon, I think that you are a humbug,' the Professor said, opening masterfully the doors of the renowned

Silenus. And when they had established themselves at a little table he developed further this gracious thought. 'You are not even a doctor. But you are funny. Your notion of a humanity universally putting out the tongue and taking the pill from pole to pole at the bidding of a few solemn jokers is worthy of the prophet. Prophecy! What's the good of thinking of what will be!' He raised his glass. 'To the destruction of what is,' he said, calmly.

He drank and relapsed into his peculiarly close manner of silence. The thought of a mankind as numerous as the sands of the seashore, as indestructible, as difficult to handle, oppressed him. The sound of exploding bombs was lost in their immensity of passive grains without an echo. For instance, this Verloc affair. Who thought of it now?

Ossipon, as if suddenly compelled by some mysterious force, pulled a much-folded newspaper out of his pocket. The Professor raised his head at the rustle.

'What's that paper? Anything in it?' he asked.

Ossipon started like a scared somnambulist.

'Nothing. Nothing whatever. The thing's ten days old. I forgot it in my pocket, I suppose.'

But he did not throw the old thing away. Before returning it to his pocket he stole a glance at the last lines of a paragraph. They ran thus: '*An impenetrable mystery seems destined to hang for ever over this act of madness or despair.*'

Such were the end words of an item of news headed: 'Suicide of Lady Passenger from a cross-Channel Boat.' Comrade Ossipon was familiar with the beauties of its journalistic style. '*An impenetrable mystery seems destined to hang for ever. . . .*' He knew every word by heart. '*An impenetrable mystery. . . .*' And the robust anarchist, hanging his head on his breast, fell into a long reverie.

He was menaced by this thing in the very sources of his existence. He could not issue forth to meet his various conquests, those that he courted on benches in

Kensington Gardens, and those he met near area railings, without the dread of beginning to talk to them of an impenetrable mystery destined. . . . He was becoming scientifically afraid of insanity lying in wait for him amongst these lines. '*To hang for ever over.*' It was an obsession, a torture. He had lately failed to keep several of these appointments, whose note used to be an unbounded trustfulness in the language of sentiment and manly tenderness. The confiding disposition of various classes of women satisfied the needs of his self-love, and put some material means into his hand. He needed it to live. It was there. But if he could no longer make use of it, he ran the risk of starving his ideals and his body . . . '*This act of madness or despair.*'

'An impenetrable mystery' was sure 'to hang for ever' as far as all mankind was concerned. But what of that if he alone of all men could never get rid of the cursed knowledge? And Comrade Ossipon's knowledge was as precise as the newspaper man could make it – up to the very threshold of the '*mystery destined to hang for ever.* . . .'

Comrade Ossipon was well informed. He knew what the gangway man of the steamer had seen: 'A lady in a black dress and a black veil, wandering at midnight alongside, on the quay. "Are you going by the boat, ma'am?" he had asked her, encouragingly. "This way." She seemed not to know what to do. He helped her on board. She seemed weak.'

And Ossipon knew also what the stewardess had seen: A lady in black with a white face standing in the middle of the empty ladies' cabin. The stewardess induced her to lie down there. The lady seemed quite unwilling to speak, and as if she were in some awful trouble. The next the stewardess knew she was gone from the ladies' cabin. The stewardess then went on deck to look for her, and Comrade Ossipon was informed that the good woman found the unhappy lady lying down in one of the hooded seats. Her eyes were open, but she would not answer anything that was said to her. She seemed very ill. The stewardess fetched the chief steward, and those two people stood by the side of the hooded seat consulting over their extraordinary and tragic passenger. They talked in audible whispers (for she seemed past hearing) of St. Malo and the Consul there, of communicating with her people in England. Then they went away to arrange for her removal down below, for indeed by what they could see of her face she seemed to them to be dying. But Comrade Ossipon knew that behind that white mask of despair there was struggling against terror and despair a vigour of vitality, a love of life that could resist the furious anguish which drives to murder and the fear, the blind, mad fear of the gallows. He knew. But the stewardess and the chief steward knew nothing, except that when they came back for her in less than five minutes the lady in black was no longer in the hooded seat. She was nowhere. She was gone. It was then five o'clock in the morning, and it was no accident either. An hour afterwards one of the steamer's hands found a wedding ring left lying on the seat. It had stuck to the wood in a bit of wet, and its glitter caught the man's eye. There was a date, 24th June, 1879, engraved inside. '*An impenetrable mystery is destined to hang for ever. . . .*'

And Comrade Ossipon raised his bowed head, beloved of various humble women of these isles, Apollolike in the sunniness of its bush of hair.

The Professor had grown restless meantime. He rose.

'Stay,' said Ossipon, hurriedly. 'Here, what do you know of madness and despair?'

The Professor passed the tip of his tongue on his dry, thin lips, and said doctorally:

'There are no such things. All passion is lost now. The world is mediocre, limp, without force. And madness and despair are a force. And force is a crime in the eyes of the fools, the weak and the silly who rule the roost. You are mediocre. Verloc, whose affair the police has managed to

smother so nicely, was mediocre. And the police murdered him. He was mediocre. Everybody is mediocre.
Madness and despair! Give me that for a lever, and I'll
move the world. Ossipon, you have my cordial scorn. You
are incapable of conceiving even what the fat-fed citizen
would call a crime. You have no force.' He paused, smiling sardonically under the fierce glitter of his thick
glasses.

'And let me tell you that this little legacy they say
you've come into has not improved your intelligence.
You sit at your beer like a dummy. Good-bye.'

'Will you have it?' said Ossipon, looking up with an
idiotic grin.

'Have what?'

'The legacy. All of it.'

The incorruptible Professor only smiled. His clothes
were all but falling off him, his boots, shapeless with
repairs, heavy like lead, let water in at every step. He
said:

'I will send you by-and-by a small bill for certain
chemicals which I shall order to-morrow. I need them
badly. Understood – eh?'

Ossipon lowered his head slowly. He was alone. '*An
impenetrable mystery. . . .*' It seemed to him that suspended in the air before him he saw his own brain pulsating to the rhythm of an impenetrable mystery. It was
diseased clearly. . . . '*This act of madness or despair.*'

The mechanical piano near the door played through a
valse cheekily, then fell silent all at once, as if gone
grumpy.

Comrade Ossipon, nicknamed the Doctor, went out of
the Silenus beer-hall. At the door he hesitated, blinking
at a not too splendid sunlight – and the paper with the
report of the suicide of a lady was in his pocket. His heart
was beating against it. The suicide of a lady – *this act of
madness or despair.*

He walked along the street without looking where he

put his feet; and he walked in a direction which would not bring him to the place of appointment with another lady (an elderly nursery governess putting her trust in an Apollo-like ambrosial head). He was walking away from it. He could face no woman. It was ruin. He could neither think, work, sleep, nor eat. But he was beginning to drink with pleasure, with anticipation, with hope. It was ruin. His revolutionary career, sustained by the sentiment and trustfulness of many women, was menaced by an impenetrable mystery – the mystery of a human brain pulsating wrongfully to the rhythm of journalistic phrases. '... *Will hang for ever over this act.* ... It was inclining towards the gutter ... *of madness or despair.* ...'

'I am seriously ill,' he muttered to himself with scientific insight. Already his robust form, with an Embassy's secret-service money (inherited from Mr. Verloc) in his pockets, was marching in the gutter as if in training for the task of an inevitable future. Already he bowed his broad shoulders, his head of ambrosial locks, as if ready to receive the leather yoke of the sandwich board. As on that night, more than a week ago, Comrade Ossipon walked without looking where he put his feet, feeling no fatigue, feeling nothing, seeing nothing, hearing not a sound. '*An impenetrable mystery.* ...' He walked disregarded. ... '*This act of madness or despair.*'

And the incorruptible Professor walked, too, averting his eyes from the odious multitude of mankind. He had no future. He disdained it. He was a force. His thoughts caressed the images of ruin and destruction. He walked frail, insignificant, shabby, miserable – and terrible in the simplicity of his idea calling madness and despair to the regeneration of the world. Nobody looked at him. He passed on unsuspected and deadly, like a pest in the street full of men.

THE END

penguin.co.uk/vintage